DONT CLOSE YOUR EYES

Don't Close Your Eyes,
Stay up reading instead!

V. Lynessa Layne

Also by Lynessa Layne

DCYE: Complicated Moonlight

DCYE: Mad Love

DCYE: Dangerous Games

Acknowledgments

To my editor, TK Cassidy. She is a published author of several novels, over a hundred children's stories and the recipient of Guam's Maga Lahi award (named for the ancient Chieftain of the Chamorro. TK has a Bachelors in English & Library Science, a Masters in Library Science and an EdD in Virtual Education. She's also great at tough love. I couldn't have gone this far without her support, guidance and invaluable friendship. TK, thank you for pushing me out of the nest and every comfort zone. I found my Forrester.

To AJ, my associate editor and consultant. AJ has a Bachelors in Communication-Journalism. He served five combat tours in Iraq and Afghanistan and over twenty-four years in the United States armed forces. Thank you for your leadership, friendship and willingness to allow me ugly moments of frustration. I'm grateful you never gave up, never surrendered and taught me to follow suit when I wanted to throw this manuscript in the trash and never look back.

To my children. You better not be reading this until you're adults, but each of you pushed me to never give up. You've pressed me forward knowing I wasn't writing for children's eyes. You loved me for me, the sloppy, clumsy, imperfect woman who felt she never measured up to other mothers, but in your hearts surpassed them all as I unknowingly brought you peace with the sounds of my fingers on the keyboard; music in the background, chores completed while having living room dance parties, family meetings around the dinner table. You allow normalcy to bless you. In turn, you bless me far beyond this and anything I write. This series was a personal goal, but YOU are the dream and my most valued treasure. My quiver is full.

Most importantly, to Yeshua. I wouldn't be here if you hadn't seen me next to death in the darkness, taken me by the hand and said, "Talitha cumi; damsel I say unto thee, arise." (Mark 5:41 KJV
You are the breath in my body, apart from which I can do nothing, but with you I can do anything. I am forever grateful for your boundless love, mercy and forgiveness.

For AJ,
the Lieutenant Commander who taught
me to take control of my life and
crap from no one.
Thank you.

&

For you, dear reader.
Typing made me a writer.
Publishing made me an author.
You make every word worth sharing.

Cast of Characters

- **Klive Henley King** – mysterious anti-hero. Also known as Complicated Moonlight & Kinsley's pirate. Double life as businessman & hired gun
- **Kinsley Fallon Hayes** – Protagonist. bartender, college student, renowned sprinter known as Micro Machine
- **Jase Taylor** – Navy SEAL, bar singer, lifeguard
- **Rustin Keane** – Jase's childhood best friend, combat veteran, Cop
- **Nightshade** – Crime Syndicate
- **Inferno** – Biker gang crime syndicate comprised of dishonest firefighters rivaling with Nightshade for power
- **Joey** – Klive's Personal Protective Detail (bodyguard)
- **Tyndall Taylor** – Jase Taylor's little sister, Kinsley's best friend
- **Andrew (Andy) and Clairice (Claire) Hayes** Kinsley's parents
- **Bayleigh & Garrett** - Kinsley's co-workers
- **Marcus** – Kinsley's boss/manager
- **Jarrell & Gustav** – lead bouncers at the bar
- **Rock – N – Awe** – Jase's band
- **Constance** – co-lead singer with Jase, Kinsley's friend
- **Ian Walton** – Kinsley's personal trainer and track coach
- **Lucy (Looney Lucy)** – track team manager
- **Adrian Miller** – Kinsley's elective art professor
- **Sara Scott** – Kinsley's co-worker, Patrick Scott's wife
- **Patrick Scott** – Inferno prospect

Reader Key – Character Point of View

♂ - Male sex symbol Klive King POV

♀ - Female sex symbol Kinsley Hayes POV

♂♣♂ - Jase & Rustin POV

1 | ♂

Murder was never my intended occupation.

Twenty-seven stories below, the *Jose Gasparilla* anchored in the center of the glittering water of Tampa Bay. Through a scope, I searched scores of smaller boats dotted around the majestic pirate ship until spotting the bright yellow cigarette boat dubbed *The Banana Hamick*.

I scribbled precise grid points onto a small notepad, shook my head.

This idiot can't spell hammock, yet stole two million worth in cocaine?

The take, disguised as cheesy gold coins, brimmed from an open treasure chest at his feet where he stood waving to the crowds gathered onshore. I rolled my eyes and collapsed the scope. *Too easy. Where was the challenge, adrenaline, thrill of the hunt? Why hire me to kill this arrogant prat when a Dade City meth head would do the deed for a fraction of the price?*

As I locked my office, a lone janitor paused his vacuuming. "Wow!" he gushed. "Great costume, Mr. King. Enjoy wooing the wenches at Gasparilla, you'll have a hard time keeping them away."

"Thanks." I chuckled. "But I plan on enjoying the festival from the safety of a parade float." *And sharp shooting from a crow's nest.* I boarded the elevator. "There's a bucket of beads calling my name. Cheers, mate."

He waved as the doors closed. I leaned against the wall and fished a Bowie knife from my coat to check my eyeliner in the shine. Coal smudged beneath my finger when the elevator halted only five floors down. "What the?" My words died as the doors divided on leather pants, round hips, corset, cleavage, slender throat, parted lips.

1

The knife fell to my side while my mouth dried and fell open.

"Whoa!" She backed away. Beautiful green eyes, clouded with smeared mascara, widened. "I didn't expect anyone else." She shook her head, top hat firmly in place. "I'll catch the next one."

"Nonsense, I don't mind sharing," I said, swallowed.

"That's okay," she said, "I'd rather be alone. Thank you."

The doors closed, but I shoved the blade between them, sliced them apart.

"Oh, no!" Her palm shot out while she stumbled back. "No! No, thank you! You go!"

"Wait. It's not what it looks like!"

"You leave, or I'll call the cops!"

"No, love, I didn't mean to use the bloody knife to open the lift! Gah! I mean *elevator!*" After living in the United Kingdom, certain words still slipped out.

High-heeled boots dashed behind the vacant reception desk. "I mean it!" she yelled. Fingers fumbled with the phone until the receiver clattered off the edge. "Oh, shit!" She sprinted down the hallway, tested office doors like a bimbo in a B-movie. The cell phone in her hand made little sense considering the phone she'd left dangling from the desk.

"Look, I'm leaving!" I pressed the elevator button for the next floor down. "You have *nothing* to fear!" I sheathed the knife. *Pathetic girl. I ought to shake some sense into her! Show her how to escape a killer rather than cornering herself!*

I shouldn't have gone after her. I didn't allow her to know I was, but no way I'd risk a police report bearing my description when I had a target to paint. The hell if I'd forego tonight's bounty when I relished ridding the world of that stupid criminal, retrieving the drugs and taking his boat as a bonus.

Exiting the elevator, I jogged back upstairs into the reception area. I padded across the lobby to re-cradle the screeching phone receiver. In the silence a woman's voice drifted as a distant echo. *The lavatory!*

Office doors were locked tight. Darkness showed beneath sets of closed vertical blinds subtly shifting with the blowing air conditioning.

Every whispered step closer to her amped up an adrenaline rush so exhilarating, I refused to heed the voice of reason shouting at me to flee as if *I* were prey.

My ear pressed to the door of the ladies' room. Overhead, a florescent light twitched. The buzz mixed with the young woman's voice leaching through the wood.

"Daddy, something—" She strangled a sob. "—*awful* happened at the festival!" Sob. "Nate, he, well … gosh … I have no idea where to begin or what to do!" Whiny, squeaky, hoarse cry. I jerked away from the wretched pitch before braving the door with my ear again. Throat clearing. Sniffling. Stronger tone. "Look, I'm okay. Emotional, but okay. My phone is dying. If you can't reach me, don't freak out. I might stop at a friend's place before I come home. Wanted you to know. Love you."

The beep of disconnection echoed against the tile walls. Unable to see her, I assumed the smack afterward was her phone against the granite countertop.

"Stupid, Kinsley! Stupid! Stupid! Stupid!" She shouted as if her voice might shatter the mirror. I cursed under my breath. Silence. Sniffles. Lower tone.

Kinsley ….

I pressed harder to hear her, hoping she wouldn't scream again. She released a heavy exhale. "Okay, Kins. Quit being a coward. Call the cops. Let them deal with those creeps and the psycho with the knife, then go home. No one will know it was you. Totally anonymous."

Shit. Cops?

Anger scorched my gut as I clutched the door handle. *Was I the psycho with the knife? I hadn't done anything!*

She blew her nose, sniffled again. I lost my give-a-damn and strode to the lift.

Let the foolish girl report a pirate in a building! The police had thousands to sort through tonight. She wasn't the daft fool, I was in thinking her fear mattered. Screw taking the stairs. I had nothing to hide!

3

I pounded the call button, pulled my pocket watch and cursed about how long the damn thing was taking to travel back upstairs. The halves of my watch snapped shut in my fist at the sound of her gasp.

"You said you were leaving," she said.

"And *you said* I was a psycho with a knife. Therefore, we are both liars." The lift arrived with a ping. I kept my back to her as I boarded, then turned with a scowl on my face to inspire something real for her to fear. "I came to check on you, however, I now find it best to leave you to your assumptions. Good evening." *And good riddance.*

Under my unconcealed disdain, her eyes dimmed with shame. They weren't a mess anymore, but her nose was pink. The color bled into her cheeks.

"You followed me?"

Dumb question.

"Did you need to go downstairs then? Because I do." I stabbed the 'door close' button.

What the hell? I jerked when the girl rushed inside just before the doors sealed. She reached for the panel of numbers. Without thought, I threw my arm out to block her.

She yanked back. "What the hell?"

"Your makeup was a mess before I startled you."

"What?"

"Your eyes." I gestured with one hand, pocketed the other. "You fixed them, but your mascara was all over your face. *Before* I came along. Wasn't me you needed to call the cops about. What happened tonight?"

She stared, her only movement a swallow and an artery jumping at her throat. She'd stopped breathing. Several red splotches painted her chest and neck that had nothing to do with embarrassment.

"Please answer the question."

Her chest fell with a harsh exhale of all that trapped air. "No. It's none of your business. Why are you carrying a knife like that in a place like this?"

My head angled. *Was that all she could think of? My knife?*

"Perhaps this *should* be the business of the one carrying the knife. You see, love." My hand rested on my costume. "In case you couldn't tell, I'm also attending a festival and plan on protecting myself while I'm there."

"You use Mace to protect yourself at a festival, not a machete."

The space filled with my unexpected laughter. "Pepper spray? Is that what you used to fend off the bloke who left those fingerprints on your arm?"

She gasped and slapped her palm over the exact spot. A pink glow expanded up her temples. My jaw clenched and lifted while I stood straight to look down on her.

"Who hurt you?"

Her gaze collected worry as she studied our confines with the dawning of a cornered creature cursing her stupidity.

"It's not like that," she argued.

"Then what *is* it like?" I all but growled. The thief in the *Banana Hamick* may not be tonight's only target.

"I don't want to talk about it. I don't even know you."

Determined, she reached around me for the button. Again, I prevented her by stepping between her and the column altogether.

"Ugh! Come on!" she pleaded.

"Hey. If someone did something, I'd rather take care of it than not. You're safe with me, but don't protect some asshole."

She narrowed her eyes with a mute implication that I was the asshole for the moment. A brave sign she was willing to test my word.

"Nothing happened. Not in the manner you're thinking."

"Right." I clenched my jaw as I held firm. "We're not moving until you elaborate."

She drilled a scowl through my skull like her problem was hers alone. I stalled, allowed silence to expand the interrogation. She caved in less than a minute. "Fine. My boyfriend stood me up. I put on this stupid outfit because he loves Gasparilla. We arranged to meet three hours ago. I waited for two-and-a-half past that and admitted defeat."

"How did you end up here?"

"Good grief," she spat. "You want my life story, too? My father works here. So, you see, I was running to Daddy because my boyfriend hurt my *wittle* feelings. Happy now? I guess I should apologize for wounding your precious pride."

On an aggravated whistle, I hammered the button for the car park, then balled my sweaty hands inside the deep pockets of my pirate coat. If she were going to a different floor, she could press her own button for grating against mine.

"I'm sorry." She deflated.

"So, pout about it."

"Hey, you asked! I told you I didn't want to talk about it." She peeked at the red indicator, then pressed the next floor. "I don't need your trash." Seconds later, she jumped off like I was diseased. The doors closed, and I let them. I didn't need her garbage either. What did that little wench even matter? *Leave her be!* But I couldn't. Nor could I define why I shattered the silence on a slew of curses and stabbed a button three floors further down.

The moment the doors cracked, I darted into the stairwell. Racing heels clacked down the stairs. The concrete echoed with her hoarse sobs. I let the heavy metal door slam. She cursed as I heard her turn to jog the other way.

"Come on! It's only me!" I shouted up through the space where the railing wound around each level. The clattering paused. She leaned over from two floors above.

"Oh, and that's supposed to make me feel better?" she shouted. "Leave me alone."

"Yeah? And leave you at the mercy of a pervert lurking in dark places like these?" I snapped back.

"You mean like *you*?" she asked.

"I mean like the wanker you're covering for! Blast!" I leapt out of the way as she spit. Her saliva missed me and continued down the fifteen remaining flights. A moment later, a steel door slammed. No more footsteps. *Hell no! Now it was personal.*

I ripped the exit open and stormed to the elevator, mashed the button. The floor indicator ticked down. Once the doors split, I half-expected her not to be inside, but there she stood, hands curled around the bar against the back wall. Her glare blazed with anger, but there flashed something challenging. Mine mirrored the sentiment.

"I didn't deserve that." I gave her my back while I pressed for the garage once more. "Any of it."

"The hell you didn't," she stammered. "You shouldn't have left the elevator, I told you to leave me alone, and I'm not covering for anyone. You were chasing me for goodness sakes!"

My eyes flared, and I turned with incredulous disbelief at her foolish bravery. "*Chasing* you? Shame on me for trying to be chivalrous."

"*Chivalrous?*" She scoffed. "You call that chivalry when you practically wore the inconvenience of all this upstairs? I wasn't planning on you interrupting me either, bud."

I shook my head, unable to help my disgust. "No wonder your bloke stood you up."

She flinched like I'd slapped her. The heaving in her chest returned. Lunging forward, she halted our progress just to grate on my nerves, then twisted to face me, bucking-up. Her bravado soon wavered under my silent scrutiny.

"Young lady, I haven't time to play these childish games." I reached toward the panel. She jolted back against the column of buttons before melting down on the marble beneath our feet. Multiple floors lit, but that didn't strike me as much as her presumption that I'd strike her. *Was I that scary?*

"You're right." Her voice cracked as her face fell into her hands. "I deserved it. I'm a terrible girlfriend."

I hadn't an umbrella adequate for this absurd rain of emotion. With a sigh, I knelt and cupped my hands beneath her arms to lift her to her feet, bracing for the spit likely to splat in my eye.

"Forgive me if I scared you again, love, but why not spit in his face instead of mine?"

"Why would you assume I won't?" she asked in bitterness.

We stopped on the first of twelve additional levels. She stared at me, I stared at her until the doors closed once more. Interesting. She'd just conceded a perfect moment to escape. With eleven bloody floors to go, I prodded her places of pain.

"Let's pretend I believe you. Why meltdown over this bloke? Were you together long?"

"Long enough, or so I'd thought. I guess in light of tonight, we were together too long." She looked everywhere but at me. "I wasted so much time on him." Her eyes ran out of space and traveled up to mine, big, beseeching, apologetic. "I'm sorry I've wasted yours."

That look loaded the bullet in a mental game of Russian roulette. *Drop this pistol and leave the risk!*

Fresh tears added to her a different vulnerability that unsettled my normal control. Even if I knew she was lying, I'd been an insensitive asshole. *Fix it. But how?*

The doors opened again. *No way was I was doing this ten more times.* I herded her from our cell to press the button for the other one. She argued the whole way out, bargaining for using the extra floors for contemplation.

"You mean for wallowing? There's nothing to contemplate. If something is finished, let it be, and move on," I commanded. The indicator counted from the parking level. The bell chimed, the doors split open, but she didn't budge.

"I'll wait for the next one," she said. "Thanks."

Pft! No way in hell I'd concede with the visual and emotional target she'd painted on herself. Add the foolish fight-or-flight responses, she was prime for the wrong prick. *Not on my watch.*

"Nonsense. Come now." Plying her was like taking a stubborn jackass for a walk. After another verbal battle with her attitude, the bloody doors that kept trying to pinch us, my patience snapped. I spun her and cinched her waist in my grip.

"Oh!" She gasped while she grabbed my shoulders. I somewhat lost my head as the ribbons crisscrossing the length of her spine danced like feathers in a bow over my fingertips. Her body shifted closer, whether

I'd tugged her, or she'd leaned in, I couldn't say. I only knew I wasn't getting enough oxygen as her chest brushed mine. Her fingers laced together at the nape of my neck. My lips parted to release a long steady breath. Her eyelids fell a fraction as she watched. When I stroked my thumbs against her waist, she bit her lower lip as I felt a tremor travel through her having nothing to do with fear. Tension compounded as the doors sealed us inside the private cocoon. My tone firm yet gentle, I powered through.

"Look at me, love." Look at me, she did. Up close, her irises heated like the blood pounding my veins. My gaze strayed to her gnawed lip for relief.

I hardened my expression and resolve while I warred with pressing her against the wall to taste the cinnamon of her breath.

"Enough of this," I said almost to myself. "Don't waste your time drafting excuses for someone else's misbehavior. Quit looking for your father to coddle you. For the sake of your self-esteem, stop dating little boys. They've no fortitude." My mind clouded with dangerous inspiration while she searched my face. Angry tears glazed her eyes like puddles of gasoline while my desire sparked like a pyromaniac holding a Zippo lighter. One strike may cause a beautiful explosion.

No woman had ever looked at me like I had the power to put away her pain even though I'd had a hand in causing hers. *Why did she?*

"I swear," I whispered aloud what ought to remain in my mind, "you would be so strong with a real man." *With me*, I finished with my eyes.

She gasped, conflicted and offended. Her brows dipped while she read my eyes like she understood the words written in my mind. I sensed the same about reading hers. *This* young woman didn't need a kid causing drama. She needed the adrenaline rush of being shoved to the precipice of a cliff, then yanked back to safety by someone who couldn't resist her before he brought her to combustion.

"Come to Gasparilla with me," I blurted, mutinous against my priorities, my bad side, those who controlled me.

"No." She released a shaky breath.

Curse that damn word again!

She broke my grasp to push the garage button I'd neglected.

"I don't date strangers," she said like she'd hardened her own resolve.

"Perhaps you should."

She arched her eyebrow. "Nope."

"Coffee then?" I asked. "To get to know one another?" The floors ticked down like a time bomb closer to detonating and obliterating every conflicted second with her!

"The coffee shop is closed on Saturdays."

"I know. We don't have to go to this shop or the festival. We can go anywhere you want." I shifted to close the small distance between us, desperate to be near her once more, but she shook her head.

"I think you've gotten the wrong impression of me."

"Ditto."

She scrunched her nose. "No, I mean this." She added space between us and gestured to her attire. "This isn't me. For starters, I don't dress like a 'ho', I'm not easy and dating isn't that simple. I don't need a consolation prize. I need to get away from *you*."

Ouch! How could she say that when she'd been wanton in my grasp moments ago?

The lift opened on the parking garage. Humidity glued to our skin as thick and uncomfortable as the chemistry between us. We surveyed the dimly lit expanse. Few cars remained. She was lucky I was here, though my pride ached to hell.

"Great," I said. "I'm too complicated to give you consolation, nor do I date. I was merely softening the bruise to your ego." I propped one hand against the door. My other gestured she exit first. Under normal circumstances, I'd have relished wounding someone who'd wounded me, but I loathed the flush of pain in her expression. No different from what she'd done to me, but this stung.

"Anyone ever tell you what an asshole you are?" High heels hammered the concrete as she left.

I swallowed. "All the time, love."

"I hate this. I'm done with men and their drama. It's all the same. And *you're* ...." She trailed off in search of a word that might match how low I measured, inspecting me for flaws. Rosy blossoms on the apples of her cheeks betrayed her. *That's right, love, I'm not alone in this inexplicable attraction and misery.*

"I'm what?" I taunted. "Grown up? Mature? Too big a prick?"

Better if she hated me to escape my attention. Safer for both of us.

"Too *old*?" The corners of her lips lifted like that mental Russian roulette revolver. Her expressive eyes spun the cylinder as I stared like a victim realizing too late his own number was up. Victorious knowing fired from her irises, nailing my contempt, bleeding my strength. She turned and stalked away, determined to hold the power over me tight in her little fist. *Not so fast.*

"You're not done. If you'd had a man instead of a boy, you'd be done with drama, because real men don't have time for theatrics. Nor do real men hurt women. You're finished with temperamental kids. Maybe ring me when you're not one anymore." I strolled behind her enjoying the line of her legs in Puss-in-Boots stilettos.

"What are you doing?" She spun so fast I stumbled into her. Her squeal echoed off the concrete pillars while I grabbed her to keep us both from falling. Warm hands wrapped around my neck. Fiery eyes blazed mine with accusation. *Uh, huh. Two can play this game.*

"Did you do that on purpose?" I grinned.

"Ha! You wish." She stabilized and threw a finger in my face. The weak girl vaporized to re-materialize into a dominating woman. Pure beauty. This young lady, *Kinsley*, was *the* Anne Bonny to my Calico Jack ... *Kinsley King has quite the ring ....*

"I asked you a question." She interrupted my reverie. "What are you doing?"

I blinked hard. *What was I doing? Hell, what was I thinking?*

"Dangerous to be alone in a parking garage at night dressed so sexy." I nodded toward her costume. "Here. Take this." I shrugged out of my pirate coat.

"Oh, the chivalry angle again?" She stared at my offering with a stubborn lift of her chin. When I raised my eyebrows, she grimaced and yanked the heavy crushed velvet from my hand. She shrugged into the sleeves much longer than her arms. Anne Bonny looked mighty adorable in my coat. Too adorable to sport such a venomous attitude.

"Lead the way," I told her.

She snorted. "I don't think so."

My finger rose this time. "I'm walking you to your car."

"Why? To put me in my car seat and buckle my belt?"

"If you need it, sure, but I figured you'd at least graduated to a booster seat." She was so frustrated I barely contained a grin. "In those heels, I bet you can even reach the pedals."

"Insults coming from Peter Pan in a Captain Hook costume? That's cute."

I winced like she'd burned me before my wicked smile spread. "Oh, come now, love. At least grant me a solid Captain Morgan."

"Yeah, I could use a few shots of rum after being around you."

I chuckled. She turned to keep walking. Her pace quickened. I kept up, and she grumbled as we narrowed in on a shiny green Civic. The unmistakable feeling of watching eyes skittered over my back, raising goosebumps on my neck. Glancing around like she sensed danger, too, she pulled the coat closed. Her eyes held mine for a ghost of a second. We were being observed. She rushed to her car with new urgency while I scanned for threats.

She had my knife. I'd rather not pull my pistol unless I had to. Improvisations formulated as she unlocked her car, the lights flashing once. I reached for her door, but she spun with a scolding index pointing at my face again. A great effort with the sleeve.

"No," she said. "You don't get to open my door. Funny how you don't have time for childish games, yet you're the one playing them."

"Am not—"

"Are, too. Know what I'm done with? Fear. Everyone knows boys have a fear of commitment. I shouldn't be heartbroken about being stood up. It's always *coming* as long as they're not allowed to. And here

12

I have a man—" She poked my chest. "—arguing like a child while lecturing me like I'm the weak one, when he'd likely walk away for the same reasons? It takes real strength to hold out for what you want, so admit it. Which of us is weakest? Who's the kid? Be honest."

"Whoa!" I stammered, amusement confiscated. Hers was, too.

What had this bloke done to her? Dumped her over sex? Forced her without permission after she'd changed her mind?

Her finger stayed in place. I wrapped my hand around her fist and leaned in to convey the severity in my gaze. "You're *wrong.*"

She snorted and speared my eyes with a dare to prove otherwise. "You're weak. You're afraid. You're all the same." Anne Bonny shoved me aside to open the car door by herself and plunked into the driver's seat. I grabbed the door before she closed me out. My bravado challenged, she was testing me, but I was too angry at my imagination and her comparing me to that boy.

"No," I measured, "I'm not. It's complicated. *I'm complicated.* I will say no more on the matter." *But I wanted to!*

"Ha! Well, that makes two of us. Walk the plank or call me when *you've* grown up." She tossed her hat at my feet before yanking the door from my grasp.

"I need a number for that!" I shouted as she drove away. The peal of tires cut off my retort.

No more banter. No more ball-busting bitchiness or vulnerable softness, sweet perfume, coconut-scented lotion. No more cinnamon on her breath near my lips. *No more Anne Bonny and Calico Jack!*

I cursed the empty silence while my eyes drifted to the ground. *How to proceed?* She wanted proof, action over words. Impossible for too many reasons, but if I failed to act, someone else would, or worse, she'd ignore my wisdom and run back into the arms of someone who may have attacked her in his need to have what she'd refused. *Did he stand her up before or after? Or had someone else attacked her after she'd been stood up? Why would she protect them?*

Who the hell cares because she's gone!

Gone!

Why did she matter?

Was I a bloody masochist because she made my palms sweat?

After long years on the job, nothing rattled my cage. She not only pried at the bars of my prison but sent an earthquake through the very foundations setting free the possibilities of life. I was so damn screwed.

I grabbed the hat and dusted off the brown felt. A burst of bay breeze carried her scent from the accessory. Instead of emasculating myself and lifting the perfume to my nose, I trudged to the Range Rover to drive away from here and this experience. I opened the door as a shield, yanked the gun from the holster at my back, pulled back the hammer, and spun to take aim on another pirate.

"Freeze!"

"Shit! Easy, King!" Joey cried. My personal protective detail's hands flew up beside his temples. The feather on his cavalier hat waved in the wind. My barrel poised to fire two inches from his face, but he whistled with the wry grin of a card sharp holding a royal flush. He may as well have been. He had enough to run to my superiors and out my interlude with the girl.

"You're mighty brave, mate." I lowered the gun and thumbed the safety in place. "Lucky you didn't come any closer."

Joey dabbed sweat from his brow. "I'd say you're the brave one. She's mean. Aren't you lucky I caught these in case you needed a witness?" He held his phone up as I holstered the Sig. His display lit with several images of Bitchy Bonny flaying my heart. I masked my excitement. "She looks cute and harmless," he said, "but for a second, I thought I'd need to step in and defend you. Especially when you armed her. She has the coat. The coat has the knife."

"Maybe I prefer a fair fight," I joked. In truth, I was glad she kept the weapon in case she needed to castrate whoever left the prints on her arm.

Joey chuckled as he emailed the photos to my inbox, then deleted them until arriving on the final picture.

"The good news is … drum roll please …." His thumb scrolled. Kinsley's license plate centered on the screen. "Guess you got that number after all."

Regret replaced with promising reprisal as he sent the photo then hit delete.

"Ready to go hunting?" he asked.

My lips spread into a villainous smile. "Damn right."

2 | ♀

Coach Walton roared across the track, "Faster, Micro Machine!" My spikes dug harder against the rough texture. "Dammit, Kinsley! Where the hell is your sprint?!"

The girls beside me gaped as we ran across the finish line together. I glared. They looked elsewhere while I swiped an arm over my forehead to curb the sweat dripping into my eyes.

The women's track coach inspected me, but allowed Ian Walton, my personal coach and trainer, to dole the scolding while she focused on the hurdlers.

"Kinsley Hayes, you *see* this garbage?" The vein between Walton's eyebrows protruded from his red face while he shoved the stopwatch too close. "This is NOT scholarship timing! Any high school superstar could outrun you! What am I doing here?" He threw his hands and the question out to the rest of the team.

"Great question since I'm not going to the Olympics!" I tossed back. Walton ripped the hat from his head and held the brim as he pointed at me.

"Keep up the attitude and see what happens," his voice dipped.

"That a dare?"

"That PMS?" He placed the cap back over his sweaty hair then gripped his hips and waited for me to pop off again. I forced my lips into a thin line. He nodded his triumph in having the last word and sauntered to the water cooler. When I growled, three fingers waved over his shoulder. I cursed and gripped my knees. He may as well have flipped me the bird.

My father watched from the stands, having taken the afternoon from work to offer motivation. Without looking, I sensed him jogging down to 'coddle' me, though I wanted to be alone with my angst. Instead of waiting on him, I changed into cross-trainers and started the three-mile punishment Walton had flipped me off with.

Daddy joined in the next lane a moment later.

"Kinsley Fallon. This isn't like you." Both names. Yay.

"Want to talk about it?"

"Nope." I pushed faster, forcing him to speed up to punish him for his concern.

"This about Valentine's?" he pressed. He didn't stick his nose in my business when he figured I'd come clean on my own, however today his nostrils seemed brown. "Nate didn't get you anything?"

Ha! Unless the rose tucked beneath the windshield wiper on my car was his idea of resting a flower on the grave of our relationship.

"No."

Nathan wasn't worth mentioning or speculating and seemed a minor issue with the new chaos scrambling my thoughts.

"Daddy, I suppose it should be, but this is about me growing the hell up."

Dad winced at my curse. "I'm not sure what that means."

"Don't you?" I gazed at him in accusation, ponytail slapping my shoulder. Unfair, but in my current mood, I resented that he'd raised me to expect better of men. What a crippling fairytale. And I must appear a fickle child if he figured a lack of Valentines from an ex could turn my sprint to crap. *Couldn't he be honest?*

Daddy ignored my tone but quickened his pace in retaliation. "Didn't he apologize?" He metered his breathing. "It's not like him to leave you hanging. Perhaps he had car trouble? There must be a reasonable explanation. He wouldn't just abandon you."

"It's been three weeks since he stood me up." I spoke between controlled huffs. "No apologies other than a lame voicemail. Nathan's silent, and driving fine. I'm reciprocating. Besides, I've got two more years of graduate school. Screw giving it up because I misjudged a jerk lacking the balls to break-up with me."

"Easy on the vulgarity, Kins. Love isn't sacrificing your dreams. They can co-exist. Just because he wanted to get married doesn't mean dropping out. He might've lost his nerve."

"Lost his nerve?!" I screeched to a stop. Daddy halted and tugged my elbow, which I effin' hate, so we were out of the way. *"Marriage?"* The word tasted like Dial soap in my mouth. *Hadn't matrimony been what I'd daydreamed of only a month ago?* "Does it appear that he was thinking of proposing?"

"Well, I think it was a reasonable step after over a year together. And …." He worked to form words. "Nate loves you, Kinsley. He's a good man. It makes no sense for either of you to give up a great thing over one missed date. Forgive him. *Fight* for him. I don't understand your defeatist attitude. It's out of character, even if he upset you. You're not a quitter."

"Pft! Fight for him? Forgive him? No. I'm not quitting. If something is finished, let it be and move on." He looked stung, but how did he think I felt? He had my mother and a white-picket-fence relationship, the freedom to entertain romance. My generation seemed intent on murdering what remained of men willing to work for a woman's attention, not to mention the women who still made them. If he learned the true reason Nathan stood me up, the danger he'd led me into, I doubted he'd push the issue.

"It's simple," I said, "Nate doesn't have what it takes. He's a coward. When the right guy comes along, I'll fight for him. Until then I won't awaken love before it so desires. Shouldn't *you* be spouting this?"

"I'm sorry, honey. You seem … *different*."

I was *different*. That pirate had effed up my entire world when he'd called me to the carpet and revealed the type of alpha male I'd thought had gone extinct to really be an endangered species.

How had a stranger ripped to shreds the relationship I'd viewed as perfect the day before Gasparilla?

Psychoanalysis didn't punch a dent in reasoning why the encounter haunted me, or the rationality of co-mingling fear and attraction. The less sense this made, the more I tried to make up a sensible explanation and the more I obsessed about the pirate. This was ridiculous, but psychological definitions had nothing on a host of undefinable sensations. My whole Psychology major seemed upended, like seeing photos of a roller coaster and reading a person's account of their rush. Coming away from those things thinking you're an expert on their experience because you've studied the evidence to the fullest.

When the pirate had lifted me to my feet, gripped my hips, tugged me close enough to touch, the caress of his thumbs against my waist, looked ready to kiss me … I'd fallen down the first rapid drop before several loops and corkscrews and now walked in the shoes of the roller coaster rider with the disheveled hair and huge smile, lingering butterflies and nausea in my belly. Whether I rode the ride again wouldn't erase the experience and the craving to get back on. Not once had Nathan's full kisses made my toes tingle or knees weaken the way the Pirate's touch had. Never before did I have the desire to kiss a stranger. I'd like to blame heartache for a lapse in good judgement, but was that fair?

Nothing about the encounter lined up with the person I'd created myself to be. Now, I thought of my every action and reaction compared with my peers'. I thought of my standards and questioned whether they were too high or low. Picked myself apart to be someone better than before. Wondered what made me a kid versus a woman in his arrogant, condescending eyes. *Why the hell would my body thrill at such an attitude problem? What the hell was wrong with me?*

Dad eyed me, and I realized I'd spaced out.

"I see why your trainer is angry. Something more than Nathan is bothering you, and your sprint is suffering the consequences. I'll respect your privacy, but I'm always here. Don't harden your heart again, baby. You've come so far."

I sighed in defeat, knowing I wouldn't hold out for long before confessing. We didn't keep secrets. "I hate crying, Daddy. Bitterness is easier. Give me some time. I'll come around."

"If that's what you need, I'll give you space."

"Yes, please. And thank you."

Work, school, track, repeat. For two years I found my adrenaline in winning races, climbing the ranks and amplifying my moniker's reputation. When I wasn't training, interning or studying, I lost myself serving Jack, Jameson, Jim, Johnny, Sailor Jerry, and ignored the lasting image Captain Morgan left in my mind.

"What cocktail does Frat Toy look like?" I now asked my fellow bartender, Bayleigh, her opinion. She giggled at my label for a regular flirt who frequented weeknights.

A group of his fraternity brothers gathered at the bar around him, each of them waiting for their drinks based on our evaluation of their personalities. Bayleigh narrowed her eyes on a hot one and began her assessment.

"Kamikaze, baby. This is for you."

The headliner slapped money down, interrupting our playtime. He licked his lips, and they lifted at the corner. "Sorry, guys." Jase Taylor was a lot of things, but sorry was never one of them. He gloated because they hadn't a shot in hell at hook-ups when he was in the building, although Bayleigh and I seemed the only two he didn't aim for. Jase assessed the group as I pushed his drink across and thanked him for the tip.

"Thank *you*, sweet Kins." He kissed my cheek to spite them and flutters engulfed my belly. When he pulled back, Jase focused on the frat brothers while I collected my breathing with feigned indifference. "You boys keep your hands to yourselves, ya hear? Would hate to schedule a meeting with you in a dark alley after work."

"All right, Jase. You've made your point," I told him.
"You're welcome." He grinned, zero shame in scaring them away.
"Any song requests?" he asked as he picked up the drink.

I cocked an eyebrow. "How about …" My finger tapped my chin. "*Cold Little Heart*?"

That got a hearty laugh from him. If Jase had the choice, I'd have empty pockets and no dates.

"That your boyfriend, Micro Machine?" Frat Toy asked as Jase headed for the stage. I giggled at the absurdity.

"No way. He's my best friend's older brother. She's attending FSU. When she's away, he extends the relation," I explained. "He's home on leave, but y'all better do what he says, because you don't want his trouble, especially in Kamikaze mode. There's a reason I dubbed him with that drink."

They weighed my seriousness and whether their pride was worth defending.

To distract them, I leaned close to Bayleigh again and dubbed the frat boy of choice, "LIT and make it strong." He nodded his approval like I'd given a flirtatious compliment. She chuckled at the inside joke. Long Island Iced Tea was almost all liquor, but in my experience, the drinkers always requested I make theirs 'strong' like they had something to prove.

"We'll all have one on me, but water theirs down. The pledges can't handle their alcohol like we can," the hot guy said. His buddies laughed, and throughout the evening honored Jase's threat, aiming further flirtation at Bayleigh. None of them asked me out, but not only due to the hulking singer hiding lethal skills greater than performing the panties off patrons. Rumor was, 'Micro Machine' was scary on the track, therefore undatable.

Rumor also was, Jase Taylor might be home for good this time. In that case, I'd better prepare to be a poor old maid.

3 | ♀

Two days later, I dodged cat calls from the day-drinking fogies playing cards and dominoes as I trotted into the bar.

"Tell Marcus we approve of that new uniform, Kins," one teased. "Yeah, yeah, go for the full house," I told a veteran, peeking at his cards in passing. He cursed and they folded while I rushed to the register behind the bar to clock-in.

"Hey, powder puff," barked a voice box full of gravel. "Make me a proper Rusty Nail when you get a chance."

"Mm-hmm," I hummed and pounded the buttons harder than necessary. A glance over my shoulder, I regretted agreeing before assessing the Inferno biker sitting at the bar. He needed cutting-off.

"Thanks for coming." My manager strode from the hallway and paused to stare. A dumb whistle followed.

"I don't want to hear it. My uniform is in my locker. When mommy has a tea party, girly dresses the way mommy wants or else she might have to move out and pay rent."

He chuckled and held his hands open.

"What? You look hot. Mommy needs to have more tea parties before I call you in early."

"Marcus."

"Not the dress, but the rest, yes, please. Taylor's gonna eat his balls for breakfast when he sees you this way."

I rolled my eyes at his referencing Jase Taylor. Marcus wasn't going to butter me up. "Had to skip track practice *and* teatime with my mother and her froufrou friends ...." I trailed off and looked up into his face, pretending I wasn't thrilled to be relieved of the obligation. Too bad I couldn't have changed clothes first.

"What's the delay?" The biker slapped the bar. I no longer had to act irritated.

"I'll make it worth your while." Marcus lowered to a whisper. "Water his drinks down after Sara leaves."

"She's still *here*?" I asked in kind. *Why was this a secret?*

"In the back with a friend of Taylor's while she grabs her stuff."

I finished with the buttons and looked at him like he was the crazy one. No one goes in the back but employees, and what was one of Jase's friends doing here? Jase wasn't even on the clock to perform for a few hours, and they all knew Sara was married.

"He offered to walk her to her car. Given the current audience, I'm cool with that. Feel me?"

"Marcus, is her son sick, or was I called in because she's bailing on yet *another* shift? I hate being lied to."

He sighed. "Name your price."

"Really?" He knew what I wanted. I quirked my eyebrows.

"Dammit, Kins, you know Valentine's Day is always packed."

"I can clock-out and leave you till my real shift begins. After all, winning doesn't happen on its own, and my mother was threatening to vis—"

His hand chopped my voice. "Deal. Find someone to take your shift that day, though. I don't know why you don't want all the extra tips, and you know you'll be spoiled with gifts. Girls love junk like that."

"Mmm, most girls love junk like that," I corrected and walked over to the liquor counter. Pretending to stash my clutch, I grabbed an empty bottle of Drambuie from the recycling bin and slipped the new one behind the fluff of my dress, swapping the full with the empty. "Think you can handle this long enough for me to change?"

Marcus rolled his eyes and waved me past him to the hall where I handed off the bottle. "Brilliant move, Little Red. See why I need you?"

"Right." I paused before the hallway to peer at the biker. "When I'm in uniform I'll make you a fresh drink, okay?" He nodded. The veterans started a fresh round of cards while I promised them a fresh round when I was changed.

At the end of the hallway, Sara pushed through the door to the rear parking lot, a man following. I couldn't park back there today because of my stupid attire. Gravel and heels don't mesh well.

I sighed after stuffing the froufrou dress inside the locker. Either her son had a new immunity issue, or Sara was hiding something. She'd been flaky for the past three weeks. Since I was the only one available on short notice, I took the hits.

"Oh, come on!" I pleaded, ready to boot the lower locker with my stupid heels. Since I didn't go home or to practice first, I didn't have a spare set of tennis shoes. My toes were already complaining. This was going to be a long shift. *No good deed, eh?*

I stuffed my arms inside the top to stretch the Lycra as much as possible, but the fabric molded back to every curve. I spun in the mirror to see my back in the reflection and shook my head. "This is too risqué for off-season," I muttered. Even when we had to wear heels when Spring Break hit, I skated by with platform wedges. "Ready for a new type of unwanted attention, Micro Machine?"

"Red heels go great with that new embroidery," Marcus goaded in open appreciation a few minutes later. He smiled at my deadpan, knowing how I hated I couldn't remove a name tag to swap the new shirt with a larger size. Grrr.

"If my parents ever catch me in this, they'll kick me out into the real world and I'm blaming you."

Marcus's laughter faded as he disappeared into his office. When I moseyed behind the bar, I noticed the biker's heavy eyes fall like anvils to the high heels.

"Oh, no," I whined and produced the biggest innocent eyes I was capable of. His face changed as I turned the empty liquor bottle upside down trying to pour a drop into his cup. "Marcus, do we have anymore Drambuie?" I yelled.

"Are we out already?" he called back. "The next shipment won't be in till Tuesday."

"Looks like you cleaned us out, sir." I shrugged with empathy. "I'm sorry. You come in tomorrow and I'll make you a proper Rusty Nail. Deal?" I never worked Tuesdays. He'd be Marcus's problem.

The wasted biker wavered on his stool and stared like awful things ruminated in that mind. My palms tingled as I evaluated the room in case this guy did something stupid.

The cowboy who'd followed Sara through the back door now leaned beside the digital jukebox in a pair of vacuum-sealed Wranglers. A toothpick churned circles between his lips while he, too, watched. He tapped the touch screen a couple times, and I stifled a laugh when his song selection began, the genre opposite his appearance. His voice joined Nick Jonas's to provide comic relief. He sidled upon a stool beside the biker, singing *Chains*, rather well, by the way. His radiant eyes followed my movement as I made a till for my lap apron.

The biker's slow stare bent to consider the cowboy with disdain. He called him a foul name, then stumbled off the stool, curses about our bar and staff flooding from his slurring mouth all the way out the door. *Thank you, Jesus!*

"It's a shame he had to leave, eh?" Country flirted, pausing his idiocy.

"A true shame." I nodded and tugged the tap to fill a pitcher of beer for the vets. "Seemed a sure thing among the oldies, but I guess I was wrong."

He chuckled as I went onto the floor to deliver orders and clean vacated tables littered with empties. The best way to keep in touch with town happenings was to listen to old men gossip, and the moment I bent to wipe a table, I hit pay dirt.

"That hick right there's gonna get himself tangled in a nest of vipers flirting with Sara first, now Kinsley," one old-timer said to another. "Everyone knows whose turf this is. I don't have to agree with 'em, but Nightshade takes out the trash."

"Yeah, but they're all criminals."

"Now, Ned, you know the rumors just like I do. Nightshade been dealing Oxi to the locals like Robin Hood. We elderly need to have something to kill the pain of old age. Not like we're sniffin' or cooking somethin' on a spoon or what have you."

"Shhh, lower your tone, brother."

"Marcus don't care. He knows the difference between the way Nightshade conducts their company versus the company Inferno keeps. And by keeps, I mean imprisonment for sex trafficking. I don't care what you say, bad may be bad, but at least Nightshade don't sell humans."

"Well, I heard Sara say she had trouble with one of those damned hooligans that comes in wearing an Inferno vest like the one on the guy that just left. I think that was one of his friends. Trouble flocks together."

"Nothing new," another injected. "You ask me, the Infernos are a disgrace to fire departments and bikers everywhere. A gang of firefighters who can't control their hoses, spraying corruption on the good reputation of honest emergency responders. Ruins the whole system."

"Greed, politics and bad actors always do," an oldie said in bitter wisdom. "Selfishness is the root of all evil, and the men in those vests care nothing for saving any lives but their own."

"Amen, brother. Then you have these girls holding their lives in their hands when they work jobs like these in uniforms like those."

A stern finger pointed right at me. I hated when they talked as if we weren't in the room, or like we were 'asking for it'. Guess in their minds men had no control over themselves in the face of cleavage? Although I agreed with their views on selfish desires and the trashy reputation of Inferno. Interesting perspective on Nightshade, although in my mind, wrong was wrong.

"You're looking' mighty pretty today, Kins," the older veteran told me, sheepish for the trash talk I overheard.

I bent to retrieve his glass. "Thank you, sir. My mama made me look like a proper lady, but I don't think these heels convey in this uniform quite the same as they did with my dress. Since I got called in before I could grab my tennis shoes, I'm stuck marching like Minnie Mouse." I kicked up a heel. He and his pals exchanged glances and nodded. I almost pressed them for details on Sara but decided to mind my own business. "Don't y'all go getting me into trouble with my daddy for it either." My gaze met the eyes of the guilty parties one at a time, and I earned a salute from a Vietnam cap.

"Yes, ma'am."

A pair of shriveled fingers from the Korean cap handed me a dollar bill to keep. My smile came like he'd gifted five dollars, and I traveled back behind the bar. The singing siren on the stool spun to face me again, a new song playing that I crinkled my nose to. He scoffed and stood like I'd issued a challenge. My head shook as he went back to the juke box.

"Hey, girl. This here's musical communication at its best." His smile radiated hayfields and sunshine while his cocky walk in those tight jeans spelled a certainty in his ability to get into any girl's pants he desired. He'd best take those snakeskin boots out the door if he thought to aim for my panties.

"Hey, *boy*, how many guys do you think we get in here trying to serenade us with that machine? And if that's the best, guess I'm left with something to be desired."

With a call of my name, the corner table lifted their empties. I dug inside the cooler for a couple Buds.

Country ignored my tone. "Worked didn't it?"

All right, he had me there. "It did. Thank you."

"If you don't like *Chains*, what do you like ?" He squinted to read my name. Or gawk at my boob. Hard to tell which. I covered the embroidery. "Ah, come on, that's not fair. How will I order from you?"

"I don't take orders, I make them." I grinned while several veterans lifted their hats and nodded their approval. Barn boy howled with a hand over his heart.

"Quick on your toes, ain't you, Red?"

"You might say that."

"Was that your sister?"

"No."

"Better be careful. A man may confuse the two of you in dim lighting, flirt with the wrong woman."

"That's what she's got *me* for, Jarhead." Jase Taylor's voice boomed as he walked into the bar from the employee's hallway with the swagger of a champion boxer ready to deck a challenger in his ring. "This perv giving you a tough time, baby?" I swallowed hard as his honey irises glazed over my face before squaring up on the stranger.

"Hey, Squid, I don't want no trouble. She wanted a song. Gotta give the girl what she wants if she can't get it from the singer." *Oh, hell*.

"Now I *know* you're full of shit." Rather than throw a punch, Jase's hand clapped loud against the blond's, and they pulled each other into a guy hug. *Wait— whaaat?*

"Kins, put a round for them on my tab, please?" a veteran asked in a one-eighty shift from his previous disapproval.

"Sure. Um … anything else?" This made no sense until I recalled Marcus saying this was Jase's friend.

"Yeah, you keep these boys in pain, ya hear? Don't let either of them steal your virtue."

I laughed and saluted the man in his Vietnam cap the way he'd done me. "Yes, sir. No worries there."

"She always knows precisely where to aim to take a man down a couple notches," Jase joked with the veterans as he and his friend traveled to the table to thank them for the drinks.

"Ah, son, be grateful for the dose of humility," the veteran teased. The group shifted into acronym style military speak I didn't comprehend, but Blondie's fluency proved he was a military man who now claimed his flirtation with Sara and me was a diversion against the bikers.

When Jase walked back to the jukebox, the blond said he was trying to find a song that depicted *Red*, then said, "Did you realize there were twins working here, and *you* didn't tell me? Two stacked redheads and nothing but oldies to entertain them? You've been holding out."

Jase's laughter filled the space, making my breath stutter. "Why do you think I called you?" He winked over his shoulder while I fought a blush, then he turned back to his friend. "And *I'm* not old. Sara isn't natural. Kinsley is. That's Red's name, and you don't choose a single tune for this chick, she's too colorful. Why do you think I'm here singing twice a week? Always hunting for the right song." He grinned in my direction, but I resumed wiping the bar as if unimpressed, praying the blood would drain from my cheeks in the meantime.

He asked the vets for requests and one called out a mixed drink. Jase selected non-committal blues tracks for them, then glanced at his friend. "Gotta set the tone before I set the stage. The band should roll in soon if you're interested in singing some blues."

They claimed the stools across from me. Jase removed his cap with the flourish of someone who could just as easily remove his burdens. He laid the hat between us and leaned onto his muscular forearms just as I left to deliver the drink. "Well, butter my biscuits." His eyes shot to the heels, then traveled slowly back up as I pretended not to notice or hear, though I wanted to pump my fist. *Score!* Guess I could tell my mom that her torture paid off in unexpected ways.

"You want your norm, sir?" I rounded behind the bar and posed against the polished wood knowing he would do his best to focus on my face. Even if he'd just checked me out, he cleared all appreciation as fast. This horn dog didn't mind his manners with anyone else. He played, but kept me at a distance, then allowed sluts to climb all over him on performance nights. This was a rare moment of female monopoly on his attention.

"Meh, I'll do beer later. What's your read today, baby? Do us both." He grinned, one side of his mouth tilting up. Jase could stop the pacemaker on an old lady's heart with that grin. I licked my lips, then gnawed my lower in contemplation of Jase's current assertiveness. His lips mimicked mine, but his silent gesture baited like a lure tossed into a lake.

"Hmm …." I grabbed the top shelf vodka since the band wasn't on the clock yet. Jase would have to pay for his own drink, and I'd make him pay for false flirting. After shaking the ingredients in the tumbler, I faced them and poured each an expensive shot, then slid Blue Ribbon cans beside them, snapping the tabs with a smug mug. "Kamikaze shots and cheap beer, gentlemen." My empty hands found the edge of the chunky wood surface and held tight like I could hold to this faux confidence the same.

"Aw, I don't get anything different?" Jase pouted.

"Not when you refuse to change," I quipped. His friend held a fist over his grin.

"The cheap beer is different, what're you trying to say, baby?"

I didn't answer, just tapped my temple and smirked.

"Well, Rusty, I see you've made a lasting impression on my future wife." Jase grinned at his friend.

Tease!

"Or mine." The friend grinned back. They clinked shot glasses in a toast, then downed them in tandem. Country boy hummed at the flavor of the shot, then winced when he sipped the Pabst. "Should go down on one knee seeing you make him pay for his pain, but something tells me you're the type to take it slow." He winked. "Rustin Keane, at your service, Miss. Pleasure to meet the one woman Jase *can't* have." He removed the ever-present toothpick. His smile beamed radiant and clean. His free hand gripped my own in a shake I respected. No jelly. He returned the sentiment. "Firm grip. Nice." Rustin's eyes smiled as I rolled mine and made Jase another at his request.

The bell jangled over the door while I pushed Jase's glass in front of him. They turned to study a biker vest striding up to a stool. "Well, well, well. Kinsley. You're here early, darlin' and looking mighty fine!" He ordered a draft, and his fingers danced bare from the tips of leather riding gloves in a taunting wave at Jase. "So is tonight's jester. Wonder why." Silence expanded between the five stools that separated them.

"Because I asked my favorite *headliner* to keep me company," I lied, knocking this perv down a notch. Jase quirked his eyebrows at him, then cast his smile at me.

"Where's Sara?" the biker asked, all business.

Rustin piped up before I could answer. "She had to leave."

"What's it *your* business, corn-fed?" he demanded.

"She'll be back tomorrow," I offered to stifle the brewing pissing match. "Want peanuts with this?"

He glowered at the guys for a long moment as he decided whether to pursue his issue. *What was his issue, though? What was Sara's?*

"Yeah. Sounds good." His gaze roamed my body. I didn't have to look. I felt the disconcerting sensation when I bent for the nuts beneath the bar, wanting to twist his in my fist and hear his pitch rise in panic.

"You should come in early more often, Kins. Wouldn't hurt my feelings or my eyes none." My skin crawled as I slid the bowl to his chest, then grabbed a towel to begin wiping tables.

"Don't count on it," I told him as I walked away from the bar. "This isn't my crowd."

I'd only been here for an hour and hated day shift already. *Why was Sara doing this to herself when she was the star who'd trained me?* None of this made sense with her character.

He whistled and cursed as he twisted on his stool to watch my advance on a vacated table. "'Specially in them shoes. Could stand to see you and Sara together again. Tips must pour in when twins are on-duty."

"Ugh, why does everyone keep saying that?" I muttered. Sara was four inches taller, ten years older, two cup sizes larger, and had a good fifteen-to-twenty pounds on me. I wasn't trying to be a snob in my own mind, but I didn't work out for twenty hours a week to be compared to someone who barely did.

"Who said I was meaning' you and Sara?" the jerk asked.

I discreetly wrapped my fingers around the neck of an empty bottle. Jase didn't miss the movement.

"That's enough." His stool scraped across the wood as he stood. The veterans lowered their cards. "Kinsley, say the word, and I'll deck him." He didn't look at me, though. His gaze trained on the biker in ways that went deeper than this one instance. "It'll cost ya lip action instead of that cheek tonight, though."

"If he keeps it up, I'll do it myself, and you can kiss my cheek for doing you a solid."

"Everyone wins." The biker grinned at my threat, his glance prancing over the bottle in my hand. He tapped his cheekbone to show where to aim. "You hold his leash? I always assumed it was the other way around."

"That's it." Jase moved, but Rustin did, too, like a man bent on diffusing a bomb, to block his friend. His eyes warned me to stay put and ease my white-knuckled grip on the glass.

"Jase, he's not worth spilling blood Kinsley will have to clean up." The anger in Jase's eyes held and trained on his friend's face while the biker snickered. "Save it. Go prep the stage." Rustin's voice remained level. Jase's eyes shifted to mine for permission that I subtly nodded. He did, too, then resigned and patted a watchful veteran's back as he went to the stage.

"Yeah, go play with your instrument," the douche poked. "It's all you're good at."

"Hey, he's not the only one. If we're keeping score, *I'm* the best at beating off!" Relief hit as Jase's drummer, Mel, slapped the A-hole's vest in greeting, then wove his tatted arm around my waist. His pierced lips warmed my cheek, and his mouth drew close to my ear. "Someone needs his ass kicked. You okay?"

"I'm fine. Glad to see you. Is Marcus back there?"

He nodded and drew in again. "The rest of the band is out back unloading the trailer, but we scoped three other Infernos in the lot. Marcus's out there keeping score and making sure the one doesn't drive drunk." *The other one never left? Creepy.* "I'm gonna make a phone call so Jase doesn't get dirty. Sound good?"

"Damn right."

4

The snowbirds and vets trickled out. Twenty-somethings mixed with middle-aged patrons as the early evening crowd filed in. While I looked for cops or Mel's connections, Jase's irritation simmered down as his local fan base filled tables near the stage. Rock-N-Awe's Blues gig drew crowds to this place on Monday nights, but their Thursday night Alternative performances produced twice the turnout. This crowd spelled great things for the upcoming tourism season.

At the far end of the building, Jase's buddy aided the band in setting the stage, making small talk with the other members and curious barflies. I marveled at his ability to keep Jase in check and make him smile again. Jase's sister, Tyndall, might be envious, and I itched to call her and ask about him.

Bayleigh clocked-in, then shuffled to my side to catch up on orders until she spied him across the way. "Who is *that*? And can we keep him every week? Is he part of the band?"

"His name is Rustin, I don't know if you get to keep him, because I don't think he's part of the band. And from what I have gathered, he's an old bestie of Jase's from some hillbilly town in another state. With a drawl like that, I'm guessing Tennessee or Alabama."

"He has a twang to match those jeans? Aye! Might be Texas ...." Her hope trailed with a bite to her lip. She had a thing for Texans.

Garrett, the other bartender on shift, clocked-in and scoped Rustin with narrowed eyes lined in Urban Decay thicker than my own. He wound his thumbs beneath a set of red suspenders and snapped them, the definition in his biceps flexing with the movement.

"Straight?" he asked. His chin lifted as he grabbed a rum bottle, tossing and catching it behind his back for the ladies. Garrett always made that flair look easy.

Bayleigh beamed, seconding Garrett's question.

"Oh, yeah," I said. "He's straight. Keep rocking that eyeliner, bud. Your buns are safe."

We giggled, and Bayleigh leaned against the liquor counter, ogling Rustin unraveling cords he plugged into amplifiers. "See how TDH handles those cables. Bet he does wonders with rope."

"Bayleigh! Shame on you." I grinned. "Should be TSH."

"What do you mean? What's the S for?" She smiled.

"Instead of Tall, Dark, and Handsome, he's Tall, *Stupid*, and Handsome. He would flirt with our mop if we convinced him there were boobs somewhere in there."

She cackled, earning gawks from a group that bellied up to the bar with an open tab. "All those boobs are paying him ample attention, though. Makes sense," she told me as she scooped ice. "Bet you he crooks a finger and they come running to save a horse. I sure would," she admitted. I chuckled at her allusion to a popular 90's country song. After doling refills, she cupped her chin in her palm with a girly sigh. I knocked her elbow from beneath her. She snapped out of her appreciation and shot a glance at the hallway.

"What's up with Marcus tonight?" she asked.

Between mixing drinks, I filled her in on the biker's behavior and the Rusty Nail who came before him.

"Okay, uncomfortable, but it's not as if we don't deal with bikers, and you know anyone with testosterone is going to test Jase's. He's too muscular for Neanderthals who want to see who has the biggest club." She backhanded my abs and nodded at where Marcus stood. He had both meaty arms crossed over his chest evoking the bouncer he used to be. "He looks extra pissed. Did the guy actually scare you?"

"Meh. I was more nervous about Jase wasting his energy on a bark with no bite. Just another scuzz, ya know?" I shrugged, then turned to thank one of the bar-backs for lime refills. She nodded and echoed my thanks.

A guy in a Tampa Bay Buccaneers cap muscled through the cacophony. "Coke. Cherries on the bottom, grenadine, please, love?"

"I've got it." Bayleigh filled the Brit's order while I poured a quick row of shots.

"Now *that's* an accent, woman!" I told her without looking at the Brit at the bar. "The other's a slower form of speech so TSH's mouth can compensate for his brain."

"Brutal!" She giggled and tossed Garrett a towel when there was a sloppy spill near the end of the bar. The night was shaping up to be busy, but I found my eyes following our manager more than the musicians. Bayleigh made a good point. Marcus gnawed his toothpick hard enough he could shoot splinters at the next person to piss him off.

I leaned in on a free moment. "It's possible Sara had an issue with another guy from what I'm guessing is Inferno. The oldies were here gossiping about it earlier. They mentioned a vest, but you know how the rumor mill goes. Don't quote me on that."

"Makes sense, though." Bayleigh cringed and peered at Marcus. "Two Inferno assholes in one day? Wonder what Nightshade thinks about it."

"Excellent question." We tried to spot Nightshade members surveying the damage. Unnerving, because members were difficult to discern, but I'd be willing to bet that phone call Mel made was to someone connected since I didn't see a single cop in the crowd.

"No way they aren't involved somehow," she mused. "Turf wars are ugly. Let's hope the scumbag keeps his hands to himself. Marcus looks ready to throw punches."

We shared a knowing glance. He had to restrain himself anytime an Inferno jangled the bell over the door since they had their own bars. Inferno came for the pure enjoyment of causing a stir. For the time being, Marcus was talking with the guy Bayleigh said she'd just served. "Oh, Kins, did you see him?"

"Who?" I asked, distracted with drinks.

"The British babe! He was definitely TDH."

I scoffed and shook my head, rarely the double-take type of girl.

"You should have," she said, "it's the perfect contrast: Rustin is Neutrogena clean like pure sunshine, but the *other one* is dark and broody like he's shrouded in moonlight. Damn hat hid his eye color though. Wonder how Marcus knows him."

"What do you mean?" I asked and garnished a pair of mojitos with mint sprigs before passing them across the bar.

"I mean Marcus is chatting with him like they're familiar."

When Marcus caught us staring, the man's head snapped our way as if we'd shouted his name. "Yikes," we said in unison. "That's our cue to deliver drinks."

We loaded a tray full of the band's faves, and I lifted the heavy disk over my shoulder to begin the bumper car trek through the crowd.

"Check. Check. One-two," Jase chirped into a microphone. His fans clamored for seats and tables like a mad game of musical chairs. Those at the bar held mugs and bottles up with shouts and cheers. Jase took his stool at the helm of the band as they settled into their places and tuned instruments. "Thanks, baby," he said as I set the tray near his feet. I turned for more drinks, but his sharp whistle pulled me back. My cheeks heated, knowing what was coming. "Kiss, please?"

A twinge of excitement rushed to the palms of my hands as Jase swung his guitar to the side to dip down to me. I angled my cheek, prepared for the familiar warmth of his cushy lips and the scratch of stubble. Instead, warm fingers curled around the nape of my neck, and heat prickled the corner of my mouth. My eyelids fluttered closed on a deep inhale. My head tilted against his hand. Tingles shot through my chest depriving my lungs!

"Do I get one next?" Rustin's voice sounded too close.

I opened my eyes and pulled away, determined to pass drinks around like all was chill, controlling the release of my breath. "Ha! That's his for good luck. Our kiss is ritual. *Not* free."

"Guess I should start singing, then." He smiled. I had the uncomfortable urge to back up for how near he stood. I could smell his cologne, see the fine lines at the corners of his mouth, the variations in his vibrant eyes. His pale hair enhanced the bronze tan on his skin. He snagged a brew off the tray and handed the bottle up to the bassist. His arm hadn't needed to brush my breast. God bless Jase, he reached between us and cupped my cheek to thank me and reassure that he would have a great night.

"Yeah, you better." I smiled at him and turned a 'kiss my butt' glare on Rustin. He propped against the stage with a bottle in hand and held eye contact with a smile in his eyes as he took a sip. *Give me a break.* "You guys signal when you're empty."

Jase teased the strings on his guitar, his tatted-up bicep and forearm flexing with every tantalizing stroke. He nodded, and his gaze rested on mine longer than usual like he was doing math in his head. I tilted my head, puzzled by why Rustin's flirting with me didn't bother him, but everyone else's did?

Meh, I had orders to fill and no time for dwelling.

Drink requests shouted my way at the same rate song requests were thrown into the large Mason jar at Jase's feet. Greenbacks colored the band's tip jar beside the requests, and my pockets filled well for an off-season Monday. The band's cover music became the soundtrack to my work while they warmed up. Jase made a game of prodding men to call out songs for their significant others, ones that got away, or 'bitches who'd broken hearts.'

Bayleigh applauded when one came in for her from a regular with a crush. He loved the pain, she loved shooting him down, then picking him back up. This was fun. The same fun that kept me from quitting on the bad nights, or the nights when I felt guilty for all the skin my uniform showed.

"I'm tagging someone else in," I told the bartenders when at last I returned behind the bar. "I need a breather."

Jase finished another song, then dug through the papers in the request jar. "Hold, please!" a nearby voice shouted.

"Hmm … what might *that* one be requesting?" Bayleigh hummed with a finger at her lips. Marcus's friend waded through the mayhem waving more than a few dollars in his hand. Jase joked with his band mates about big spending.

As the guy reached him, Jase leaned down and whistled when the wad of cash and written request exchanged hands. "We've got ourselves a high priority tune, ladies and gents." Jase's eyebrow lifted as he read the title. He looked back at the band like *you've got to be kidding me.* "No wonder you gave me so much scratch for this, man. Gonna make me go there. I may have to kiss that barmaid again afterward to resuscitate my masculinity." The crowd laughed with uncertainty, and I grinned on a wave of my finger. He was very flirtatious with me tonight. Made me curious. "I'm gonna bring in the extra help of my way-back-buddy, Rustin, who knows this song much, *much* better than I do."

Rustin hopped on-stage, showing as much curiosity as the rest of us, but introduced himself with a country flourish and took a mic and guitar from the nearby stand. The audience welcomed him before he leaned over to hear the song title from Jase.

"To be clear, does that say what I think it says?" he asked.

"That it does, my friend, that it does …." Jase trailed off while Rustin guffawed. *Hmm.* "Think you're up for it?"

The duo shared a nod and warmed the horde with small talk while they adjusted instruments. Someone from the floor offered Rustin a stool of his own. Marcus was in my ear checking to be sure I had nothing to report. I tugged bottle caps in quick succession while downplaying my earlier discomfort.

"We need you safe, all right, Little Red?"

"Safe from what, Marcus? Perverts? What else should I expect with the new uniforms?" I shrugged and flashed a bright smile. He ignored my dig and didn't buy my blasé explanation. I focused on the band to dissuade him from pressing for more. He delivered bottles to the barstool patrons and cut me slack.

"Hey man," Jase called out to his requestor, "who is this for?" The patron's muffled voice broke through. Jase snickered, then came back to the mic. "He says it's complicated. Did you break her heart?" Everyone struggled to hear the response. "Ah, someone else did. He endured the fallout. Hey, we're here for you, boss. Marcus ought to make sure you aren't attacked in the parking lot if she's in here somewhere." The entire place erupted in laughter, me included. There was another muffled exchange. "She's *here*? You've got balls of *steel,* dude."

Everyone looked around for this mystery woman, wondering if this would end in happy reunion or a drink tossed in the brave soul's face.

"Who is Complicated Moonlight, and does he do therapy sessions for broken hearts?" Bayleigh mused as she toweled beer foam off her hands. Jase looked over at Rustin as they worked out the notes to a song that had the masses in riotous laughter. Jase's huge smile stole his ability to get the first lines out.

"*Big Girls Don't Cry*?" she snorted. "Fergie? That's messed up."

"Agreed." I giggled. "This is happening. Keep an eye out for claws to mar what *you* say is a pretty face." I choked on another laugh when I caught Jase zeroed in on me. Bayleigh didn't miss his focal point, either.

What the hell?

He closed his eyes to belt the chorus.

"Ouch. This plot thickens ...." She trailed off, trying to stay light for me, but knowing something more was brewing. "Is it disturbing that Jase knows these lyrics and notes like he does this one on his own time?" She had a point, and I smiled, but what was up? Shouldn't that offend me if he was staring at me while singing that song?

"Holy crap, Kins! Are the claws *yours*?" Bayleigh snatched my wrist to halt my reach for a liquor bottle. "Moonlight! He's looking over here! What if it's for you? Do you know him? What's complicated? Did you break down and punish him for it?" She shook me as if I held information she needed to save the world.

"No way ...." The breath whooshed from my lips like a pregnant woman in Lamaze. Peering where she insisted he was, I didn't have a clear view of the man she'd dubbed Moonlight. He was back-lit. His face was a mystery.

It's complicated.

But ... what if?

I'm complicated.

"Nope. No. No. No. Not possible," I told myself. Bayleigh clung to every morsel. "Wait, didn't somebody call me love earlier?" *A British accent! Oh, hell! No one with an accent had ever called me that before the elevator or since! Until tonight! What an idiot, Kins!*

I wanted to rush out into the crowd and rip the hat from his head! To glimpse the face that haunted my decisions for the past two years without the veil of a costume! The asshole who was just dick enough to come to my job and call my childish crap even still! *He recognized me?*

When I skirted around the bar, the man vanished, and I spun until connecting with Jase's hawkish eyes. *What was happening?* I sensed turbulence, although everything appeared the same on the surface. The hidden undertow scared me. Jase was deeper, more flirtatious, and that kiss had been the furthest he'd ever dared. Rustin seemed to be pushing Jase's envelope. Three men in competition all at once. Two passively telling me to grow up. One doing so from his screwed-up sense of humor, or who the eff knew?

Forget waiting for the end of the song! I collected my things and clocked-out for the night before anyone could convince me to stay. I hustled to the car, grateful I'd taken an earlier shift rather than staying for Jase's break. Not to mention, the questions Bayleigh wanted to ask about the developing dynamic, but I didn't think she'd have to ask to understand what had just happened.

The ultimate in agonizing encounters had found me, and I wasn't sure how our future would play out.

Five a.m. came too soon.

I tumbled out of bed desperate to punch the lights out of the snooze button. Ugh. By five-fifteen, I'd risen from the dead, clad in a sweatshirt and track shorts, secured my hair in an ugly bun, and double-knotted the laces on my cross-trainers. The bun jostled with my lethargic steps to the kitchen. I covered a long yawn while my left hand fumbled inside the cupboard for an energy bar.

"Come on, please be the dark chocolate ... please ... not the fruit chalk flavor ...." I prayed as if playing a tiny lottery that controlled whether the day would be crappy. Don't ask why I always bought the gross ones.

The luck of the draw, I suppose.

With a banana and a water bottle tossed into the mix of essentials, I shouldered a small knapsack and trotted down the stairs to my car. The brisk sting of cool air jolted my eyes wide open with a rush as effective as a cup of coffee. Or maybe the thrill of the pirate coming into the bar to call me back to the battlefield lit a fire beneath my feet.

En route to the beach, my thoughts replayed the unforgettable interlude two years prior. Was the pirate handsome without his costume, or plain but influential in that way you don't notice he's not attractive? One thing I did know, he was ballsy and knew how to make an entrance. He also had the best cologne in the world, along with a grip that reigned in my attitude rather than scared him.

I swallowed some water and fished for the power bar.

"Hell, yeah! Today's forecast is ...." I drummed against the steering wheel when luck hadn't failed, and I bit into a peanut butter bar. *Oh, happy day!* "Thank you, Jesus." I turned up the music to force my head out of pirate-shaped clouds and into the frame needed for a five-mile jog before the obstacle course.

Familiar lamps brightened the sidewalk like the warmth of an old friend's smile. After parking across the street, I killed the ignition and got out to savor the rumble of waves, salty breeze against my face. I closed my eyes through a deep breath and opened them to survey the deserted obstacle course sitting to the right. I gathered my water bottle and smart phone, locked the car and coiled the keychain around my wrist.

Though dawn threatened to nudge the moon from its lazy haze, buttery light floated over the gulf, reflecting with the shimmy of the currents. The waves ferried beams ashore then retreated into the spray. Damn Bayleigh. Moonlight would never shine the same. He might not be that pirate at all ….

I forced him out and concentrated on my warm-up, stretching before hitting the sand.

Rather than insert earbuds and drown nature's solitude, I jogged in the ambiance that paused all else on my brain, the continuous rush of water, seagulls fighting for fish while plover and ghost crab dodged my footfalls in their quest for periwinkles beneath the sand. No competition here. My rare quiet place. In the natural turbulence of this feminine mind lurk the troubles emotions bring, *could I maintain my grade point average until graduation, would Eliza be angry if I hurdled faster than her, was this guy into me or was I reading too much into things? What had Sara flustered enough to change to day shift? Did Inferno have her inventing excuses to leave? Was she in danger? Was Rustin warning about someone mistaking me for her?*

Shut up! Quiet place!

Just me and the run. Just me and the run.

I veered further from the shore to where the sand wasn't as firmly packed. The difficulty of running in powder silenced all thoughts of anything other than the pain of the push against the resistance. My breath steamed in hot, even pants as I trekked past each lifeguard post. When I turned around at the two-and-a-half-mile mark, or ten lifeguard stands along, the sun crested above the horizon to the east. My favorite part, something only a few other early-bird joggers and I shared as I soldiered on toward the obstacle course.

Sunlight painted the sky in orange sherbet. Distant barges illuminated against the horizon's infinite edge. The gleam of metal monkey bars stole my attention as I neared phase two.

Finishing with a full sprint, my heart thrummed like a snare in my ears as I pitched my water bottle into the sand and huffed onto the obstacle course.

Today was my first morning back since before Christmas. I expected to be rusty. Earbuds in place, I opened a music app and rapper, Nate Feuerstein, set the mood as I rolled my shoulders like my fists should've been taped for a fight.

'I swear, you'd be so strong with a real man.'

Get out of my head 'Moonlight!' Screw needing a man to be strong!

I tapped the stopwatch app, secured my phone and bolted through the tires with the fervor of a starving cheetah racing after a gazelle. Slinking up the rope climb, across the monkey bars, I ignored the raw pain in my palms while the music pumped with my adrenaline. At the pull-up bar, I squeezed out seven, then bounded up the large net and warred with the swing and sway as the braided nylon threatened to toss me off in front of a couple of voyeurs drying their faces with towels. At the top, I lunged over the block wall the net secured to, stuck the landing on the other side, and proceeded to lather, rinse, repeat. As I leapt to the ground a third time, a guy stretched at the tires, dark hair, expensive sunglasses and workout wear, a sleeveless tank showcasing definition (despite the chilly temp).

His routine differed from mine. We didn't cross paths often, but at the pull-up bar he eased himself up a dozen times as though he could've asked me to pick a number, any number. *Grrr...* I forced my pride and noodle arms to strain through another seven and ground out an eighth in spite. Even as my muscles trembled when I dropped, I gave myself a fist pump. *What a great morning!*

He smiled before running to the rope while I sped to the net again. Causing his smile made *me* smile, too, especially since his demeanor conveyed a thread in common: he didn't seem to be one to entertain fools during a workout. Neither was I.

This guy was fast, because soon he was on the net. The ropes rocked harder as he rambled past me (and my pride) with an effortless vault over the wall. I touched down behind him with a new surge of determination. My reward was an impressed nod that in no way delivered credit because I was a girl. *Eff yeah!*

The victorious adrenaline I loved propelled me into a bonus lap. Wasn't he kinda challenging me to workout *with* him?

This time, however, two more men occupied the equipment, and my challenger force-fed me his dust for breakfast. *Dammit!* I hurled girly stupidity into the seashells, fell behind, but pushed myself harder to prevent having my buns whipped by these other beasts.

I drove harder as I shimmied down the rope and jogged to the monkey bars, following another attractive torso across, though his hair was blond and matted with sweat.

While I wondered where the dark-haired guy went, I now dreaded that stupid pull-up bar. With these men sweating and the humidity compounding with the sunrise, the metal was nasty and slick when I jumped to grasp the bar. My fingers slipped off. Strong hands arrested my fall and lifted me like a child to regain a firmer grip. Before I popped off, I turned and looked over my shoulder. *Jase Taylor!*

I read the, "Morning, baby," from his lips. He nodded with a smug grin that read my accidental attitude loud and clear, then cranked out pull-ups beside me. Since this was a bonus round, I did three and left him there doing—well, I lost count after eleven. The other guy made them seem as easy with his James Bond build as Jase did bulging like Captain America.

I pushed that sculpture from my mind and ran to the net. My turn to give an appreciative smile when Jase landed right behind me.

I left him and huffed over to the shorter girly bar for core work. My sweatshirt rubbed like a Brill-o pad against my sweat-stung skin. I shrugged from the stifling sleeves to peel the drenched collar over my head and tossed the discomfort to the sand, then chugged the remaining water from my bottle. Although the air chilled the soaked tank to my body, I was overheated. Several men roamed the beach shirtless and two ladies jogged in sports bras for the same reason.

An old treasure-hunting couple wandered close to the shoreline to sweep a metal detector over the sand and collect pretty shells. I focused on them as I gripped the bar and hooked my knees over the dew-dampened metal, dangling upside-down to make my abs scream. After pumping crunches well beyond exhaustion, I dangled, pulled an earbud. Rays of sun glittered against the soft waves, a pair of pelicans above coasted on the breeze. Sand Pipers skittered around the old couple as they sought periwinkles beneath the sand. The metal detector beeped and scattered the tiny birds.

I smiled as the old lady bent over. The man nagged her about letting him do the digging.

"Nonsense," she griped. "You just want the credit when we find the Spanish gold."

"Woman, I know how to share. Been doing this for over fifty years now, haven't we?"

She waved him on and stood with annoyance that didn't convey in her smile.

Adorable.

I wasn't sure how long I let the scene steal my thoughts, but I startled when a hand waved in front of my face. Jase cast a disarming grin, his elbow propped on the bar. A bare eight-pack, protruding biceps, and popping pecs gleamed with perspiration like a freshly waxed car after a sun-shower as he combed his fingers through sweat-soaked hair.

I tugged the other earbud and dismounted to stand before him, squinting against the sun.

"Hey!" I breathed. "Thanks for the help back there. The pull-up bar was kind of slimy." I cringed, dorky by mistake. Inside, I face-palmed at the thought of him singing that I be a 'big girl now'.

He chuckled. "Agreed! Wonder what *nasty* jerk spilled his fluids without cleaning up?" He glanced over his shoulder. "We should blame Rustin," he whispered with a thumb pointing to the obstacles.

"Ha! That's so gross. Deal." Figures cocky Country was who I'd admired on the monkey bars earlier. Good thing he didn't earn a vindicating look to inflate the ego he sported.

"Did you guys have fun last night?" What I didn't ask: *why did you stare at me while you sang that song?*

"We did pretty well for an off-season Monday." He seemed casual enough. "Although, it just wasn't the same after you left." He winked and peeked again over his shoulder. "I think I watched the fire go out of more than a few of the men in the room, including Rustin, when you walked out the door."

"Aw, not you, though?" *Crap! Mouth diarrhea!* "I'm sure you both had partners waiting in the wings to cheer you up."

"Yes, *me,* too. That's a given, Sweet Kins. I don't like when you work early because you leave early. My muse." He sighed with a pearly grin at the Heavens. "People throw food at me when you aren't working. I wish they'd pick something softer and tastier. I hate broccoli, but at least it fed the horse's ass over there." He snickered and tickled my ribs.

My cackle burst louder than I wanted as I jumped back. How bizarre to have his open attention. The only things thrown his way were bodies, bucks, bras, and bikinis. You better believe he made a lot to headline at the bar *twice* a week, and he turned dimes to dollars in our pockets with every show. *No complaints here!*

"FYI …." He leaned close like we shared a secret, "No company but each other's last night." He waggled his eyebrows and another embarrassing too loud laugh joined with my slap to his sweaty arm as my flirtatious alter-ego presented.

"Ah, the gay card. Makes sense why you've never asked me out." *Oh, no! Abort! Abort!* I didn't want my heart broken when he confirmed *any* reason. Hell, I didn't want my heart broken at all, and

Taylor Street was a one-way lane of heartache only the moronic traveled.

His grin faltered. *Uh, oh. Brace yourself. Stupid Kins!*

"Wait, what?" *Come on! He wanted me to explain?*

"Well, you know, you flirt a lot, but ...." I gulped, begged my nerves to calm. *Did I even want anything?*

For goodness sakes! What had I just done?

Cleaving to my endorphin-induced confidence, I glanced at my phone and picked a song, jammed an earbud back in.

While I panicked inside, he tugged at both ends of the towel slung around his neck and chewed his lip like *he* was the nervous one! *Whoa! I had never seen that expression on him before!*

The brilliant blond jogged over and broke up the awkward moment. Jase seemed relieved and disappointed at once. I felt the same.

"Damn, guys, I'm happy to see you, too." Rustin panted. *How had I not recognized him when I was working out next to him?* "You, Red, are a *tough* woman!" His beam framed a deep set of dimples as he tossed his chin toward the course. "That normal for you?"

"Affirmative."

"How come I haven't bumped into you before?" Jase asked, glad for the change in subject. "I'm always here for lifeguard training."

"That's right. Tyndall mentioned you were a lifeguard. Maybe lifeguards aren't the early risers I am," I teased. "Can't force dedication." He rolled his eyes, so I slacked up. "Just playing. I hate when guys come onto me or women give me the death ray because of my drive. I try to wake up before the perverts and haters. True story."

"Makes sense," Rustin said. "Although, I don't think perverts adhere to time constraints. It's kind of a twenty-four-seven preoccupation." Rustin squinted at me then fired a grin at his buddy. "Better keep your eye out."

Jase's hands came up in surrender. "Hold up. Did you think I was hitting on you? Because I wasn't. I was just being friendly. Can't cross paths and not say hi. That's rude." His lips clamped shut at Rustin's sigh. "You come out here *every* day?" Jase wondered.

49

I fought the sting in my cheeks at his admission.

"Not *every* day, but when Track season is upon us, I'm here every opportune morning for extra conditioning." I supplied an invitation I shouldn't have written.

"That's right, Tyndall mentioned you were a runner." *Touché.* "We're about to jog down the beach. Want to join? In a platonic, friend-zone sort of way?"

Rustin nodded beside him, a dangling tongue the only thing absent from this dog's mouth, hope dancing in both sets of eyes like wagging tails. *Good grief.* Last night, I'd booked out to avoid them in my confusion. Today, I'd clipped leashes to their collars and given them names!

"Sorry, guys, I get my run in before the obstacle course, and I have class. Another time?" I had no classes today, but big girls had more to do than flirt with boys, and apparently, I'd read too much into Jase's flirtation. *Sigh.*

Best to bolt. When they expressed their regret and pleaded, I smiled and turned them down. *No more mixed messages for me today, thank you very much.*

I plucked the nasty sweatshirt from the ground and tucked my other earbud in as I shook off sand. To my surprise, the guy—my expensive handsome challenger —granted a polite nod from behind his ever-present sunglasses as he, too, made his way toward the parking lot.

Not wanting to seem rude, I removed my earbuds as we fell into distant steps in the same direction. The silence expanded with my mute plea for him to talk to me. I'd sworn-off dating, but there was something about this guy I couldn't put my finger on. He'd sent all the signals, and how vindicating if Jase saw that maybe I *hadn't* thought he was coming onto me.

"Impressive pace on the course," I prodded before we reached our vehicles. *Come on, dude! What am I missing?*

"Ditto."

I inhaled. I loathed that word.

50

"Ditto, huh?" I uncoiled the bracelet from my arm, unlocked my Civic catty-cornered to the Tesla he cruised up to. His head rose. I longed to smack the sunglasses from his eyes to see them when I called him out.

Suspicion slammed into me when he smiled, not the same smile he'd given before. This one enjoyed a private joke remarkably like the man who'd followed me to my car in that parking garage two years ago. *The same arrogant asshole? No effing way! The pirate had used that stupid word, too!* My heart drummed, but my pride shouted louder.

I cleared my throat and anxiety, noticed the similarity in the way he carried himself just the way the pirate had. *Well, hell. Here goes.* "A minimal effort word from a *man* who outperformed me on the course? I am disappointed, and had you asked *today*, I would've had coffee with you. Nothing too *complicated* about that." *Boom. Mic drop.*

A gorgeous smile cracked his catalogue-model-cool. If he *was* the pirate, how fabulous to be driving away from him again? If he was not, still awesome to demand a guy man-up.

The fan of my fingers as I drove away was a crap-calling bonus.

6

That evening, time crawled at a sloth's pace as I agreed to work a much-loathed Tuesday evening shift I had sworn off. Being nice sometimes sucked. Marcus knew I hated open mic night but promised I could have Valentine's Day off without even covering my shift. Said he would work my shift himself if he couldn't find a replacement. Though the Hallmark holiday loomed a couple of weeks away, who could say no to that? The confusion swimming through my mind over the guys was enough without the added anchor of turning down gifts and invitations to go out with men I'd not trust to feed my mom's cat.

Tonight's patrons buzzed low and laid back without touching the mic. We listened to the juke on free play and helped Marcus tick off inventory. For now, the biker I'd promised a drink to hadn't shown, which was nice. Bayleigh and I kept up with orders as Garrett refilled coolers with cases he hauled from the back. A bar-back refilled the trays of cherries and wedges of limes, lemons, oranges. He tossed us the ugly cherries to snack on. I worked the stem of one in my mouth with a smile as I thought of men trying to impress us with their knots.

The toe of my sneaker tapped along to the crooning of *Bad Moon Rising* like a cheerful omen as Moonlight bubbled into my head while Marcus simultaneously asked about Blue Moon bottles. The iconic sound of CCR faded while I traded Fogerty's voice for Jase's.

Two men on my mind at the same time. On top of that, I hummed along, picking apart Jase's and Rustin's odd dynamic on the beach this morning. *Were they competing for my attention?*

"Both dogs chasing the same ball, but the one to catch it first can destroy it all by himself? What do you think?" I asked Bayleigh after the replay. She called the Blue Moon count to Marcus. He asked Garrett to bring a case. Bayleigh double-checked the fruit arrangement as the bar-back replaced the lids over them. I spat the knotted cherry stem into the trash.

"Meh. The only person Jase has fooled is you," Bayleigh said and checked the olive bin. "Whether you're plain blind, or off-limits due to your code of ethics, I can't figure out, so neither can he. I say keep him confused till he makes his intention obvious." Nausea soured my gut. *Was she right?*

"And Rustin?" I asked. "It's weird. Where does he fit in? And why?"

Marcus took the case of Blue Moon from Garrett and strode behind the bar. The bottles jostled as he set the box on the bar, then pat his bulking bicep to make us laugh. "Rustin could be the final straw, or Taylor's excuse," he injected. "He's close to making a move. I'd bet money on it. Seeing you all prettied up yesterday must've got the caveman going with all the competition. I keep trying to tell you, wearing heels might take you off the market."

"Ha! Sir, you need to hush."

Bayleigh and I shook our heads but smiled.

"True story. Pretty legs in a set of heels, a little skin—"

"A *lotta* skin." I called his crap with a dry edge. He never paused.

"— will make a man ignore a butter face all day long. And if she is a butter face, that vanishes with each passing shot. It's a win-win for the bar."

"You should be ashamed of yourself," I told him.

His turn to chuckle. "You'll never have that problem, Little Red, so my advice is maybe leave your options open?"

"Thanks, but what's that supposed to mean?"

"It means," Bayleigh intoned, "he *knows* Complicated Moonlight. And that even if you grow old and fat, you'll be the opposite of a but-her-face. Your face will be pretty when everything else fades. You'll be a butter body." She cheesed and elbowed Marcus for holding out. He studied her like WTF while I laughed but thanked her.

"Hold up. Complicated Moonlight?" Marcus asked.

"Yeah. The crap-calling song requestor from last night. The Bucs hat." *Buccaneers. A pirate.* "Admit it, he requested that song for Kinsley, didn't he? You're doing the chummy guy thing where you watch out for your wing man, and he's doing that thing where he pokes the girl with the stick, so she'll smack him. You never forget the boy that pulls your hair and pokes ya."

They all snickered as I shook my head in disapproval, but what a thrilling idea from a man who had decided I'd been too young on our first round in the ring!

Garrett weaseled in to tell Bayleigh to catch the order at the end of the bar. "You want the rapid low down in real guy speak?" he offered with a gleam in his eye. "Jase is a slut in love. Rustin is a redneck pervert. You two invent stupid names for patrons, and your TDH has come in sporadically over the years, enjoys Michelob or Captain and Coke with cherries and grenadine. But when you're on-duty, Red Running Hood, he usually leaves or settles for cherries and Coke. He either wants to control himself around you or avoid you. Think he suspects you're the wolf?"

"Garrett! You brat!" I cackled, but everything came to exhilarating life at the idea that he'd been under my nose all along. *But why wait all this time to reignite our sparring match?* "What's his name?" I asked.

Neither man spoke.

Garrett cleared his throat and glanced at Marcus for a beat. "I lied. TDH is here for Jase, and Jase is in love with him. Rustin is the jealous lover come from afar to stake his claim before all is lost forever to some childhood sweetheart." His forearm covered his forehead like a damsel in distress, while I gaped at the terminology pertaining to my role. "Thus, ended the fantasy of every bartender working last night and praying they might be a big girl now. Don't you remember about fifteen other women sitting right in front of the bar? You guys make this too easy. Ooh, speaking of TDH ...." Garrett's voice trailed with his eyes as they followed an exotic Latina model-walking toward the stage. He rubbed his hands together and wished us well with our PMS and angst.

"Looks like she needs instructions for holding the mic. I'll whip you up some chocolate martinis when I return."

Bayleigh and I stared him down while Marcus called, "Take your time, Garrett. These things can be complicated!"

Garrett grinned over his shoulder. "You know it, boss."

"See what I mean about them heels, girls?" Marcus jeered. We exchanged a look. Marcus was watching out for bros before hos, confirming her point.

When he asked about the liquor bottles, we gathered the almost empty liquor bottles and used them to assemble trays of dollar shots, then yanked the pour spouts. Marcus went to grab the new bottles.

Bayleigh proposed, "Next time they come in, I'm feeling the situation out. Pass the lime wedges?" I grabbed the bucket and pushed them her way. "Thank you." She arranged them for the server who came to take the tray. "I'm hearing a lot about Jase and Rustin, but you're suspiciously quiet about the one I'd go for, which makes me think you'd also go for Moonlight. It's okay to admit, at least to me. What's not to like? He's mysterious, older, and *not* Jase." She and Jase equaled two sluts of the same feather with little else in common and a sibling rivalry dynamic. "Or maybe you *should* pick the dude who serenades you while every other woman, besides me, envies you through your oblivion. Kind of feel bad. Jase's certainly tortured himself long enough over you."

"Ugh! I hate this!" I stammered. "He doesn't serenade me. If you can't even make up your mind, how can I be expected to? Forget it. Graduation. Internship. Track. Grades. My IQ is dropping by the day."

"Right. That new internship you're hoping for might be great when you get it, but can it make you—"

"Bayleigh. Pass the bonbons because I'm not listening to your sex talk. Jase is a fool if he makes a move. Same with Rustin. And if Moonlight is older, he's worse than them. No one will ever stay faithful because they'll be too busy cheating with hookers to be in a celibate relationship. Let's not go there."

"Au contraire, mademoiselle. An older one has the restraint that a younger guy doesn't. If they've got their junk together, they can keep it together. Their wild oats are sown. They recognize there's more to the savor rather than devouring a quick bite. Assuming *you* can stay celibate, he may not have as hard a time waiting …."

Grrr. I chewed my lip in recollection of the things the pirate said to me before I left him in the parking garage. *Hadn't he implied something similar? Was that part of why I ought to stop dating little boys and opt for men?* Jase and Rustin weren't exactly boys anymore. Jase was almost thirty years old. Before hope turned me into a girly idiot, I forced myself to remember there was a great divide between words and action.

"Celibacy is for pussies who can't close the deal," a crass voice barbed. I turned to see the dreaded biker walk up to take a stool. *Ugh.*

He eyed the new bottle of Drambuie while I peeked at the time to see how many hours I'd have to endure his BS.

"You didn't think I'd forget, did you? You promised me a drink." I hated drunks who retained memory.

While I set to work on his rusty nail, Bayleigh walked around the corner to, I assume, grab Marcus. The biker's deceptively kind smile lifted from my butt to my reflection in the mirror. "You ever been on a motorcycle?"

I cocked an eyebrow. "No."

"That singer have a bike?"

"Not that I know of," I told him, trying not to show exasperation. I saw where this was heading. "Last time I checked, to join a pissing match, you have to be a shoo-in for the competition. Bikers aren't my type. No offense."

"I'm not offended." Seemed true enough, but that gleam in his eye soured my gut. "I can't fault you for your inexperience. Like sex. How can you judge something you've never had? Who doesn't appreciate the lure of a virgin? It's like pay dirt. Especially to that singer."

Ouch! My cheeks stung and I over poured his Drambuie like a nervous novice. He noticed and chuckled.

"Besides, you think you want celibacy, but *you* need a bad boy to keep the worse boys away. Your singer talks a big game, but he's weak over you, and that makes him weak period. Bikers can be scary when they need to be."

"Bikers can also be nice rather than creating a poor image for the rest," I ground out and slammed his drink on the wood before him. "And you know nothing about the singer. Back out of my business or leave the bar."

"Well, well, well …." He took the drink and gulped the entire thing in three swallows, then mimicked how I'd slammed the glass, making me flinch. "Maybe I was wrong." A slow smile took over a sinister undercurrent I hadn't spied till staring at him. "That weak singer could use someone like you to keep him safe."

I jumped and squealed as the bottle of Drambuie shattered near my feet.

"Damn. That was the only bottle in this shipment, Kins." Marcus cursed and bent like he was cleaning the mess. I hadn't even realized he'd walked behind me! When he stood, he had the neck of the broken bottle in one hand, his empty trash bag in another, but there was zero missing his threat. Bayleigh tossed the biker's glass in the sink, then crossed her arms over her chest as she stared at the pervert.

"What a shame," the biker said. He made a show of duck lips as he considered the liquor bottles, then said, "Rusty nail ain't my only drink. Good thing there's a whole bar. How about … a Blue Moon. Bottle not draft. Careful how you hold that, man. Looks like a threat."

Marcus held his gaze and nodded. "Yeah, you're right." He shoved the shard inside the bag. Garrett picked that moment to come back. The pep in his step faltered somewhat when he took in everyone's expressions and body language.

"You asked for a Blue Moon? Did I hear that right?" Garrett chimed, diffusing the static. "Bottles are still warm. I'm gonna tap the draft, okay? Hope you don't mind plastic."

"Yeah, that's fine." The biker grinned right at me like he knew something I didn't.

"Kins, since it's slow, you have bathroom duty," Garrett told me while he placed an orange wedge on the cup. I nodded and grabbed the mop, wanting to throw the wood like a stake into this vampire's heart. When I got around the bar and into the bathroom, I glanced at my reflection to see my cheeks alight. Turning the tap, I scooped some cold water to pat against them, then stared to talk myself down. Bayleigh came in a second later. Her hand soothed over my back as she scoped my reflection.

"Don't listen to him. Not all men are whores. Your singer is weak for you, but I think Jase keeps that guy afraid to misbehave the way he'd like to, and that's why he's pissed."

"Sometimes I really hate this job."

"No, you don't. You hate perverts. If every biker were like him, you could hate it, but you know most of them are good guys wanting to look dangerous in their leathers." We both smiled, me reluctantly. There were some adorable men who came in feeling like a million bucks with their swaggers and their *ol' ladies* beside them, even though we'd seen them two nights before in collared shirts discussing stocks and golf games. She was right. That part I did love. "Don't let one jerk-off and his trashy gang ruin it for you."

"Thanks, Bay. I don't know why he rattled me."

"We both know that Jase sleeping around bothers you. Unfortunately, it's not hard to unsettle a good girl about something that would naturally upset her." She scooped my hair over my right shoulder and bent to rest her chin on my left. Her blue eyes met mine in the mirror. "Jase isn't the only option. Just for you, next time Moonlight comes in, I'm knocking that hat right off his head and unmasking him. Would you like that?"

I rolled my eyes, but my cheeks grew warm again as I nodded.

"I'm going to prove that it's all shadow illusion. That he's unattractive in the daylight hours. No booze. No shade. Male pattern baldness is a good reason for the cap. I feel much better now. Don't you? Glad we had this talk." She clapped her lips shut and smiled. I reached up and cupped her free cheek, then turned my head to kiss the other.

"Thanks for helping with Inferno. You're a good friend, Bayleigh Blue."

"Thanks. Just don't tell anyone, my reputation will be ruined." She moseyed to the door, pausing as she grabbed the handle. "At least if Moonlight's unattractive, you'll have an easier time narrowing a winner."

"Pretty is as pretty does, Bayleigh. Looks aren't everything."

She chortled at the ridiculousness on her way out. I took a long look in the mirror, thinking of my morning. If he proved to be whom I'd suspected earlier, Bayleigh might knock me out of the way to take him on herself. Memories of his athleticism had me ready to run away to a convent to hide. What was that saying about corrupting a nun?

God, help me! I prayed and started mopping.

7 | ♀

For the next two weeks, school poked along while not a single guy worth flirting with came into the bar. Fortunately, not an errant biker did either. Work was blissfully boring in that regard, but a dangerous restlessness had taken root. Existence in a classroom with my nose pressed to the glass lost some luster. Had there always been this many couples mingling around campus? Had I gotten so used to wanting to gag myself at their public displays of affection that I'd ignored them altogether?

The days passed in a blaze of dedication but lacked adventure. Didn't matter if I blocked out Bayleigh's sex talks. My mind was captive. Not by the act of sex, but the anticipation and subtle hope that a worthy partner may be riding over the horizon. Even the flavor of victory during meets needed spice. Nothing compared to the adrenaline rush I'd enjoyed the night Complicated Moonlight made a request of the man Bayleigh swore was serious competition for him.

Was he brazen enough to make another request, or would he turn out like the wussy guys I sat near in today's Color Theory course? They tossed glances, but never met my eyes.

All little boys, love.

Mr. Miller, the *one* adjunct professor that demanded we call him by his last name, owned the only set of XY chromosomes in the place that made eye contact without shying away. A man. Also, the only professor who didn't treat his students like petty subjects begging at his throne of wisdom and precious time. I got the impression he did this job as a hobby more than survival, which might explain his evident enjoyment versus those so pressed to pay the bills they exhausted themselves teaching almost twenty classes a semester.

The errand boy from the staff office wormed his way into our lecture, delivering flowers and gifts while the girls reacted like an ATM spewed free cash.

Crap! My throat dried. How had I forgotten Valentine's Day? I *hated* vulnerability, and I *hated* that I had no reason to get roses from anyone but my father.

Still…

Shushing my inner girl, I refocused on the awful slides projected up front. The art professor's poker face was worth the course. I didn't need the class. Jase's little sister, Tyndall Taylor, was an Interior Design major. To better understand my best friend, I'd opted to appraise ugly art in an attempt to see the same beauty she insisted was there. Wonder what she'd think of Miller and his slides of the most ridiculous canvases. I snorted to myself. Tyndall would be too mesmerized in checking Miller out to notice the slides.

Meanwhile, these minions attempted to impress him with feigned sophistication. Pathetic. He knew they were brown-nosing and exploited their ass-kissing like a bonus sociology lab. I rolled my eyes.

"Ms. Hayes, your opinion on this piece?" he called my crap. I considered the single yellow line in the center of a black canvas that unjustly made the big bucks.

"That's easy." I smiled to cover my embarrassment, glad for the dim lighting.

"Oh?" he asked. A snobby jerk from the table beside mine stared to see what *I* could *possibly* contribute. Okay, not everyone avoided eye-contact.

"Yeah." I gestured to the screen. "That's a light saber. Although, the artist should have made the handle easier to spy. Luke's great, but I'm a Han Solo fan myself. Add a classic Harrison Ford somewhere in there to liven things up. Some Chewbacca fur to give this extra texture. *I'd* be ready to mount that baby on the wall."

Miller tossed his head on a pleased laugh, and the class followed suit, except for the snob, this was serious business.

"Interesting perspective considering this piece predates the era of *Star Wars*. Perhaps the artist was a time traveler?" Miller teased.

"May I?" the snob asked, righteous indignation all over him. Miller nodded. "You see—" snob gestured toward me, then the slide "— this symbolizes the light beyond the door closed off to the darkness of the world."

Several students hummed and the class shifted to deep thoughts of the shallow minded. Why he'd singled me out, I wasn't sure.

"Ooh, I like that," I admitted, unfazed. "Although, if the door were completely closed, the light would emanate from the bottom, whereas this yellow stripe is vertical, therefore the door is cracked open. The question is whether the person in the dark is pressing the door open to peer into the light, or vice versa?"

Another hum throughout the student body. The snob sneered. Miller spoke up. "How very Hermann Rorschach, Ms. Hayes, Mr. Anthony. Each piece, much like an ink blot, is subjective and dependent on your view of the world."

"Always have to outdo everyone, eh, Hayes?" the snobby Mr. Anthony whispered as he leaned into my personal space. "Maybe we'll get lucky and you'll sprain an ankle this season."

"Aw, is that a bruise on your ego, Anthony?" I growled under my breath. "Or just the shadow of the demon living inside your black heart?"

"If it is, are you gonna grab your Bible and perform an exorcism on me?"

Miller cleared his throat and shot us a warning look. The sting went all through me while Anthony wore an innocent expression.

"You know, class, art is also a fantastic tool for mature dialog on differing perspective with exceptionally low risk for personal threats and name-calling. Therefore, should you encounter such a virulent art critic, consider ousting their toxic temper or else your perspective may become tainted by the same poison."

Damn! My eyes bugged at Miller's passive aggressive threat as I stared at the table.

"In conclusion, Mr. Anthony, did the artist's child cause a happy accident on his father's canvas, or was this simplicity created on purpose to expose us as the deep-minded frauds we think we are? The world may never know, so each one of you are correct. Next." Miller clicked the remote in his hand to produce the next slide. Several heads turned to look at us, fists over their grins.

"Actually." Anthony leaned close again when Miller's attention focused on the slide. "I'm pretty sure that's the shadow of doom as the dwindling Valentine's cart passes you by."

I shrugged while girls, and a couple guys, gasped in gooey awe as they received flowers and cards, balloons and stuffed animals.

Miller sighed as he stepped aside for the frazzled delivery guy. "We may as well address the elephant in the room." The lights came on, spotlighting the cornucopia of leftover love.

The remaining empty-handed women perked like premenstrual poppies eyeing fudge brownies.

Miller brushed the long hair from his face, scanned the insane floral arrangement gifted to one of the most beloved sorority girls. To be facetious, after asking permission, he plucked the card, then read aloud the love note in the most melodramatic manner to make the class laugh. I couldn't stop chewing my lip as the squeaky wheels rolled past.

No worries, Kins. The day isn't over because you leave campus empty-handed. This jerk has no say in whether you're wanted or not.

My fears subsided when cart boy halted and placed an enormous vase of lavender roses before me. I peeked at the girl nearby, ready to slide them to her. He pinned me with a look and flicked the label. *Kinsley Hayes.*

Tears crystallized my vision of another vase crammed with orange calla lilies and white roses. He tapped my name on that envelope like a smart-ass, but I cupped my gasp in girly awe not even Assholio Anthony could steal. Orange calla lilies were my favorite. *Had Daddy taken pity?* The guy dragged a giant bear from the bottom, then a bunch of balloons fastened to the lily vase jostled free and smacked him. Now, I chewed my lip to stifle a grin while he muttered and tossed

64

several cards and a box, then slid a vase over to the girl along with a couple cards.

Holy crap! Look at this stuff!

"Wow, who knew I was such a beloved bitch, yeah?" I beamed at the jerk-off, but you better believe I was praising God for this wonderful vindication even if I knew I shouldn't.

Miller homed in on his next victim. "I can't speak for everyone else, Ms. Hayes, but I'm dying to see what's inside that wrapping."

The girls leaned in as I took the wrapped present in my hand. The foil paper shined with scrolls of red and silver. He glanced at my fingers as I picked at the edges.

"You save wrapping paper?" he asked, a light in his eyes. I nodded. He reached for a nearby paintbrush, then slid the tip beneath the folds. No damage. "All done."

"Thank you." I avoided looking anywhere else as I held the only jewelry box I'd ever received from someone other than my father. He didn't buy me things that came in flat velveteen boxes. "Wow." I sighed, uncertain how to digest the gift I revealed as I opened the lid.

My teacher whistled amid the coos. The sorority princess jogged over, eager to be in every limelight— one of few girls not intimidated by me. *She* intimidated *me,* though. When she offered to clasp the necklace around my neck, I sputtered a 'yes' and ponied my hair aside.

"This is magnificent, Kinsley."

With deft piano fingers, she adorned my throat with a dainty vine of emeralds and diamonds. She was right: the piece was magnificent, and too generous!

She and her sisters gabbed about pairing the jewels with dresses and shoes. I fought tears, fuzzy and yearning to know what fool spent such money and didn't leave a note.

Mr. Miller cleared his throat while I held to mine. "Analogous color pallet with your eyes, Ms. Hayes. I'd surmise someone bought that to compliment your irises."

Oh hell. What a deep statement.

I studied the leaves and flowers between my finger and thumb. No more denial, I wanted butterflies and sentiments, pining and playing, affection and romance, to make others want to gag themselves over my public displays of affection with someone. *Dammit to hell!* This jewelry had the strength to kidnap my resolve as long as I wore this collar for someone's leash! *Get this green Kryptonite off my neck STAT!*

"Coach Walton is going to be nervous if you have a boyfriend."

"It's a good thing I don't," I sang.

"You might after this. Someone in that stack could be the lucky winner."

The sorority sisters speculated like high rollers making wagers with a bookie. Teach winked as I rolled my eyes, then he moved to the next Valentine victim, quoting Shakespeare from her bouquet. *The Sisterhood of the Traveling Pants* followed him to gush elsewhere.

"You were saying?" I cheesed at the sobered face beside me.

"Guess some men enjoy castration."

"Well, let's hope at least one of them has cojones big enough I can't fit my snips around."

He snorted with a reluctant smile while I removed the necklace and reflected that Mr. Miller had summarized every reason for my dedication and why I wanted none of the rumor mill. Being myself was bad enough without adding a relationship or love interest to the drama. Guy beside me: case-in-point.

The warm and fuzzy faded after I replaced the necklace with the care of a surgeon.

The cards were a myriad of corny and adorable, with heart candies strewn on elastic included inside of one from one of the guys Jase had threatened at the bar. *Wow. Guess Jase didn't scare everyone?* I read the verse from the card on the lilies but didn't recognize the handwriting or the source. A pretty poem about never leaving.

Finally, I addressed the arrangement of lavender roses—three dozen of them—that I'd tried to ignore like the nag of intuition. As I leaned up to smell the soft purple petals, I spied a card wedged deep between the blooms, *tied to a pumpkin spice Keurig coffee cup!* My heart slammed with hope.

When I ripped the envelope open, Moonlight confirmed with his unmistakable message:

Kinsley,
Not simple or easy, love?
I'll buy that, but you failed to mention you were fast.
Keep those spikes on.
X- Complicated

8 | ♀

When class ended, I was tripping over the balloons to get out and call Tyndall during practice! I needed to run! *Can we say exhilaration overload? Moonlight used my name! He knew my name!*

Miller insisted on helping me to my car because he didn't want me mugged for the necklace. "Excellent point," I agreed, but couldn't kill the dumbest girly grin.

"I've heard your face can freeze like that," he teased.

"That's a good thing, right? Who wants a stick up their butt like the poser from class?" I tried not to rush him as I lost control of my rapid pace. "How do you handle art snobs? I prefer my Han Solo poster much more than that last piece. But if you paint a line and make a million who's the real idiot?"

He chuckled and shook his head as I forced the giant bear in the messy backseat. "It's possible Walton will like this development. Hard to slow you down, Hayes."

"That's good stuff, make sure you tell him if you see him."

"Sure, but you've been forewarned: he's not happy today. I figure he'll try to take it out on *you*."

"Sounds like you know him well," I said. We teamed to shove all the balloons inside with no success. "Thanks for the advice, Mr. Miller, but I don't think even pissy Walton can bring me down right now."

The pain in my cheeks confirmed how idiotic I must've appeared. When I bent into the front seat to tuck the necklace in my purse, I snagged a pocketknife, then shoved the bag beneath the passenger side. I came up brandishing my weapon of choice with mischief. Miller's smile grew.

"Screw it." Grasping the lot of strings tied to the balloons, I sliced them free, and we watched them sail into the sky with my spirits. "Like blowing out candles on a cake." I sighed. "All those wishes. You should make some, too."

"No way. Can't keep up." When I smiled back at him, his phone was up, and he'd snapped a photo. "You mind? School paper? I assist the journalism department where I can."

"Fair enough. Thanks for your help and the lesson in sophistication today." My smile tamed in shame. "I'm sorry for my petty part in the lecture. I should've ignored Mr. Anthony. I didn't mean to disrupt or disrespect your time."

"Think nothing of it. I was more bothered by him wishing someone injury over their differing perspective. Might be worth reporting?" he suggested. Immediate dread caulked the cracks in my happy moment. I shook my head.

"Maybe if I wasn't so close to graduation? Not worth the flack that might come as a result, but if he becomes a problem, I'll keep the idea in mind. Thank you."

"All right. I won't press." He turned away after a wish of good luck with Walton. "Oh, and happy Valentine's Day, Kinsley."

"You, too, sir!"

I locked the car and headed for the locker room. Ten minutes later, I had earbuds in. While Coach thought I was running to my warmup music, I gushed into the mic to Tyndall like a dang fool.

"So," Tyndall said, "you're telling me you think the guy who requested *Big Girls Don't Cry* is the workout dude from the beach who is *also* the pirate from the elevator two years ago? If so, this guy sounds suddenly very persistent. How do you know it's him? Did you hear an accent or something? By the way, I love that my brother had to sing that." She snickered.

"Right?" I giggled then cleared my throat. "Well, there *was* an accent at the bar, but what I recognized at the beach was uh … um …."

"Was what?" she demanded.

"It's hard to put in words."

"BS! You have too many choice words for me when it comes to men in my life. Out with it, woman!"

"His *cologne*," I blurted. "It's so delish, I can't forget it. He wasn't wearing it when he was working out, but when he opened his car door, the breeze picked up and I smelled it when I was getting into mine. Like it was trapped inside." Heat hit my cheeks even if she couldn't see me. How embarrassing. "Don't make fun or give me crap, unless I call you upset that I was wrong! Please be super happy with me? Tyndall, the asshole pirate is maybe admitting he's ready to man-up, and that he *likes* me despite my being a jerk!"

"Ha! Or he thinks *you've* grown up." *Nice*.

"Kins, this is crazy. Two years is a long time to wait to make a move. A very long time to think about someone. Maybe he was married and got a divorce for you."

"Ugh. Don't say things like that. How awful."

"It's seriously awesome he remembered you after so long, which means he never forgot you. I'm envious. You know I'm the first to admit that girls get a little dumb and reach for coincidences that mean more than they do, but I'd never fault you for loving his scent. We should pay a visit to the perfume emporium and exhaust ourselves trying to find his cologne so I will know what to buy you for your birthday."

"All right you …."

"Psh. You'd love it. I bet you'd spray it all over his coat and wrap yourself inside like your favorite blanket."

"Because that's what you'd do?" I shot back and grinned.

"Whatever. You need to hide this from your dad, but how will you wipe that ridiculous smile from your face if I can *hear it*? You're too obvious!" *Crap*.

"He might buy that I'm thrilled, because I wasn't a troll who received no gifts?"

"Like me?" she asked.

My face fell and stride faltered. No wonder she'd made that snide remark about Moonlight divorcing. *Double crap*. Walton picked up on the motion at once. When I went silent for too long, she forced a laugh.

"I'm kidding. Why do the untouchables send you flowers, but the only one you *want* flowers from is too dense or high to realize it's a holiday? And I hate carnations. They remind me of my grandpa's funeral."

"Oh, Tyndall. Please tell me you're not still slaving over the same man-child you told me about last year. I thought we were past him."

Walton jogged up the track to intercept my misbehavior. As though this were a game of football, I juked and maneuvered around him. *Hell, yeah. Thank you, Daddy!* "You should watch men's sports and learn a thing or two. There's more than running really fast, coach!" I tee-heed and told Tyndall he had smoke billowing from his ears. "I have to go, but we're revisiting your relationship issues later. He isn't good for you. You're too great for someone trashy."

"So are you," she retorted. *Gasp!* "Easy, girl. I'm talking about my brother."

"That's mean."

Did they have an argument? No secret Jase was an overprotective asshole who cock-blocked his little sister like his favorite sport. I didn't mind. She was too pretty for a douche who wouldn't put down the drugs and video games long enough to notice her. *Maybe Jase was onto her?*

"Sorry. We're reversed. I hate Valentine's this year, but I love that you don't. Thank you for the chocolate."

"Hey, only the best for you, baby." I mimicked her brother. "And those came from him. Not me."

"Right, because Jase remembers holidays without the help of women. Oh! I have to go, he's beeping in!"

That wasn't Jase she hung up on me for, but the sleaze. Though this sucked, I felt better for my foolishness.

Walton laser-beamed the worst of evil eyes. I ran around the bend where the hurdlers practiced, and called for my girl, Eliza, to move as her teammates started. She shifted lanes in time for me to clear the first hurdle. The girls beside me hauled more ass than they typically put forth during practice. When I cleared the tenth and final hurdle in the hundred-meter row, I sped past Walton with his stopwatch. "My time?" I asked with a smug grin. His finger rose, but his lips thinned when he read the clock. Yeah. He didn't have to say. "Didn't even have my spikes on for that one." I cheesed and beat my chest, then did a high kick like a cheerleader.

Walton fumed, but lost his fight with the smile I provoked. "Eliza! Hundred-meter hurdles! *Now!*"

"Thanks, show-off. Now *I* have to suffer," she muttered. "Want to run beside me? I think it'll help my sprint."

"Sure! Same here. Mind if I put my spikes on first, or would you prefer the edge?" I teased. She giggled and shook her head, gesturing up at my face in question.

"Kinsley, you look like you just won the decathlon. You're radiant. What gives?" I had no choice. I told her about the card and flowers. "In that case, get those spikes on, girl!" She beamed excitement and looked around. "Hell, he might be in the risers somewhere!" *Oh no!* My face fell.

"Oh," she hurried, "I didn't mean to scare you. Forget him. Hop to! Walton's gonna get onto you!"

Too late. Walton blew the whistle far longer than necessary. Eliza leapt into action while I hauled to the duffel I'd left in the stands to grab my spikes.

The stuff Tyndall said about my father rang true. If he realized the guy from the 'lift' drifted back into the picture to cloud my eyes with hearts, he'd turn into a worrywart. The only pirate he'd entertain me falling in love with had better be on the Bucs football field scoring us box tickets. His words.

How to hide this happiness? A sneaky call to my dad. He answered on the first ring.

"Happy Valentine's Day, honey. Will you be hungry after practice?" He'd prepared for our annual dinner to make me feel like I didn't need another guy yet.

"Pops, do me a favor? Take Mom somewhere romantic just the two of you instead of our third-wheel norm? I got called into work tonight."

"You sure, Kins? You never work on Valentine's Day."

"Positive." *Negative*, but when I wished them well and hung up with my dad, I called Marcus, so I wasn't a liar. After arguing that we'd made a deal and he wasn't one to go back on his word, I assured him that I'd like to help. He sighed, then sounded like I'd made his whole week. "You short-handed?" I asked.

"Something like that," Marcus told me. "Things need your brand of cheer, Little Red." The background noise drowned his voice.

"Say no more. I'll be there, sir." I hung up and laced my spikes, then pulled the earbuds and tossed them with the phone in the bag.

The whistle piped to such an incessant extent, I worried Walton may pass out. I suspected he had an underlying reason for today's attitude, perhaps the same angst I'd experienced in Miller's lecture and possibly Mr. Anthony's attitude problem, too. Couldn't hurt to blend respect into my sarcasm.

As the zipper traveled the tines on my duffel, I looked to the stands. My breath stuttered as I spied a Bucs cap in the top corner. Same color. *Moonlight?* A single red rose rested against the stranger's smile.

One of the track team's managers, my biggest fan, (Looney) Lucy ran behind me to grab water and wave at someone. The Bucs hat waved back, and my heart regained its normal rhythm. *Not Moonlight.*

He was here for her.

"*Blocks! Now, Micro Machine!* I swear, girl, you're going softer than an infant and a puppy wrapped in Charmin toilet paper!" My heart leapt to my throat at Walton's berating. I caught another smile from the guy in the stands, this time with Lucy nowhere nearby. "Get out here before I mummify your ass with it!"

Jeez. Walton and I exchanged silent anger as I stalked to the blocks.

"Got your number, bud. Now you take mine." I quirked my eyebrows.

"There's the bitch I know and love. Stay away from babies, too. At this rate, you're likely to get knocked-up in the prime of your career."

"Walton! How dare you? Because it's not like *I* have a vested stake in my career! It's all about *you*!" He smirked and nodded while I bent and positioned my spikes on the blocks. "If it weren't for me, you'd still be doing private sessions instead of assistant coach while ours is on maternity leave. She might decide to take more time with her baby and pass you the job, so man-up and quit being a coward!" I shouted as he jogged down to the hundred-meter finish line. He kept me in suspense on purpose. "Your fear is showing, and that's more contagious than any baby! And since we're on the subject, I'm sure she'd love to hear your opinion of them!"

He blew his whistle. I shot from my spot, determined to make him eat his attitude. When I finished, *he didn't even clock my time!*

"You make an excellent point about cowardice, doctor. And maybe after putting up with you for the better part of four years, I don't want this job. Now get the hell off this track, so I can train your replacement if you screw up. Oh, and happy Valentine's Day." He looked right through my shock and awe. "Overheard the others saying you got some serious merch this year. A fancy necklace? Watch out for guys who buy jewelry. Big price tag, big expectations. Keep em' closed, Micro Machine." *He was serious!* Not an ounce of humor. And he never used my name when he was angry. "*Go home*, dammit!"

"Fine. You want to play that game?" Shoving past him, I trudged to the duffel bag and traded for tennis shoes, then trekked up the hill to the car. I wanted to look at the stands so bad, but my pride refused the pleasure.

Coach meant to scare me off, but he was wrong. While his crass bitterness stung a little, I could see his misery wanted company, but my company was too joyous to keep, even after his rant. And … maybe I could see some paternal fear overshadowing his professionalism. He was like the stepfather I'd never needed. About twelve years younger than my father, but he'd invested a great deal of his time and care to my personal career. In addition to crafting workout regimes and after care came the responsibility of what I ate, when and if I could drink, and even the negative effects of dating.

When I had a weakness, Walton bore the burden of building my strength and worked me through the emotional and physical setbacks. He'd never missed a single race, meet or invitational from the day my father had procured his exclusivity during my brief desire to be just like Allyson Felix and take home an Olympic medal. Although I'd changed my mind about going for the gold, even fired him to keep him from wasting his talent on me, he'd applied for an assistant coaching role and scored to keep me in shape. When I tried giving up on him, he'd never let me give up on myself. He'd never left my side.

Now, I was graduating in a few months. A lot going on there for him.

When I strode back on the track, I hauled that stupid bear and the lavender rose bouquet with me. Bayleigh was right. If a chick wanted answers, she had to reach for them on her own. If Moonlight *was* watching from the stands, and one-in-the-same as the pissy pirate, this ought to provoke him.

The girls stopped practicing to come ooh and aww. I'd taken the card out and tossed the sentiment on the passenger seat. When Eliza bent to smell them, I asked her if the guy in the hat was looking our way. "He is," she said. "Hard to tell if he's watching us or not, though. Too much shadow over his face. The rose is tapping his lips." We shared a private smirk while I coaxed stems from the bouquet to hand them out to the team. They were beautiful. I hated giving them away but loved their smiles. When Lucy took hers, she blushed in flattered excitement. I cast careful indifference and turned my attention on Walton, forcing the bear into his open arms.

"Who are those from?" he demanded, awkwardly fumbling with the stuffed animal. "You better be worried if these are from the same guy as the jewelry."

"Walton, I have no idea, that's why I'm okay with spreading the love." I smiled. "My guess is *you've* gone as soft as that bear. You need to take the stuffed animal and give it to whoever she is before she goes home thinking no one wants her, because *you're* too big a wuss to tell her. If total strangers can give gifts like these to someone who scares them, you have no excuse. And I'd like to just accept some happiness rather than worry for now, thank you."

The girls cleared out at his order. Eliza whispered that the man left, but that he'd delivered another surprise. "Come visit me later, yeah?" I asked her. She turned and nodded, then headed to the locker room.

When we were alone, Coach thanked me the way one guy might thank another. No eye-contact. A nod. I slapped a hand on his shoulder and warned him to double check that nothing with my name was in there before he gave the bear to her. "Even add your own card with a handwritten note?"

He sighed. "What if she doesn't like it? Doesn't soft repel girls? Nice guys finish last and all that? Girls like guys who treat them like crap."

I chortled and shook my head but couldn't deny inside myself that Tyndall was a perfect example. "Not true. Never treat a girl like crap. No one would ever accuse *you* of being soft. You're not an all-around nice guy, and since when do *any* of *us* finish last?"

He grinned at nothing in particular. "Touché, Hayes."

"If you promise not to slack up, go for it. I'll promise the same. For the record, Coach, sometimes going soft doesn't mean you're weak, it means you're ready to face the danger. Courage is irresistible."

9

Wednesdays were country nights at the bar. Valentine's Day served a mixed basket of date night couples and singles crying tears into beers or looking for other lonely hearts to copulate with. Should be interesting to see who'll be picking a bartender's brain tonight. If there wasn't some douche in an Inferno vest, I was all ears and patience.

When my tires crackled over the gravel parking lot, I noticed the employee spots filled to the max, and included Jase's truck after his hiatus to help Rustin move. Neither of us were scheduled. This was a pleasant surprise.

My car fit into a tiny spot. I wished for a sunroof to climb from instead of the skinny shimmy I performed to get out. After readjusting the outfit I picked rather than the skimpy uniform, I reached for the rose bouquet that had rested on top of my duffel after practice.

Eliza better show if she'd watched him put those there!

The bump of bass beating the walls of the bar foretold a fun night ahead.

My boots crunched all the way to the sidewalk at the front, where Gustav, one of our bouncers, stood guard by the door. He whistled as he took stock. I measured right at his elbow. "Looking cute tonight, Red Running Hood. Are you working?" The low depth of his voice vibrated in my chest.

"Yes, sir, I am. Thank you." I pulled a rose and passed the flower with a wish for a great night.

"Bless your tiny heart. Have fun, Kins. Got y'all covered for the evening."

"Always reassuring when you're on, sir." I grinned over my shoulder and peeked at the row of cars. A bright white Tesla glowed from the best spot in the lot right beside the bar. I said a giddy silent prayer.

He tugged the door open on a band of men covering Shania Twain's *Any Man of Mine* and the bar singing every word. Gus and I snickered. I wasn't over the threshold before a drunk girl draped me in her arms.

"They're wild tonight, girl. Good luck."

"No joke," I muttered and wrapped a supportive arm around Lucy. Dammit.

Eliza tugged her away with an apology. "Think you're her Valentine, Micro Machine. Catch ya on a free moment when I'm not babysitting?"

I nodded. She pointed at my boobs and mouthed that they were cute. We giggled as I thanked her. My shirt brandished a smiley emoji with hearts for eyes. You can guess where the eyes sat.

"Dunno, I like those shorts and boots, myself." Rustin's drawl hummed near my ear. I turned, and he stole the flowers, passed them to Bayleigh, then captured my waist. His other hand grabbed mine to guide me onto the dance floor in an expert two-step. Bayleigh fanned herself and cracked a fake whip behind his back.

Rustin spun me beneath his arm and pushed the small of my spine in different directions as we got into the groove of the quick music on the chorus. The live band was silly, and I looked up to see Jase doing backup vocals with the country headliner. My head tossed with a cackle. "What the hell?" They both smiled down at us while they harmonized like a couple smart-asses. "If you guys bust out *Man! I Feel Like a Woman,* I might have to dance with you later!"

Jase's eyebrows quirked in the middle of lyrics. Rustin hooted and told me I'd just sealed my fate.

"That one's been done."

"No freaking way!" I cheesed. "I'm bummed I missed out, and since when does Jase sing any of this?"

"There's much you don't know. Now snap to, girl!" He navigated us between too many dancers and did so with an impressive grace.

"You're kinda good at this, ain'tcha, Country?" My drawl mocked his. After I spun so my back met his chest, I watched our toes to prevent stepping on his.

"Not kinda, Mizz Hayes. Very," he told me over the music. His mouth brushed near my earlobe. "I'm impressed you're able to keep count. Thought I'd have to put your feet on mine to do anything with you."

"Smooth! What's that they say about *ass*umptions?" I grinned over my shoulder and took his hand holding my waist to unwrap his grip as I spun away and into the waiting arms of a nearby stranger standing around. Before he denied, I goaded him onto the floor. Rustin's smile brightened. Undaunted. Challenged as I left him open and alone.

"*You*, sir, need another beer!" I craned my neck to peer up at my new partner. Before he flirted or came up with a cheesy line, I took his empty and steered him toward a wallflower watching the crowd and wishing to dance. She perked up, and I slinked behind the bar to clock-in, then grabbed a full tray and let Bayleigh catch me up on drinks and tables. "Did you get a rose, Bay?"

"Only about two dozen from different patrons! Hey, Chad came up here a few minutes ago looking for you. He said Eliza told him you'd come to work tonight." *Hmm* … Chad, my favorite deejay, wasn't on schedule for a couple more weeks. Never pegged him for coming in on a country night, either.

"Did he say what he wanted?"

"Think he needed to ask you something for the paper." She yelled over the juke beginning *Redneck Woman*. The crowd sang along like a choir, and I loved their contagious spirit. "He's around here somewhere. If I see him, I'll point him in your direction—oh! There he is! And there *he* is!" She spun to face me and took my hands from the tray to lean in till our chests touched over the bar. "Give a discreet look to your right when you lift your tray. Chad is talking to Moonlight! I'm giving you a beer for Chad, and you can say one of these chicks bought it for him."

"I'll do you one better. Add a rose and I'll tell him they're both from me. Gonna pretend not to notice Moonlight unless he says something." We shared a wicked grin. Butterflies practically flew from my mouth.

"Hey, baby." Jase's baritone sounded before I had the chance to lift the tray. I whirred to face him, tingles choking adrenaline straight to my throat.

"Happy Valentine's Day."

"Happy Valentine's Day, Jase." My speech was too breathy, and I swallowed sudden anxiety. "I had no idea you guys were back in town."

"Who's the flower for?" he asked. I gnawed my lip and hated that I had to tell him since he and Chad didn't talk.

"The guy over there from a patron. Bayleigh put it on my tray," I lied, feeling awful for not getting him something. *Why? We'd never exchanged gifts before* .... "Can I get you a drink, Jase? Cool you're helping with country tonight. Didn't realize you knew any. Let alone that you were willing to toss your pride and panties out to the floor."

Gosh, this was like my freshman year in high school all over again!

His lips crooked into his sexy grin. He put a palm on the bar and stepped closer to cage me. I swallowed and backed against the wood. Another server came and swiped the tray I'd arranged, vexed as she took in Jase's proximity. *Yikes.*

"Who's that flower really for?" He pressed, his eyes smiled, his lips straightened.

"Chad," I confessed. "I brought enough for the employees." *Why was I jumpy?* "There's one for you, too, if you want."

"Thought you said you didn't know I'd be back."

"Jase! What's with the interrogation?" He drew close. The heat of his body collided with mine.

"Ready to own up to that dance?"

Um. "Depends." I smiled to disarm him. "You the type who likes to put a choke hold on your partner while you two-step?"

"Nope. I reserve those for the dudes who mistreat chicks." Okay, I now noticed he must be several shots in, goofy, flirtatious. Odd he cornered *me* out of all the women in the bar on such an opportune night. "If I don't manhandle you into a headlock, you want to dance with me?"

"What if I put you in one?" I teased his buzz. His broad smile came out, and his hands wove their way around my waist. I squealed when he lifted me to plant my feet on his. I had no choice but to throw my arms around his neck to keep from falling back.

"Guess I don't mind, but thanks for asking first, sweet Kins."

"Nice." I wanted to ask him questions about why the unusual desire to prove he could dance, but he got to the floor and told me I was leading because he didn't know how to do this. "Seriously? Need the sister to help a brother out?" My smile brightened as I stepped from his feet and instructed him to take proper form.

"No Junior High weaving back and forth?" His lips quirked into that crooked grin before his lower lip popped in a pout.

"Nah, middle school boys are too touchy-feely for their own good."

His fingers dug into my shirt. "That how your ex behaved when you were sweet and innocent?" His eyebrows rose. I almost giggled at how protective he seemed over the kid I used to be.

I shook my head and stepped back, forcing him to follow in a leading way.

"You saying I'm no longer sweet and innocent?"

"That I can't figure out. You seem to be but leave just enough doubt to keep me guessing."

"Which means you don't pry Tyndall's brain for information," I teased, but inside I cheered because he wondered about me!

"That a dare?" he threatened in big brother mode.

"Really, Jase? I was playing. Can we please not discuss exes? I'd rather forget. I'm in too good a mood and I'm certain the two of mine are nothing compared to your too many to count." We continued to move, and he didn't once grind on my toes with anything but his mention of my high school ex, Jack Carter. "Did you get any cool valentines?" I shifted subjects.

"As a gift, or for someone else?" His head tilted.

The jukebox changed, and while the dance floor crowded with canoodling couples, Jase's neck snapped at the song that came on as if someone jabbed a finger in his shoulder. A cover of *All I Wanna Do* by Halestorm. I looked at the music player to see what rattled him. Chad leaned against the wall beside the glowing touch screen with a gutsy grin but shrugged and gestured over his shoulder like another had picked the music.

"That guy ...." Jase trailed in irritation. "Confessing his intention, eh?"

I scoffed at the absurdity. "Now I know you've had too much to drink. He's a deejay. It's Valentines. He may not be on the clock but knows how to get people on the floor. However, I am on the clock and I'm going back to work."

"You mad at me? Sounds like you're saying I don't know how to get people on the dance floor."

I gazed up at him with a soft smile, my hands on his chest. "Don't put words in my mouth. Take a flower and quit being big brother. Have fun." After a placating kiss to his cheek, I turned and strode up to the bar, asking Bayleigh to hand me another rose for Jase and an update.

"Everything okay over there? I can tell you were catching crap. Guess what that means?" Bayleigh grinned.

"When he thinks Chad is coming onto me? Yeah. Big brother mode, Bayleigh. Enough said."

"Right. I'll play blind, but can we adopt a seeing-eye dog?"

10

"**Afternoon, Mr. King.**"

"Good afternoon." I greeted one of the parents at the Children's Cancer Center. He rushed to hold the door while I juggled flowers and bags into the lobby.

"You're gonna make the rest of us look bad," he joked.

I chuckled and shook my head. "On the contrary, you're a warrior. I'm just an awed bystander trying to help your fight."

"I appreciate that. Are you volunteering today?"

"If they'll let me," I told him.

"Well, I know Evan will be glad to see you," he said of his son.

"Ditto. Tell him I'll be in after a bit."

He nodded and meandered down the hallway.

"Oh, Klive, how sweet of you to think of this place today. Don't you have someone special you should be with instead?" Nurse Lynn rushed from her place behind the reception desk to remove several shopping bags from my hands.

"Only you ladies." I grinned.

"That's too bad." She smiled before peeking inside a bag filled with rainbow acrylics. "I'm assuming these are for today's art therapy class?"

"They are, and these are for all of you." I set a large vase on the desk beside colorful fliers and schedules.

"Thank you!" Lynn gushed. "They're beautiful!"

"Indeed. Tie-dyed daisies are perfect inspiration for today's class," the art therapist said as she joined us. "Maybe we should bring these into the art room as a visual aid?"

"That's a great idea, Greta," Lynn told her. "He came bearing supplies, too."

Greta thanked me and took the vase while Lynn carried bags into the hallway. I headed back to the car to grab stacks of old newspapers, but threw two new ones on top, then hauled them inside to the art room. Multiple bald heads and bright sets of eyes turned my way. Several siblings and parents dotted the chairs beside their loved ones and held paint brushes in anticipation.

"Klive! I'm happy to see you!" Ten-year-old Hannah clapped her hands and waved me to sit beside her and her mother, Adeline.

"Give me a moment to pass these out, then I'll come over, all right?" She nodded.

"Here, don't want you taking all this weight on your own," sixteen-year-old Evan said as he walked up. His eyes smiled above dark crescents. I shook my head as he tried to remove half of the stack from my arms.

"You're a good man, Evan, but the only one I'll let you help me with is the one on top. I happened to circle and highlight some points of interest," I told him with a wicked lift of my eyebrows, grin to match. His expression shifted to an adventurous glee as his teenage interest piqued. After double-checking to see if his father heard us, he gently raised a paper from the top while his dad was in conversation.

I sauntered over to Hannah and asked her to take the other one from the top and read the front page.

"Okay," she said. When she collected the paper, she noticed the ones beneath were different.

"Trust me. Just read. Let me know what you think when I come back."

The art therapist greeted her class, then placed a CD in a cheap player. She told everyone to visit while she prepared. Instrumental harp thrummed a calm and contented vibe into the room before she dug into the bags of supplies I'd brought. Cabinet doors opened and closed as she rummaged for items and stowed others.

The kids and parents nattered about life as only they experienced the unpredictable days and weeks. Two other volunteers passed out cups of water and paper plates. I paused at each station and spread newspapers beneath the tables and below canvases on small easels, spoke with each family while I went.

Only one soul here today knew life without the sting of cancer. A first-year medical school intern. She busied opening tubes of acrylic paint and dotted paper plates with the color pallet.

I'd never had cancer, but my little brother, August, fought for two hard years before winning when he was fourteen. Our lives took on such a different meaning that we existed like aliens who visited the Earth of shallow problems and humans every time we finished a hospital stay or chemo treatment. As a result, I feared hospitals, but faced my fears when donating marrow and finding a match at the Cancer Center. A child. Hannah. My first mission to save a life rather than taking one. Atonement.

I knelt near Evan and spread papers beneath his area. He folded the newspaper I'd given him. "King, do I want to know why I'm reading about a gifted university track star in her final season? Is this supposed to inspire me since I'm in my final stages of chemo, because the only thing you've done is caused new pain if you feel me. The one you circled is hot. Her teammates are too."

"Where's your dad?" I asked from my hands and knees.

"Getting wet wipes from the teacher," he said.

"The girl I circled is the one from the elevator. Bitchy Bonny," I said so only he heard. "Kinsley Hayes."

His jaw dropped as he slapped the page with her photo. "No way. *The* Anne Bonny from your Gasparilla story? She looks too wholesome to dress the way you told me. Even in that uniform and letter jacket."

"Ha! You haven't seen her at work." I fished my phone from my jeans and showed him a photo I'd taken while Kinsley leaned over the bar. Her shorts climbed high on her thighs; calves checked from standing on the tips of her toes.

A dumb grin mingled into the shock in his face. "You have to bring her to visit."

"Who?" Evan's father asked. I yanked the phone under the table and shoved the device back in my pocket. Evan cleared his throat as I stood up and placed paper beneath his canvas. "Oh, I know this girl." Evan's father pointed at the paper. "The one that's circled. Kinsley Hayes. She goes to the same church as my wife's sister."

The medical intern squeezed in next to Evan and dotted paint onto his paper plate. "Ah, Micro Machine. Her cousin is in the medical program here in town. I've never met her, but everyone's afraid of her except him. He swears she's nice, but you know how legends grow. Apparently, her drive caused her last track coach to go into premature labor three times before she quit her job and gave it to the personal trainer Kinsley hired for the Olympics. They say she was vying for a spot on the US team but chickened out because she's never lost a race and is too afraid to lose."

I laughed before I noticed her lack of humor.

"Don't believe me? Go to a meet and see her temper for yourself. But don't let me steal the moral from the story of the article. That writer knows the rumors as well as we all do, and he's always on the lookout for something to redeem her character with. Supposedly, she's gearing up to fight the diabetic crisis one child at a time as a nutrition counselor. Admirable, considering she's not taking the typical Kinesiology route that athletes on scholarships usually do, but I hope she has a better manner with children than she does toward her peers on the track."

I couldn't assess whether this girl feared or admired 'Micro Machine'. Perhaps a mixture of both with a large dash of ignorance.

"Why not talk to her?" Evan asked her. "You know, see for yourself if the rumors are true?"

His dad gave a more-or-less nod of agreement and we all looked at her. She shrugged. "I don't know. I'm just a lowly undergrad who can't even jog for thirty seconds without coughing up a lung. She's about to graduate with an advanced degree and an athletic ability that makes the papers. What would I say?"

The girl moved onto the next table and seemed to move on from the subject of Kinsley just the same. Evan's dad shook his head in wisdom and said, "What a shame. Never know what you *won't* know."

Evan grinned at his dad and told him he made no sense, then he looked at me. "I think legends are the stuff that drives explorers to the ends of the Earth in search of the truth in them. Ya know? I've faced down chemo and death. I'd talk to this girl in a heartbeat. She doesn't scare me."

"Atta boy, mate. You got yourself the makings of a brave man," I told Evan's father. Evan grinned in knowing. I left them in order to continue laying my paper trail until finally settling on a stool beside Hannah.

Spinning her paintbrush, she made a whirlpool in her water cup while awaiting instructions from the art therapist. "Here, Klive," she said. "You can share mama's canvas."

Adeline and I smiled at one another and shook our heads. "You know," Hannah's mom whispered, "she's just nervous we won't see you anymore when she triumphs over this disease." A mite of doubt clouded the smile of certainty in her words. Adeline was nervous she wouldn't see her daughter much longer if this disease won the war.

I glanced at the art therapist as she apologized to the class for the delay. Only a few more minutes, she promised, she forgot something in her car. Out of the room she dashed, and I took that moment, due to the fear in Adeline's eyes, to pull a tiny velvet box from my pocket.

"Oh, Klive, no. I wasn't implying—"

"Shhh, Adeline. It's not what you think, dear. You both know one woman has my heart, and today I came to show her to you."

"Is that an engagement ring, Klive?" Hannah asked in excitement. I urged her with my hand to lower her voice, double-checking to be sure no one overheard and created a new rumor. The others were too busy talking amongst themselves, thank God.

"This, Hannah, is something I had made just for you as you enter the last leg of this race against cancer." They both gasped as Hannah opened the box. A white gold bumble bee perched atop a dainty white gold band. "Do you know that because of the weight of a bee's body, science itself says it shouldn't be able to fly?"

She allowed me to place the ring on her middle finger, the thickest of her bony digits.

"Is that true, Klive?" she whispered in awe as she stared at her gift.

"Would I lie?"

They both granted big smiles and shook their heads. I continued. "Do you know why it flies?"

"Nuh, uh. Why?"

"Because no one told the bee that it couldn't fly, the bee flies anyway. Now, look at me and listen close." I held both her tiny hands in mine. Her skin was cold. She leaned in like we shared a secret. "No matter what you believe to be impossible *can* be possible if you believe. When you feel weak, feel yourself second-guessing the pain of the fight, your endurance, you look at this and let it remind you of the truth. All things are possible with faith. Do you understand, Hannah?"

She nodded. Her whole face brightened. "Is that why you also gave me the story about the runner? How she's so short she shouldn't be able to run so fast, but she keeps winning anyway?"

I sat up and marveled at how she noticed what I hadn't. "Fantastic observation." In the picture featured in the paper, Kinsley stood with her relay team. They each smiled in their uniforms and college letterman jackets with medals around their necks, but Kinsley was at least half-a-foot shorter than the second shortest woman in the bunch.

Picture in hand, I pointed at the star of the article and said, "May I introduce you both to Calico Jack's Anne Bonny?"

"Shut up!" Hannah squealed and threw her arms around my neck the way a grown woman might've after being gifted a ring in a velvet box. But she thrilled for having a face to her favorite character now. How many times had she asked me to retell her the story of how I'd fallen for the meanest, prettiest girl at the pirate festival even before I'd gotten there? An edited for children version, of course.

"Oh, Klive, have you talked to her? Did you get her a present for Valentine's Day? Why are you here with us when you should be on a date with her? Oh, my gosh! Oh, my gosh! Oh, my gosh!" She plunked down on her stool and clapped her hands. I'd never seen her brown eyes shine with such radiance. *What a feeling!*

The therapist rushed back into the room and introduced her Valentine husband to the group. She held a huge vase of red roses and wore the most wonderful smile comparable to the love glowing in Hannah's face. The class awed. Adeline leaned closer to look at the article and the ring on her daughter's finger.

"Thank you, Klive. That ring is perfect. We couldn't be more excited for you, right Hannah?"

Hannah sighed with the most romantic look up at the ceiling, and I chuckled. "Oh, you hopeless females. Whatever shall I do with you?"

"Bring her by to meet us?" Hannah rushed. Her mother nodded and agreed.

The art therapist asked for everyone's attention. Adeline handed me a spare paintbrush. We each dipped into the blue for the background and touched our bristles to her canvas. While Hannah followed directions, I said low for Adeline's ears only, "I haven't yet spoken to Kinsley. I sent her two sets of roses then watched her give them all away."

"Why on Earth would she do that? Does she know they're from you? Or that you even exist?"

Adeline speckled shades of blue while I dappled bits of white clouds to hers and Hannah's canvases.

"I believe she gave the roses to others who hadn't received any gifts, because I noticed she gave away a bear I didn't buy her. She knows who I am, just not by name because I'm playing secret-admirer games with her. I get the impression she's not the type you fawn over, and she comes running. Considering the venom with which she told me off during our first encounter, I don't quite know what to expect."

"If the rumors I overheard are true, and what we've gathered from your story and reading, confidence goes a long way. To strong women, heck most women, nothing is a bigger turn-off than insecurity, Klive. You're the least insecure person I've ever met. Your confidence alone instills it in others and makes us all question why we ever had a doubt about a good outcome. It's one of the reasons we love when you visit or participate. I don't see how she couldn't use someone to continue that confidence as her life is changing. Just be yourself."

"Changing? What do you mean?"

"The article said this girl is graduating. I haven't gone to college, but I remember being scared about graduating high school for what comes next. If I were her, I'd be worried about my plans for the future coming into the present, especially when she leaves that running career behind. Oh, crap, they've moved onto their flower and we are still painting hearts in the sky. Here, hurry before she sees!"

Adeline grinned and rushed to rinse our brushes before we attacked the stem and leaves while the therapist made her rounds to our side of the room. When her vibrant face looked into mine, I relished the true friendship in her expression, rather than unrequited love. I'd never confide this weakness for Kinsley to anyone else.

"Hey, Klive, do you think Mrs. Greta would be upset if I added a bee to my flower when we're done?" Hannah asked all aglow.

"Well, Hannah, you can ask me yourself, but I think that'd be a great idea. What gave you the inspiration?" Greta asked, her hands behind her back as she appreciated our work. Greta's eyes smiled as she ruffled my hair and praised Hannah's ring. "Yes, I believe the whole class could benefit from adding a bee to their daisies, and after class is over, Klive, you may hand out your daisies to each of them. This way they don't wilt on our desk."

Later, after the last flowers were handed out, Hannah and Adeline hugged me goodbye. They each took the remaining two daisies. Adeline asked how I felt.

"Quite content. Why do you ask?"

"Because Kinsley gave all her flowers to others. Now, you see why you shouldn't take it personally. Happy Valentine's Day."

Good point.

"Happy Valentine's, ladies. See you soon. Text me when Hannah's next treatment is scheduled, and I'll come visit."

"Will do. Goodnight!" they called out to the art therapist and her husband.

The room emptied. Only the sound of instrumental harp chimed through the air. I helped stuff the spackled newspapers into trash bags while Mrs. Greta and her husband washed paintbrushes. Her husband gathered the filled garbage bags and headed to the dumpster outside.

"We go to church with her family." Greta said over her shoulder. "She's not as scary as the kids at school make her out to be. She works the nursery with her cousin and babysits for us when we want to go on dates. I'd say she's better with children than with her peers because children haven't yet learned the cruelty of the generation she's cursed to be part of. Think about it. They'd rather have everything handed to them on a platter, so they don't have to work. They judge anyone who works for what they have as being given something they've never had. That's why I love this job. These kids and their parents live for what matters."

"I couldn't agree more."

"Kinsley is dedicated at a level her peers can't understand because they come to Florida to party at the beach between classes. A pity she didn't become a doctor. Always nice when you get the physician who graduated with ropes and honors rather than the C student. I don't know your beliefs, but you're welcome to attend church with us anytime if you'd like a proper introduction." She focused on stubborn red paint stuck to the neck of a brush to avoid the response she guessed was coming.

"I'll consider it," I said, rather than outright refusing. She needn't know that God and I weren't exactly kosher.

"Klive, you don't have to stay. I'll help her with the rest." Greta's husband returned and kissed her on the temple. His arms folded around her waist. "I can think of no better date on Valentine's than serving alongside my beautiful bride," he said against her temple.

She giggled and turned her face to his for a kiss. I rushed outside to gulp the humid breeze. I didn't want to think about God or the impossibility of the situation. I'd rather pretend that with Kinsley my own advice would prevail, that all things *were* possible.

The parking lot held only three cars: Greta's parked beside her husband's and mine alone on the opposite end. I felt like my car, isolated while Jase parked nice and close to the girl I wanted parked beside me.

11 | ♀

"Is this for me, Kins?"

"To you, from me, yes, siree. Don't let your ego read too much into it," I teased Chad. The rose rested on the bar between us.

Most couples were on the dance floor and hanging out at tables. This afforded me a small lull to chat. He sat on a barstool opposite, enduring the country songs, claiming they'd be better with his special twist.

"I think they sound great." I shrugged.

"Oh?" He pinned me with skeptical amusement and an accent straight from Down Under. "And your bias has no bearing whatsoever." He peered at Jase and regarded him with similar suspicion as Jase did him.

"The roses? Any idea who sent them?"

"Roses?"

"Yeah, the ones you received during Miller's Color Theory lecture. Lucy couldn't wait to tell everyone how you showed up to the track with them." I rolled my eyes and sensed Lucy's boring into me this moment. "If Micro Machine has someone special cheering her on during her final season, it's more for fans to cheer about. Everyone loves a happy ending."

"Good grief. Chad, I have no idea. Secret admirer." My lip sucked between my teeth in debate. *Should I ask him who Moonlight was?* He'd flip for even a mention of the 'Complicated' story I held to.

"Secret admirer … sounds intriguing." He grinned like a guy who saw I held my cards close. "Playing. I won't write about it unless you confirm."

"I appreciate that. The song? Someone else, or were you trying to drive Jase up the wall?" I tested, my poker face in place.

Chad chuckled, pleased I asked, but we both knew there was something unsaid hanging in this game. "Both. He's tipsy. So protective of you. Easy equation. Did *he* give you a gift, by chance?" Nice. He wasn't giving me anything on Moonlight unless I gave him something.

"Hmm … I suppose it's possible the roses might've come from Jase, but no. Nothing I know of."

Chad nodded in contemplation. His fingers twirled the red stir stick in his drink. He looked out at the stage and the crazy crowd.

"Before you ask—no—the blond didn't get me anything, either, but seriously drunk patrons gave me a bunch of corny gifts and inappropriate invitations." We both laughed, but I found intrigue in how hard he searched for a significant other to write into the picture of my life. *Why the sudden interest?*

"All right, I'll let it go for now. I only came to drop your article. Figured it might be positive publicity for you and this place. I noticed police reports released for this location about Inferno incidents. That's not you guys' fault. Hope it helps." He tapped a stack of papers he'd placed at the corner against the wall beside where he sat.

"That's nice of you, Chad. Even if it *is* weird having a spread on my career. You're making me soft. How will I remain tough to get the job done?"

Chad scoffed while I slid a pair of Blue Hawaiians across for a couple a few stools down.

"I know you too well, *Kinsley*." I loved the sound of my name from his accent. He knew and screwed with me all the time. "You've got that down whether or not you're soft for a split-second. Hope you like the feature, darl. I'll see you around campus. Take caution with Inferno." I nodded and let him kiss my cheek. He snickered as I leaned away to look at him. "Taylor is frustrated. Have fun with that. Fill me in when he takes you off the market that way I can really piss in his Cheerios."

"Chad! Shame, sir. Behave."

"Never." He stood from his stool. "Happy Valentine's, Micro Machine." He handed me the rose I'd gifted him. "From me, to you." The bud tapped my nose before I snatched the stem from his naughty hand. I shook my head. Bayleigh tsked with disapproval as she wound behind the bar to grab a full tray.

"I can't wait until this day is done!" She shouted over her shoulder. Chad's attention diverted. "If I get one more stupid, grammar school Valentine or box of chocolates, I'll need a bigger uniform!" Her joke was hollow. She seemed bothered even as she tried to sell her humor. Chad waved her off, disappointed she didn't have something more interesting.

After his departure, the tension in the staff became more obvious as time wore on, I was no exception after a few hours. My smile was real, but I made orders like a machine. I lost myself in contemplation over the things Chad had said. *Police reports for this address about Inferno. As in— there had been more than I'd realized. How come no one mentioned anything? Why hadn't Marcus put together a meeting or told us whether Sara was absent, or had officially quit?*

In another bout of generosity, I stayed through closing, hoping someone might gossip when the crowds deserted, but no such luck. Everyone was tired and serious. The fun vanished from the bar. Usually during clean-ups, we'd put the jukebox on free play and dance with our brooms and mops, trade lyrics during sing-alongs, choreograph the rare routine to pull customers.

Not tonight.

Jase gave an excuse to stay, but made Rustin go when the country band finished packing. Even he seemed sobered and somber. The quieter everyone became, the louder I wanted to shatter their silence with a scream. *Did they all know what the hell was going on and refuse to tell me? What purpose could that serve?*

The hallway was empty, the locker room clear, the dishes done, and the glasses rehung. The floor mopped, tills counted, tips divvied, and everyone filed out. Jase walked to my side and grasped my hand with an expression that asked permission. My smile tired, I took what he offered. The night was still except for crickets chirping as we trekked outside. When we got to my car, Jase stilled me with his hand at my cheek. I memorized the callouses and texture of his fingers. His eyes held emotion, *exhaustion or more?*

"I missed being around you, Kinsley."

Oh!

My breath hitched, and my cheeks plumped with the stretch of my lips. "What a wonderful thing to say, Jase. Thank you. For what it's worth, work is lacking when you aren't on the schedule." No way I could be as forthcoming as he'd been without my face catching fire. Thank God for darkness. He looked at the gravel for a second, but his grin reflected mine. How flattering to make him look this happy.

"Will I see you at the course, or, you know," he cleared his throat, "outside of work?"

My smile tamed, and I bit my lip. There was a weird vulnerability between us. Like when you're growing boobs, and the boy who saw you as another best friend, sees you differently. I swallowed and nodded. "We'll see."

"That's good. My workouts haven't had the same punch these past few days."

"Ah, you need a woman to run you off the course, eh?" When I beamed up at him, he looked away and his Adam's apple bobbed. *What was happening? Should I stop this?*

"Something like that." His hand left my cheek and traveled to the nape of my neck. My head tilted back. "You're a little maddening, Kinsley." When I gasped, he leaned in and our lips met. Thick fog stole my rationality and goosebumps broke out over my skin. No way in hell could I stop this. His warm mouth was soft, patient, sweet, slow … *ooh.* My body burned to lean against him and increase this drag.

When he broke away before I felt ready, his lips quirked. "Sorry I didn't get you anything. Figured something homemade would do the trick there."

My laughter filled the surrounding emptiness, ours were the only two vehicles left in the lot. My hand found his arm. "If it was from the heart, that's what matters," I jested.

He cleared his throat again and shook his head. My face fell.

"Believe me, Kins, it'd be a lot easier if it wasn't." For the second time tonight, my breath was stolen. "And if all I wanted to do was make love to you, I'd fulfill my lust somewhere else to keep you intact. In case you gave any credence to Chad's song when we were dancing. Not that I wouldn't give my right nut to make love to you, just, damn, could you shut me up?"

Whoa! My smile erupted while I covered his mouth and tried to harness my elation before my heart jumped off my face into his hands. He smiled against my fingers and cupped them with his, then dipped them down and licked my palm like he was French kissing. I cackled and wrestled against him till he released me, then I caught his face and smeared my wet palm over his cheek. He chuckled and snatched my hand then placed a sweet kiss to the back.

"Happy Valentine's Day, baby."

"Happy Valentine's Day, Jase."

He stayed until I got into my car then watched me drive away. Holy crap. *That just happened.*

That night, sleep was more like a nap. Snooze wasn't a choice since I slept through the alarm. My rigid schedule shattered as I joined the land of the living at five-fifty. In the haze that followed, I tripped twice while wrestling into a pair of shorts and a sports bra, pulling my sweatshirt on backward by mistake.

"Gah!"

The drive to the beach was as foggy as my brain, I forgot my water, and the protein bar ended up being fruit chalk! *I couldn't effin win!* Like a dog with peanut butter, my mouth was sticky and parched, and my tongue kept traveling over my unbrushed teeth to remove that filmy feeling.

Once I parked, the soupy morning and humidity made the sweatshirt a misery. I shucked the fleece, cursing myself for not grabbing a workout tank. Call me a prude, but I felt over-exposed and inappropriate, much the way I did at every track meet—that uniform being as sparse as the work uniforms would be once spring break hit. From then through Labor Day tourist season packed the bars, beaches and restaurants.

So much to be pissy about!

Ironic, considering how crazy awesome yesterday had been. Gifts from a secret admirer *and* a crush kissing me goodnight on the same day? Guilt ate away at my happiness for loving the attention of two men and having no idea which I wanted more. I'd never been in a triangular predicament before.

I tipped my head back and my neck popped. Yeah, the tension was everywhere. The key chain coiled up my arm and sunglasses guarded eyes heavy with yesterday's eyeliner and mascara against the burning sensation of the rising sun.

My stretch cut short when a jogger halted his run too abruptly, and knelt to tie his shoe, checking me out the way a thief spies the perfect car stereo to pawn. A knot formed in my belly as he untied the shoe before retying the laces. His gear seemed too new, especially his shoes. The white laces and swooshes on the sides glowed fresh and unused like the white of his t-shirt. No sweat ring around his neck. I'd never seen him here before, but maybe this was his normal time of day, or his first time gaining the courage to jog in public? But he didn't match his clothing. They didn't fit his vibe and came off as more like a costume.

I chewed my cheek trying to plan my options. *Should I jog my usual route, or go the same way as him? Which one would help me seem less like a scared animal he might want to chase? Maybe I was thinking too much of nothing!*

"Good morning," I offered. Taking in my surroundings, I cast him a dismissive, but polite, smile. He barely nodded as his eyes ate at my body like the starving homeless. I might've dismissed my fear if he could tear his gaze away from my exposed flesh, but I'd come up against a look like that before. At least this guy was alone.

My throat dried in remembrance of the Gasparilla festival two years ago. Two jerks had openly trapped me between them in the chaos of drunken throngs. The groups of costumed festivalgoers had been so thick no one noticed or heard my pleas for the men to get their hands off me.

I cupped my arms at the memory of how the one forced my arms to my sides while his fraternity brother tried putting his hands down my corset. I'd screamed and shouted for Nate, knowing he'd never allow them the liberty. Nathan had beaten the shit out of them once for trying to force me into their room at the last frat party I'd ever attended. The brothers took their revenge in the open with the threat that I go ahead and tell and see what happens to my reputation. With all my might, I'd kicked the tip of my boot into the shin of the guy holding me. When he'd let go, I'd ducked and backed my elbow as forcefully as I could into the other guy's ribs, then took off running as fast as my sprint in

102

high heeled boots could carry me to my father's building. Their vows of vengeance had assaulted my ears in the mayhem. I remembered looking over my shoulder expecting them on my shadow, praying to reach my daddy's office before they could catch me again. They couldn't hurt me if my daddy was there.

I'd run into a knife-wielding pirate instead.

I released a shaky breath at the memory of his presence, the fearsome command to tell him who'd hurt me. A look like his conveyed action over threats. I'd cried the whole drive home, swiping tears from my eyes with the sleeve of his pirate coat. The first man aside from my father I'd ever— nope. *Hush, Kinsley Brain!*

The pirate wasn't here. Neither was Daddy, but I wasn't in heels or a stupid costume restricting my breathing or movements, either.

Here and now, I scanned my surroundings. The obstacle course was my best option for safety in numbers. Jase, Rustin, or even beach guy might show up to work out. *Who was I kidding? Beach guy is Moonlight. Moonlight is Beach Guy and my pirate.* Thinking of the way the pirate had put the fear of God into me when he'd held that knife, I was ready to run behind him and point this creep out to him. Wish I had that knife on me now. Maybe I should take the Bowie from beneath my mattress and keep the blade in the car for things like this.

God, please don't let this creep do something to me!

The guy stood up, pulled his phone and pretended to be busy enough to figure out which direction I might go. Or, so I guessed. If I returned to my car and left, he'd see what I drove and my plate numbers. I sighed and stalked to the water fountain, a passive eye on him the way he eyed me, like a standoff. *What the hell?*

The course would fill sooner than the beach. Against my athletic judgment, without a warm-up, I turned and trotted through the tires with cold muscles. My breath rasped harder than normal, a sweat broke over my skin that had nothing to do with exertion, and I kept resisting the urge to peek over my shoulder. By the time I jumped down from the block wall, the man turned to walk the way he'd come. I landed with the grace of tossed bricks. He peered over his shoulder, still hesitant. I jogged again to the tires, conceding for my safety.

First work? Now my favorite workout spot? Was nothing sacred?

My right triceps locked tight when I climbed the rope. Fun times trying to slink down without dropping or shredding my palms to ribbons. As a result, I skipped the pull-up bar, and aimed for the net, resigned to jump the wall and go home. The treadmill was a better option today. This time when I jumped, my ankle twisted on impact and my bottom met with the sand in a flash of white pain.

"*Ohhh shit!*" I cried, the injury only part of why tears rushed to my eyes. I pushed my foot out to inspect any swelling. Strained weeping followed with visions of my career flushing down the toilet before the season had barely begun.

"*Whoa!* Heads up!" I had no hope of scrambling away. Someone landed with a curse while I shifted away as best I could. "Kinsley? What the *hell* happened?" Jase demanded, rushing over, bending with concern.

"My ankle." I whimpered, desperate for this not to be real.

"We need to move you. You're lucky I took the one side. Rustin will be over the wa—"

Jase dove over me like a protective shield. Rustin landed against him in an impact I deserved. Jase cursed. Rustin cursed *at* him, demanding to know what the hell kind of moron— "Red?" He cut off. "What are you doing like this?" He shoved Jase's arm out of his way. The first time I'd seen anything but flirtation on his face. "Man, Jase. Now I'm sorry for the foot up your ass."

Jase shifted to squat beside me, shaking his head at Rustin. "She's twisted her damn ankle. Make sure no one else comes over that wall before I can move her. We need ice," Jase told him. "Here, put your arms around my neck, baby." With a nod, I did what he said and let him lift me.

"It's all clear," Rustin called as Jase walked us to safety. "Where will we find ice at this time of morning? The businesses are closed for another few hours." Rustin studied the quiet boardwalk, but Jase trudged toward the frigid waves, the fog stealing the sun's shine upon them. Jase's head looked in Rustin's direction. "Good idea. That water is still cold. You want me to remove her shoes?"

"No." Jase placed his chin against my head. "I'm sorry, baby. This will hurt, but you're used to the occasional ice bath against sports injuries, right?"

"Doesn't mean I *like* them!" I almost howled when we went in. Jase barely flinched as the freezing water swallowed his calves. He was smart enough to recognize my attitude wasn't toward him but resulted from fear and pain. "Oh, gosh!" He dropped to his knees. My legs and bottom submerged all at once. I sucked my teeth and gripped the hell out of his neck, squeezed into his warm body out of desperation.

Mascara melted into the crook of his throat as my tears stippled black droplets to his skin. My body burned for different reasons than last night.

"Shhh …." he soothed. "A few days of rest, and you'll heal. I can drive you to school if you want to visit the sports medicine doctor?"

Rustin waded in, wincing and cursing, making me giggle during crying against Jase's stubbled Adam's apple. Jase's chuckle joined mine, and Rustin's hand went to the foot I hadn't hurt. He lifted the drenched shoe from the ocean. As my sock rained water, he said, "See, it's barely even got anything wrong."

"Wrong foot, Country."

"I knew that." With a scoff, he gave me his smile, the only visible sunshine on this dreary beach. My injured ankle rose in his hands. The dripping sock carved patterns into the swollen grayish pink flesh. He averted his attention toward the shoreline to avoid my eyes. "You've got some concerned spectators."

My gaze shot over Jase's shoulder. *The beach guy!* Moonlight stood at the water's edge with three others looking on with worry. Part of me thrilled over his concern. Part of me was ashamed, considering whose arms held me.

The reasonable part won out, seeing the attention as a negative. "I need to get out of here with no one knowing I'm hurt. Chad put that article out. I can't afford speculation I might not be able to perform. People love negative publicity and too many would love to spread some on me."

My tone was rough, angry, frustrated. Rustin nodded like I had a great point. Jase studied my expression.

"Jase forgive me. I need my daddy. My coach will freak, and I don't want him to unless it's real. My dad can take me to the doctor, then I'll deal with the result."

Jase nodded, cleared his throat and asked Rustin for a favor. "Yeah? What's up?" Rustin asked, his hands on his superhero hips, his shorts wet up to his thighs. They shared a look. Rustin walked up and reached beneath me. My arms transferred around his neck, and for the second time today, I was uncomfortably close to too much exposed skin that even water this cold couldn't steal the heat from. There was something in how Rustin was a stranger that made this more inappropriate. He fought the waves to get us to the shore, and I looked over my shoulder to see Jase dive below the surf. When I winced in sympathy, Rustin chuckled. "Lifeguard. Remember?"

"Ah. Well, crap. Hope it doesn't look like I needed rescuing," I cracked. My ankle was numb, but my pulse thrummed in the swollen tissue.

"Ha, I think *he* needs rescued, Miss Hayes." I didn't lean into Rustin's chest or neck the way I had Jase's. I didn't want the onlookers getting the wrong impression.

"She all right?" Moonlight asked him with the faintest hint of an accent, the concerned citizens waited for an answer.

"Yeah, things got a little too hot between them, if you know what I mean." Rustin flashed him a grin. My jaw dropped, and my hand snapped against his chest. Moonlight shook his head and looked at me from behind sunglasses.

"You all right?" he demanded, scary and soothing at the same time. Like that night in the stairwell. I found my voice.

"I'm all right, thank you for asking." He gave a tight smile and a curt nod. The others I vaguely recognized from morning routines also nodded and went about their business.

I tried to quit studying him. My mind homed in on the pain in my ankle, focused on every panging nerve rather than looking like an ungrateful slut in the arms of another.

"Rustin, will you please set me down? I think I should try walking."

"No ma'am. Not until we get to the picnic table, Mizz Hayes. Want me to toss you around a little to make it seem like I'm not overcompensating for your injury?" Before his offer registered, he shifted me in his arms and tossed me up and caught me like a child while I squealed in laughing surprise against my will for all the butterflies set loose. He tossed me again while I giggled breathlessly and shouted that he put me down.

"Fine. Have it your way." He set me on the picnic table. While I caught my breath, I provided my car key and instructed him to get the phone from my console. In the meantime, Moonlight did rounds on the course. His sunglasses seemed to aim in my direction multiple curious times. Dark hair matted with sweat the harder he pushed himself. He was doing pull-ups when Jase walked up with a kiss for my cheek. Jase took to the course like he wanted me to watch him instead. The pain bloomed thick with my embarrassment at getting caught and passively called out.

Rustin, breathing a little hard, slapped the phone in my empty palm with a triumphant ray of sunshine printed over his mouth. Wagging that tail …. "Thanks, Rustin. Excellent job, boy, now go play." I teased him, then dialed.

My father answered on the first ring. "Daddy? Have you left for work yet?"

13 | ♂

A man I recognized stalked across the sand like a bloke on a mission to retrieve his little girl positioned between two shirtless men.

What caused Kinsley's injury?

Her agility had given my own a great run, yet the bee was at risk of no longer flying. *Nonsense!*

I moved about the course as her father knelt for her to hop on his back. She smiled like a happy girl. Too good at that facade. When I jogged from behind the wall to the tires, he helped Kinsley into the passenger seat of a BMW. I took that moment to walk over and shake Jase Taylor's hand.

"I hope your girlfriend is all right."

"Girlfriend? Now there's a foreign word with a ring to it." He grinned and thanked me. "I hope she'll be fine, too. If I have time, I might go check on her later." Envy was hard to conceal. "Something tells me she won't be serving my drinks tonight, though." He looked to his friend, and his face was grim.

"Mind if I come watch you perform?" I asked. "Afterward, perhaps we might discuss the happenings at the bar?"

He gave a knowing look, then introduced me to his friend, Rustin Keane. We shook hands.

"Pleased to meet you. Wish under better circumstances," I offered.

While assessing me from behind shades, he returned the sentiment then agreed the recent events at the bar were, "Escalating and unavoidable."

Taylor rested his elbows against the picnic table, his legs open as he squinted against the dull light of day.

"Yeah, I'll see ya later, King."

I didn't expect to see of them until the evening, nor did I, but I did see Kinsley.

The end of lunch break had me dashing onto the lift to head up to my office, attire expensive, hair sculpted, impatience showing. About twelve floors glowed on the panel of buttons. I added mine, then weaseled into a corner for spare inches, desperate to keep space between myself and a notorious loudmouth who thrived on sexually harassing co-workers in ways difficult to prove beyond hearsay.

Before the doors closed, Kinsley and her father joined the crowded box. The others barely noticed due to their phones. A cold rush gripped my ability to breathe while her father checked whether his floor was lit, then shifted her toward the back. He glanced knowingly at the man nearby and cast me an apologetic smile when he tucked Kinsley inside my personal space in order to place himself between her and the pariah. For the first time, the invasion of my bubble did not bother me. I wished I were free to pull her closer, to hold to her as I had that fateful night of Gasparilla. *Oh, to make this crowd disappear!*

Breathe in ... two, three ... out ... two, three ....

I almost closed my eyes to recall with vivid clarity how the curves of her hips felt beneath my fingers.

"Daddy, you don't need to do this," she whispered. "I don't even need to wear this stupid thing." His arm secured her waist, she had a splint on her ankle, and she argued that she could stand by herself. The doors shut. Without bumping me or her father, she wrapped her hands around the bar at our backs. *Oh, memories.* At least she didn't want to rip the metal from the wall to beat me over the head this time.

"Mom can pick me up, then I can drive," she insisted. "The doctor said the swelling will go down soon. He even cleared me for work."

"What does that doctor know?" he said under his breath. "He's younger than you are."

"He is not. This splint is nothing more than a melodramatic placebo. Useless and attention-grabbing."

"Kinsley Fallon, there's no use arguing, young lady. Don't make me pull this elevator over."

She snickered while her father fought a grin then cleared his throat.

"I'm taking the day. I'll make calls from my desk at home. This way I can keep you off your feet, and *you will not* work. What happens when someone bumps you or steps on you and turns this into a full-blown injury?"

Excellent point.

I reached for my personal phone to text Marcus to give her the rest of the week off. When I brushed her by mistake, her head turned in apology, where she did a double take. Her chest inflated. *No way she recognized me in this capacity, right?* But she exhaled in a manner I mimicked, blood rushing to her cheeks and pounding in my ribs. What madness being this close and playing indifferent, especially since her father picked up on her shift and eyed me in speculation.

"Forgive me," I rushed and refocused on my device, determined to throw him for both our sakes.

Marcus sent an angry emoji. As I explained, he quit firing questions. When I finished, half the elevator had emptied—meaning we weren't sardines, only a school of fish. Kinsley's father busied himself talking shop with someone I gathered to be a colleague. Kinsley stepped inches away, apologizing and looking down at her foot while she forced the splint to go with her. She didn't glance up, but she spoke.

"Your cologne smells very nice, sir."

A full smile stole from my indifferent sham. My hands traveled to my pockets as I studied the veins in the marble floor so her father—and everyone else— might not notice my elation.

"Thank you. You're the runner from the feature, yes?" My voice was quiet and drowned under the conversation around us, but she nodded without any hearing issues. "I hope your foot is okay." I gestured.

With a tap to her Mona Lisa lips to silence me, she nodded once more. Her hand dropped to her side next to my own.

"I'll be at my meet without an issue." The Mona Lisa transformed into Rembrandt brilliance, then shifted right back. "Looks worse than it is, because my daddy won't quit coddling me."

She had me. I smiled at the wall to stifle a laugh. Her father hadn't heard a word, but we dwindled by more than half of our school. Further communication had to be covert.

What a delicious thrill! What did she think of me without my costume? She was much shorter in flip flops than she'd been in her boots.

A woman in a pantsuit lowered the phone she'd buried her head in and breathed a sigh of relief as the pariah stepped off. When the doors closed, she said, "Oh thank heavens he's gone. He makes me uncomfortable." Several agreed with her.

She looked at the mirrored ceiling in praise, then gasped at the reflection. "Oh, Kinsley, your foot. Andy, what happened to her?"

Amazing what people missed due to social media.

Kinsley sighed as the woman faced her father. I brushed my fingers against the back of Kinsley's hand. Electric shock. Her breathing changed. A muscle jumped in her neck while I clenched my jaw. We had something thick. If this ride didn't end soon, we'd be exposed.

"She's okay," her father supplied like he knew his daughter was having trouble talking for the moment. "She was running cold on that obstacle course at the beach because some pervert almost accosted her. She had the fortitude not to go to her car so he wouldn't know what she drove, but still."

I inhaled my anger so deep, I had no choice but to add something. "That's unacceptable." I met the eyes and expressions studying our proximity. Kinsley's cheeks flushed while I worried. My instinct to protect her showed too obvious, but hell if I knew how to erase the anger the way she masked her emotion.

"I agree. Absolutely unacceptable," Kinsley's father stated.

They shared a look before the woman picked back up. "What's this world coming to when a woman can't even go jogging in a safe area?"

"I keep telling her to carry a can of wasp spray with her," her father said. "Hose them down from a distance. Get 'em in the eyes. It's not a weapon, court shouldn't be an issue."

Nice!

"Easy to jog with. Nothing odd there," Kinsley injected. She snickered along with the others, the sound thawing in the warmth of her timbre.

"Did you report him to the authorities?" I asked. "Or at least carry pepper spray?" I couldn't resist the dig.

She choked on her giggle and swallowed before shaking her head. Her eyes big, round and guilty, if not shocked I'd spoken directly to her before these people.

Her father studied us then focused on her like a man frustrated and wanting the same thing.

"No. I didn't think of it and I don't remember him well enough," she told me. A lie. She was lying to my face in fear while I grew agitated. *Had my words in this very building two years ago meant nothing to her?*

"That's a shame. Should you remember, get a sketch and a report this. If you expose roaches, they run. Though your father's bug spray idea is brilliant. Way further reach than pepper spray."

We chuckled together as I attempted to erase the tension.

"See?" Her father nodded.

"Yes, sir. Thank you," Kinsley said.

My anger vanished at the stung look on her face. *Dammit. I didn't want to embarrass her!* I wanted to squeeze her hand and tell her I'd squeeze the trigger of my gun if this happened again. Things were becoming dangerous at the bar with Inferno, now the beach. I had more than enough suspicion to merit a tail without being a stalker. *I should have gone to the beach sooner, dammit! I might have caught that wanker red-handed and dealt with him then and there! Was Inferno responsible for this? What the hell was their angle?*

The lift opened on their floor and her father bid the rest of us adieu. He aided his beautiful daughter through the doors. Her limp resulted from some bastard making her scared *and trying to steal my bee's wings. This was not okay!* Hannah was looking to Kinsley as a source of proof in doing what you shouldn't be able to. Two powerful reasons to fight for one person's safety, activating my powers of evil for good.

Kinsley peered over her shoulder with that bloody silent plea that wrapped my fealty and fury around her tiny finger.

Anything you want, love.

Could she read my answer?

The doors closed. I avoided the dancing eyes studying our magnetism. Pantsuit lady was sure to gab to her entire break room at the earliest opportunity.

When I got to my office, I locked the door and grabbed my other phone to call the only man I trusted for this job.

"Christophe, I need Joey for an exclusive amount of time," I told my private investigator.

"Concerning?" He multitasked in the background.

"A protective detail."

"He's on yours."

"Not mine. A woman's."

"A woman?" He stopped everything. The background noise muted. "Who will watch *your* back? I'm too busy managing the rest of my staff, and Joe is the only one who knows your double trouble." *Double life.*

"I suspect this is pertains to the double trouble. Not a direct threat, but one great enough I need an extra set of eyes protecting this girl. I want to hunt without distractions. May I have him, or not?" I struggled with my exasperation. The stack of messages on my desk proved there were many things to take care of before I went to the bar, if I got the chance, and I didn't need to add more to the list.

"I'll move him at once. What's the name? And you never answered my question about *your* back, King."

"Eric can watch mine. Her name is Kinsley Fallon Hayes. She's mid-to-high profile." I referenced the article and some of her background, then told him about the bar and this morning.

"Klive, is your interest professional or something more? Be honest."

I didn't want to hear shit about how dangerous a romantic attachment was. I knew every instance with her could equal a target on my head if I couldn't recruit a replacement in time.

"Professional. One of my bartenders quit this week. I won't lose another because some prick can't keep his hands or knob to himself."

He whistled. "Professional. Right. Joey's texting now. He'll be on point in about an hour. You have a phone number to trace?"

"Not without going through personnel files at the bar. Have Joey text Marcus. He's got it."

I hung up, my jaw clenching, palm tingling to do permanent damage. Something larger was afoot. *My* bar. *My* staff. *My* girl. *Who could know that, though?*

If only I could ask Kinsley what this asshole looked like. Before I went off the deep end, I had to admit some degenerate could have targeted her at random. She revealed more skin than usual this morning, but that shouldn't matter. Damn near every female jogger in the Bay area revealed more skin than necessary, and that was their prerogative and shouldn't mean writing an invitation to some tosser.

My fist pumped a stress ball before flinging the foam across the office. *In ... two, three ... out ... two, three ....*

Thirty minutes later, I received a text from Joey: *Target acquired. Bitchy Bonny back on the radar* ☺.

I rolled my eyes.

14 | ♀

Moonlight is here! ❤

Bayleigh texted from the bar during the shift *I should have been* working. Missing one of Jase's performance nights was as weird as the developing relationship between us. I giggled when she sent a picture taken near the stage. Jase sat on a stool with his guitar and the mic in front of him. Rustin perched beyond. But, in the left corner, at the coveted table, sat a man wearing a black fedora with a red ribbon.

B: *Sexy, huh?*

Bayleigh Blue! Get to work! Quit being a creepy stalker. Marcus will notice :P.

B: *Creepy stalker is in the job description. How else would we memorize everyone's drinks? Tonight's drink of choice is Captain and Coke with cherries and grenadine.*

Wish I was there. I sighed.

B: *So do I. They do too. Get well. Xoxo.*

"All right, girly. What's got you smiling that way? That's not just any sigh." My father sat on the porch swing beside me. My feet rested on his lap. He had removed the splint to alternate massage with cold compress. The tissue was tender, but nothing I couldn't have walked through. Still, I'd spent my day doing school work from my laptop on the couch in his study and trying not to daydream over the intriguing reunion I'd had with my pirate, not to mention how scary attractive he was in business mode. No fear of ticking me off in front of my father, either, that one.

Daddy's intuition had been fired up ever since, and he'd disappear only to reappear with a snack or soup like I was sick, then peek at my notes or my screen expecting doodles of hearts with a boy's name or something. Poor guy.

"It's Bayleigh texting me from work," I told him. "The music's good tonight." I showed him the picture.

"Ah. Mike's boy." *As in Michael Taylor.* "I noticed Jase on the beach with you this morning …."

"Ha! That's because it's hard *not* to notice Jase on the beach, Daddy." I gestured at his physique since Jase and my father had comparable builds, my father was a mite smaller and less defined in his late forties, but I earned a laugh out of him the same.

"True. Is that normal?" *Oh, boy.*

"Meh. We have similar workout regimens. Nature is preferable to the gym, yeah?"

"Yeah." He nodded and rubbed while I tried not to wince at the residual pain. "All right, I have to know. Are you dating?"

"Daddy, how in the world did you get that idea? You know I'm waiting until after I graduate. Jase and I are friends."

His laughing outburst nearly knocked me off the swing. I clawed at the wooden armrest like a cat falling from a tree and gaped as though he were crazy.

"For real, I'm *not* dating."

"What about the guy from the elevator?"

"What?" I gasped. Heat warmed my cheeks. "The pirate? What about him?"

"Pirate?" He leaned back to study me. All humor vanished. "I meant today. The man you stood next to. You looked at him like you recognized him. *He* seemed uncharacteristically coy beside you, not to mention candid and protective once he learned what happened. Is *he* the pirate you told me you met in the elevator?"

"Uncharacteristically? As in, you know him?" I danced away from the question.

"Why? Are you pushing for more information? Because for the right price, I may have what you're looking for."

"Daddy! Stop. No, I don't want his information, (*liar!*) and I have never seen him before. He was … scentastically pleasing and *uncharacteristically* handsome, sir. I mean, cut me some slack. I'm still a woman, even if I'm behaved. If I got the caveman going in a man like that one, wouldn't be the worst thing in the world, eh?"

He stopped rubbing my ankle and put his face in his hands.

My nose shriveled. "That's gross. Who knows where my feet have been?"

"Scentastically?" He laughed. "It's a good thing you earned that scholarship, because the words that come from your mouth …." He trailed off and grabbed my feet again but didn't rub. "I love you, Kins. You're too pretty for your own good, and that's not my biased opinion. The whole office was talking about it in the break room after reading the paper. Everyone's praying for you to nail your season. I downplayed your injury."

"Thanks, Daddy, but that's because there's barely an injury to downplay, but that's sweet of them on all accounts." I chewed my lip for a moment. "Today was scary. Thank you for coming."

He grew angry in a snap. "The man in the elevator was right. We need to report what happened to you, and maybe it's better that Jase was around. You should time your workouts so he's there. Not trying to—"

"Whoa. Slow your roll, Pops." I set my phone on my belly and lifted my hands. "I didn't mean the weirdo from this morning. I'm not going to report him, because it could've been my imagination going crazy, but better safe than sorry. I meant my career disappearing in an instant. It got me thinking about things I've been ignoring."

"What do you mean, honey?" I winced when he traded the warmth of his bear paws to the cold compress.

"I mean I've been working hard at being the best and staying that way, but what happens when it's over? Not like I haven't known this time would expire, but what comes next? What do I have to show for myself aside from a room full of medals and good grades? Is work and scholastic achievement everything?"

"Oh, boy." He sighed, deep and aging, weary of holding a facade. "Kins, do you remember when you were little, and we'd go to the park?"

"Yeah, Dad." I grinned, being a smart-ass. We could see the playground from our front yard. Old-fashioned streetlamps illuminated the empty swings, merry-go-round and seesaw. Most of the kids who'd moved into the neighborhood when we were all little were teens or grown. Now, the main use for the slide was a make-out spot. On occasion, neighbors gathered to grill on one of the barbecue pits or play soccer or football in the undeveloped area. "Do we need to go swing over there?" I teased.

"When you're able to hobble over," he cracked like a smarty.

"Nice."

"Anyway. When we bought this place, you were only five years old. I couldn't wait to get you on the swings and the seesaw, but you had no interest in the equipment. You loved making me chase you through the oaks. You'd reach up and try to touch the hanging moss, even if you were twelve feet shy." We chuckled. "As much fun as I had, I wasn't sure I'd catch you in time if you tripped over one of the roots on the ground. At first, that's all I had to fear. Then, you discovered the open field. That grass hadn't yet finished growing. Divots and dips everywhere. It didn't matter. Once you got your feet under you, you were a quick little thing even back then."

"What happened? Scraped knees?" I grinned. "A tantrum?"

He smiled as he looked at me and shook his head. "No. I was that good." He winked. "You were the best practice for keeping me in shape."

"You're such a humble man, Dad."

"Thanks, your mother tells me the same thing all the time."

She walked out, then arched an eyebrow at our position. Dad and I pursed our smiles. I pulled my legs off his lap to let her sit there. After asking how I felt, she handed me a cup of decaf.

"Am I intruding on anything important?" she asked.

"Of course not, Claire. We love when you join us."

She snorted but snuggled up to him and ran her maternal expression over my face.

120

"Daddy is getting all sentimental on me and talking about the playground. Me running away from him. Think he's afraid I will do that now that I'm growing up?" She and I shared a laugh while he shook his head with a wry grin.

"Young lady, that wasn't what I was getting at."

"Pray tell, Andrew, let's get down to it," my mother said. Her fingers wended through his hair like he needed soothed. "It's late, and your *grown-up* daughter is a night owl, but *you* are an early bird who has to be back at work tomorrow, mister. No more days off before vacation. You don't want to upset your boss."

"Yes, ma'am." He sighed and gave me a pointed look. I cringed. "As I was saying: the real danger wasn't in the obvious roots and things. You ran right over them. It was when you discovered the open field. You'd take off like lightning, throw your arms out and stare up at the sky like a bird about to take flight." *What was the point in this story?* He read the confusion on my face. "The running wasn't the problem. It was that you'd close your eyes and run, enjoying the mystery in where your tiny legs might take you. I'd have to predict your steps to keep you from tripping or running into the street. The harder I had to work to keep you safe, the harder you giggled. Like it was all a dangerous game."

"Daddy—"

"No, Kins, honey, hear me out. You're about to graduate. I can tell today startled you. Men are coming from the woodwork like they knew you wouldn't date until you had your degree. There's a field coming. You're about to be in the open, and this time, I can't predict your steps. If you trip, it won't be fair of me to save you. Lord knows your mom is right. You don't even think of yourself as an adult and you're in your mid-twenties."

"Daddy …." I swallowed hard, unsure what to make of how serious he was, or how my mother stared at the chains on the swing instead of me. At my father's prodding, she stood up. He did, too. "If you guys want me to move out, you can just tell me."

"No, honey. Don't miss the point."

"What's the point?"

"Kinsley Fallon Hayes, don't play dumb with your father."

I sighed and looked at my toes instead of them. Lonely feet with no more lap to lay on.

Daddy kissed the top of my head and wished me a goodnight. I gave him a pleading look.

"I'm sorry for whatever I've done. I love you. I don't want to upset you, and I'm not dating. Honest."

"But you will be, and it's okay. I'm not upset. You've done nothing wrong. And you're not the only one here who has to grow up and move forward, baby." He grasped my mother's hand, and her eyes softened, no longer avoided mine. "Just do me a favor, Kinsley Fallon?" he asked.

"Anything." I nodded, a lump in my throat.

"When you want to throw your arms out and fly, don't close your eyes."

Between Marcus banning me from the bar until Monday, and coach ordering me to stay home until the same, I was going stir crazy. By Sunday morning, I needed out. When my daddy saw me come into their house for church wearing heels, he threatened to march me back up to my garage apartment to make me wear flats.

"Dad! My ankle is fine!" I all but pouted. I didn't care about the heels. I was making a point.

"No, ma'am."

"Yes, sir," I countered, my eyes determined. "It's this or working out. I'm not sitting around and getting fat on all your sick food."

"My food is not sick," he argued in mock offense. I couldn't hold my anger with him, and he knew that. "You love me. Be a good girl. I'd be more comfortable with you doing a *light* workout than walking in high heels."

"Deal."

"Uh, uh. A light workout. Promise me."

"I promise! What do I need to do? Spit in my hand before we shake?"

He chuckled and ruffled my hair before we shook hands. I marched outside and up the stairs, into my place for those flats and another run of the hairbrush. At church, I felt like a Hobbit for how short I was compared to everyone around me. My dad liked the contrast. Jase's dad did, too.

"She's miniature without high heels!" Mike Taylor gushed and threw a brawny arm across my shoulders. Jase's tiny mother, Bianca, stood the same beneath his other. He and my father joked about our statures and made small talk after the service finished. My mom gabbed with all her girly tea party friends and discussed plans for their next frilly event. Itching to get out of there, I was practically pulling on my dad's sleeve, urging he take me home.

"You doing the potty dance, little bit?" Mike teased. My dad grinned and filled him in. Mr. Taylor nodded in understanding. "Jase is at the beach. You should stop by his stand and say hi after your workout."

"Already?" I asked in surprise.

"Yeah. He's helping with lifeguard training and prelims."

"I might do that, you know, after I get the ants outta my pants."

"Guess I'd better end her torture, Mike. It's always good seeing you. Perhaps your son will join on a Sunday soon?"

"Always working on that one. He's stubborn. Think a reminder that sweet Kins attends might be in order?" Mike asked. "Jase tells me you got flowers on Valentine's Day."

"Did she?" Daddy asked. My eyes closed. *Dammit*. I'd given most of them away and assumed my father had gotten me the calla lilies since the card they came with seemed a passive way of begging me to never leave.

"Hey, how did Jase know?" My forehead creased in confusion. He'd only seen me with the red roses, and I recalled telling him I'd brought those for the employees.

Mike dipped close like we shared a secret audible to everyone. "Young lady, if there's one truth you can always count on no matter how old you get, it's that your parents will hang you out to dry when grandkids might be on the horizon."

My jaw dropped, and Mike's play morphed to triumph. Daddy's riotous laughter drew attention as he tipped my mouth shut. My mother's hands clapped and cupped to her chest.

"Did I hear something about grandkids?"

Ugh. Now, I was crazy ready to get the hell out of there! At this rate, the church gossips would have caught the tail-end of that conversation and been fast at work spreading a pre-marital pregnancy that didn't exist with a man who hadn't attended in years!

Daddy ended my humiliation after they shared a few more jokes. Mike and Bianca kissed my cheeks, then pumped me up about their daughter's plans to visit during spring break. "Hey, I'm playing," Mike said. "But if you married Jase, I'd have the perfect sister for Tyndall." His elbow tickled my ribs. Jeez. Gloves off.

"Yeah, no pressure there," I teased with a dry tone.

Minutes later, I scooched into the back seat of my dad's Beemer. "Come on, Daddy! Before you guys plan my wedding! My proverbial tie is too tight, I tell ya!"

"Our evil plans worked!" He cheered. Mom slapped his arm as she grinned over her shoulder.

"You'd make pretty babies with that one," Mom said.

"Are you crazy? Could you make it more obvious you want me to end up with Mike's son? It's like I'm in junior high, only in junior high Jase was the boy you'd have warned me about. Suddenly, it's okay to have his children?" I crossed my arms over my chest. "This is an alternate universe."

"Welcome to the wonderful world of what you call 'adulting'."

"I don't use that word."

"Well, little rebel, now you know who got you flowers on Valentine's Day," my dad offered.

"Psh! For all I know, Jase has no clue he got me those flowers because you and Mr. Taylor hatched a plan to make him look good the way I did with Tyndall's box of chocolates. I mean, how else did he know my favorite flower, Daddy?" My eyebrow arched as he glanced in his rearview mirror. Mom chuckled to herself and looked out the window. *That woman* … I had my answer. Had she had sent that necklace? I asked, and my dad almost stopped the car in *OH HELL NO!* panic.

Mom's hands rose in surrender. "Easy! All right, I confess! It bought the necklace! She's too tomboyish. I just wanted her to look like a lady."

When we got out at the house, she shot me an expression that said she'd saved my ass but had *not* sent jewelry. I played along. We watched dad go inside to make lunch and her nails skimmed my arm.

"May I see it?" she asked. Her green eyes searched mine in seriousness. I nodded and so did she. We went into my apartment. She dug through my fridge for coffee creamer while I grabbed the velveteen box from the bedroom. When she turned, the box rested on the island. She looked at the velveteen like she needed a newspaper to kill a gigantic roach. I'd not seen that look since I'd sprained my ankle in ballet.

"Kinsley Fallon …." She opened the box, a reverent gasp following. "This *wasn't* Jase. It's not a crush purchase." Her French manicure ran over the diamonds and emeralds. "Someone's either interested in your heart, your purity, or the combination. Someone rich. This is not cubic zirconia. You be careful, Kinsley."

"I will, Mama."

She evaluated my expression for a few beats before yanking me into her arms and kissing my head. "Oh, my baby. Here I am telling you to grow up, talking about babies, and I … I … I'm not ready. My baby. I know you hate this. Just let me hold you for a minute without any sarcastic comments. Just be still and know how I love you."

"Mama."

"Nope. You hush."

I hushed and let her hold me for three solid silent minutes. She released me, stole my creamer and closed the door behind her before I could argue. Alone, I looked down and traced the necklace the way she had. Mom hadn't looked confident that I could handle who might come out of hiding. *Had Moonlight bought this? Why not leave a note like he had for the roses?*

Rather than let the unease expand, I snapped the box shut and hid the treasure once more in the back of my closet, then changed from this stupid dress back into my skin.

16 | ♀

At the beach, I chopped my jog by more than half as I dodged increasing towels and umbrellas once church services let out.

Shirtless men dotted the obstacle course while ladies out to trap the sun's rays hovered like flies as they gawked at the chiseled physiques. A woman sporting an Iron Man tattoo worked out in her swimsuit like an audition for a body-building bikini contest. I joined their ranks while my tank and shorts appeared reserved as sun-worshipers all around shed their layers to absorb the heat.

Even if I'd babied myself and my limits, I'd made fantastic progress. When, at last I finished my core work, I flipped from the girly pull-up bar, and ran an arm across my forehead to keep sweat from dripping into my eyes. My torso drenched proof-positive with victory. I'd kicked my twisted ankle's ass, and triumph over that fear of failure carried an endorphin high that couldn't end yet.

I thought about what Mike said about Jase and the lifeguards. Jase conducted training like the drill sergeant in charge, and I'd skirted past him undetected on the way in. That meant to get to the car, I would have to pass back by. Now I dreaded the jog, not because my ankle hurt, but because the eye candy in red swimsuits obeying every order from the man who had to watch their every bouncy flounce. Maybe why he liked being a lifeguard?

Ugh. Let the torment of relationships and crushes begin. *I hated this junk!*

When I happened upon his realm, the lifeguards took a group break. Jase leaned against the ramp of a stand, his tan darker than most of today's beachgoers. Aviator style sunglasses rested on his nose, whistle nestled between his glistening pecs, his free hand clutched his hip above red swim trunks.

127

Rustin, the ever-present sidekick, chattered beside him with one of the *Baywatch* bunnies. Jase laughed at something she said.

Go time.

Should I jog in front of the stand, or behind it like I'd done when I'd come in? Translation: was I a wuss, or did I have the balls to say hi?

Abruptly, my ugly bun felt like my hair gave ugly a new name. I tugged the elastic holding my hair and let the sloppy waves flow. Now, he'd have no choice but to notice me.

"Hey, Jase." I grinned with a small wave and kept jogging like I was doing my routine. His chin turned my direction in a way that gave me flurries.

"Oh, no you don't, baby!" He laughed and piped his whistle as if there were a life in danger. My steps faltered. I screamed when he captured me and vaulted me over his head without warning.

"Jase!" I squealed. He didn't put me down and shifted like he would do presses. "You freaking show off! Me Tarzan, You Jane much?"

"No, that's a different position, sweet Kins." He smiled wicked as hell, the innuendo screaming louder than I had. "You all better?"

"I'll be better when you put me down!" I shouted, unnerved by heights and precarious balancing on the palms of someone's hands!

"Oh, yeah?" He teased, then pumped his biceps. I flew up before he captured me in his arms. I pushed away from his hold, but he molded me against his heated skin. "Want to do real-world scenarios?" He looked back at the trainees. I gasped and fought him while he cracked up. When I took stock of our position, we were about ankle deep in the surf and continuing. "Hey, Matt, will you grab her shoes as a matter of safety? Watch her right ankle."

"Jase Taylor!"

"Kinsley Hayes!" He kept going, and this was nothing like when he was icing me down with my swelling ankle. Jase's body-double jogged over and took a swipe at my shoes before dodging my kicks.

"My ankle is fine, and I have no desire to go swimming, sir. You and your twin better turn your bottoms around and remove me from this water right now." I unfolded my arms from his neck to cross them over my chest. Jase and this guy, Matt, chuckled together like I was joking.

"Or else?" Jase asked.

"No more kisses for you." I gave a smug lift of my chin. Matt winced in play pain for his fellow man.

Jase was undaunted. "Is that so? Hmm … last chance. Shoes on or off, baby?"

My jaw dropped. I tugged my sunglasses away.

"You're not serious. You won't throw me in, will you?" My eyes widened from the horror. He shook his head, but not in denial, he seemed affected. *Score! Welcome to my world, bud!* He continued walking, and I jerked as the fangs of chilly ocean bit into my bottom, soaking my shorts like spreading venom, the pain following. My grip tightened as I tried to pull myself up.

He tsked. "Sweet Kins, seems I got you wet. Guess there's no turning back now." One of his eyebrows lifted with a devious grin, then *he threw me into the dang water!* Pins and needles didn't have jack on this.

Sputtering in shock, I surged free and dove for him. "Jase Taylor! I cannot believe you did that to *sweet* Kins!" Hoisting myself up to his shoulders to push his head down, he went without a fight. The water was painfully cold. His skin had been hot, but he didn't seem to care since he came up smiling when shoving the droplets from his face. One wicked glance in my direction had me fighting the current for safety, but Jase dove and caught me, bringing me back under, pulling us both up together.

"You can run from me on land, but you cannot escape here. This is *my* element, baby," he boasted with a splash.

"You are *such* a player. I'm not falling for this. It takes a lot more than that, mister." I splashed him back, then dove underwater, swimming through his parted legs, rising behind him.

He turned and scooped me up. "I have no idea what you're talking about." Charm oozed from the most adorable look of innocence, making me laugh at the mere absurdity. Tension ensued when he dropped his play. Pressing me against his chest once more, he brought his face close enough to kiss me, but held his position. Great. The breath caught in my throat like he was about to follow through like Valentine's Day! The tantalizing memory of the last kiss he gave me floated like a ghost between us. *Could I handle another?*

"Oh, c'mon. It's working a little."

With superhuman strength, I grabbed his chin to shake his head no. "Afraid not, sir. I'm immune to your charm." *Psh! May I shake the hand of the woman who was?* One glance over my shoulder showed there were a few pissy women still on the beach suffering from an addiction to his charm, and they wanted their fix. *Not too keen on sharing, huh, ladies?*

"You mean I'll need to use my superpowers *in public*?" Jase asked. "Kinsley Hayes, this is a big deal. I only whip those out for crime fighting, baby, but you're criminal when you're plastered this way …." *Cheesy idiot.*

His smile vanished, replaced by sudden gravity. When this time he descended, low and slow, I gasped expecting another kiss. What I got was an anything but innocent Eskimo kiss, his nose running up, then dragging back down to tickle the tip of my nose. My eyes closed to the thrum of an escalating heartbeat when his forehead rested against mine, his deep inhalation indicative of a desire to take this much further. Millimeters separated our lips and warm heat emanated from both our mouths.

What was going on when the king of easy lays was taking a pointed interest in me? *Me!*

"Let's restrict those for crime fighting from now on." My voice wasn't as strong as I willed. Whatever his intentions, we were both affected. I was glad for the pain of the chilly water. I'd bet he was, too.

He cleared his throat. "Yeah, I only pull them out in emergencies. Keep that in mind for next time, ya hear?"

I'd have asked how many emergencies he'd used that move in, but before I had the chance, he threw me back into the surf.

17 | ♀

Monday wouldn't come fast enough! The dichotomy of anticipation and trepidation for seeing Jase sing at work, not to mention being hot on my toes once more, had formed knots I couldn't untie. Spring break season—all of March—didn't kick off until the end of the week, but the first Alternative night was always crazy packed. Everyone had the itch for fun. They brought their chaos to the bar and lined my pockets while rocking out with the songs Jase's band, Rock-N-Awe, performed.

The beach was on pause since Coach allowed one workout only, and that workout was under his supervision. He wasn't a jerk, I wasn't a bitch. We didn't fight. I hated to admit that maybe there was something to Coach Walton's incessant lectures about getting enough rest. When I zipped the duffel on my spikes, Walton and I shared our relief, though I knew he fought a silent war on whether to allow me to run. I wasn't saying a word. My sprint was healthy like nothing had happened.

But so much had happened.

With Jase.

Angst hadn't been an issue until the drive home to get ready for work became a mental rehearsal of scenes with unpredictable endings. Who the hell knew how to play this game I avoided? Most girls, I supposed. Like the type of girl who gave a crap, I used every tool in my arsenal for transforming a hoydenish athlete into a bar-maiden babe.

An hour later, I tied the tiny lap apron over the black shorts and admired the bonus of training in the sun. Five-foot-two never looked so long, lean, and cut when the sun kissed all the right places. *Whoop, whoop!*

My father turned into the driveway. Well, hell. To delay until he went inside, I double-checked the pearly whites, applied texturizer to tousle the layers in my hair, added more eye makeup than normal, and spritzed perfume in extra places. When I peeked out the window, I growled. He and my mom sat on the swing which meant he'd had a long one. *Dammit*. I scanned the land mines of laundry—*I should have done that when I was in relaxation mode*—and jerked okay smelling track pants up my legs to cover the shorts. That called for more heaven in a bottle to cover the hell I'd have taken if he'd seen me dressed in this.

Earbuds. Yes. Good plan. I picked a rock song I hoped Jase would play tonight and pretended to be running late as I locked my door and jogged downstairs to my car, tossing a wave with a kiss to my parents. When I was out of sight and on my way, I sighed in relief.

The parking lot up front was half-full and filling quickly when I drove in. There was one spot in our employee area. I snagged the space. Seeing Jase's truck sent adrenaline bursting through the tips of the fingers I drummed on my steering wheel. The clock on my dash read four. Thirty minutes before go-time.

I pulled the vanity mirror on the visor and snapped at my reflection. "Kins, you can do this. He's only a guy. A flirt who can't help it. Get out. Get with it."

I exhaled as I opened the backdoor. Jase's voice carried over sound checks, joking with patrons as the band set up. The locker area was empty but gave me an extra space to remove my pants and put on my game face.

When I sauntered out to the floor, the band goofed a cover of *Don't Fear the Reaper* while they asked for certain mics to be turned up, drums down, etcetera. I tucked myself behind the bar to help dry glasses and Bayleigh hung them up since she could reach without a stool.

Her eyes bulged when I failed to stop singing when the band stopped playing. "Crap!"

"No wonder you don't come on karaoke nights!" Bayleigh stooped down to have a laugh attack, egged on by a patron shouting for "More cowbell!"

I slapped my forehead and felt the heat light my cheeks but score on supplying comic relief. "Hush, you witch!" I whispered. Her face burned pink against the boundary of her bleached blonde hair that bounced with every quiet shudder. When her snorting ensued, I knew we were in trouble.

"Bayleigh, I've gotta fevah—"

"Kins, cut your crap, and clock-in," Marcus barked, apparently not a fan of classic SNL skits. "You know I hate when you help off the clock. It's illegal. Bayleigh, get your ass up and back to work, or I'll put you on clean-up." She shot up, still super pink, fighting the giggle loop, cringing at me with bright, smiling eyes. He paused in his tracks to point a finger at both errant children before him, the band pausing like siblings to watch. At least this stole the attention from my public fail, yeah?

"Aye, aye, captain." Bayleigh's tone trembled with laughter.

"I can't hear you!" Rustin called over the mic in the stupidest signature to make the whole patronage join when Bayleigh repeated herself. Jase and I shared an incredulous smile at their blatant misbehavior, but we also knew Marcus was a sucker for anything that got the patrons going. They were now a party to our mischief. His finger pointed in our faces.

"Since I'm babysitting a bunch of children on my staff tonight, make sure you're at your best. It is obvious it's scheduled to be a big night. Big nights, bigger fish. Bigger fish, bigger tips, and bigger trouble. Should I continue, or can papa go to work?"

He didn't wait for an answer. Garrett whistled when he sauntered up to clock-in, a huge smile on his face, waiting behind another server doing the same.

She seemed less amused, and closer to Mr. Krabs. Bayleigh sneered and rolled her eyes. Oh boy, drama, drama, drama. On my way to the beer cooler, I gave her a small kick and an order to behave.

The first group of many spilled in through the front doors manned by two of our bouncers. If they were here, chaos was in the forecast, but this evening shaped up to read like a page ripped from the album of our best nights. People who hadn't trickled in since the Labor Day bash made their ways over with hugs across the bar, requests for buckets of beer and shots to bump their Etch-A-Sketch buzzing. All the extra compliments on my appearance proved I'd nailed my intended mark.

Bayleigh's exuberance radiated all over her demeanor when she returned from taking orders near the stage. "We should begin our shifts with a joke every day! I'm on fire tonight, babes!" She shared a booty bump and giggle, then we hammered out the band's alcohol before five-minute call. "This crowd is great!" With that, she disappeared and reappeared before the drums with the drinks we'd made. She may have had an infectious attitude, but her flirtation wasn't enough to cancel the disappointment Jase shot my way.

Well, damn. A blush crept into my facade. *He was fine without his kiss!*

Who had time to worry about love interests when demands for booze had me scrambling in the best ways? Tuning him out was impossible when he greeted patrons. The bar went nuts with clapping, howling, whistling, and chanting. Beer bottles and mugs pounded tables in time with Mel's drumming to go with Jase's pep rally. No way he could hang onto disappointment with such motivation. Even Marcus stood against the frame of the back hallway with a huge smile on his face. Marcus's grin gleamed bright next to his dark skin, which meant I didn't need to stress over bikers and assholes. Such a relief.

"Who came out for a good time tonight?" Jase sounded over the cacophony. We bartenders cheered when he asked to see who'd brought their cash. Fists full of whatever wadded into wallets, pockets, purses and bras shot up, and Marcus put his fingers in his mouth to do the whistle that always had us covering our ears. Jase gave his lopsided grin like a reward, turning his head to laugh away from the mic before coming back to speak. "All righty, boys, and girls, I say it's time to play in the rain." The beating, chanting, hollering resumed, and the blissful sound I'd missed drained into the rush, flooding the entire bar.

Mel spun his sticks on his fingers then beat the drums. Rustin strummed his guitar. Bass chords from a guy I had yet to meet complemented the Shaun Morgan-esque crooning that signaled *Six Gun Quota* straight from Jase's sexy rasp. He was magnetic and appealing to watch as he stroked his own guitar.

"Kins, honey, I need eight margaritas! Top shelf!" one guy called, yanking me back to the here and now. "Extra salt on the side, please!"

"Babe, I need four Buds and a whiskey sour!" another yelled over the song. "God bless runners! Your legs look great tonight!"

"Thank you, sir!" I shouted into the wonderful insanity, watching Garrett twirl bottles over his wrist before running them along shot glasses like a gunslinger. He'd pocket that bottle the way a cowboy holsters a six-shooter, then he'd pull another in a blur. I made drinks beside him and in his spare moments he'd pass them over heads I couldn't reach. When I thanked him as well, he said, "No problem, T-Rex!" and grinned back, eyes lined, top hat and suspenders in place. *What? No monocle?* Garrett had been the one to shop for my costume that fateful day when I'd met that asshole pirate. Steampunk was a way of life for him. I loved Florida freaks.

"You know, between you and Bayleigh, I should have no self-esteem left!" I teased.

"You have so much to be insecure about," he said. Two large tipsters extended money and compliments with an order to keep 'em coming. Garrett pointed at them in playful warning to keep me clean. That only led to comments about getting me dirty. Anyone could see they were playing, out for an enjoyable time that had nothing to do with having their asses beaten for sexual harassment, no harm no foul.

Bayleigh rushed behind the bar in a fluster of wispy hair and flushed cheeks.

"Hey! Trade places with her, will ya?" Garrett called over to her, tossing her a water with an order to drink.

She nodded and recapped the bottle after she chugged.

"Garrett! They're teasing," I argued.

"Who said it was for you? I need a break from passing out your orders, and you could use time doing it yourself without trying to reach too high."

"Ass."

"Closed for business." He snickered, ordering me and a full tray out to the floor while Bayleigh called out the table numbers. I liked that he kept me from going stir-crazy behind the bar, but sometimes Garrett was protective like Jase, though flirtation came with the territory. My point was, there was no point.

Along the way, agility was my weapon against the animated talkers who flailed their drinks around with their hands, couples dancing near tables, and passersby looking for the line to the restroom to break those seals. Music vibrated the wooden planks beneath my feet while friends and familiar faces greeted in passing. A couple of vulgar comments about my buns or breasts normally came in the concoction consumed during rotations to and from the bar. Full tray, empty tray, back and forth like a worker ant. The queen was the coveted table at the front nearest to the stage, not reserved unless you had an in with the band. Since they must've been Jase's buddies, I went the extra mile.

Didn't hurt that Jase had a full view of my hustle, and I of his. When I was able to blend in, I watched as he hugged the mic with his lips and played his guitar beside Rustin who'd join in on background lyrics. His talent was obvious. Rustin caught my eye with a smile that I returned.

Time breezed by with each song they performed, each tip to my pocket, each drink I made and served, the obstacles I avoided, and best of all, no residual pain in my ankle to haunt any of the tight-rope walking to keep from tipping trays. *What a damn good night!*

Between songs, Jase drained a mug of water, replaced the empty, and cleared his throat. He wanted his refill and his hydration had better come from me this time. He then spoke over his loyal subjects:

"This next one is a cover from a band who knows how it goes when you're sent overseas. Though I'd have to kill all of you if I admitted the things I've done." He paused with a flirtatious grin aimed at the ladies in front of the stage. "I promise, I'd make it slow and sweet for you, girls." The men went nuts, egging on the dog. He laughed away from the mic while Bayleigh rolled her eyes. She loaded another round on my tray while I re-hydrated.

"What gives, Bay?" She didn't give a damn about him.

"The way he watches you, then he does that, and it's like he can't pull his head from his ass long enough to go for what he wants. Why else would a headliner perform in the same place twice a week, Kins? Think of all the places downtown he could sing at during the off-season, not to mention the bank roll during the rest of the year."

"Seriously, though." Jase's voice stole any response I may have given. "Cheers to the heroes who came home under the stars and stripes. To all you who have worn and still wear the flag on your shoulders. To those who pledge allegiance to it, hang it high in your yard or at your business. And to those who stay here awaiting your soldier's return and everything that comes with the mission."

The pounding, whistling and chanting was deafening. Military of all branches stood at his urging. Marcus nodded in our direction to say shots were to go out. He hid a cringe for the moment, but his smile would split for the result.

That small hit would turn into thrice the gain.

Damn!

When I heard the opening chords to Five Finger Death Punch's rendition of *Bad Company*, I turned and exhaled. Jase had such a smooth edge to his voice and persona when he performed this one. He'd flip that into tough and badass on the chorus like he wanted every chick to know that he could be whatever guy you wanted.

As the band got into their music, I trucked along and swatted away naughty hands that tried to steal extra shots.

Once the shots were complete, I had a lot of orders to refill and catch up on. Jase's could wait a tad longer. I stacked a tray for another table near the stage. To venture close was comparable to braving the current of the ocean on a red flag day. My knuckles turned white as I fought to keep from spilling anything as I navigated the throng. The music was so loud, I had to shout to make confirmations. That's when a guy tipped me with a twenty.

"I can't accept this!"

He nodded with a smile, even as I shook my head. "Come on, Kinsley. I insist. It's not for anyone but you!" he yelled.

"Huh?"

He flipped the bill to reveal writing on the back, then grasped my hand to wrap the money inside, curling my fingers over the top. "Call me! I'd love to pick your brain sometime."

What the hell did that mean?

Tucking the tray with a ballerina spin in the opposite direction, I saw Jase smile down on an 8–chord break to destroy my uncertainty about letting other men down. *How did anyone have the nuts to flirt with me at all?* He was here. Watching. In ass-kicking military mode. Creeps beware.

When they finished that song, I stood holding all things that needed replenishing, and passed ice water up. He handed the drained glass back, then beer was next as Rustin, Mel and the bass player transitioned to another song. Jase extended the empty bottle just in time to grasp the mic and sing with a scratchier timbre. His eyes closed, and I became a captivated fangirl. The 'V' of sweat across his chest narrowed near his navel, soaking through his shirt like a brand of superhero waiting to reveal the true valor beneath. *Hot!* So was the temp under these stage lights. Whew. I fanned myself.

A chick beside me placed empty glasses on my tray with a request for two more Cosmopolitans. Back to business. Hustle the drinks, fight the flow, rock out with the men behaving as little boys on stage. Repeat every hour as they flew by.

An edge filtered into the air as the evening progressed, putting the staff on watch for thieves, public fornication, penis-measuring contests that risked breaking out into brawling.

"Anyone down for grown-up babysitting?" another server muttered as she passed by to clock-in. She eyed a group of men sitting at the bar. I stayed behind while Bayleigh traded with me. "Who wants to buy me a drink to help me endure my shift?" the rude bartender asked. Somehow, guys loved her mistreatment. Emasculation wasn't my thing, but whatever. She snatched money for two shots with little thanks, and not one had a problem with her attitude. Marcus never had an issue with us drinking on the job if we didn't get tanked, easier to accept a patron's generosity than to turn them down. Drunk pride being dangerous to wound and all.

She took up a tray I prepared, and once she had the table numbers, the guys' eyes followed her as she left.

Another group of masochists bites the dust.

When the band announced a break, we were so slammed I couldn't get away long enough to bring them drinks. Minutes later, an order for two shots and two beers rang out as this bartender extraordinaire manned the liquor in ways that made Garrett proud.

"WHAT KIND?" I yelled without turning.

"VODKA, PLEASE, ABSOLUT!" the customer strained over the crowd.

"BEER?" I shouted, then twirled to face him. Jase leaned over the bar with patrons buzzing around him like a hive of stirred up bees. I smiled as I grabbed the beer he drank and held the bottle on display. "YOUR HEADLINER WOULD LIKE A DRINK! WHERE IS TONIGHT'S LUCKY BUYER?"

The lively group competed for the chance to help a brother out. I took money from a handful of random women at the end of the bar and glanced from the register to Marcus's hallway post knowing he'd love me charging for the band's drinks rather than giving them out for free.

My smile vanished.

Intense familiarity slammed through my adrenal glands!

In the flesh, mere feet away, Complicated Moonlight stood in his signature cap with his arms crossed, leaning against the wall. He scanned the crowd like a stand-in bouncer, his lips drawn into a tight line. The light dim, the bill of his hat cast shadows that concealed the sharp details of his face, but this one wasn't happy.

When he looked over like he felt me staring, our eyes locked, and he caught me.

18 | ♂

Here a conflict, there a conflict, *everywhere* a bloody conflict if Kinsley Hayes was near. *How was she all over everything, yet unaware?*

Meanwhile, Jase Taylor pandered to the clientele packed inside the bar like cigarettes he lit up and consumed. They were his nicotine, their gleeful sounds inhaled through every breath he sucked between lyrics, and fiery embers of his voice ate away their stressors. He was a gifted performer, but my attention waned away from him while that hot little woman delivered the strongest buzz in town. When she tended bar, alcohol wasn't necessary. Sobriety was safer. What an ironic twist of fate that Kinsley was an employee Marcus had hired long before I did regular check-ups.

Under my nose all that time.

This place wasn't near my typical realm, more a hole-in-the-wall establishment at risk of going out of business years back—a lucky find before I'd moved to Florida. The owner had a nasty habit of cooking the profits rather than paying the piper. Unable to deny the potential, and seeing opportunity where Nightshade's profits could increase, you might say this place landed in my lap when I became the piper he had to pay. *Stay in school kids, don't do drugs.*

Nightshade drank here back then, and once revamped to entice a friendlier (and cash affluent) crowd, they still hung out, only with a less caustic facade. Jase Taylor was old news to them, but he'd be an absolute source of power and jealousy in no time.

Three Nightshade members, my most important, wormed their ways into the crowds, blending like everyone else.

Joey wasn't Nightshade, but he was also here if I needed an extra hand with the two Inferno bikers dressed as civilians rather than donning their signature vests. They behaved, but the way the one

141

watched Kinsley screamed ulterior motives. He communicated with his friend whose silent vibes confirmed my suspicion.

When she breezed around the bar, her warm high met with my cold front and stirred a tempest of conflicting emotions whirling like a fearsome twister. Macabre fascination had me on edge like a storm chaser attempting to understand the thing that could kill him. Every bit as futile.

"A picture lasts longer, and it's said one's worth a thousand words. Judging by your expression, I'd bet they're all dirty." Marcus handed me a stack of paperwork. He looked over and chuckled. "You approve the uniform choice, boss?"

"I do."

"She's cute, huh? Little Red?"

Ha! She was nothing shy of vodka-down-the-wrong-tube-sexy at work. When she ran at the beach, she wore no makeup and her hair tied up and messy. Tonight, red waves cascaded down her back and her carnivorous eyes were sorely feline, gnawing and gnashing on the desires of men I had no right to guard against, yet here I was.

"Cute. Sure, Marcus, she's a regular kitten. Adorable, sweet, claws at the ready." She'd been vicious in the lift the first round, and last week when I'd confronted her about reporting the creep from the beach, her eyes ignited like green flames even as she played polite. I wanted to dangle toys all around to make her bat at each one with no luck to piss her off again. She was fun to provoke. "So far, based on what I've seen, the servers are doing a great job. Place is running well, aside from these few hiccups with Mrs. Sara Scott. Honest opinion— is she prepared to quit, or does she need firing for the safety of others?"

Marcus rolled a toothpick between his lips, his good mood dimmed. "She's not coming back unless by some miracle her issues resolve themselves." When he shot me silent askance, I shrugged.

"If it's about their marriage, I'm not risking relations between Inferno and Nightshade over personal matters. Too dangerous."

"Oh? And when these two stalking Kinsley act on their plans to deliver a threat to Sara, will you react then? When it's too late?"

"What makes you think I even care? Fire Miss Hayes for her own safety, too."

He scoffed in offense. "Klive King, do you know how valuable Kins is to your establishment? How much *Nightshade* values her service? You let it leak she might be in danger, one of them may start a war you don't want on your hands, anyway." I turned in surprise, and he gestured out to the crowd. My first lieutenant, Eric, scoped Kinsley with a protective eye, itching to haul these two snooping men out back. "She's a figure-head around here. Taylor's in love with her, but your guys, they're loyal to the staff. Why couldn't you join that?"

Thank you, Marcus! What an interesting new twist on a pivotal part of my escape plan. Divine providence?

"How about this, I will act on her behalf under one of two conditions."

"Sara trained her. You have four-in-one with Kinsley because you had four-in-one with Sara. If we solve the problem, she can continue here—"

"What are you on about? If Sara has negative affiliations, I don't want her on the staff. Do you want to hear my conditions or not?" He waited in pointed silence. We paused as Jase pumped the Veterans. Marcus grumbled when I ordered a round of shots on the house for the servicemen and women. Why not? Jase Taylor was my candidate for replacement, so I needed to honor the things that mattered to him, this was part of that. So was Kinsley. "See how happy your kitten is?" I grinned while he stewed.

"*My* kitten? You're not fooling anyone, King. Have fun with that since you're eyeing Taylor. How in the hell does flirting with one man's treasure make him more willing to like you? Anyway, get on with these conditions," he told me.

"If she's a weakness, I want to know. I don't need a lovesick puppy. I need a bloody hell hound. Kinsley Hayes is an excellent catalyst for feeling him out. My conditions are: if one of these Inferno pricks is planning on waiting until she's leaving to make a move, I will let

Taylor act and see how evil he may be. If one leaves before, I'll go hunting."

"What's the other condition? That sounded like two, but it was one condition with two variables."

I tugged my brim lower when Kinsley headed this way. She wrapped behind the bar, this time to stay, taking wads of cash, calling charges to another server as she and Garrett made drinks as if they had a running race.

The band opted to take a break, and Jase stopped to shake hands, take pictures, listen to praise. But when the man who had taken Kinsley's hand earlier offered his up, Taylor created a space between them. *For the stalker's safety, or his own?* Marcus noticed, too.

"Looks like Taylor's trying to decide if he wants to spend his break trying to go see her or whipping this guy's ass."

I nodded. "The other condition I'd become involved is if Kinsley flat out admitted she was afraid. I'd do it for her. There. Balls out."

"So, she has a first name that he knows." He looked at me with impressed surprise. "King, I knew you had a heart in there somewhere," he teased.

"Oh, but there's a catch."

"What's that?" he shouted since the bar area grew too loud. Taylor cut a way through patrons and snagged a sacrificed space right behind where Kinsley poured rows of shots. Marcus smiled when she auctioned Taylor's drinks. Jase didn't care about the beer as much as trying to get her to notice his existence.

"For her to make a request of me, she has to know she's in danger!" I told Marcus over the volume.

When I looked up, Kinsley stared right at me. She didn't look away or blush. She had a request, all right, but the only danger on her mind was whether I'd unveil myself after our games.

Here kitty, kitty, kitty ...

19

"Hey, Garrett, get over here and let her take a break, please?" Jase yelled. "Also, a shot of rum—she deserves it!"

Both men ignored my protest. Garrett placed a shot glass in my fingers and warned of no chasers to follow. In other words, no spitting the liquor inside a bottle. I downed the rum, then Garrett handed me a cocktail napkin to wipe the dribble.

"I didn't spill," I said. Garrett peered around my back, then scoffed. "What?"

"It wasn't for the rum. It was for the drool over the guy you're scoping as Romeo busted his ass to make it over here to spend his break with you. Loyalty, Kins."

He earned a slap to his bicep, and I avoided looking at the cloak-and-dagger gentleman. "We aren't together, you brat, so I am free to scope whomever I want."

"Touché, grasshopper. I forgive you, but one at a time." At least he grinned, then ordered that I take fifteen and stay close to Jase. "No questions, just frigging go. I've got work to do."

"Okay, jeez." I turned to Jase once more. *I will not scope the guy in the cap!* "Hold on and I'll come around, okay?" Jase shook his head no, stood to his full height, and hoisted me over the bar as I giggled in shock. The drunken entourage surrounding us erupted in dirty catcalls. *Yikes.*

"Baby, they are harmless. You're safe. Now, turn around and put your feet on top of mine the way you had to do with that two-step," he said at my ear. I cupped a laugh. His arm was strong at my waist, the other came out to shove naughty hands while we duckwalked toward the stage through the rowdy mass. He didn't give them a tough time since he claimed responsibility for their … *enthusiasm.* Is this what busy nights were always like for him? Who cared? All I sensed was the heat where our bodies connected! The spiritual warnings were barely audible in the buzz of electrical charge.

When we got to the stage, I mingled with the band. The new bass player, Dan, though shy, introduced himself to me and the three women who'd glued themselves to Mel. After shaking a few hands, they resumed. Rustin had his arm around a pretty waist as he drank a beer on the steps and added to their conversation, careful not to leave her out. Mr. Taylor, however, situated himself apart.

"Hey you!" I raised my voice and face to him with an elbow digging at his ribs. "Should I go back to work and let you partake? You're so quiet!" He grinned down in answer, shaking his head, his brown hair dark and wet near his scalp. The rest of his tresses tangled with his eyelashes so that he tossed them like an afterthought.

"Kins, I swear, one day we will drill it into your head you're my favorite girl!" he yelled. "If I can spend my break with you, why waste it on anyone else?" There was such a legit notion in his face, I had to glance away. His turn to elbow my ribs. He smiled like he didn't need sunglasses to shield his eyes from the blinding inferno erupting in my cheeks. "Do you want to go back to work? I mean if this makes you uncomfortable …?"

Gotta appreciate a man who allows a tinge of his vulnerability to mix with yours. His relieved laugh at my emphatic head shake added a tingle to my palms as they wrapped around the edge of the stage while I hoisted myself to sit upon the wood surface.

"Excuse me." He leaned over—*against* me—to reach his beer.

The insane intimacy was in that my thighs were apart, him standing between them, and when he lifted back up, he didn't move his hips away. Just dipped the bottle to his lips then placed the sweating Bud near my right hip, his other hand rested beside the left. Inner conflict raged with the inappropriate desires that sparked to life. Pretending I was unaffected and focused on the stories he told of various other gigs, was futile until the others joined. About ten minutes in, cackling at their tales came as easy as the desire to let down my defenses.

"Gosh, I pray I'm never in one of these!" I teased and smacked Rustin in the stomach for what he'd added about some chick. He gave me a line of flattering bull, stole my hand without letting me pull my fingers away, and asked about the small calluses to distract me. As he resumed talking, his fingertips played over them. Jase had no issue, so I resigned to allow Rustin's flirtation.

The crowd's impatience grew too obvious to ignore, so before leaving them, I produced the Valentine card that had been on the calla lilies. "Will you read this and tell me if you recognize it as a song?" Rustin snapped the cardstock from my grasp first, but Jase swiped the poem, his eyes narrowed. When he looked back up, his right eyebrow rose.

"Kins, this looks like it came from a floral shop. Someone send you flowers, baby?"

I chewed my cheek as if I didn't know he was the guilty party (thank you, Michael Taylor). "Well, these calla lilies came in a mix of a ton of other stuff …." I grinned like an excited idiot thrilled to get something.

"A ton of other stuff, eh?" Jase pointed the card at me with his big brother authority. Great. "I'm gonna investigate this since it seems familiar, but you need to watch the ones that don't leave information. Never know who's watching you, okay?" *Um, a dig at my cloaked secret admirer asshole pirate, perhaps?* "Mmkay, creepy. Thanks, daddy." There was a reflective smart-ass in his grin. He licked his lips.

"Daddy isn't my style, baby, but we can see how things pan out when the moment presents itself. For you, sweet Kins, I'll keep an open mind." With a salacious gasp, I slapped his arm that rose to high-five Rustin.

"You, sir, are far too presumptuous. Time for you to go back on, and for me to mix drinks."

"Uh, uh, uh … not so fast, woman. Your first order of duty is to accommodate these poor patrons who've had to endure my off-key songs because *you* never kissed me." Jase gave a mournful look at the antsy crowd and placed a bereft fist over his lips at the travesty of it

147

all. I cackled once more and reached out to pull his hand away from his mouth.

"*I* didn't kiss *you*, huh? So now we've switched?"

"Well, you kissed me that other time, so I figured you'd want to again." He shut up when I grabbed both of his cheeks. His expression transitioned to a kaleidoscope of hope, surprise, victory, all manner of uncertainty, but he leaned in without hesitation. He expected my lips on his and groaned when they planted instead to his cheek. His chest expanded as my kiss lingered. I felt his lungs deflate when I disconnected. The desire to try for more showed in how he licked his lips and looked at mine. Gosh, I wanted him to, but he restrained his temptation.

I vaulted off the stage. He grabbed my hand and tugged me back with an urgency in his expression.

"Kins, any requests?"

We held eye-contact for a beat. "Surprise me," I challenged and walked away before he responded. *How deep would the shallow Jase Taylor push himself when he wanted something?* A Navy SEAL had more willpower than I'd seen of him with women.

The pirate was right. I was tired of boys and empty flirtation and watching my best friend's brother stay the epitome of such when there was more. Why not discover whether he could put his money where his mouth was? The worst that would happen was I'd end up thinking of him as shallow as I did now.

By the time I went back behind the bar to resume my shift, I noticed the ball cap guy disappeared. Jase downed a bottle of water while the band resumed their places on stage. Recapping the empty, Jase took to the mic. "All right, all right! Sorry, I broke longer than usual, but have you guys *seen* that cute bartender?"

I slapped hands over my face. *He didn't just do that*! Bayleigh knocked my fingers away and forced me to endure the roar in agreement.

"So then, you forgive me?" he asked them, yeah, they forgave him. "For those of you who may not realize, I *love* surprising people."

Oh, no! No, no, no, no, NO!

"I consider myself a humble man." He couldn't keep a straight face in the ensuing crap-calling. His guitar strap lifted over his head. The instrument rested against his hip, and his left-hand pat his chest in faux sincerity. "When I get a request from a beautiful woman, my humility takes the back seat to please the requestor, especially when she wants a surprise. I need audience participation for this song. Anyone ever work a tambourine?"

Good grief—about every female in this place. *Argh!*

This man! Careful what you wish for.

He pointed, and three clamoring chicks tripped over each other in a tizzy before the victor trotted on stage in heels too high for her to pull off a seamless strut. Okay, she was amusing and impossible to hate for trying to look cute, but after that cat spat, she was a hot mess. She straightened her dress and smoothed her hair as he held the tambourine out to her with the same humor on his face. "Congratulations! You're tonight's lucky contestant," he teased. She leaned his way to take the instrument, eyes all a bat, breasts and booty bubbled.

Jase played indifferent even as he moved close to ask her a question. *Hey, baby, how'd you like to shake this for me later?* One could pray my imagination scripted worse than reality. Whatever he asked, she nodded with a huge grin.

He turned to the rest of the group, and said something inaudible, pulled the mic up to his mouth, and his free hand pointed at me. *$%#&!*

"Kinsley, baby, this one is for you!" The crowd cheered as the tambourine shook. Dan strummed the familiar bass chords to Jet's *Are You Gonna Be My Girl*. Mel joined in on the drums, Rustin shared a fist bump and a huge smile with Jase, then came in right on time while Jase *screamed* into the mic!

"You're kidding me!" I cheesed at Bayleigh. She set about dancing as she served drinks behind the bar. "Who'd have ever pegged him for a British Invasion, yeah?" (Yes, I know Jet is Aussie, but I'm talking style here.) This was mucho impressive!

"I'd agree, I don't think he's joking!" she shouted. Jase winked at me, producing a fit of giggles. Bayleigh giggled along, because he was such an animated fool all the while—changing the lyrics to 'cute black shoes' and the color of hair to red, counting off the numbers with his fingers, and a '*but you won't date a single man, yeah!*' to replace the debacle in the radio version. Bayleigh was so right, and this naughty headliner made no mysteries as he grabbed his heart because I kept shooting him down.

She rubbed her throat in empathy. "He's gonna need more water after this!"

"For sure!" I grinned and tried to focus on serving.

The whole band rocked the stage like this venue was much larger and their names glowed in flashing lights. We're talking dancing with the mic stand idiocy! The level of passion and fun they threw into their performance was contagious, so there was no choice but to rock out with Bayleigh and confirm myself as the one he was singing to when Captain Obvious left the building the more alcohol these patrons consumed.

The relationship questions were awkward. What should I say? We were not together, but was that my fault or Jase's? What would happen if—*nope*—the brakes slammed hard on those thoughts.

The most rational option was to enjoy the moment. The adoration from smiling too much gave me away. Jase was so silly, confident, sexy, talented, take your pick! After that screaming, his voice would be the raspy I loved.

When he went to his knees, flipping the damp hair from his eyes, the last lyrics of the song screeched across the speakers and his finger rested in my direction. Pregnant silence ensued where the normal applause would have erupted, and my throat seized in a panic! *Holy hell, did they expect me to answer that question? Now?!* Instead, I settled for whistling between two of my fingers and cheering as that 'woo!' girl. The bar followed while Jase picked himself up off the stage with a knowing corner of his mouth smiling at me like he'd accepted a challenge—he *wasn't* backing down.

20

Bayleigh leaped to my side to fill a mug with foamy brew. "You can't avoid him forever. He asked you out." She was right, but I stalled.

"Bayleigh, he sang a song. What he's paid to do. It's common knowledge he is a chronic flirt. This buys them more tips." Glancing at the stage, Jase studied me while downing another bottled water, then took a swig of beer. He turned to talk to the band.

"Oh, yeah. You're the flavor of the evening," Garrett added. He dipped between us for some cherries, my attention back on making cocktails. "And Bayleigh isn't into that tatted punk on the drums, either." She and Mel had been, er … eye-*loving* … each other for most of the night. Garrett took an extra cherry to toss and catch with his mouth for the ladies he wooed, then another, and they all oohed and awed when he produced both stems tied together.

"Show off," we grumbled.

"Say what you want, see what you will," Garrett called as Jase spoke to the chick onstage with the tambourine again. "Women are too hard or dense. What the hell does a guy gotta do for a date?" He looked at the ladies in question.

Jase cleared his throat over the mic and curtailed the lecture Garrett prepared to give, hushing the captive audience along with him. "All right. Just so there's no confusion, that song was for Kinsley Hayes. This next one is for the redhead working behind the bar."

I gasped and looked up with slack-jaw shock as the band covered Buckcherry's *Next to You*. Jase's smirk was full of vindictive confirmation as he threw in with the rest and started singing. Well, hell! Garrett leaned in to pop off.

"Enough, mister!" I snapped in his face and commanded him to, "Shut it!" He and Bayleigh fist bumped while I rolled my eyes and hustled drinks. Marcus came to help at the liquor counter, happy and irritated all at the same time as he snatched bottles for me.

"I'll say this for you, kid. You sure can reel 'em in." I did a double take when realizing this wasn't a compliment.

"What the hell? Are you insulting Jase?"

"Garrett, call the other two bouncers to assist Gus and Jarrell with this crowd. Line's out the door, and at this rate, the damn fire marshal might walk in and close us down."

"Since when does the fire marshal care about this place?"

Marcus ignored my questions. "We've got two brawls on our hands, and one cat fight. It's a *Monday* night. Shouldn't happen until next week!"

Garrett agreed and set about following orders. Jase was making a romantic fool of himself to my right. Marcus frustrated with me on my left. Bayleigh at my back trying to keep from stepping on toes, and tipsy jokers sat in front of me. Talk about surrounded.

"Kins!" Marcus addressed me. "You know I like Taylor. Means you're doing an excellent job, but as soon as Romeo finishes his little stunt, you are going home."

"But I—"

His hand sliced the air between us, cutting me off clean. *Did he seem too liberal with granting time off as of late*? Under normal circumstances, he was the exact opposite. *Why this recent change*?

"Kins, don't argue. I'm not mad, want to keep you safe with all the attention."

Chewing my cheek, I tried reading between the lines regarding what he *didn't* say. This was the second time he'd sent me home early in the past month.

"This about that creep from Inferno who harassed Sara? The guy who gave me crap about men on motorcycles? Is he in here tonight? Because I'm not making him a damn Rusty Nail. I'd rather hammer a rusty nail to his forehead."

Marcus chuckled. "What if he was? Does that scare you?"

"What?" He almost seemed like he was goading me for a certain response. "If he has bad intentions, yeah, I guess it does," I sputtered. "I mean, Rustin pointed out how we both have red hair, how in low light I might be mistaken—" I broke off. "Wait. Is this about Inferno, or is it that guy with the ball cap that keeps watching me? You guys were talking, maybe you warned him or something? I mean he's never here, then suddenly he's here on the regular. Garrett claims he's come in over the years, but this is the first I'm seeing him …." My mouth ran away on tangents meant to provoke him as we shouted over one another. That guy wasn't the creep, nor did he creep me out, but damn!

A cat call shifted our attention down to the end. "Always great service, Kinsley. You know just how to light a fire, darlin'. You have my number," a dude called then disappeared out of our back entrance. Marcus growled and narrowed his eyes on me after staring him down. *Ugh! That was the last thing I needed right now!*

"The man in the hat *isn't* a danger to you. He recognized you from the paper, that's all. Happens all the time. I think it's obvious anytime you're featured we get perverts."

"So, he *is* a pervert, then?" We both knew Complicated Moonlight wasn't who I'd accused him of being, but Marcus was hiding something.

"Kinsley Hayes, I'm warning you now, if you don't stop, you'll hear a fat lady joining Taylor's singing." My lips clamped shut. Marcus had never threatened to fire me before.

"I'm going to work the floor. Bayleigh cover me?" I asked in disgruntled frustration.

"No, young lady, you're behind the bar for the duration," Marcus ordered. "It's my job to keep you safe, it's your job to make drinks. Two on the end are empty. Bayleigh, take the floor, and Kins back to work."

Jase stole away the fit I prepared to throw when he wrapped that song, and the bar came alive with rhythmic clapping and stomping while chanting for more.

"Oh, you want more? Don't we all?" Jase quirked his eyebrows at me, causing a heart rush and a little smile in the mix of my pissy. He turned and cued Rustin, who busied with changing guitars as he nodded. "Give this go-go girl a round of applause and drinks for working that tambourine!" She bowed after he kissed her cheek and sent her fluttering off stage with a delightful story and more cocktails than she could drink in one night. "This gem goes out to my sister's best friend, wherever she is."

I bit my lip through a bigger smile as I split lime wedges for martini glasses.

"Who is his sister and is he talking 'bout this redhead on the last song?" A white-girl-wasted drawl shouted to Marcus. "I'm so confused!"

He pinched the toothpick he chewed and arched an eyebrow at me. "No, he's talking about someone else, and he doesn't have a sister. You must've heard him wrong!" Marcus pronounced each syllable like she was hard-of-hearing. I laughed at her scrunched face, tilted head, duck lips and Marcus held his arm up so I could snuggle in for a side hug. "See," he hissed by my ear. "Crazies don't only come with male appendages."

"Point taken, boss."

There was an anticipatory lull when Rustin spoke into the mic, "I apologize for being rusty." He paused for us to laugh at his pun, then said, "Here goes nothing." All clapping for him came down with the hand he lowered inch-by-inch until their volume was nil. A cough was the only sound when Mel beat the drums on an introduction. Rustin's pick pinched between his fingers while he prayed over his instrument, willing the guitar's compliance, then the sliver of ivory metered out the iconic *Eruption* of Van Halen's, *You Really Got Me*. Both hands worked like simultaneous brushes scrolling in different directions to paint the same harmonic picture. He chopped at each note but held that guitar like a reverent man in love.

Jase gripped the mic and watched his friend instead of me until silence hung again as Rustin's final note laid over the heads watching.

Jase strummed his own guitar, and the band joined him and Rustin. The performing prankster disappeared to morph into a man on a mission. He sang these words like meaningful facts, natural, effortless, and alternated between holding the mic between both hands and going at his guitar here and there.

I assisted patrons while I watched Jase more so than the earlier two songs, but the ghost of crushes past played memories in my mind as my body went through the motions. History swirled around Tyndall's house. I tried recalling signs her brother may have shown back then. No, that was dreaming for the dorky romantic I'd been as an idiotic teen. The reality of how much I should enjoy Jase's show for *that* part of me slapped my insecurity out of the picture! *This was amazing!*

"Your boyfriend is so hot! Hope you don't mind us saying so!"

"Kinsley, you're so lucky, how long have you two been together?"

"Is this what it takes to win a date with Kinsley Hayes?"

"What about the roses I sent you?"

"Who knew Jase Taylor was so romantic!"

"Did he plan this?"

"Does he sing to you when you are alone, too?"

"If you'd worked on a karaoke night, I would have done this for you! C'mon! Just a date. Just one date!"

"No fair! You've tied each other down!"

"I thought you wanted to have coffee."

"Does this mean Jase is off the market, or can I still sleep with him?"

"Should I get my panties out of his truck, then?"

Okay, I admit, I imagined the last two questions there, but interviews I'd given to papers for track or scholastic achievements weren't as intense. Factor in the crowd had standing-room-only with both Marcus and Garrett taking and passing drinks as fast as I could make them. Faces blurred in the lucrative mayhem, and Marcus's expression fished for gratitude about ordering me home early.

Wait—*coffee? Roses!* Record skip! *Had Moonlight come to own up?*

"Marcus, did you see the person who mentioned coffee?"

"Huh?"

Applause erupted when the song finished, and I clapped, flattered by all that was happening, but *he was here!* Oh, dammit all! What a mess this evolved into.

Jase placed his hand on Rustin's shoulder. "I can't take all the credit on that one. Please give it up for my best friend and amazing guitar player, Rustin Keane, ladies and gentlemen!" Soon Jase and Mel wouldn't be the only ones with a following here. Rustin fanned himself for more with a huge grin on his face.

"All right, enough about him. Let's return to the real star. We're slowing it down."

Even though Marcus asked me to repeat my question, my throat was too busy closing as Jase set a stool near the mic and sat down. An acoustic guitar replaced the electric he'd been playing on. Rustin placed his onto a stand and grabbed the tambourine while adjusting the other mic stands. Mel came around to sit in front of his drum kit with a little bongo between his legs. He lowered the mic until he greeted everyone and reminded the crowd that 'he was just the drummer in the background'. Dan kept his bass guitar but shared a mic with Rustin. *Hmm ....*

Jase cleared his throat. "This next one goes out to the girl I had a crush on in high school."

"Nope, I'm done," I said and tossed my towel to the bar. I could handle no more. This wasn't real. This was a successful publicity stunt. "Marcus, can I go now?" I felt ready to have a panic attack. I didn't want that *Carrie* moment when I learned this was all an elaborate hoax.

"Shhh … let the man finish. If he hurts you, we'll take care of it," he teased, flexed his bicep. He spun me by my shoulders and kept his hands there like reassurance while I waited for whatever Jase would say next, whatever he would play.

"A girl who starred in my thoughts, if you know what I mean, and distracted me anytime she came around. When I listen to this song, I think of her, and when I sing along, she's who I'm singing about."

"I can't," I whispered.

"You *are*." Marcus tightened his grip like he needed to keep me from bolting.

"Ladies and gentlemen," Jase continued, "I'm sure by now you can guess who I am talking about, but this one is for the adorable redhead with the short hair, braces, the cutest blush, and the most beautiful smile all the while." His eyes held mine as he took a long drink of water. Mel counted to four for the band, then beat his wrist on the bongo. Rustin had something small in his right hand that sounded like a rain maker he began to shake while simultaneously hitting the tambourine against his knee with his left hand. Jase started strumming a song I absolutely loved.

Tears prickled, and Marcus kept me in place. This was overwhelming, and too much of a good thing almost hurt.

A rendition of Mr. Big's *To Be With You* floated through air that had grown stale with the stench of sweaty pheromones and booze. The whole band harmonized with Jase's rasp that melted into these lyrics so well, but as he pulled from his stomach to belt his vocals as they climbed in volume and passion, the voice that delivered rock and blues could steal the hearts of angels. How did mine stand a chance?

Slow-dancing couples took to the floor where lusty women had been minutes before.

Drops of perspiration rained down the sides of his stubbled cheeks, and his shirt molded to his torso. Every lash of his fingers against his guitar flexed his biceps. He was beautiful, each word that poured from his mouth drew straight from his heart like a tightened bow and shot like an arrow that pierced mine with bittersweet pain. Jase didn't sing ballads too often, so catching one was comparable to trapping a butterfly in a jar.

Did Tyndall tell her brother of my love for 80s rock and my associated weakness for bad boys being sweet?

Jase grinned and held my eyes while telling me he wanted to be with me, been waiting in line to be with me, and hoped I felt the same. Part of me knew he was taking a punch at the pain my ex-boyfriend from high school, Jack, had caused me, and I knew now while Jase sang that he'd wanted me then.

A flash of his brown irises colored in pain during what I'd thought the worst moment of my life played on a private reel with his voice as the soundtrack:

"I'm sorry, Jase. I'm so ashamed. This is nothing compared to what you have seen and gone through. Please, forgive me for my petty, childish shit."

"I appreciate that. Kinsley, it's okay to feel pain. I don't care who you are, what you've been through, we all have our scope and tolerance levels. If the shit hurts, it hurts. We can't help how we feel when it happens, right? Is there some gauge that says having your heart ripped out should be less painful than death? It's like death, right? In its own way?"

"I feel like I will die. What is left of me? Who am I? What do I have to offer? What is there to look forward to now?"

He'd rushed to capture me, and he'd carried me to safety as the brave soldier home on leave he'd been those years ago.

Real friends let you crash and kept you protected like a safety belt. They didn't take the belt off and allow you to slam through the windshield, shattering to irreparable pieces. They didn't deny that the crash was imminent. Jase had buckled me in, never feeding me BS lines to lessen the impact, but I'd always assumed he'd comforted me out of obligation to his sister. How crazy. Even reflecting on that day put a debilitating lump inside my throat.

Oh, Jase. Dammit. I swiped stupid tears from under my eyes.

Bayleigh looked at me like I was in for trouble. I widened my eyes in agreement as she handed me a tissue to sop up the mascara streams.

I bore the full weight of the reverent stillness when he finished holding the final note for an awe-striking amount of time. He sat unmoving, and the bar sat with him.

21 | ♂

The next half-hour of my life consisted of watching Jase Taylor pine in ways that showed the patronage in the bar that Kinsley Hayes was more than a one-night conquest. As a red-blooded male, seeing was believing. Landing that woman would take more than positioning himself between her thighs and her kissing his cheek.

He was a dumbass on that stage, I'd give him that. A clever way to win her over. Even *I* laughed a few times, so who blamed her for the gorgeous smile? Didn't keep me from wanting to knock her off her certainty about him while knocking her off her feet for my own. If he wanted her, let's see him prove the hell out of his worth.

Where his friend, Rustin Keane, fit into that mix would have to flesh itself out, but I hadn't missed their private communication during the break. Kinsley cackled the whole time, never suspecting that Deputy Keane had dropped his companion to grab her hand as a passive threat to the Inferno voyeur I edged closer to now.

Eric, Joey, and I passed one another, shifting and communicating. Seemed Marcus's wish may come true. An Inferno biker signaled another, then Gustav flagged me. Joey walked out the door with eyes on Kinsley's vehicle in the lot. Eric followed the biker. That left me with tonight's most wanted. The remaining two Nightshade members gazed at me to ask if I needed aid. I shook my head.

Marcus eyed the guy and did his best to keep Kinsley distracted, but he was praying this stalker would give me the excuse to kill him. When the wanker leaned against the hallway in the same place Marcus and I had been standing not so long ago, possession sizzled my veins. From there, you could see behind the bar and every rise Kinsley made onto the tips of her toes, the muscles in her legs, the way her shirt rose and exposed her midriff when she reached for the glasses. He checked her out like ticking off an itemized list of things to get off on. I ticked off murder tactics.

"… as soon as Romeo finishes his little stunt, you are going home," Marcus said loud enough that the bloody stalker and I heard. I glared, but Marcus sent that scowl right back while Kinsley gave him a slurry of attitude. At least he stepped in to block the bastard's view.

"Is this about that guy who harassed Sara? Is he in here tonight?" she fired off.

The Inferno voyeur enjoyed a subtle laugh of sick victory! The prick wanted to die. My jaw clenched at the bullshit stunt Marcus had pulled, but he kept going.

"Why, does that scare you?" he asked. Fabulous. Her expression softened, and her eyes grew to that same plea that made me go after her when she'd fled into the stairwell. When I shouldn't have, yet here I was—again—chasing shit that upset her!

"If he has bad intentions, yeah, I guess it does. I mean, Rustin pointed out how we both have red hair, how in low light I might be mistaken—" she broke off. "Wait. Is this about Inferno, or is it that guy with the ball cap that keeps watching me? You guys were talking, maybe you warned him or something?" Off she went on an insulting tirade.

A whistle wrenched my attention off her to narrow on the asshole. "Always great service, Kinsley. You know just how to light a fire," the stalking asshole hollered. "You have my number."

Marcus glared at him, then me before settling on 'Little Red' like the whole incident had been her fault.

As I watched the prick stalk down the employee hallway, Kinsley prattled off, changing tones and attitudes and opinions faster than the wind shifts. She knew better. If she was spooling up, she feared something and was likely taking aim at me for what that creep had just done.

Joey texted to add to this bullshit: *He went for her car till he saw me smoking. He's hostile. Let's deploy.*

Even if Taylor stopped performing right this instant, he'd still not arrive at her place in time to stop the stalker. I shot Marcus a confirming look and listened to him argue with this little woman, back to a bratty girl.

Perhaps my anger surged too strong, or was the idea of those fingerless-gloved hands on my girl just too damn much? If I rushed after him, I'd make a mistake in this mental fog. Another song *should* have made me jealous but didn't. Jase's stunt gave me a chance to think, to calm, to plan before I allowed emotion to lead my better judgment.

When the patrons at the bar fired questions at Kinsley, I threw some of mine in there to torment her the way she tormented me. "What about the roses I sent you? I thought you wanted to have coffee."

She turned to Marcus with genuine panic and disappointment written all over her face to ask if he'd seen me. Good. She deserved the torment. Taylor may have been gunning for her heart, but *I* was about to *pull my gun* in her honor. Let's see Jase do that. Then I'd consider whether he loved her. Until then, time for the gloves to come off.

Marcus looked my way. I tipped my hat and stormed out the back door.

***

Kinsley's neighborhood epitomized the American Dream, well-to-do houses, manicured yards, basketball goals in driveways, flowerbeds that won best yard of the month awards, jogging paths. Her family's Craftsman style home with the cliché white picket fence and porch swing slept at the top of a curving incline with a panoramic view of the park. Large oaks draped in moss flanked either side of the residence and dotted the playground in front.

I parked on the other side of the playground and inspected the sets of French doors lined by Juliet balconies through my night vision scope. So far, no signs of life. Neither the three balconies in the main house nor the two at the front of the garage apartment showed a single shift in the darkness or the flicker of a light beyond their sheer curtains. No cars in their circle drive. No movement for the past ten minutes except for a randy couple kissing at the top of the playground slide.

A large branch hung close to the garage apartment Kinsley took residence in. The good and bad thing about hundred-year-old oaks, they withstood weight, a man's weight was nothing. A horny boyfriend could scale that tree like a cat, so an Inferno firefighter would nail that entry point in seconds. I would not do the same. Too predictable.

I reached into my back seat and shrugged into a college Letterman jacket sporting the surname of a frat jerk that owed Nightshade money. Next, I pocketed my Sig and its silencer, snapped on black nitrile gloves, and tucked a garrote away, just in case.

Time to go to work, and fast. Kinsley's stalker may not have been foolish enough to try anything tonight, but as I made my way past the couple with nothing more than a 'sup man,' I felt that intuitive tingle.

My eyes narrowed at the edge of the road, looking up to the window roughly two feet away from the thick branch beside the garage. The sill appeared open at the bottom. Curtains inside billowed with the breeze every so often. Confirmation that Kinsley Hayes needed a hard lesson in protecting herself.

I made a sharp right at the pavement until the park was no longer visible. One advantage of their lot being over-sized, on a curve, the next-door neighbors' homes faced away from the property on both sides. When I saw no traffic on the street or camera systems on the neighbor's house, I circled back and traversed the outdoor staircase leading to her front door. A knowing sensation lifted the hairs on my arms, the back of my neck, prickling my scalp. I wasn't alone, I practically smelled the unmistakable stench of nervousness culling from inside.

Kinsley's shift didn't end for another forty-five minutes. More than enough time to pistol-whip and haul the prowler to the Rover under the guise of a drunkard needing a ride in case a neighbor noticed. The dirty work would continue elsewhere.

Reaching for my kit, the thought dawned that I may not even need to pick the lock. *Please let me be wrong!*

The cool metal doorknob revolved beneath my glove, confirming my worst fears for Kinsley.

Every murderous instinct I'd restrained for the last two weeks came undone.

22

Marcus grabbed my attention.

"Kins, you can stay. I'm sorry I took my stress out on you." My manager looked down at me while I wondered what the hell had changed his mind. Bayleigh's hand gave another supportive squeeze before she mixed a gin and tonic. Marcus lifted his finger to signal Jase this had better be the final song of this stunt before he got back to his normal performance sets.

"You want one more?" Jase asked the intoxicated assembly, understanding. They cheered in answer of Jase's broken silence. Deep emotion still swam in his eyes, but they lit with enthusiasm. "This last song is from a band I cover often called Seether. This goes out to the only woman who holds my attention whenever I'm here, whether or not I am working," he said. He gazed at spots nowhere near me that had me searching in curiosity. "A woman I hope will at least give me a date after tonight. Perhaps even one day her heart." He stared at me that time. The resounding, "aww!!!" from every female in the bar, including Bayleigh, made me smile. Made me nerve-eating nauseous, too.

"Bayleigh Blue! What has gotten into you?" I turned away from Jase to pin her traitorous googly eyes.

"What? I'm still a woman, aren't I? If you don't give him a date, you will come off like a total bitch!" She pointed at him while her hands crossed over her chest. "Never thought I'd say this about that man, but he's *smart*."

She was right. I'd look awful if I turned him down. When I spun to face him once more, he gave that lopsided grin, melting the trouble he caused down the drain. I loved when Jase performed anything by Seether, but what song could such a hardcore band have in their albums to convey anything sweet enough to dedicate? Was I about to be offended?

"Song's called *Never Leave*." Jase said. The electric guitar was back to replace the acoustic, pedal near Jase's perched feet. Mel took his regular spot at the drum kit. Rustin tapped his toes to the counts his bestie measured with each note he strummed to life, then he joined in as Jase took to the mic in his sexy rasp. This one didn't have the same sweetness. More a rough vulnerability and angst. Interesting shift. He scratched along in his sultry signature about being nervous, showing excitement and wanting more, like the Valentine. *Oh! Like the Valentine! The poem! Loud and clear. Never Leave. Aw!*

"And ... *there's* his permission to pass Go and collect." Bayleigh elbowed me on her way past as she worked the bar. I shook my head and stood rooted while Jase sent a knowing smile and owned up to sending *that* bouquet. His plea was a powerful appeal to never leave his company, that I'm the one who keeps him excited and begging for more, but always at bay, that he would keep trying for me. He feared putting his heart on the line.

Risk was worth the reward.

Well, I was out of excuses. All those miserable shifts of Jase Taylor treating me like his little sister had been to push me to a safe distance. How had this fine specimen had a crush on the bad haircut, brace-face Kinsley Hayes in this alternate universe I'd stumbled into?

The song grew as heavy as my reality. *What if this didn't work out?* Tyndall had acted so cavalier, but say I wrecked Jase's heart, or, more probable, he shattered mine? Where would that put her? Or this friendship I'd always counted on with Jase?

The song ended with a single note wafting over the air, and once more, silly Jase had left in favor of the contemplative deep thinker.

He studied me, helpless to have to go into requests for his next set without seeking me out. Part of me wanted to run through the crowd like the end of a corny chick flick and tackle him with a million yeses. But did I only want him because he was a crush for years? Because he was gorgeous and sexy and everything wrong? Because my father seemed okay with the idea?

There was much to consider.

I untied my apron, counted my till and tips, divvied them up to share with the bar-backs and dish washers in the kitchen. Marcus walked up as I grabbed my bag from the locker area.

"What are you doing, Kins? You can stay. You should."

"I'm leaving, Marcus. I don't want to give him an answer because everyone expects me to. He deserves better than that. When I respond, he'll know it's real and not for show."

"I can respect that, Little Red. Pray about it, or whatever you do," he told me in awkwardness, but I loved his thought.

When I opened the back door, he followed me while insisting I could stay, even as a patron, adding that I should face my fears. *Did he want me to give Jase a chance? What happened to that junk about making Taylor work his butt off?*

"No, Marcus. That crowd is crazy. Besides, with the Inferno stuff going on with Sara, it's best I leave while the bar is full. You were right earlier, and I'm sorry I gave you crap."

He sighed and ran a palm over his forehead, then jogged ahead of me. Jarrell paused his bouncer duties at the door to join us. His hand touched the small of my spine while he paid strict attention to everything.

"You guys okay?" They walked me the entire way to my car, making me paranoid.

"Kins, I don't want you scared. I promise we'll talk, but not yet. I'm still working some things out," Marcus assured me like a father pushing away questions from a five-year-old. "For now, save your energy so you can keep running from Taylor's hot pursuit."

There he is ladies and gents! What the heck?

"I'm not running! I'm thinking. There's a difference."

Jarrell's laugh echoed over the empty vehicles. I almost demanded an explanation, but my mind was so heavy, I conceded. Marcus's laughter joined. "Right, when you earn *that* metal, you show it so I can slap him upside the head if the rock is too small."

"Back and forth. Honestly, you guys need to make up your minds. Nice pun on the medal, by the way."

Marcus asked me to stay once more, but I shut the door on further arguments and watched him in the rearview until the bar faded.

23

The air inside the small apartment should have hollowed with dead silence, but the quiet filled my ears like cotton. I sensed an invisible presence occupying space, shifting and blocking the ticking of a bedroom clock and the conditioned air heaving through a vent.

The front door pressed closed at my back. I released the knob with the same calculated millimeters that I had used to open the portal, assessing obstacles while my eyes adjusted to the darkness. In the living area, golden light from a neighboring streetlamp spilled through sheer curtains over the two sets of French doors. Two couches covered in pillows and throw blankets faced each other and a vase with dead flowers adorned the coffee table between them.

To the left, blue digits on the microwave displayed the wrong time. A curtain was drawn over the window above the sink. Dirty dishes lined the length of the counter. The kitchen island filled with mail and papers, a laptop, candles and the crystal vase from the roses I'd gifted her for Valentine's day.

The interior door beside the refrigerator leading to the garage below locked tight at both intervals. *Sure, love, secure the entry that doesn't matter ….*

I joined the pistol with the silencer and crept toward the shallow hallway. Movement! I jolted into a bathroom, nearly tripping as I wrapped my foot in a pair of panties!

Me. That was *my* own bloody reflection in a full-length mirror at the end of the hall. *Tosser!*

At least the shower curtain wasn't drawn. No one hiding there.

The washer and dryer across the hall sat between open accordion doors. Kinsley's laundry flooded the floor. I bent and yanked the knickers from my ankle and tossed them back into the mess.

This meant the wanker lurked behind one of two cracked bedroom doors. Each flanked my reflected image. Carpet absorbed a repeated struggle with another pair of Kinsley's obstinate undergarments! *This bloody woman and her laziness!*

Rather than tossing the booby-trap, I hung onto the bra. My patience expired! Instead of kicking in doors, I strode to her front entry and ripped the door open with a resounding slam shut a second later. "Kinsley, baby!" I called with no accent, mimicking Taylor. "Did I beat you here? You left your door unlocked." Unwilling to dance in the dark, I flipped the light switch that supplied enough glow to illuminate the living, kitchen, and hallway.

With the gun behind my leg, I marched straight to both doors and kicked the right open. Her study rested empty except for a corner desk and the normal at-home office supplies, sleeping desktop computer. The curtain billowed before the open windowsill. "Guess no homework tonight?" I taunted. "What a shame, I wanted to play the naughty teacher again. Figured that serenade hit your target, baby."

I traversed the laundry pile like a mountain goat, then drummed my fingers against the other door. The hinges yawned as I pressed into her bedroom. "Perhaps you're ready and waiting in there? This is a sexy game of hide-and-seek." *All right, that sounded fun.*

Would Kinsley know where to hide or defend herself from men such as the one who peeked like a nightmare beneath her bed? Come on. *What was I working with, here—a total amateur?* Without a doubt, in the tritest of hidey-holes, I spied the unmistakable sheen of metal glinting in a telling gray against the light spilling into her room.

"Oh, naughty girl. You're keeping a secret. Perhaps I am not enough for you?"

Just as he took aim, the steel toe of my boot kicked the gun from his hand, and the cruel grain of the textured sole ground onto his fingers, ripping a cry of pain from his lips. Lucky for him his face wasn't within reach. He had no choice but to expose himself.

I strolled into her en suite to give him a sporting chance and check that he was flying solo. My quarry rolled into the open with a clumsy dash for the hallway. Endorphins rushed like a feeding frenzy with the thrill of the chase!

"Not so fast, you sick—" Threats and names rained from my American imitation until I pinned his wrists behind his back by C-cups and straps. Wadded panties stuffed in his mouth muffled his pained screams. Each knuckle-bruising blow to areas of great reaction, with no exterior bloodshed, sent tingling pleasure spiraling like foreplay for the torment that lie ahead for him while I imagined the happy endings that lay in store to keep him from getting his hands on her. "Shall we take this back to my place?" I asked with suave sadism as I placed him into a chokehold and chopped his neck and shoulder with a brachial stun—pausing our cat-and-mouse play as he crumpled, passed out.

Hoisting his frame of no meager size over one shoulder, no sooner had I turned off the lights, did light of a different type shine into the windows and curve onto the walls before vanishing. *Someone was home!*

Shit!

The man's limp body jostled with my hustle into the study to pry that window wide open. He *had* come in this way because there was no screen to keep me from dropping him from the second story to the sprinkler damp soil below. Had I not written him onto the list myself, I may have felt sorry for the shoddy landing with nothing to help break his fall. Who knows? Perhaps the impact had done the rest of my job for me?

Now to get the hell out of here and inspect the bastard!

At the sound of her humming and the thrum of every step up the stairs, Kinsley had arrived, and our fates were in peril if I didn't find a place to hide this instant!

24

The driveway was empty.

"Thank God no one's home." I sighed with relief. I'd be able to slink back into my apartment without Daddy spying my naughty appearance. A late weeknight never stopped my parents from having fun with their friends. When my mom's SUV slept inside the garage, that meant that they'd gone out for drinks. If she took her vehicle, she left the garage door cracked at the bottom. No cracks tonight. Daddy was designated driver. Mom would be a handful.

So glad Daddy couldn't pester me about my evening at work with Jase.

Across the street, the slutty teen-aged dream from a few doors down was sucking face with a guy at the top of the slide. His hand was up her shirt. Her father would shoot him if he realized she wasn't the angel asleep in her room on a school night. "Hey, guys, you mind keeping it clean for the littles that play there in the morning?" I called, never having much tolerance for watching someone trash their self-esteem.

"Aren't *you* one to talk, daddy's girl," she sneered.

Huh?

The guy took off with the promise to call her. She gave a prissy pout and flipped me off while I shrugged her attitude off and mounted the stairs. *What was her damage? She should be thanking me for doing her a favor.*

When I walked inside, I swiped at my eye makeup and smacked the light switch with frustration at my sloppy mistake. I turned to snap the deadbolt. *Wait! I hadn't used my keys to get in!*

"What the hell?" I whispered and held my breath. Nothing moved. The only sound came from the ticking clock. I rushed to the refrigerator, then sighed with relief, hand to my chest.

No creamer. Mom must've stolen my coffee creamer again and forgotten to lock up after herself. "Thank you, Jesus, but good grief is mom a hypocrite."

Irritated and relieved, I spilled every heavy cent and business card from my apron onto the coffee table, then heaved the tight shirt over my head. I shifted my shoulders as I adjusted the girls inside this crazy bra, half-tempted to pull the heavy curtains and unburden myself of this under-wire and lace. All I wanted was a shower and sleep.

"Son of a bitch!" I toppled over my own feet and caught myself against the floor as I tried to peel my legs from these damn shorts. In a bit of a fit, my tennis shoes flew from my feet against the baseboards in the hallway while I vented about Marcus's uniforms the way I wanted to. "Let's dress Marcus in nothing more than Spanx and see how his frank and beans feel after being smashed and outlined for hours with women copping feels! What am I saying? He'd love that. Ugh! I hate reeking like a beer-drenched skank!"

I peppered the laundry pile with the stinky uniform, then sank down before the mirror at the end of the hallway like my reflection was my only friend. "You look tired." My fingers reached out to touch the glass where wisps of hair rested against my forehead.

"Isn't life just so charmed because you make bank on tips? And all those metals! My, how many do you have now? Like a hundred? Oh, a hundred and two? My mistake. You're lucky. You don't even have to try. Scholarship, good looks, outrunning everyone in everything, aren't you babes? And isn't it just heaven how Jase Taylor sang to you? I bet you're not even grateful and probably still won't sleep with him. Then again, it's common knowledge you're a snobby prude who thinks you're better than everyone else around you. Poor thing. Alienated on that island of achievement with no one to keep you company."

I touched my face and pushed the wisps away like my mother would, tried seeing myself from her eyes. She'd been so afraid of that necklace. I grinned at my reflection.

"But wait!" I said to myself. "There's more! Hold, please."

I sought the velveteen box and opened up to show my reflection the necklace inside. She gasped and asked, "Is this real? Who gave you such pretty jewelry?" I tossed my head on an uppity laugh and waved my hand like this were nothing. "Why, I haven't a clue, love," I told her in a British accent. "But perhaps they came from the expensive man in the expensive suit with the best cologne in the world. Who's that you ask?" I scoffed at her and removed the necklace, secured the clasp at the nape of my neck, then admired the way her chin lifted and how her heavily made-up eyes sparkled with the emeralds and diamonds. "He's dangerous," I said, my chin and voice dropping. "Like this necklace. And the way you stare at me from stranger's eyes. Where's your innocence? You are scary."

I ran my fingers over the jewels, the flesh plumped by this bra, trailed my hand down the line between my abdominal muscles, stopped at my navel.

"Who are you and what do you really want?"

How many times I'd asked myself that question at crossroads, but never in this capacity. As a grown woman. No more *where do I want 'this' to take me in adulthood?* I need a solution.

Does Jase have a place in the new phase, or will his recipe for a relationship call for sacrificing dreams? Do we even match?

My previous internship ended three months ago. Now I'd received letters of acknowledgment and consideration from the ones I'd applied to. Suspense was a nasty thing. I could always become Daddy's assistant. That also kept me here for Mr. Taylor if the internship downtown wasn't mine. The other one was upstate.

Was Jase ready or capable of hanging up that notched belt for a long-distance relationship neither of us knew would work?

Mom would have smacked my bottom at the direction my thoughts headed.

"You talk and think too much," I muttered to my reflection. Rather than remove the necklace, I wore this persona while I closed the heavy drapes in the living room, then scooped the tips in my hands and hauled the money to the lock box in my closet. The change went into a five-gallon jug. On the way to my room, the twenty-dollar-bill with the writing fluttered to the floor. I squatted to read the handwriting: *"Kinsley, you're a fire starter. Call me. Pat."*

"Ugh! Do guys think this works? I can't believe he had the nerve to say that to me before he left. Hmm … Jase pro: he's big and mean enough to scare jerks like this. Then again, that could also be a con for my guy friends. He might scare them all away. Which doesn't make sense because this guy, Pat, had been in front of Jase and had no problem giving me this with him watching."

I rolled my eyes and scaled the mountain of laundry.

Only—?

Fragrance sucked through my nose like I should have had lines chopped on a table and that twenty as a straw. I'd never done drugs, never would, but I wasn't an idiot.

"Oh, God, please tell me he brushed off on me somewhere! How had I not smelled him before?"

I rushed into my bedroom and dumped the change on the foot of my bed, then hastened out to the laundry pile. On my knees, I flung dirty clothes, not caring where the stray twenty landed in the mayhem. "Where's my shirt? It must be around here! For goodness sakes! I smell him now!"

In the elevator and stairwell, the pirate had *the* most wonderful cologne I'd ever gotten my nose close to. His scent was a stain on the pirate coat I'd never wanted removed but faded after some months. Since then, I'd been on a secret quest to pin his fragrance down in stores without luck.

At my father's building, I'd smelled him twice since. The first time I hadn't given credence because he hadn't studied me with an ounce of recollection. Days ago, I'd complimented him, and he'd brushed my hand with his fingers. We had an undeniable chemistry, and he knew who I was and wasn't running away. Instead, he played games like a guerrilla fighter. Dart in, dart back out, repeat. To what end?

In my madness, I cursed about Jase, about the pirate, about men such as Rustin, and who I expected Jase to still be. Every stale liquor-stained uniform made me cringe. After five minutes, I realized there was no single article of clothing. Tears collected in my eyes as I stared down my reflection in the mirror again. That dangerous queen reduced to a desperate princess, she appeared confused.

"Longing for something you can't have? Shouldn't have, and won't have if you respect the man who poured his heart out tonight?"

But here, I didn't have to pretend to be a better person. That reflection could be whoever she wanted to be, and deep down, the give a damn was getting harder to care about along with every 'should'.

When the phone rang, I ran to answer as if the person on the other end would pull me from this defiance and place me back into the skin of the good girl I'd always been. The one who'd choose a longtime crush over a mysterious stranger and never keep expensive gifts she could never wear in the light of day.

25 | ♂

Time's up! Kinsley's coming!

As I grappled for a place to hide, I understood why the rogue fireman picked such a childish space to conceal himself; there was nowhere to hide! I settled for the window and was about to take the branch when a teen shouted down the street as she looked back this way with her finger in the air.

Bollocks! Because things weren't perilous enough!
The closing windowpane slammed too loud. *Shit! I was damn near tempted to reveal myself and deal with her!* She was closing in on a situation that neither of us wished for. *Marcus was supposed to keep her at work, dammit!*

Instead of being as cocked-up as the Inferno novice, I leapt into the laundry area, whittled into the small space between the wall and the washing machine, at war with the clothes pile as I wrestled the accordion doors closed. Several articles of clothing hung from hangers on a bar over the washer and dryer, and I silently slid them close to further conceal myself. My fingers touched crushed velvet and I knew. *My pirate coat!* I pat the inside pocket for the Bowie knife but found the pouch empty.

Through the slats, the living room became visible when she hit the lights. A terrifying thrill came with being able to see her without her seeing me. Like a two-way mirror, so long as she kept the bloody doors closed. More trepidation, not of the thrilling variety, accompanied the ways this might end. *What would I do if she caught me?*

Bile burned my esophagus when Kinsley turned to examine the door she'd slammed shut and placed a hand to her chest. *Had she not left the door unlocked?*

As she disappeared into the kitchen, visions played of these doors pulling apart. My hand smothering her scream of horror while she

181

tumbled back against the wall or into the bathroom, every soft emotion vanishing with the instinct to survive. *Would she run? Fight? Faint? Would I knock her out, try to reason with her, mistakenly kill her in the mayhem?*

The idea made me shudder, but which would win out? *The Caveman or Casanova?* Ha! Both if I knocked her over the head and trapped her in my lair. Coming home from work would be far more invigorating! Nice thought, but the more consumed I became in this infatuation, the more rid of the passion I longed to be.

Thinking straight within her realm was impossible, and her presence played cricket with my conscience, swatted my contrasting emotions back and forth between wickets!

No! This wasn't happening! Please, God ….

She crossed into the living area and ripped the top over her head.

My mouth became as dry as the Sahara. I didn't want to be this peeping pervert, but how could I resist? My eyes squeezed shut, but the gentleman gave up while the male gave in and relished the bottom half of the uniform peeling past her hips, down her muscular thighs, revealing cotton panties. The full curves of her breasts threatened to spill from her bra as she bent over and manipulated the stubborn material.

My fantasy paused, her hum replaced by frustrated grunts and curses. I stifled a laugh! Not at what she said. That part was hard to make out—except for Marcus's name—as she toppled over her own feet. She caught herself and wrestled the shorts off in a tizzy, kicking her legs as one swats at a bee invisible to everyone else, her shoes flying into the wall close by. Perhaps I should tell Marcus how pleased his star server was with her new uniforms. I cupped my laugh at her bitching about his 'frank and beans' being outlined and felt up.

The haze of lust dimmed as she spoke to herself, revealing a very raw and intimate peek into that mind. I stared through the slats, riveted on every word, until she vanished and reappeared with a square jewelry box she presented to her reflection. My breathing seized when she removed the most exquisite necklace encrusted with diamonds and emeralds she thought came from the expensive man in the expensive suit. *Me?* She had mentioned my cologne, unless there was another who wore cologne she loved. *Who the hell else could he be and who was he that he bought that anchor for her neck?!*

The purpose of this visit clicked back in place with a new type of anger so alien, so … so … hell, *what is this?*

Ponder later! Get out! Kill the dunce eating the daisies in Kinsley's flowerbed, then figure out where the hell this necklace came from!

She set the box on the floor. I nearly sagged against my coat when she ran her hand over the jewels then her body, down, down. She stopped shy of those panties and gave a magnificent view when she charged into the living room to scoop change into her palms. This bra was good, but she'd be lethal in lingerie, especially with that necklace. Some emerald earrings set in black gold to mimic her eyes. *Shit!*

She paused in the hallway when the money the Inferno asshole had handed her drifted to the clothing pile. His handwriting chunky and legible in black marker. She groaned after reading his words. I agreed with her irritation. If this were the sort of flirtation she received on a regular basis, shouldn't be too hard to knock her out of her knickers with a respectable effort. Shag her with that necklace on to spite the buyer!

My breath caught as she rose, but stopped midstride, inches from where I stood. Her head angled to inhale the oxygen deprived of me, and a foolish mistake as green as the irises peering my way glared me in the face: *wear nothing scented when entering another's domain!*

I wanted to throw a childish fit as she'd done but holding still remained my only option. *Kinsley ... back off, love ... don't open the doors!* I prayed hard while she sniffed to find the source.

"Oh, God, please tell me he brushed off on me somewhere!" She ran into her room. I breathed for the split-second she took to drop the change, then drop to the floor near my feet! *Oh, to have her this way under different circumstances!*

"Where's my shirt?" Kinsley begged. "It must be around here! For goodness sakes! I smell him now! Why, God, what are you doing? My pirate! I know he's the guy from the beach! The elevator! I know they're the same man and he's so freaking fine in every capacity and we match and that's bad because I know he's not as nice as he looks, and he's as dangerous as the necklace he placed around my neck! Maybe he knows I'm not as nice as I look, either. You know I don't mean to be a bad girl and have bad thoughts. That's what this has to be right? Some rebellious crisis before graduation like the cold feet a bride gets or something but come on! Jase Taylor is the last person I should ever end up with!"

She vented in a fury, ripping dirty clothes up to her nose, gagging at what she found. I breathed as shallow as possible, relieved, yet disturbed that she did think I was the buyer. All of this didn't stop me from being interested in what swam inside that wondering mind of hers. These insights gave me an unfair advantage over Jase Taylor, but I never professed to playing fair. Ironic she thought Jase to be the last person she should end up with when I was, but she knew better. Like fruit in the garden, a woman always desires most what she's denied.

She slumped in defeat, inhaling, sighing to the heavens and pleading forgiveness from her Lord for her thoughts. I smiled, flattered with how she loved my scent and longed for more of the knots I'd tied her into. I wondered if she might be as angry as I imagined were she to discover me. *Ha! Probably worse, considering our first encounter.*

"What is it about wanting what you shouldn't have?" she asked God. "That is why Jase wants me, why Rustin has a stupid crush, right? It's weird. Lord, how do I do this? And what about this man? Like you combined my favorite posters into one person." Her head tilted on a groan. *Score!* "Show me what to do. Who to pick beyond my foolish bias?" She huffed, then reached up for the handle on the accordion door in a horrific twist of irony!

Music filled the silence. Kinsley bolted as her phone rang.

Hallelujah!

Every tense muscle sagged against the wall at my back, a silent praise going up to the textured ceiling.

"Constance!" Kinsley cheered and placed the phone on speaker.

"Kinsley effing Hayes!" her friend's voice sounded through the apartment. "I came to see you after my gig by the beach finished, but you're not at work. Where you at?"

"Aw, I'm sorry. Marcus keeps sending me home early from the crap that happened with Sara. He hasn't told me much, but I'm not stupid."

"Give me a break." Constance snorted. "What bartender hasn't endured harassment by a biker or five? Goes with the territory. Sara can't complain when she flirts with anyone who carries a wallet."

"Ugh. You sound like the day crowd down-lookers. They talk open trash about the bar, our new uniforms, are terrible tippers. If they don't like the place, why not go somewhere else? There is no way Sara pays her bills with the early shift." Kinsley broke off. "Are you smoking?"

"Yes, just one, and I don't want to hear about how much prettier I'd be if I wasn't. We all have vices. Let's skip to the cool stuff. Everyone's gossiping about how the headliner serenaded you tonight! He's almost done, but I can tell Jase's deflated without you here."

The first of several squeals followed that statement.

Shoot me now.

Constance exhaled what I guessed to be smoke against her phone. "The whole bar is talking about it. But as your purity partner, I need every detail to gauge your level of risk. Sounds high if these sluts are any sign. They're ticked."

Purity partner?

Kinsley sighed. "Oh, Constance, I wish you'd been there. Why weren't you? Your name was on the schedule."

"Stick to your story, then I'll explain."

"Jase was so romantic …" Kinsley gushed and rushed through the events the way a child reads a Christmas list to Santa.

Meanwhile, in my mind, every recounted song translated to a sexual position Taylor planned once Kinsley dropped her panties.

Slaying my disappointment proved difficult considering how hard a time she had given *me*, a stranger, on the lift. But here she was, able to shift from sad to giddy in a flash. The way she'd plastered her smile at work then come home torn up said everything. This young woman concealed her true feelings, but why?

"How do you feel about it?" her friend asked once Kinsley came up for air.

"Happy. Who wouldn't be?"

I rolled my eyes, desperate to shake the truth from her.

"Agreed," her friend said, "but I'm weirded out by it." My interest piqued, and Kinsley queried in kind. "Jase was the one who taught *me* you never, pardon my French, shit where you eat, or piss where you drink. He's going against his own rule by pursuing you."

That's because Taylor has a bigger male pissing all over his territory.

"Makes no sense. Don't hate me for this, Kins, but it's no secret you're a prude, and I don't care if he says he's had this thing for you since you were teenagers. What's he going to do when you won't give it up after a few dates, or at all? *You'd* better hold out after all the years of sacrifice."

"Constance, I've been wracking my brain about this for the past month!" Kinsley's cheeks flushed pink with the same sadness I'd seen of her in the laundry pile. As she stood before me once more, I expected her to collapse into the mess like she'd slumped when she'd arrived home.

"Past *month*?" Constance gasped. "There's more and you haven't told me? Kins, this is more dangerous than a single serenade."

What followed was a fair and informative debate on my prospective protégé's conduct and revealing on Kinsley's not-so-strong suits.

"Maybe I'm wrong, and it's possible a man can change." *Give me a bloody break!* "Kins, your choices are your own, but if you get with Jase, you need to get dirty and clean up."

"Come again?" she asked.

"Jase is a dirty man, but he is a neat freak OCD style."

"I thought you said you never—how would you know?" Kinsley breathed, dread straining her voice.

"Ease up, I haven't, but I still broke his rule by accident. And ours …."

"Constance … what are you talking about? Is it why you weren't performing with him?"

"Yes, Kins! I am working my ass off to behave, but I'm a twenty-eight-year-old woman with needs, desires, living in the twenty-first century of free love!" Constance had vanished and given way to a whiny girl. "I'm not sure I even want a husband one day, and what if you don't either? Have you ever thought of what will happen if you fall in love with your career and decide you don't want to get married? Are you staying celibate forever? Can't I sacrifice smokes instead of sex and still be your purity partner? I can't keep doing this! Once you start it's so hard to stop!"

Kinsley growled at Constance's meltdown while I wanted to do the same. *Some of us had people to kill and a nap to take before the office in the morning.*

"Get a grip, Constance. Tell me what happened and how it pertains to Jase!"

Kinsley bordered on tears like Taylor had already broken her heart. Her chest heaved. Oh, to yank her into my arms and order her not to love what was bad.

I was bad, dammit, but what did it matter if she would fall into a set of bad arms either way?

Constance cleared her throat. "I didn't sleep with Jase, and I never will, though you should check and see if Sara has. I bet her customers are getting jealous of one another. Maybe that's why the bikers are suddenly interested in finding her."

"Constance! What the *hell* has gotten into you? I know you two don't get along, but damn. I don't trash your friends that I hate. Quit deflecting! You slept with someone, and I'm irritated, but it's always meant more to me than it does to you."

They both huffed and sat for thoughtful seconds.

"Okay. I deserved that. Look, I slept with Rustin. Jase wasn't pleased when I came downstairs to make breakfast and didn't wash my dishes. Not to mention how pissed he was that I was even at his house. I mean, like we haven't been friends forever?"

"*Rustin*?" Kinsley interrupted in shock.

Constance cleared her throat. "Yes, Kins. The sexy blonde with boots made for walking all over you in the bedroom. If I'd known he was staying, let alone planning on joining Rock-N-Awe, I wouldn't have given him more than a smile. It was a desperate moment, and tequila makes you do things those whiny country songs aren't lying about. Now I'm so nervous, I've been avoiding Jase, and I think I might have burned a valuable bridge, or at least set it on fire. He's mad at me and he's a huge source of networking my gigs. If I don't make amends, my gigs might dry up."

Kinsley rolled her eyes. "First of all, you give him way too much credit. You have a gift. Sure, he's introduced you to great contacts, but your voice is what books your jobs. Second, he's *disappointed*. Two of his good friends making a bad judgment call. Who can blame him? He'll be in the middle if this goes sour. Third, you've been holding this crap in for like a month, so we're even. Sorry I made you feel you couldn't confess."

"It's not only disappointment. I'm telling you, he has Obsessive Compulsive Disorder bad, which means you need to quit calling out this tiny splinter in my eye and clean up that plank of an apartment in yours. And thank you, but, for real, you will be a huge disappointment to me if you go to bed with him after all your effort."

"I'm not going to bed with him. And my apartment isn't dirty." Kinsley merged the land mines into one major obstacle. "You can ask my mom because she was here. Stole my coffee creamer. Having zero rent is nice, but I have no privacy. So, you see, even if I was going to screw up and sleep with Jase, it's impossible because the parentals see and know everything. She even left my door unlocked when they're always on me about that."

Constance laughed and blew another breath against the phone. "Your apartment is dirty, and I'm surprised your mom didn't do laundry and take the creamer as payment. And you can complain about zero rent and no privacy, but seriously, your dad still makes you breakfast. Your mom hides meals in your refrigerator and does your laundry. If you hate it, you can come split rent and utilities with me."

"Psh, whatever. She didn't do my laundry because I planned on washing clothes when I got home. Your call interrupted my chores."

"I can come over and help."

"That's sweet, but I am cleaning then going to bed. I may sleep in tomorrow."

"Wow, you *never* sleep in. I hurt you. Forgive me for letting you down," Constance told her.

"Forgive me if I end up letting you down."

"Kinsley Fallon Hayes, what do you always tell me? If you leave room for failure, you'll fail. But you always have my forgiveness."

Kinsley sighed and sauntered into the hallway holding the phone in her palm and checking for an eyelash in the mirror. "I just feel like everyone is alive in motion around me while I'm sitting still. Not trying to fail, just have less and less in common with the people around me. I'm lonely. That's stupid isn't it?"

"No. Not stupid. But you're tired and have a lot on your mind. I doubt you're sleeping enough. How much have you had to eat and drink?"

Kinsley covered her stomach and cringed. "I just ate, and I've got a bottle of water I'm nursing."

"Right … you never eat or drink enough. You're gonna put yourself in the hospital. Maybe you should sleep in and report back tomorrow. You may not feel lonely or envious of your peers with a clear mind," Constance reasoned. "Go. Hang up. Eat. Drink. Sleep. We'll talk. Bye, babes."

"Bye, Constance." Kinsley tapped her phone and leaned her forehead against the mirror.

I couldn't help wishing to steal these petty worries from her mind and make her something to eat. At the same time, I both envied and related with her, unable to relate to my peers for the restrictions on my lifestyle and continuously staying on the move to the point of burn-out and hunger.

She turned and the door in front of the washing machine yanked open. Every scenario of what came next swam like lottery balls. *Whose would tumble forth? Hers or my own?*

27 | ♂

Kinsley flung the lid open on the washing machine, her hand inches from where my body suctioned against the wall. She pounded buttons the same way she'd hammered the ones on the lift. *The same lioness in desperate need of taming.*

We were both pathetic contradictions. Me: saying prayers being the killer I was, the illegal stalker in her apartment, trespassing on her realm and the territory of a far better man. Kinsley: the image of Sister Christian cursing the likes of the sailor who'd sang her into a fit of confusion and now conflict with a good friend.

"I'm so tired!" she shouted, kicked the metal washer. "And that freaking cologne isn't helping, dammit!"

Easy, love. Those feet are valuable ….

She took a long look around, trudged into her room, and I expected her to shower. I prayed to escape, but instead, I heard music—older music. Whitesnake was probably the last band I would've expected. As the beginning of *Slow an' Easy* sang into the silence, Kinsley appeared at the mirror a moment later, eyes mean. With a dip of thumb against her tongue, she ran the moisture along her lash line a few times, repeating on the other side.

God would not grant me a reprieve, he would torture me to the fullest, and he would use one of hell's angels to do the job. She smirked at the mirror with makeup smudged like a sloppy slut three sheets to the wind, ready for bed, but not for sleep. The lyrics sang into the space between us and her fingers walked up the mirror, over her reflected figure until she brought her hands over her head, rose to the tips of her toes, then took two graceful steps back. Her foot angled like a ballerina to the pile of laundry she stood upon. Her toes grabbed a shirt, and her foot rose like a crane, toes pointed and gripping as she used sheer muscle to extend her leg out beside her, and there she dropped the garment inside the filling washing machine.

Damn!

"Yes!" She cheered and broke form. "Still got it."

After that, she bent for piles to shove inside the machine, slammed the lid shut, did a graceful turn on her toes with her arms bowed over her head, then relaxed and yanked the accordion doors closed. On the drumbeats, her hands found her hips and she high kicked into the living room before dipping back and plucking a throw from her floor. The blanket wrapped over her shoulders as she pranced to the couch where she let the fabric fall off her flesh the way a satin nightie might melt to her feet in my mind. She needed more than taming and *Slow an' Easy* like the song's title, wasn't the way to go!

The sweet remission to my cancerous evil revealed her own cancerous side when her temper flared, or while alone with her music and chores. I no longer cared that she was a slob. If this was how she cleaned up, I'd go home and destroy my house to hire her to dirty the place like an 80s-glam rock video!

What a shame she didn't have a larger apartment. She was titillating motion and danced in ways beyond average. I didn't want to miss a second of how she held her body, turned on her toes, rolled her hips, ran her hands over her skin, or pointed with objects she took up to put in rightful places after belting lyrics into them.

Not a modicum poorly done except for her vocals.

Which made this worse. Like adoring a stripper.

I loved how she flipped her mane and fluffed the waves to make them huge, mimicking the hair band era. *Hells bells, what woman went to her knees in an air guitar?* If she didn't stop soon, I'd be in the worst danger of my life.

My cap crushed in one fist, the other tangled in my hair while I leaned almost against the slats to see her, risking myself, but unable to restrain my desire to watch. The heat of my body from watching hers was far too hot to be wearing this bloody jacket, and I longed to strip and take her down the way she needed.

192

In only a few bruising songs, the apartment sparkled. This introduced a new work hazard that stirred me at thresholds of *deep blue* and had me seeing red over that damn Inferno pervert and any other. Who the hell knew where Taylor fit into that lot? I'd never felt this level of possession over another person. Such an intense need to protect and preserve, not to mention please.

Jase may have known her for longer, but he'd taken his blasted time until I'd come into the picture, hadn't he? Just who was pissing on whose territory? Was Taylor pushing back as I vetted him for Nightshade? Did he suspect my interest in Kinsley wasn't only a facade to screw with him?

When the music turned off and the shower turned on, I should've been relieved, but my body begged to join her. Didn't matter if doing dirty things clouded my mind, I knew how to handle this woman in every sense of the meaning and trusted no one else to do the job. I needed an outlet for my anger and frustration. Clamoring to escape as soon as she disappeared, I relished the thought of unleashing on her stalker.

I darted into her home office and shoved the window open only to find that my victim had vanished! To make matters worse, I was about to climb out for the branch when a niggling reminder ate at my brain. *The bastard's gun. I'd kicked it from his hand, but in the mayhem, hadn't retrieved it! No way in hell would I leave one of those behind again.*

Hours ticked by with me trapped in the dark study, her music now a soft lullaby I fought against to stay awake. Kinsley being a night owl concerned me since she woke up before dawn to run on the beach. Her friend, Constance, had a point about her lack of sleep and basic self-care.

When my head knocked against wood, I smashed my fingers to keep the damn door from slamming closed. What the— *Shit! I'd fallen asleep! For how long?*

Kinsley!

Was she crying?

I fired to my feet when she cried out again. In a fog I shot toward her bedroom like a discombobulated fool wanting to go to prison! *Had the Inferno stolen back inside without my hearing to complete his job?*

The room was black, but I saw movement on the bed. She was mewling, thrashing, legs flailing. I struggled to make out the offender attacking her! When I reached down to yank him away, I didn't meet with a male, but *she* seized my shirt.

"*Please! Help!*" she begged with tears in her voice. My everything locked tight, mouth tried for words, but none came. Like a robot, I sat up, no one else in her bed, and she held to me instead of beating my ass and screaming the way I expected. "Don't let him hurt me." That voice. The desperation. Unnerving.

"Where is he?" I whispered in confusion. "Are you hurt, love?" My heart and eyes raced to spy anything, to make sense of her fit, her current response to me. "I swear to you, I will not harm you. You're safe with me."

"Oh!" She hiccupped against my neck, her sobs dwindled, her arms tightened when she should have pushed me away. *"You're* here." *What?* She seemed *relieved.*

"I am, where is he? The man threatening you?" I searched the darkness, one of my arms wrapped around her, the other hand holding my silenced gun.

"You scared him away."

"Then I need to find him." She refused to let go. I pried her arms from my neck, her whining like a child odd and out of place, much like everything about this moment in time. "Here, lie down. I need to make certain he's gone."

"No! Don't leave me!" She cried out and reached for me after I made sure the space under the bed was blank.

"Kinsley, trust me. I will say no more on the matter. Stay put." The situation was too urgent to role play just now. She conceded, rested against her pillows, folded her hands on her stomach. Again, odd. Minutes later, I'd cleared her apartment, and when I returned, I expected a slew of questions.

She silently gazed up at me. "You came back."

My head tilted in wonder. "You aren't afraid?" *What the hell alternate universe had I stumbled into?* Her player still hummed with 80s rock, now a ballad. *Silent Lucidity* appeared to be on a loop. The singer said something about a bad dream, and I peered at her in wonder. *Is that what this was?*

"Should I be afraid of you?" She gave the faintest of smiles.

Considering I'd kill you if I knew what was good for me, yeah!

"You should be, but I'm not here to hurt you. Only protect you from anyone who might try."

"Like a guardian against naughty boys without the Captain Hook costume. I love this dream …." She sighed but smiled. *Oh, madness*! *Was I the one dreaming*? "Stay." Her voice soft, her order firm. I pinched the hell out of my arm. Not a dream. That meant I still had a gun to collect from somewhere on her floor, but when the woman of your dreams gives you a command while amid hers, you obey. *How to handle this?*

My elder brother, Lachlan, was a sleepwalker. Perhaps Kinsley was, too, but how lucky could one bloke be to screw around with two people during their sleep?

"I can't stay, love." *Damn, did I want to!*

"I can't let you leave again," she whispered. "You keep running away." Her hands ran up and gripped my collar. She tugged, but I stayed. My desire expanded at a dangerous pace. When I didn't budge, determined to be stronger than an emotion, she rose against me, and I knew. She *was* dreaming, and I'd garnered a starring role.

Her nose skimmed my throat, she hummed at the scent while my head tilted. A weak moan came when she breathed small kisses against skin untouched for *years*. I dropped my pistol to keep from gripping the trigger by mistake. Her comforter squeezed in my palm as she made her way to my ear while I fought tremors. "You smell so damn good, sir. What's your name?"

Her lips brushed everywhere that burned beneath her feather-light branding. I was weaker than I ever recalled as evidenced by my panting. *Oh, to lie down and join her dream, to rest in this hypnotic haven, to break from denying my longing for her.*

"Would you like to know me, love?" I asked in acute pliability.

Her mouth wove along my jaw. She gave a faint laugh. "In every sense."

"Ohhhh ...."

She swallowed my moan. My tongue joined hers, arms wrapped her waist, and she crawled against me till I fell back on top of my gun, her falling on top of me. Didn't matter. Nothing did. Just us. Our body-heat, her soap mixing with my cologne. Hair running like silk through my fingers. Her nails scrubbing at my five o'clock shadow. She wasn't the pure innocent. Miss Hayes needed to face that dirty music she loved. She wasn't a little girl anymore, and her desires, her curves, her scent, her sounds were all woman. The lust pressing at her shorts, all man.

Kinsley, all mine. She had to be.

She wanted to be mine, wanted me to be bad with her, to quit dallying around our chemistry. She said these things while her mouth tasted, tickled, tempted areas so sensitive I felt virginal under the sensational overload.

Bloody hell, I wanted to heed her every command, but *not like this*! I employed every ounce of restraint to break the seal of her kiss, her naughty hands traveling down my torso, my grip bunching her top, to pull myself away instead of pulling the camisole off her altogether. She protested and knocked me down. Hmm. *If she did something against* my *will, she couldn't accuse me of doing anything against* hers, *right? No!*

"No, love. Not like this." My words garbled against her urgent lips. "How will I tell you my name if you keep smothering my mouth with yours?"

"Your name?" She sat up with the glee of a giddy teen. I wanted to smack my forehead. This was like handling a Schizoid! Personalities everywhere. I clenched my jaw, hefting the full weight of responsibility amid her vulnerability. Once more, I applied the strength she'd bitched at me about before leaving me wanting in the car park two years ago: *You're weak. You're afraid. You're all the same.*

I'd told her she was wrong. I'd prove her wrong and be stronger, deploy more courage and be different than the type of man would savor this, which was why any other man needed preventing from such self-indulgent misbehavior. The danger in the fireman trying to get away with what I had now angered me beyond the desire I fought. *What if he'd already done something like this?* I could barely handle the agonizing idea of such a violation. He had to die.

"What's your name? I'm dying to know. Please, sir?"

"Henley." I confessed, and prayed like mad she wouldn't remember, the way Lachlan never recalled why he woke up in various places with mum's makeup all over his face.

"Henley." She tested my middle name, the best sound apart from my first name, from the best source.

"What are you going to do to me?"

Dear Lord, I'm not strong enough for this ….

"I will put you back to bed and be the man you demanded," I insisted rather than granting her a list of all the dirty things pounding through the wrong head. "Isn't that what you want?"

"I want *you*." Her voice became rough, her hands on another mission to test my will. I reached out to grip them and growled in aggravation because she loved my dominance!

"What about Jase?" I bucked to throw her off and flee her before I did something I'd regret for the rest of my life.

"What *about* Jase?" she quipped in a bitter shift, her winds dying, another personality showing up. "Weren't you the one lecturing about boys?"

"He's not a kid. Nor are you. Quit playing games, young lady. I'm willing to have coffee with you, nothing more."

The hourglass on this dream state contained dwindling grains of sand.

"You don't want me?" Her lip came out in genuine sadness, and I chastised my reprimanding tone. *Soften … soothe her.*

I released her and pinched her chin between gentle fingers, a soft order to look at me following. She sagged against me. Her huge eyes skittered over my face in the dim glow of her phone. *God, please!*

"Kinsley, love, I want you very much, but this thing with Jase seems inevitable, therefore I will grant that wish for the time you need to get him out of your system." When she argued, I stymied her protests with a few gracious nips at her lips until she hummed. I leaned away determined to maintain control. "Kinsley, when *I* take you, you'll be my own and no one else's. You'll plead for me when you're wide awake. You understand? I need you to behave."

She nodded, offered her lips, but I kept her chin and demanded her eyes. "I want to hear your answer, Kinsley."

"Yes, sir. I understand."

"Young lady, no one else in your dreams had better have what belongs to me. If another appears, you deny them and call for me. Who do you belong to, love?"

"You, Henley. Yours, now may I please, please, please have more?"

She whined when I said, "Not yet, but I'll kiss you once more. Would you like that?"

"Yes, sir, so much," she said.

"Ditto." I smirked and allowed her tongue to seek mine a few more salacious times, allowed myself to relish the sensation and flavor of lips I'd dreamed of kissing for what felt a thousand lonely nights.

"Henley, you make me so hungry for things I've never eaten."

My lips curled. *Ditto, indeed.* "Now, that's what I like to hear," I told her. "Bedtime. No arguments."

She rested back onto her sheets. I tucked her in with the reassurance I wasn't asking anything of her I wasn't doing myself. *Mutual torment was only fair, dammit.*

The Sig found my pocket while the shadows helped disguise my reach for the gun near her wall on the floor. That bastard. I should have strangled him right here when I'd had the chance. *How the bloody hell would I keep her safe from herself?*

"Goodnight, Henley." The angel sighed. Her eyes watched with the heaviness of impending REM. They also pleaded for her pirate to stay longer.

Were she to wake and I still be here, she'd never want to see me again.

My thoughts and voice softened as I knelt beside the bed. "Close your eyes, Kinsley."

"I don't want to," she mumbled. They fluttered shut against her will as I ran my hand over her tresses, committed her to memory, then slipped from her room.

I snagged that twenty-dollar-bill with my target's information scrawled in bold Sharpie, exchanged for a clean twenty-dollar-bill and a card for my favorite restaurant. I wrote a date and time over the logo, stashed the tropical-themed cardstock in the pile of business cards I placed inside her apron.

Not too often I used my lock-picking skills to relock a door, but I did and jogged to the safety of my SUV under the darkest light before dawn.

28

No one else in your dreams had better have what belongs to me.

That sentence haunted the next couple of days. Don't you hate when you had an amazing dream, even thrilling, but when you wake up only bits linger in your memory as a few foggy pieces of awesome? What mysterious, intriguing, mesmerizing words! I wrote them on cream colored paper-mache.

My Bible rested on the pillow beside me, worn from years of highlighting passages, ear-marking pages, taking random notes in the margins, and now in the place of my deepest longing to curb this lust. "I'm in a bad state," I said as I scribbled in the leather-bound journal. "I know it's only natural at a certain point, but I admit the scripture that used to read so clear is blurry." There. Raw honesty. Not like God wasn't reading the thoughts and intents of my heart anyway. "I'm having trouble seeing straight. I'm tired but having trouble sleeping. I feel like you've gone silent, Lord. I deserve your silence. I'm sorry. Maybe I've been too silent."

The small clock on my bedside table displayed six minutes after midnight. Beside the clock, *Silent Lucidity* remained looping from my speaker because I'd had the best dream when Queensryche sang me to sleep. I slapped the pen down, closed the metal hook on the journal my mother had made me herself. The pen laid on top of the Bible. My toes squished bare against the carpet as I tip-toed before the laundry area as though I kept a secret. *From whom? Myself?* Or maybe I was embarrassed at this weakness. Embarrassed that the woman with the necklace chatting to herself in the mirror was the same one calling to God now. What a defiled wretch. *How did a woman like that have the gall to speak to God? Who am I?*

The accordion doors squeaked as I plied them open. Shoving hangers with jackets and dresses aside, I reached for the royal blue crushed velvet as I had on many desperate nights over the past two years.

Complicated Moonlight's heavy pirate coat wrapped me up just like that night. If I closed my eyes, I felt his hands and body heat from the elevator, the way he'd stoked his thumbs at my waist, how his fingertips twitched against my spine while he doled stern but empathetic words. I'd memorized the mint on his breath as he'd released a ragged sigh when I'd looked up at the prettiest eyes rimmed with coal. I'd affected him as badly as he'd affected me.

I touched my lips with the memory of the dream of his hands, lips, skin, scent. My nose dipped to the collar of the coat seeking the cologne I knew had faded long ago, but butterflies burst from my belly with the huge smile as I caught the faintest hint.

"Oh, merciful Lord, how sweet you are!" I skipped back into my bedroom and jumped in bed with the coat wrapped around me, adjusted the long material until relief relaxed a modicum of the tension coiled in my shoulders. The pen and my journal slipped down the pages of the Bible with my bouncing the mattress. They tumbled down the other pillow. The companion pillow. Where I looked over and imagined a dark head of hair I might run my fingers through, over smooth skin covered by my comforter. Then, the dark hair morphed to the light brown of Jase's, an arm colored in inked scales reaching for the skin of my belly before pulling me to him and hiding us beneath tangled sheets.

This was bad. Two men on the mind. Which head belonged on this pillow beside mine?

Every time I fell asleep, carnality replaced reality like stepping through the exotic sheers in an opium lounge. Everything I'd deployed as a defense up to this point now failed. Months shy of twenty-five, I wasn't a virgin. I wasn't a promiscuous princess, either. I hadn't had sex in *years*. Constance was right, the longing lingered in the recesses of a darker place and once you started, the body craved a new high. Ah, but the body will do what the mind commands, and my body

DCYE - Lynessa Layne

obeyed coiled in chains with which my mind caged the disobedient desires.

Until now. The woman wearing emeralds and diamonds, she was pushing chains off her bound arms.

I sighed and gathered the shoe box near the Bible onto my lap.

The boy I'd loved and lost my virginity to remained in the memories of high school hallways and heartache. Since then, only Nate had gotten close to territory charted by one. Poor Nate. We'd fooled around until I'd recoil when things became too steamy to trust myself. I'd loved him, too, but I'd wanted to wait until marriage. Yup. I'm *that* girl, the one you love to talk about when she turns away. My decisions were my own, and I had personal reasons why they mattered.

From a sparkling frame, Nate's roguish smile curled full of unfinished business while mine beside him glowed full of promises I'd broken soon after the pirate told me to grow up. Though flawed, both relationships were long-term and patient. Jase's were not. He didn't even have relationships. He had no-names flings. We were incompatible. And the pirate? Who knew? He'd said he didn't date.

Bayleigh's words replayed like the song lulling me to relax.

I chunked the frame back on top of some other stupid things I should've torched in one of those breakup rituals Tyndall swore by before her latest boyfriend. I'd burn this when she burned him. She'd rather erase the past with ashes she could blow off her palm when she was done with a relationship. I mulled the good and bad, critiqued our experiences and feared if I reduced memories to ashes, I'd forget a valuable life lesson and repeat the same mistakes. Then again, Tyndall seemed to 'love' every single guy she'd ever been with until the facade crumbled into hate. I didn't love lightly, if at all.

Sharing myself was not that easy.

The more intense the battle, the harder I worked out and made sure, once again, to get out of Dodge before Jase pursued anything. Call me cowardly, intimidated, outright fleeing temptation, but leading someone on was plain bad, especially when I wasn't sure who I even wanted, and that's that!

Though her honesty was painful in places, Constance possessed a talent for playing Devil's advocate. After proclaiming her uncertainty of Jase with me, she developed a sudden shift and told me to give him a chance. "You're not leading him on. You're playing hard to get, at least that's what I'd assume. Kinsley, you have so much caution, you could loan most of it out and still have some to spare!"

Girls who had easy sex made sharing themselves seem effortless and wondered what my problem was. Even if she respected my choices, Constance wasn't exempt from that. I always wondered why my sex life mattered to anyone else.

"Kins, other than me when we are on-stage performing together, have you ever known Jase to sing to *anyone*? Do you realize all the lays he could have garnered from pulling that stunt?"

"Stop."

"I won't, and here's why. I've never seen him this way over anyone. He protects you without a second thought. Threatens any guy whose vulgarity goes over the top. He takes care of you when you're working, makes sure you get your breaks. Ever think he wasn't spending them with you before because you intimidate him?"

I laughed and shook my head. *Me intimidating Jase? How about the opposite?*

"His friend—"

"Rustin," I said.

"Yeah, Rustin, you witch. He might be a source of confidence. We all have our security blankets. If I'm willing to toss my own to be around some guy I had a one-night stand with, you can shuck yours."

Hadn't Marcus said something similar about Rustin?

"Constance, you're killing me."

"Come on, doesn't he pull out your play, Kins? He's easy. Simple. Go with the flow … everyone's doing it."

No, everyone's *already* done him.

"Original. Did he put you up to this?" I asked while she laughed at the absurdity. Best I figured, he'd offered to forgive her if she put in a good word.

204

Jase singing the blues might be apt depending on how tonight went. For the second time in the same week, angst accompanied the drive to work, along with checking my reflection while practicing a smile that seemed natural. Psh! What a joke, the amount of makeup and effort I'd put into my appearance— yet again! —said everything. I checked the mirror as often to be sure that anytime I smiled, lipstick wasn't on my teeth. Whatever, I could feel pretty if I wanted to. Jase, or no Jase. There were other guys at the bar and tips to hustle, hence some added oomph in the form of a new push-up to give the girls a boost in courage too.

Outside the car, I used the sun's glare on the windows as a mirror while I tied the apron around my waist, twisting to be sure the back of my hair stayed pinned in the knot my mom had helped me with before I'd left for work.

"Crap! I thought I'd taken these out the other night," I muttered, looking down at the stack of business cards from Monday. In the reflection, the apron was lopsided. I divided them to even out, then jogged in place, loosened my arms and legs. Nervous energy beat too fast through my body contrasting the swanky music in progress.

When I tucked behind the bar, a tag-along waited ripe and ready for training. *Thanks, Marcus. Dammit.* The sarcastic bonus? He smiled beside Bayleigh while ogling my goodies as if hitting the jackpot. Regret hovered like this dude's shadow while I clocked in and made a till for my apron.

Bayleigh walked past with an encouraging pat. I was grateful until some dude told me a tattoo would be sexier.

"*Excuse me?*" I turned halfway through a draft, foam spilling all over my hands in distraction. He cleared his throat in embarrassment. I almost punched the newbie when he removed a Post-It from just above my bottom. I tore the yellow paper from his fingers. *Property of Jase.* "Bayleigh!" I shouted and sopped the mess with a hand towel like the perfect moment to show newbie what *not* to do. On all fronts!

Bayleigh giggled and waved without looking over her shoulder, a tray over the other.

"So, who's Jase? New to the area, sorry." The guy shrugged, avoiding my eyes in favor of quick glances from my boobs to the bar.

"The singer with daggers in his eyes taking aim at you." Newbie choked on his automatic look up at the stage, confirming Mr. Taylor was watching him. What could I say? If Constance was right, then my pissy reaction to the Post-It grab probably prompted a pissy reaction from Jase.

"*He's* your boyfriend?"

"I can neither confirm nor deny, newbie. Now hush and follow leader." I smiled with a Karate chop command hand. Jase *was* watching me. I found myself sneaking peeks at his muscles flexing at each strum of his guitar, slicked hair, black wife-beater hugging the definition of his chiseled chest. "Here's what I *will* say. Don't date people you work with. It gets weird."

Newbie nodded while I accepted with a gracious smile the first beer bought for me and coached him about drinking on the job and maintaining objectivity. Any other night, I wouldn't consume the brew, tonight, I did.

Claiming Jase without committing to him wasn't so scary when he gave such a neutral interest in how things were going behind the bar, he didn't smile when our eyes met, he didn't look upset, or away, either. When he sang into the mic, he crooned slow and sensuous about loving someone no matter what they did.

Curse Constance for being right!

Jase trashed all subtleties. The air hung heavy with hormonal hell that wasn't mine alone. This man sharpened his weapons to wear down defenses by creating an atmosphere of hot, steamy calm. The showmanship of Alternative Rock night contrasted in how laid back and fluid his voice drizzled raspy yet sweet like slow dripping molasses down rough tree bark. His target clarified every time I turned and found his irises boring into me.

The crowd remained manageable. After an hour of the newbie in tow, we kept such an easy pace, I praised him for being able to handle things on his own. Yup, I saw through his attempt to seem like he hadn't gotten the groove. He earned the brush-off. He took the praise instead of a bruise to his ego, thank goodness! Now, onto Bayleigh!

"Woman, you're in trouble for that stunt, and to think ...." I paused and fanned all those business cards from my apron. "All these could've been yours ... imagine all the wealthy perverts with nothing to do but spend their money on young eye-candy."

"That's so wrong!" She cheesed with pride. "I've taught you well. You look so hot tonight, you should be thanking me for trying to keep you off the market, so you don't have all these hornballs stuffing your pockets with these offers. Now, what's in here?" Bayleigh's hips swayed to the slow music as she worked around the newbie, flipping through each card and any messages they'd left for me. "Banker, broker, real estate, ooh—car wash! Yeah?" She smiled at me like he was a winner. "Maybe he owns it?" She went on when I shriveled my nose. "There's a bakery in here for the snobby part of town, bet they have fantastic tea and crumpets!" she said with a horrible British accent and held that one with her pinky out.

"Sounds like a busy woman." Another guy chimed in, mocking her British accent with a much prettier version, wincing through his teeth with play sympathy. "Buy you a drink as consolation?"

"Kins, I'm pretty sure he's referring to you." Bayleigh laughed.

"Indeed," he confirmed. "No offense to you, dear."

"Believe me, none taken," she flirted.

"For what it's worth," he said, "that bakery has an excellent assortment of tea. I can't vouch for crumpets, but their *coffee* is to die for."

My scalp prickled, tingles electrified my toes, my palms, my heartbeat. *What the hell?* I swallowed the unexpected nervousness, focusing on my pour more than usual, counting seconds for liquor like a novice. I struggled to find my voice.

"Thank you, but I already have one I'm nursing, sir." I didn't turn but displayed the bottle. My beer trembled. Bayleigh snatched the bottle and tossed the remaining three-quarters into the trash.

"I think you want to take this," Bayleigh breathed near my ear while I gaped at the countertop to hide my shock.

"You know I hardly drink as it is. I've done enough damage. I should be thanking you," I whispered under my breath and gestured at my evident effort. She shrugged and told me to suit myself, then stole the drinks I'd been about to walk down the bar.

"Forgive my mistake. I forgot you're not one for consolation."

I gasped.

The voice that haunted my daydreams and sleeping hours lurked right behind me! *Complicated Moonlight! Beach Guy! My pirate! Here he was wrapped into a confirmation of a single man! In the flesh!*

I looked up at the mirrored wall, peeking between the liquor bottles, trying to calm my breathing. His reflection distorted, but our eyes met, and he tipped a fedora much like the one he'd worn in the picture Bayleigh had sent last Thursday. Hell. I'm a sucker for a straight man who knows how to accessorize.

The heat in my cheeks rushed over my chest, the blood pounded in my heart and ears, but I smiled down at the counter.

Newbie walked up and blocked the mirrored glass. "She also has a boyfriend, that big-ass body builder onstage. Can *I* get you something?" I bit my lip as my smile grew. He was a tad sore.

"That's all right, mate." I *heard* the smug grin. "I'm at the table nearest the stage where I can see her big-ass body builder boyfriend up close. Or rather, where *he* can see *me*."

Damn! So bold! Courageous. Bayleigh and I shared huge smiles as I risked a glance and mouthed "holy hell!" She nodded, then her eyes trailed and her whole face melted as I guessed he looked her way.

When he walked away, newbie turned and muttered about how I should have given him the same hint. Bayleigh and I fought the giggle loop. She rushed down and cleared her throat. "No, she gave *you* the hint because we work together. It's part of the job to flirt with the patrons. If you go too far, it's on you, bud," she told him. "She'd be doing a hell of an excellent job if she made him a Captain and Coke with cherries on the bottom and met that sexy attitude with the one hiding in there. Only the strongest of women make men like those compete." Her eyes swam with wicked intent ready to push me into the dating pool. "Strong bitches need strong assholes, and you are the strongest bitch I know. Think you can handle it?"

Crap. She knew my trigger. I cackled on accident as she broke all the insane tension locked tight for too long. My joy cleared and quieted when I spun to find Jase staring again. True to his word, Moonlight sat at the coveted table and there were several in his company. The crux? Many had turned on my accidental too loud laughter, his company included, but *he* had not.

Challenge accepted.

29

Rustin took a stool at the bar while my mind reeled in excitement and overwhelming apprehension for how to play this evening. "Howdy, Mizz Hayes. You seem a little tense. Let that hair down, girl, and quit trying to fool everyone."

Something about this idiot replaced the tension with the need to dominate. He looked at me like he wanted to draw out my flirt. I smiled. "What'll it be, Hickleberry?"

His blue eyes flared with amused light. "I see what you did there. Mixed Huckleberry and hick. Clever."

"You're sharp," I said.

While Rustin grinned like a player, the newbie shook his head in disapproval, confused. Bayleigh cackled on her way past. I hated that she got to go out onto the floor even if she wasn't the one delivering Moonlight's Captain and Coke. The mean server was.

Ugh.

"You want more cheap beer?" I asked Rustin.

"Hey now, Bayleigh did some readin' and she pegged me for a Perfect Pour. I think that's fitting." He pushed the empty snifter across on a charming grin, but his eyes smiled brighter. His flirtation prepared my attitude for the fearsome task of playing with my asshole pirate.

"Humph. I taught Bayleigh how to *read*. Guess I need to fail her." I grinned. "A Perfect Pour? A good sign she hasn't slept with you yet." My smile exploded.

His radiant laughter tickled my sense of humor.

"Or she has, and that's why. How are you to know unless you've compared notes?"

"Smooth. Not happening, bud. Here's your drink. Now go be a good boy." I pushed the refill across.

"Good is for the mediocre," he said, "but I can tell you're a good girl, so enough said."

My jaw dropped on an incredulous, "Oh, HELL no!" He stood and dipped a finger against his tongue to draw an invisible tally, then winked at Bayleigh as she passed by.

"Bayleigh, a bathroom break?" But I wasn't asking. I marched into the locker room before anyone could argue.

When I came back out, my eyes were midnight mean, the top button on my shirt undone, the girls in femme bot mode. Jase belted a cover of Eric Clapton's *Have You Ever Loved a Woman*. Rustin beside him was in full swing on a stupid harmonica and had a bird's-eye view. Jase sang lyrics about a girl belonging to a best friend while Rustin winked right at me. My eyes narrowed.

Who was he screwing with? Men like him made women a novelty, or in his case, another trophy like mounted deer heads on the wall. Every bit as dead after the shot nailed the target, the claim all the same.

Constance, Bayleigh, and I were just deer in the woods.

I would not be in that one's crosshairs as an easy kill. More like the twelve-point buck who'd escaped the hunter's rifle over and over. If he wanted me more, he deserved the misery.

The bitch server just finished Moonlight's table. I took her empty tray and ordered her to the bar to make more rounds. She copped an attitude. I threatened that she'd lose Fridays if she gave me more grief. She scampered, and I set about proving Rustin was just another cliché in the mix, boys all behaved the same.

When I marched out this way, I didn't think before performing. Tray folded beneath my arm, I plastered a beauty pageant smile, and nailed Jase like I should've been on stage waving to an audience while earning their adoration. His crooked grin bore a tinge of dumbstruck relief that made him miss a few lyrics.

Bam. One down.

I spent more time at tables than normal as I participated in what I avoided: shots, flirtation, a pint-chugging contest. One of the few times I didn't mind falling in second out of five chicks. Sometimes, women were more fun than men. I enjoyed playing their games instead of watching from the outside. Women rarely asked for my company, and that bothered me. Tonight, nothing did.

Each time I turned and caught the handsome gaze shadowed beneath that hat, my happy high climbed higher. I pranced behind the bar when Moonlight's table needed refills.

"He's still not drinking," Bayleigh sighed, "but his Gray Goose eyes appear to have made *you* drunk." She snorted and flew through the liquor counter beside the bitch server while they traded snarky insults.

"So, *no* alcohol? *Again?* Didn't you say he was drinking last Thursday?"

"Yes ma'am." She paused long enough to ask me with her eyes what I would do. "I vote you spike his Coke. Remember what Garrett said? It's you, babes."

What a crazy idea. "I could claim it was a mistake, but then that looks like I make mistakes."

She busted out laughing. Bitch put a hand on her hip, attitude all over her. "Mistakes? Look here, Micro Minx or whatever the hell they call you at that dumb campus. Where do you get off threatening to take Fridays away when you're not in charge? Taking my tables? And I'm so sick of this ho in disguise as the basic girl next door. I see what you are." She griped while I gaped. "The guy on-stage is a fool for you. Now you're flirting with his friend, and the big tipper at the special table? I'm reporting all of this to Marcus if you pour Captain in that guy's drink."

My hand met with my hip and gripped so I didn't pour Captain in her eyes! "Ho in disguise? You don't know me. I don't recall seeing you in high school when that guy on-stage banged everything with boobs and a skirt while I guarded my virginity. Maybe because you didn't graduate? Get your head out of your ass and wipe the BS off your eyes so you can see that his friend keeps flirting with *me*. Not the other way around. Chicks like you always put the blame on the woman. But I'm more than happy to go with you while you tattle to Marcus. Gives me a front row seat to his response."

Bayleigh whistled, grabbed my shoulders, and steered me to the tray she'd made. The bitch stood there unsure how to respond. "Easy there, Micro Minx. Keep your top on. You are drawing attention, and not the type the manager would approve of," she said at my ear. "But I won't deny I like it. You're kinda mean when you've been drinking. If we weren't on the clock, I'd let you loose and take bets."

"Where is Marcus? I want to report her."

She sighed. "So, you can tattle first? You're better than that. I can't believe you just noticed he's not here. He had a certification tonight. Gus is on as manager. Garrett couldn't make this shift such short notice. Marcus won't fire her. We need the bitch. Chill. Deliver this drink, and I'll take the heat when she tells Big Papa. A little secret?" she asked at my ear again. "I bet if you tell Moonlight his drink is from you, he won't even mind."

I sighed. "She called me a ho."

"No, she called you a ho in disguise, which means you're good at hiding it. She could learn a thing or two."

Dammit. I didn't want disarming.

"Bayleigh, do you see who he's sitting with?" Our attention shifted to Moonlight's table. "Maybe I shouldn't bring him a drink."

"Was he wearing a ring?"

"I haven't looked at his hands. I'm too distracted and far away to notice anything other than the obvious."

"Deliver the drink. Look for a ring. Hell, not just because of Nightshade. Check to make sure he's not a cheating dick with a wife. Guys like him aren't available."

Excellent point. *Why would that guy be on the market?* I snorted to myself. *Because he's an asshole. But a Nightshade asshole?* I'd once asked one of his companions about the ring he said you had to be a total badass to earn. White gold with fleur-de-lis etchings, amethyst stones mixed with diamonds. Intricate and beautiful, like the men who wore them.

We liked when they came in because the bikers stayed away. The Nightshade members who flirted with me seemed more protective than fearsome. Otherwise, I didn't know how scary they might be outside of these walls. Their business didn't take place here. Out of sight, out of mind. Besides, Marcus would never allow us exposure to risk.

"Quit thinking, Kinsley. Go. Do. Be." Bayleigh snapped in my face so I'd snap out of the zone. I blinked a couple times before reaching for the tray with drinks for the band.

The band!

Jase.

Focus! Screw fear. Full bore.

I had a view of Moonlight's back when I marched up, his body turned to watch Rock-N-Awe. I snagged that fedora right off his handsome head and placed his hat on mine with a smile at his friends.

He spun at once, stunned by the audacity. I loved how his pissy dominance shifted to pleased shock. *Ooh lala.* That costume he'd worn had hidden so much. He'd been dapper in a sharkskin suit, but in this capacity, his hair was so cute and messy without the hat.

"Gentlemen." I met each set of eyes at the coveted table and avoided Jase's. *Those daggers were sharp!*

I went around the faces, listed the drinks I'd made for them over the past hour, delivered refills they each confirmed. I recognized a few as Nightshade and a couple who weren't.

Good.

When I refocused on Moonlight, I caught him admiring his hat on my head rather than demanding a return. How flattering. Thanks to my buzz, I didn't shy away, but looked him right in the eye. "Now, you. Coke with cherries and grenadine is better than the beer you ordered earlier, also your norm. Assuming you're not tonight's designated driver, it's spiked with Captain."

"That so?" When his smile flashed, so did heat through my body. The smug asshole had taken a backseat, and he seemed impressed. "What if I am tonight's designated driver, but handle my alcohol intake better than others?" *Nice.*

The tray I'd been balancing found a place to rest nearby as I grabbed his drink and pushed the glass across. "Then you should have no problem with this," I told him. He placed his hand over mine on the glass. A rush of air left my lungs.

"Did you make this?" he asked.

"Bayleigh did, but that redhead requested it. Said she turned you down earlier and thought you might need consolation." *Damn, I was too flirty when I drank, but this was awesome, guys!* "Enjoy, sir."

His hand over mine tightened as he leaned forward in such brazen darkness, everything inside my body hummed with the current he transferred. The cologne came next. My eyes strayed to his lips, the wicked smile that split them. He had a great smile, but he had an even better voice, and that Jude Law accent hadn't been a joke. "Oh, I *plan* on it."

When I gasped, a proverbial canary flew from my mouth and into his that closed with the knowing of a cunning cat enjoying a taboo meal. His hand left mine, one finger dragged until I gripped the glass all by my lonesome. Without thinking, I lifted the liquor to my lips. He laughed with his group, but their heads turned to stare at him with awe on their faces.

Glory be! I made this man laugh! And downed his damn drink. Shame.

"Well, love, guess I don't need consolation, because that redhead allowed me to buy her a drink after all."

He tossed too much cash on the table even though his drink had been on my bill. He snagged the glass to pour a couple cherries into his mouth. "And now, I get the joy of watching her walk straight to bring me another." He gestured to the money, chewing with a smile. "That's what I'm paying to see. My drinks are on my mate, Joe's, tab."

My head tossed back on a laugh. Like a true drunken smart-ass, I grabbed his bills and gave a tiny curtsy. "Yes, your highness." The other guys watched our exchange more than the band. *Yikes! The band!* "While I'm grabbing his drink, do you all want anything else?"

"Not unless you'd care to join us?" his friend offered. Nightshade branded his left ring finger. I couldn't remember his name, but he wasn't 'Joe', and the only thing he was married to was the syndicate.

"I don't think her boyfriend will allow her." The sexy jerk issued a challenge.

I gave a sweet smile, the one I reserved for letting them down easy, and shook my head. "No can do. I'm on the job."

The Brit chuckled to himself and murmured, "Not yet."

I wasn't sure what he meant, but this felt like another private joke. Grrr.

"And, I *don't* have a boyfriend."

I sauntered to the bar, hellbent on walking straight. Bayleigh drew me to the hallway and tore the hat from my head to fan herself with the cologne we inhaled.

"You are so bold when you drink! He smells fantastic!" We were amid girly gushing when her face abruptly cleared. She threw the fedora in my hands. "Marcus's office, now." She cupped my protest and shoved me inside, then slammed the door shut.

I stood befuddled for awkward moments. *What in the world just happened?* My hand went to the knob, but the sweat in my palm alarmed me into investigating before doing something stupid. She must have had a reason for this.

Paper littered the walls with schedules and notes. The large desk held four monitors wired to the cameras, each screen split into quarters. I moved in to see the band in motion, patrons walking in the front, cars searching for spots in the parking lot, bouncers checking identification at the doors, the bitch and Bayleigh behind the bar.

Bayleigh spoke to a familiar face, but I didn't need the volume to see that the conversation and her body language appeared forced as she prepared his drink. I reached back until my fingers wrapped around the arm of Marcus's chair and drew close to the monitors as I sat down on the cushion. Something about him kept the tingle of unease humming in my palms. I bent closer to the monitor and zoomed in. Civilian clothing. Average haircut and build. No noticeable tattoos or scars. He brought a glass to his lips. Fingerless leather riding gloves.

The door opened and closed. "That guy is back," I told Gustav, my mouth dry. "That why you had Bayleigh throw me in here?"

"I came to find out what happened to my drink and make sure you didn't get sick or fall on your ass." The accent made me lurch like a child caught playing in mom's makeup.

"What are *you* doing in here?" I demanded.

"I should ask you the same. What are you looking at? Who is this bloke you speak of?" He leaned in to inspect who I'd zoomed in on. "Marcus and I are good friends. Since he's out of town, I'm helping keep an eye on the place. Should you have cause for concern, I need to know."

His face turned to mine, eyes drifted to my mouth. Warm relief flooded the stress in my limbs. He was here. In closed quarters. Alone. Us. Cologne. Safety. Authority.

"The roses were amazing," I blurted. Curiosities pinged through my head, but the only thing I mustered was, "Thank you."

His lips quirked. "You're welcome. Wasn't sure you wanted them. You gave them all away."

"Provocation," I confessed.

"Atta girl." He turned back to the monitor like exercising great effort to ignore the chemistry permeating the tiny room. The lock would be easy to flip, and with the fear of Bayleigh hiding me combining with his protective presence, the good girl left the building.

"Has he messed with you?" Gray eyes interrupted my wayward musing.

I filled him in, then shrugged. "I'm used to it. I always shake it off, but now I'm not so sure."

"And your boyfriend? Have you informed him? Did he do anything about this?"

"I told you I don't have one."

"You will."

"Provocation." I growled and rolled my eyes.

"Believe me, love, you're provocative, but I'm proving myself stronger than the rubbish you accused me of last time. 'Tis difficult when you're every bit as vulnerable and wanting as you were when we last spoke."

"Wanting?" I scoffed. His hand shot to the arm of the chair and turned me so we were eye-to-eye like he could call my crap with a single look.

"I didn't want you last time," I lied.

"Didn't you?" His eyebrow arched while his chin lifted, jaw muscle jumped, spine stiffened as he stood straight.

"Don't *you*?" I blurted. Dammit.

I remembered that storm in his eyes and the binding of the corset, his strong hands holding my waist, lips close as he taught me not to put my faith in a man … even as he made me crave to know one ….

"You didn't answer me. Does Taylor know about this?"

I swallowed. Odd to hear him use such familiar language concerning Jase. "I didn't have to tell him. He was there when this happened. If he did anything about this guy, I didn't see."

"That so?" He ripped his darkening gaze from his assessment of my honesty and tapped a key on the keyboard. The audio yelped to life. Several strokes followed, and the noise levels changed and fluctuated until we heard the conversation at the bar. The biker was quiet but searched the faces in the crowd. "Provocation, indeed," Moonlight muttered. He moved to another monitor with the parking lot and pointed at two motorcycles.

"Where's the other biker?" I whispered the question we both wanted an answer to. Disconcerting that they parked together but weren't sitting with one another.

"Allow me to worry about that. Captain and Coke. Cherries. Grenadine. As for this," his finger waved at the air between us, "our time is coming. Count on it. Until then, I need you to loosen up and be yourself. Can you manage that for me, or shall I piss you off to bring you back out? Chase you down again like some bad guy?" The slow wickedness of his smile brought one out in me.

"Are you a bad guy?" I arched a skeptical eyebrow.

He sighed and shook his head. "There she is. After delivering my drink, stay close to your boyfriend." His finger rose when I tried to argue. "Kinsley." My name from that accent. Those lips. His eyes traveled between both of mine. "Trust me."

"Yes, sir." The response came like auto correct. *I didn't mean to send that* ....

"That's what I like to hear." He flicked the brim of his hat on my head, then cast a weapon of a smile over his shoulder. When he left, the office felt empty and the cool unease returned. My eyes flickered to the hallway monitor. I watched him fan his fingers with a knowing grin right up at me, the way I had him at the beach. I smiled and followed the monitors to see him stride to the bar without a word. He set a black card in front of the biker. The biker's chin bucked as if the pirate offended him. *Interesting.*

The gray-eyed man angled his head toward his table. The leather gloves snatched the card and disappeared from the frame. The pirate then slapped money beside the biker's empty glass. A bill marked with heavy black writing.

Cold fear lanced my veins.

"Dear Lord," I prayed. "How did he get that?"

He looked up like he heard me, then vanished from view.

30 | ♀

I remained rooted for several minutes before summoning the courage to leave the office.

Behind the bar, Bayleigh's face radiated concern while my mind reeled. "Bayleigh, did you find money with black writing on it?"

"Yeah, 'Pat' says you're a fire starter and wants you to call him. So gross."

How was this possible? The last time I saw that money was in my apartment. I could've sworn I put that twenty on my coffee table. Then again, I hadn't remembered returning the business cards to my apron. Maybe I'd tangled the bill in the cards I'd fanned for Bayleigh?

"Hey, you okay?" She stared at the tremor in my working fingers as I mixed the only drink I planned to deliver. I poured rum into a shot glass and tossed the spiced liquor down my throat. "I didn't mean to freak you out. I just hated how that guy gave you crap about virginity that time. Wasn't down for giving him round two, ya know?"

"Thank you."

"Guess we know your Rusty Nail's name now. I'll still call him asshole. Want me to deliver their drinks? Kind of disappointing he went to sit at Moonlight's table."

"Relax. I'm okay. Just can't believe Moonlight's finally here! In the flesh, ya know? Who knows, if Inferno has the audacity to screw with me in front of him, he may just provoke the caveman." I poured a handful of cherries into the glass while she chortled and popped my bottom with pride. "Do me a favor though? Give the bitch her tables back? Have newbie pick up my slack while I break with Jase for a few. I'm not worried about Nightshade or the biker. Interesting olive branch, huh."

But I wasn't asking.

Her eyebrows lurched up in dawning. I wanted to say that Moonlight promised to handle this, that I trusted him to do so, that he wasn't a creep, he was keeping an eye on what unnerved me. She'd have flipped her girly crap and pressed for more. I tapped the brim of the fedora on a wink and sauntered out to the floor to shake her worry. I gripped Moonlight's irises like a life ring in the middle of choppy waters.

Upon arrival, their new addition's gaze roamed like dirty hands, and my passive-aggressive side rose. "Sorry for the delay. Girl problems." I glanced up at the ceiling, shrugged with a cutesy, adore me beam. The guys chuckled, but Moonlight cleared his throat, his stormy eyes pinned the biker's, and the asshole averted his at once. "The other server is back from her break, so I will leave her to tend your table," I informed them. Inside, my guts bounced between emotions.

Moonlight nodded his pleasure in my performance. The storm vanished as soon as he bestowed his attention on me once more. *Hallelujah, I hit that mark!* Having his intimidation factor keeping this Inferno jerk in line— amazing! As for a ring on Moonlight's finger, I'd yet to spy one.

"Thank you." Moonlight searched my uniform like he needed to. "Kinsley."

Again, he tossed a wad of cash down. Our eyes met, smiles matching. My head shook in disapproval, hand on cocked hip. "Sir, you need to stop giving me so much money to do a job I am already paid for. I walked over here very well and could've balanced a book on my head all night."

"On the contrary, love. I believe you should stop adding tricks. I may keep paying you more just to watch." He quirked his eyebrows like a total player.

"Noted. I'll bring the ball for my nose next week," I cracked. His laughter tickled my palms. "Thank you, sir." The cash folded and tucked into my apron. I turned to the tray still perched on the edge of the stage. Every drink sweating with melting ice, untouched as if the band were making a point I didn't feel up to taking.

Jase belted a final note, then yanked the piece from his ear like he could wait no longer. He grinned down at me, pointed to his audience, shucked the plastered tank over his head, tossed the sweaty fabric right on top of me.

"Just because your groupies enjoy being dripped on, doesn't mean that's how *I* roll!" I ripped his shirt away, then scrambled back near Moonlight's table to avoid the sluts who clambered to steal Jase's fifteen minutes.

Don't look at Moonlight!

I sensed his gaze and silent gravity to the extent I almost felt guilty for paying mind to Jase, even as he'd ordered me to do so. *How did this work?*

Money poured into the band's tip jar. If Jase stood any closer, those bills would be tucked in his waistband. "Thank you, so much! You are all so generous on such a slow night," Jase gushed. His thumbs hooked into his pants to draw eyes to the V of his hips and the line of dark hair from his taught navel, disappearing beneath the denim. Moonlight caught me rolling my eyes and snickered like he knew better. C'mon, who cared about the male on-stage, his muscles bunching and bulging with every bend to clear the clutter so I wouldn't have to ... *ugh! He was being sweet!*

With a miffed growl, I reached for the empties, including the brew Rustin drank. When Rustin protested, Jase snatched the bottle from my hand. Rustin tossed the smirk of a justified sibling as he took the beer from Jase.

"Okay, ladies. Make room for my girl," Jase told the brood of bubbly bunny-wannabes. He hopped off the stage. His grip snaked around my waist to tug me against him. "Hey, baby. Leave the trash for the bitch with the broomstick up her bum."

Again, I really didn't want disarming, but couldn't help smiling. He removed the burden of my collected bottles and tray with his free hand, then ran those fingers through his sweaty hair to pull the tendrils away from his face. His eyes trailed over the hat on my head. He grabbed the brim and tossed the fedora onto Moonlight's table.

"Hey! I like that!" I wriggled from Jase's grasp. Moonlight arched an eyebrow when I stole the fedora before he had the chance. Jase grasped my wrist and laughed as he hastened me back against him.

Moonlight tipped his Captain and Coke up to his smirk. I bit my lip and used the hat to fan myself against the hot flash.

"All right, sweet Kins. Looks like someone's tanked." Jase grinned. "I don't think I've ever had the pleasure."

And I wasn't sure what to do with my hands! His pecs would be the obvious choice, but I was out of my element on this one.

"I'm not so sure you'll still call me sweet after tonight." My smile was a nervous but fair warning. The humor in his eyes clouded with desire.

"Perfect. You're cute in this hat but stealing from patrons isn't your style … neither is drinking. Especially at work."

"Not falling into your trap, mister, but if you behave, I will spend break with you. I put the witch on tables to free me up." His desire shifted to joy. I loved that smile.

"Hmm … behave?" he asked. "The way you're behaving?"

After taking the hat from my hand with a warning glance, he placed the black felt with the red ribbon upon my head, then wrapped his fingers around my waist. His ploy worked. My hands had nowhere to go other than his chest. He leaned against the stage. His skin sizzled beneath my balmy palms. Jase's Adam's apple bobbed. His lips faltered for a splinter of a second before words formed shapes over a full smile.

I heard nothing but the thumping in my ears and the cackling of drunken women. His fingers played at the skin of my lower back. Excitement tingled down through my hips, weakened my knees, my resolve, my reminiscence of the pirate holding me against him as Jase bent to speak in my ear.

This contact was inappropriate. Like my thoughts. Which was the lesser of two evils? Jase's sex appeal, or memories of a mystery building only a table away?

Focus. Jase. Arms. Sexy tattoo. Muscles. *God ... would this be such a sin? How come Constance and Tyndall and Bayleigh get to have sex and aren't burning in hell from the force of a lightning bolt? Would you smite me if this happened only once?*

"You seem distracted ...." Jase's raspy voice dipped with my stomach. He put his cheek against mine, and my heart was set to explode.

"What?" I stammered.

"I asked if you'd let me take you out at least once." He stood back to implore me.

"Once?" The word stumbled over my tongue. *Take me out? A date.* "Okay, sure, but before I agree, will you please ask me again when I can think straight? I want to remember."

"It's great you want to remember, because Lord knows you never let me forget." *Huh?*

"Does it help if I tell you that inside, I'm Snoopy dancing?" His eyes flared. I cackled far too easily from that moment forward.

After clearing his throat, his hand covered mine on his chest, he said, "You didn't kiss me before I went on, Kins. I will let you slide again this time, because we are making it, but I refuse to step foot on that stage without one, you hear me?"

I snorted because he must be joking, only to realize he wasn't. "Uh. Well, if I must." I breathed and caught the go-to-hell glare of the server who came to collect the empties in the area I'd stolen from her earlier.

"Need anything to drink?" She sneered through a kind veneer.

"I'd love one, how cool of you to ask," Jase said and stood straighter. "Kins and I will have Kamikazes. You can ask the others what they want."

"Jase—"

But he pretended not to hear and sent her off. "We need to hire some new talent. I don't like how she treats you."

Aw. I side-stepped the obvious. "You know I can't handle your drink, right?" I couldn't handle any more drinks, period.

"Nonsense."

His fingers whispered up my spine as he forced my nerves to dance at attention. Beside him, Rustin observed my walls coming down brick-by-broken-brick. Jase didn't hammer them out or even wrecking ball that junk down as per his usual style. He brandished a chisel and wore away at each one with care. I wasn't sure I liked how Rustin studied me with the continuous query whether I'd try to rebuild or surrender. He saw I wasn't as strong as I ought to be.

When the Kamikazes arrived, Jase handed me a glass and took one for himself, clinked his with the neck of Rustin's interjected bottle. "To my evil plans working out …." Jase's voice vibrated low, seductive, as his eyes dared me to test his seriousness. "And the destruction of anyone else's …." He gulped back the liquor in a few swallows.

When I sipped at mine and tried to analyze, Jase tipped the bottom of the glass. I raced the threat of booze spilling from the corners of my mouth. *What did he mean? Was he joking or serious, and how should I go about handling this predicament?*

After that, he and the guys spoke, fans complimented them, made requests. The crisis seemed averted. I watched Jase's arm as he talked with his hands. Every movement made the dragon appear to coil and shift with him. There was nothing traditional about this ink, symbols hidden like a code used behind the scenes in the military to keep the civilians guessing. *Was this some form of sneaky communication?* Absurd, but sexy to imagine.

"You're awful quiet, baby." No sooner had he said that, when did a wasted slut come-a-calling. An obnoxious regular notorious for overdressing in an under-dressing way. She squeezed between the guys to drop her flirt dollars into the tip jar, overcompensating with her cash like she was a hooker who paid clients for sex. Her pitchy Charlie Brown's teacher garbles had me staring at Jase's chest to keep from popping off. Sweaty boobs rubbed everywhere as if I were nothing more than a sheet between her and the man she wanted to uncover. *Grrr.*

She spoke to Rustin but placed her hands on my shoulders to move me aside. Jase winced and his hot mouth breathed close to my ear once more. Kamikazes were great for slowing everything down, blurring my usual speed into slow motion pissed off like a *Crouching Tiger Hidden Dragon* corny cat fight was about to happen.

Jase grasped one of my wrists with a wry comment about scratching him, but I didn't hear because my other hand was shoving her tits away from my back and getting her sweaty hands off where her paws had been applying subtle force like we were taking turns.

"Hey!" She gasped when she lost balance in her stripper heels. She was wonderfully pissed off. I didn't care if she was about eight inches taller than me, nor did her skanky friend having her back intimidate me.

"I don't share. The two of you were here the other night." I snapped. "I made your fruity drinks while you shot me the evil eye during his serenade, but, funny, I *don't* remember him mentioning either of *your names*. Wonder what that means?"

Rustin whistled then coughed to suppress his enjoyment, lips plowed into his cheeks like he concealed anything. I glared at him while Jase's voice sounded over my head. Bayleigh bounded up to diffuse the situation before this became something more.

You know what they say about redheads and their tempers. Guess I was your classic cliché that way, but I didn't give a crap. Disrespect always pissed me off. Ironic that Jase even called me sweet at all. My gaze fired to his.

"Told you so."

His eyebrows rose, face glowing with pent-back amusement.

"Gus, time-out for these two?" Bayleigh belted while massaging my shoulders where the other ho's grubby paws had been. "Be glad Marcus isn't here," she said in my ear. She was right, and the bouncer moved the two outside for a cool down. I wasn't immune from his warning shot.

"Come on, Bayleigh, did you see the way she was touching me? Ugh! What is it about guys in a band that make women so stupid?" I wondered aloud, looking back at them sitting in various places on the stage, grinning at their lead singer as though he were in for trouble. "Like minds?"

"Ouch, baby!" Jase chuckled and looked over his shoulder at the others but ensnared me once more inside his bubble of influence. "Hey, you okay?" His face cleared of all humor as he tipped my chin up at him. Concern. For me, or for them? "Need to sit out?" He reached over for the ice water and placed the chilly glass to my lips with a polite order to drink. I shoved his offering.

"Good grief. I wish everyone would quit asking me that! You guys need to go back on. Now, may I please return to my regularly scheduled program?" I pressed against his chest, irritable, but he didn't give an inch. The devious glint returned, and he prepared to pounce.

"There's no need for violence, sweet Kins. I'll tell every woman in this place I'm taken. Just say the word."

"Ha! Don't you wish, mister? You won't trap me into telling you what you want to hear. That's what hos like those are for." Jase dodged before I smacked him to turn me loose.

"All right, you're not working like this."

"Says who?" I protested. *Who was he to boss me around however he wanted?*

"Says me."

"But I'm still on-duty."

"And you're drunk. You know Marcus's rules. Guess I should have listened to you," he teased. Tucking me into the booth next to the stage, he murmured, "Rustin, keep an eye on her so she doesn't go behind the bar and do something she might regret, will ya?"

"Give me a break." I rolled my eyes. *Who wouldn't have reacted the way I had? A pushover.*

Rustin took a seat beside me with a look like 'guess you're stuck with me now'—drawl included. The next song didn't require a harmonica or a singer since the band played while Jase set about finding his spare t-shirt. Before he hopped on-stage, he leaned in and whispered, "Caught you drooling over me earlier, I'll be wiping that off later."

Gloves off on the suggestion oozing from his lips!

"I'll need that kiss, and I'll wait right here until I get what I want."

I gasped. He fell back enough I could see his smoldering query. The liquor I'd consumed seemed to have driven due south. With the way he talked, I struggled to appear unaffected, but managed to look elsewhere.

"Oh, you want to play?" He half-smiled. "Well, babe, just because you're pissed at two trashy groupies doesn't mean you'll leave the rest with a sub-par performance because you refused to take one for the team, right? You're better than that."

Take one for the team? Better than that?

"Ah, Kins is most certainly a team player and a way better one at that." Bayleigh grinned and copped a squat on Rustin's nearby lap out of perceived convenience. His veiled smirk, the hands he placed on her bare legs, the stupid challenge in his eyes, they were all I needed.

"Well, if it's for the *team* ...."

If ever existed a moment in time to allow one great taste, the time to seize was now. I reached up to cup Jase's face. For a fleeting second, I paused and studied him up close, committing this to memory before diving in and kissing him the way I wanted. My every imagining paled to the physical stroke of his tongue against mine, the taste of vodka on his breath that helped release all the insecurities over my inexperience. He suctioned me against him, his fingertips digging deep into my spine. He groaned as he increased the depth and changed angles that popped the buttons from my resolve. I thrummed with triumph and reckless abandon.

Had I asked, I believe he would have called off the rest of the show to continue what we were doing, which was why I pulled away. For a second, he appeared to consider yanking me back for more, but our eyes locked like he searched for something. I neutralized against the attraction and explosive chemistry that startled me.

The lewd crowd called dirty catcalls, but the world around me vanished, save for the sweating bottle that sat on the table in front of Rustin. Jase turned to clear his throat and throw his fresh shirt over his head. He slicked his hair with ice water from the pitcher, then ran his chilled palm over his face. *What a powerful high to see Jase Taylor so affected.*

While he jumped back on-stage, Bayleigh leaned over to remove the empties from the table I stared at. "Coffee's almost ready just for you, and I think your team's winning." She looked so proud. *How was that when she wanted me to make a move on Moonlight?*

"After that kiss, I can ask Moonlight for his number." My eyes narrowed at her screwing with me. She smiled over her shoulder with a cluck of her tongue. "Now, stay put like a good little girl while Rustin takes a wiz."

"I think I can handle it."

Jase began a George Thorogood cover. I studied the crowd, stopping on bimbos one and two who'd returned from time-out.

Sloppy smoky eyes with smeared eyeliner glared at my animated wave-off. I reveled in my natural hair color by comparison to her poor dye job. This wasn't the last I'd see of her for a long while. She was a regular, but such was the nature of bartending. *Thank God Marcus isn't here!*

My gaze rested on Moonlight at the table across the dance floor. He spoke to the remaining two in his company, but wasn't looking at them, he watched Jase. Damn, he was scary hot, and my inebriated brain examined him without an ounce of discretion.

The bitch server resumed her tables and headed toward Moonlight's table with a fresh tray. When his gray eyes spied her, he sought me out, and our eyes locked.

Under normal circumstances, I'd have looked away in flushed embarrassment, but my gaze held, too.

"I'm sorry," I mimed. I wasn't sure what I apologized for. His conversation continued while his eyes rested unmoving. When the server set his drink down, blocked his view, his head tilted with a dazzling grin that widened my own.

He mouthed, "me, too," and put money down for her, but his eyes never strayed. He could tell she didn't like me. Was he feeding my attitude problem?

His eyes grew wide, his mouth stretching to an 'uh, oh' smile. Rustin walked into my eye line and stole my sinful view before taking his seat once more.

Yikes! Busted!

Rustin cleared his throat while my eyes shot to Jase pouring charisma into the mic.

"Sorry you lost."

"Lost?" I played dumb.

Bayleigh set black coffee and a handful of creamers down. "I gave the server your refill," she told Rustin, "but she said you paid your tab?"

"Yeah. One of us has to operate heavy machinery," he reasoned with a nod toward Jase. "Although I bet that kiss was more than sobering. He may not need a designated driver," he teased with a baby blue wink. "Kinsley, don't think he's letting *you* drive."

Before I copped an attitude, Bayleigh thanked him since she wouldn't need to take me herself now. Shame sprinkled like salt over my drunken wounds.

"Sorry," I apologized, embarrassed at myself. "I don't usually behave like this."

He scooted to my side and inched close enough that his blue jeans brushed my bare thigh. "Like what? *A drunk*?" He was teasing, but not being a jerk for once.

"No, *not a* drunk, hey, *I* am *not* drunk!" *I so was.*

"Mean is what I meant. I've been mean tonight, and I'm only buzzing for your information." I lifted my chin.

His finger scrolled circles in the condensation on his beer bottle as his lips twitched. "Okay, you win, you're *not* drunk. Though, if you *were* drunk, might excuse your *mean* behavior."

I gasped and prepared to drill into him when I noticed his eyes danced like a shiny fishing lure.

"Ah, ha! Woman, you're ready to blister my hide on both sides! And you say you don't behave this way." He smiled and shook his head. "You're honest in this capacity."

"All right, now. That'll be enough of that, mister. You don't even know me. Don't go accusing me of being something I'm not." He earned a playful 'oh no he didn't' wave of my finger and head bob, lightening me up as Jase went on about bourbon, scotch, and beer.

Rustin's eyes shifted to the table, then back, a sneaky smirk tugged the corners of his poker face. "You're right, I don't know you, but I'd sure like to."

My heart caught in my throat and pounded at his confession. I wasn't only drunk, I was white-girl-wasted. When Rustin Keane came off sincere? Mmhmm. Staring at blue waters that seemed deeper proved difficult. I looked down at my hands clasped over my legs. This called for a change in subject.

"You're good on that harmonica, and the guitar the other day was amazing," I offered. "Oh, and the tambourine and that shaky thing that sounds like rain. So many instruments." *Was my pitch too high?*

He swallowed a swig of his beer and chuckled. "Shaky thing that sounds like rain, eh? We can call it a rain shaker if you like, or a ganzá. Thank you, Mizz Hayes. It's my understanding you're stingy in the compliment department. I'm flattered."

"Are you being a jerk?"

He chuckled and shook his head. "You can drop your weapons, girl. I'm serious. Jase talks a lot about you and assures me your favor ain't too easy to earn. He's a mite taken with you. You ask me, any woman who makes Jase a smitten fool has my respect … and *deserves* it."

I choked on a dismissive scoff and bit my lip when Rustin's face held something too genuine to be a joke. *Jase? Smitten? Taken with me? What beautiful, sweet, gooey words!* Tyndall's brother hadn't used those. They had to come from this wing man's embellishment. *But, what if?*

"Come on, Kinsley. Why do you think I'd like to know you better?"

Remorse cooled my veins and warmed me to Rustin for how I must've misinterpreted his intentions. Maybe he had a direct approach when wanting to be friends? Gosh, I'd been such a jerk to him, and worse still, after Jase had talked about me? *Ugh! What an idiot!*

"That was quite the kiss you gave him." His drawl glazed my guilt. His face drew close enough I smelled his beer. "Just be careful. I don't know if you're the right type to handle him."

Okay, what the what?

"You're saying I can't handle Jase?" I was incredulous. 'Handle' was a trigger word. Rustin waggled his eyebrows while taking another healthy swig of booze.

Turning to face him in combined suggestion and warning, one of my nails poked his chest. "You have *no* idea what I can handle, Mr. Keane, and you never will," I said. His lungs swelled. He swallowed when I stole his beer and took a long, drawn out gulp. My confidence fizzled when I turned my whole body away and noticed Jase studying our exchange. *Jeez, why was I so jumpy because I kissed the guy? No one had committed to each other here.* Still, I expected jealousy or something, but I couldn't tell you what I saw in his expression.

Adding to this conundrum, Rustin took that moment to scoot against my back, his mouth near my ear. "I see why my friend is so enamored with you." Warm breath whistled against my sensitive lobe. I closed my eyes as confusion intensified over my inability to read him, over Jase, over how my insides twisted in mutiny.

The rich tones of Jase's Les Paul charged and crackled all around as he transitioned to singing a story of a scorned lover caught in a painful dichotomy. The slow sensual moves of couples whispered promises to each other's skin as they displayed their ballroom talents. I craved to dance again.

"Wanna dance?" Rustin asked from over my shoulder. I hated how he did that. I refused his invitation. I didn't trust him. Too unpredictable.

We watched in tense silence for the rest of the song instead. I stayed glued to my spot with uncertainty in how to escape this without seeming as panicked as I might be. I looked to Moonlight. His hand settled around his mouth in contemplation, his eyes friendly enough, but more studious when he met my gaze. A wordless urging to give him the signal, he'd take me out of this predicament. I half-expected him to rise and ply me away from Rustin and onto the dance floor. I half-wished he would.

His gaze shifted over my shoulder. Rustin leaned close once more so I could hear him over Jase's rasp carrying the current over everyone, lost in his love for his music. "He's almost finished with his final set. Last chance."

"No, thank you." My solidarity came as though I'd siphoned a powerful confidence from the gray eyes that helped me dismiss Country altogether, strength even in drunkenness.

"Have it your way, Mizz Hayes." Rustin shoved off as applause erupted for Rock-N-Awe. "May the best man win." He jumped up to break the stage down while I sat dumbfounded and debating whether I'd heard him right.

Jase's humbled laughter echoed over the mic, then he bent to shake hands before leaping down to inquire about my behavior. I picked apart whether Rustin somehow meant between him and Jase? *And what about what Jase had said earlier about evil plans? Did that mix in somewhere?*

My ebbing intoxication pared to annoyed exhaustion and impatience. I didn't want Jase or Rustin to win. That made me, what, a prize? If that was the case, they deserved vindictive torture. To become so nuts for me and *only* me they'd be ruined so other women wouldn't stand a chance. Selfishness took up residence. Perhaps the sentiment would disappear in the morning, but for the moment, I wanted to punish them for who they thought I was, for who I was tonight under the influence. *My heart wasn't a toy, and my body wasn't a prize.*

Even now Rustin played another immature game of challenge. He smiled at me while winding cable over his palm and elbow the way you replace the cord to the vacuum. His mind games dizzied me. I stood to walk away but had to steady myself against the table. "Well, hell …."

"Yeah, guess I should have given you a refill on the coffee you didn't bother drinking," Bayleigh chided. She cleaned and collected as the band packed up.

"Sorry, girl. I'm so embarrassed. Did you at least have a good night for tips?"

"Yep." She leaned close with her voice lowered when the band dismantled the drum kit. "Remember those cards you gave me? There's an interesting one for you by name. Not creepy." She took something from her pocket, then straightened without the offering. The guys added bottles to her tray. She took them with a promise to call me tomorrow to make sure Jase didn't kidnap me. She stuck her tongue out at him when he said, "hilarious."

"Kins, keep that chastity belt locked tight. Sober is one thing, drunk isn't allowed."

Jase balked. "You can't be serious, Bay. She's safe with me." He tucked me under his tatted arm the way he always did with Tyndall. Though sweaty, at least he didn't stink, and I was tired of holding to the table. I caved into his support.

"Thank you, Jase. Sorry."

"What are friends for, baby?" He kissed the top of my head, then cupped my shoulders to steer toward the exit. "Rustin, you ready?"

"As if I'd leave you to haul her out on your own." Rustin snaked an arm around my waist like I needed that junk. Excuses, excuses, along with mounting evidence to support my original theory on Mr. Keane.

And Jase had asked what friends were for.

Friends.

What the eff? What to do? Who cared when I caught gray eyes and a smirk as we progressed?

My heart leapt to my throat when Moonlight stood to shake Jase's hand and compliment his performance.

"Hey, thanks man." Jase shook his hand. "Hope we see you around here more. Great tips." They laughed.

Moonlight smirked knowing I felt the same.

"Plan on it," the handsome Brit said. He tapped the brim of his hat on my head, dipping to my vantage. Tunnel vision. Pretty lips …. "And to whom does this belong, love?" he purred into my haze.

"You, Henley. Yours." I sighed, then snapped to reality. Embarrassment lit my face on fire. I ripped my eyes from his gaze to the floor, unable to explain my blunder even to myself.

"Who?" he asked quietly, face aglow as he enjoyed my mortification.

"Henry? Is that what she called you?" Jase chuckled. "Damn, she's trashed worse than I thought. Sorry, man."

"That's all right, mate. It happens." The empathetic pirate, not being an asshole in this moment, stole the fedora to grab my attention. I chewed inside my cheek and counted the planks in the floor. He introduced his two companions but checked me over while their conversation went in one ear and out the other. I lost focus on anything but how he fanned my firecracker cheeks with the hat and pressed a cool glass against my carotid. After a wince, I closed my eyes, sagged against Jase to relish the cologne and Moonlight's soothing sweetness after I had blurted a name I'd never heard in my life.

"Sorry to interrupt," Gustav's deep voice intoned. I looked up and noticed the creepy biker hadn't been part of the chatting group. *Thank God.*

Gus waved a hand in front of my eyes. The others all looked up at him while I blinked several times. "Kins, can't help noticing you couldn't finish your shift." I bit my lip as he continued. "Are you willingly leaving with these men, or would you like me or Bayleigh to take you home?"

I busted out laughing but caught my tongue and cleared my amusement when I saw his severity. He waited with expectation, so I nodded.

Moonlight replaced his hat on my head and set his glass on the table as if an excuse to appraise my seriousness. His expression offered another silent bailout if I needed one, but hell, I knew nothing of him when I'd known Jase for a decade!

I avoided his tempting eyes, hiding how thrilled I was that he was letting me keep his yummy hat and scent. My focus trained on Gus, blinking back the bit of blur.

"Yes, Gus, thank you. I will see you tomorrow evening."

He gave a gruff nod. His scary turned on Jase, all friendship aside. "Taylor, you keep your damn body to yourself. You, too, hick." He made them both promise and didn't give a crap if his order came in front of patrons. *Yikes.*

"Kins, you have no shortage of bodyguards," Jase teased once we took to the lot. His black 4x4 loomed across the labyrinth of chunky gravel. I stumbled over the larger rocks.

"Sorry, guys, I can't believe I got so tipsy. Oh, Jase you must be so disappointed!" I didn't want to let him down. "Hell! Am I slurring?!"

I wanted to cry! What if after all this he lost the admiration I'd never realized he'd given until now? He was always so sweet, always on the lookout, always protective.

"Whoa." Jase paused. "Kinsh. You aren't shlurring at all, I'm the one shlurring." I would swear I saw his effort to seem serious … Was Rustin laughing? Jase grabbed my chin and my focus. "Hey. Baby, you'd never dishappoint me, well not worsh than when you're shooting me down." His lips twisted into that irresistible grin. He cleared his throat and looked back to the ground for me as we continued. "Tonight, was amazeballs! Thanks for not turning me down for the first time in history!"

I chortled at his stupid word while he and Rustin fist-bumped in front of me.

"Jase, you're so crazy. If I don't turn you down over and over, what makes me different from the other women you tag and bag?"

He stopped walking and his grip tickled my waist when he lifted me into the truck after Rustin opened the door. I giggled and gripped his shoulders as he steadied me.

"Kinsley Hayes, look at me." I squinted hard. "Never say that again. You will *always* be different whether you play hard to get doesn't matter. If you weren't, Rustin wouldn't already be a pussy for you."

I cupped a giggle and looked around the lot before leaning close and whispering, "You said Rustin's a pussy."

"Man, c'mon," Rustin whined.

"Truth hurts." Jase grinned. "Baby, you're it. All those other girls are to take the edge off so I can handle being around you every other night."

"Wow, um … Jase." I wavered. "How sweet. Not sure where to go from that." 'Twas a gifted guy who could spin his man-whoring into something that made me feel special. Was he serious that all I had to do was say the word, and he *was* all mine? *Should I? Could I handle that?* I hated Rustin for knowing insecurity would feast away at some point.

Jase Taylor, a one-woman man?

"You okay?" Jase tested, released his grip. His silly smile came when I nodded like a two-year-old who knew how to go potty on her own. Once I laid down on the bench seat, I concentrated on the cold leather pressed at my cheek, praying to stave off the nausea. *Don't throw up, Kins, you pathetic lightweight!*

The chime of keys igniting this beast had me squeezing my eyes shut all over again, the whirling driving me mad until the jacked and stacked Silverado rumbled to high-decibel life.

"Want mood music, babe?" Jase looked back as Drake's voice crooned about heading home. Though I managed a feeble laugh, I forced myself to listen, and gazed up through the windows at the stars as we progressed to my place. Well, my parents' place. They wouldn't be tapping their toes when I drove up super late escorted by the dueling Casanovas, but I still took hope they'd be sound asleep. I didn't want to let them down by looking like I brought men home, like the girl down the street. *Wonder if that guy kissing her on the slide really called her? Why'd she flip me off? I've never been mean to her. Well, there was that one time when I babysat and ate her ice cream in front of her because she threw that massive fit about Barbie's new haircut.* I snickered to myself.

The guys were making small talk in the front seat, barely audible above the low music. They said names I didn't recognize, though one sounded familiar, but I tuned them out in inebriated numbness.

The glowing console lit Rustin Keane's profile. There was a different air about him when he must've assumed I was asleep, because his guard was down. This relaxed light made him kinda attractive, but *why did guys do that? Turn into something else to impress a girl?* Stupid. He was *stupid.* Handsome, but *stupid.*

I turned back to the stars. The tranquility lulled me to sleep. Even if this junk was a mass of confusion, the future held a mystique and potential for the brand of romance I'd always dreamed of. I wondered when that time Moonlight said would be ours might come.

32 | ♀

The sun shined orange and veiny like a flashlight through my mascara-glued eyelids. "Wow, Guess I didn't move all night," I croaked. The fedora rested on the pillow beside me, the cologne a kiss good morning. I shifted stiff and uncomfortable, to squint at the ceiling.

My spinning fan threatened to hypnotize me back to sleep. I hefted the weight of my hangover to walk like a dizzy moron to the bathroom. No water balloon bladder bursts, thank you. *What happened last night?* Nothing much registered after Jase's kamikaze, except embarrassment regarding Moonlight and something irritating me about Rustin.

Ugh. Beer before liquor, never been sicker— a myth I felt on the verge of proving correct. *Had I puked at some point?* I gripped the vanity and squinted at my sloppy reflection. Bra and panties. *Had I tossed my clothing because I'd tossed my cookies?* Because doing laundry wasn't already miserable enough.

Plying bobby pins from my tangled tresses was like playing with Halloween spider webbing. By the time I finished fluffing my freed locks, all that was missing was a Mötley Crüe concert tee to complete my 'I love the 80's' glam. Makeup rings around the eyes and all.

The toothbrush trembled as I spread the paste. No exercise, not enough food or water, *and* far too much booze? I scrubbed my mouth like I could scrub away my foolishness, then grinned at the mirror while I rinsed (and downed ibuprofen).

The beautiful light of day didn't hurt so bad when I sauntered back into my bedroom. I cued up Crüe. *Kickstart My Heart.* Seconds later, opening Mick Mars riffs killed the silence, drenching the apartment in music as alive and wild as the evening guaranteed to be. I wouldn't allow this hangover to take me down, dang it.

Grabbing my air guitar, I slid to the best of my ability on carpet into the hallway and rock walked into the awaiting spotlight that was the sunbeam shining through the window above the kitchen sink. Didn't matter how great Rustin wailed on his stupid instrument of choice, mine was better right now. *What did he call that thing last night? Who cared?*

Jase wasn't the only one who played leftie either. I harmonized with Vince Neil as I brought a fist up and tilted my head back to belt lyrics, then pounded the mic down on the invisible strings to prepare for the chorus.

The imaginary guitar tossed aside when I entered the stage of tile in the kitchen and snatched the K-cup from the empty vase on the counter. Pumpkin spice. My favorite and what I ordered anytime I went to my father's building. Looney Lucy was the barista. Her obsession wasn't always annoying when she kept my flavor on hand for me year-round. Moonlight had to have seen me order coffee there at some point. Sexy cool to imagine that one paying attention when I wouldn't have recognized him. So glad I got to keep his hat! Yeep!

Celebration was afoot, Spring Break was in the air, and the exit of paltry-tipping snowbirds imminent. Though my own spring break vacation was a couple weeks away, others were likely crowding our beaches or on their way down right this moment. The work forecast called for rain tonight without a dang cloud in the sky! Just the way I liked! Wonder how I should go about playing up the skimpy uniform? Own it, or fight it? Heavy makeup or light? Wedges instead of heels for sure. Jase always checked my legs out when I wore my wedges with the ribbons tied up my shins.

On a drumbeat, I snapped the Keurig coffee maker shut and hit all the right buttons in time to the song, then turned to hop on the island counter and fanned my legs before hitting my knees to swing my hair like any great head-banger would. Oh, and don't forget the *Cherry Pie* crawl. Mom couldn't tell me not to play on the counters now!

Ha! What was I thinking? She would have a coronary if she found out I tainted her ballet lessons this way, even in the privacy of my place.

More reason to rock this!

After that, catharsis took over as I gave into nature and let momentum carry me with the music like the wind blowing wildly through the weeping willow in the garden. I grabbed a mug, toasted Pop-tarts, washed a few dishes until my stir spoon hit the sink. My cup slid across the granite island and I raced to capture the ceramic as an awesome finale. Holding the steamy mug in triumph, I closed my eyes, took my air mic in the other hand and turned to bow to the imaginary audience. "And that's how it's done."

"Holy shit, encore!"

I opened my eyes, shrieking in shock and horror, leaping back, spewing java lava all over myself! A slurry of curses flew from my mouth as searing pain ripped across my breasts. They were sure to liquefy like a Madame Tussauds wax figure and adhere to the bra! Although I didn't need any effing ice water to wake me from this BS!

"Can she join the band?" Rustin begged. "That was so hot!"

"*C'est un cauchemar!* You guys *slept* here?!" I shouted, infuriated. Two imbeciles perched on the edge of either couch, hair rumpled, no shirts, gaga grins.

"Did you speak another language?" Jase's tongue tumbled over his words.

"What did you say?" Rustin panted.

My eye twitched, my lips flat. "I said this is a nightmare." I face-palmed imagining what they'd witnessed when I was being my secret self.

"Psh! Or a fantastic dream! Encore?" Rustin begged as *Too Young to Fall in Love* started from my metal playlist. His lower lip quivered and popped at the same time as the Pop-tarts sprang from the toaster. These two were so moronic. I almost faltered from humiliation but opted for righteous indignation amid the irony of the lyrics. *How did someone proceed in this situation?*

My skin hurt as much as my pride.

"Ah, Kins. Forgive us. Here." Rustin located a dish towel and tossed the terrycloth to Jase. He caught the material and bent to the tile for the mug I'd shattered in the mayhem. He placed the jagged pieces into Rustin's outstretched hand and wiped what little mess was on the floor. Most of the coffee covered my torso and dripped from my drenched and cooling bra, trickled down my panties in small streams and droplets to my feet. My fists balled in a damp grip, whether to keep myself in check or in preparation to knock one of them out ... I wasn't sure.

Jase cleared his throat as he lifted the towel in silent question but failed to look at my face to indulge in the buffet of my body. "Uh ... Kins ... I can ... if you want ...."

"No!" I knocked the towel from his hand and nailed him with a frog to his left triceps. He winced but rubbed his muscles like I'd branded a reward. I threw my fist to the heavens in aggravation. "I *am* too effing young for this!" I performed the stomp of shame down the hallway and assessed this humiliating situation. *My Lovin'* was what I changed the music to so En Vogue sang the words I wanted to shout at both players fist-bumping with triumph in the background.

Couldn't they get the message and leave? Why did they stay? That was inappropriate, right? Would Bayleigh see this my way? She would tell me if I was just being the prude she coddled.

Storming into my bathroom, I paused mid-stride, then backpedaled to take in the folded uniform on the foot of my bed. The same one I'd worn home last night. No vomit. Removed. *By whom? And just how much fill had they had of my body?*

I growled and peeled at the sticky undies but changed my mind even as I turned on the shower. The water sprayed as cold as the cotton glued to my skin. I kept the water on the cold setting. I dismissed the sweet scent of my creamer and pumpkin as I crept back into the bedroom. That coffee would have been delish. I sighed and put the speaker into the bathroom to further sell being in the shower. *If they thought I wouldn't hear them, what did they say about me? Had they left?*

Tiptoeing to the bedroom door, I peeked through the crack to the mirror at the back of the hallway. I couldn't see them, but I saw Rustin's cowboy boots sitting beside the welcome mat. *How had I missed those during my stupid performance?*

Heat warmed the blood in my cheeks again, but I forced myself to concentrate on the muffled voices until they sharpened.

33

Rustin's wolfish grin met Jase's. "Survey says?"

"Depends. Wet bra or air metal?"

"Wet bra I give an eight. Air metal, a five."

"A *five*?!" Jase balked like Rustin had insulted his own performance. "Meh." He shrugged a second later, coming to his senses. "She needs proper training on how to hold that guitar and strike the right chords." They chuckled in knowing. Neither admitted the show was a ten in their naughty fantasies-come-true, though the naughtier would be training her in general. "Wet bra I give an eight, as well. It's 'cuz it was black, huh?"

"Damn straight." Rustin snickered, then ran his tongue over his teeth, craving his toothbrush. "Definitely not working with the crazy hair and brace face you first told me about. I'd say your edge is that she doesn't think of herself any different from back then."

Edge? Jase wondered. *Seemed more like an Achilles' heel. Rustin didn't understand, so in his eyes she was another chick on a level playing field.*

Jase went to the hallway restroom, listening to the shower and music from the other he wished he was privy to. He only had to go through one drawer to toss Rustin a spare tube of toothpaste Kinsley kept for guests. *Were any of them ever male?*

Rustin tossed the tube back to nail him in the side of the head a moment later. "What the hell is the matter with you? You cleared the place last night. No evidence of a boyfriend except that coat. Could be her father's. Either way, she's clutter, dude. Dangerous. Trips you up."

"Better hope so." Jase removed the cap from the paste and finger scrubbed his teeth in unison with Rustin. After splashing water on his face, but contemplating the cold shower he relied on to get through night after night around Kinsley, he accepted the pain of his imaginings, and walked back into the living room while Rustin spit into the kitchen sink.

"Hey, sorry, man. Can't be easy being whipped over and over by such a miniature brow beater," Rustin teased. "Wish you'd make a real move. Do I have to trample on your turf to get you off the sidelines? Anymore performances like that one," he gestured with a thumb over his shoulder, "and I might forget whose turf I'm on altogether. Factor in the French, and I'm ready to sue you for false advertisement."

"Not so fast, asshole. *I'm* the damn quarterback of this game." Jase glared at his friend, but they both knew he'd need some prodding before he'd make a play for Kinsley after so long. She *had* kissed him back more than once, and her hands had been all over him last night. Whether she was drunk didn't matter. Alcohol was a truth serum. *We should give her more to drink*, he thought to himself with a private smile.

"Let's look through our play book and run one! Over here, over here, I'm open, I'm open!" Rustin mimicked a 90's movie, always on par for comic relief.

Jase plopped down on the couch to fold the throw blanket that had covered a fraction of his frame overnight. Even if she tortured him when she was within proximity, he'd slept well knowing he'd tucked her in, and no one was coming through that door without going through him to get to her.

Rustin stood to put his firm hands on his friend's shoulders, giving them a rough jostle.

"Hey, Jase, where you at? Pay attention. Right here." He snapped his fingers and pointed at his eyes. "Who's got the ball, bastard?"

"Me."

"How many times have we played this game?"

"Countless."

"Exactly. She's like the rest. You've gotten shot down before. How do you handle an opponent you can't outrun?"

"Wear 'em down. Exhaustion," Jase answered. "Strike hard and fast, pull back. Recover, regroup, repeat."

"I saw that kiss last night and the way she watches you when she works. Inches, but this is a game of inches, and that's how you win." The light filtered back into Jase's face, but his brows furrowed as he stared up at Rustin.

"Kinsley isn't like the rest."

Rustin sighed. "If I'm looking at the number one team knowing they are in a league all their own, what the hell chance do I even have? You've lost the game before you've snapped the ball. C'mon! You're killing team morale! Fire it up or get out of the way and let someone else in! That's what's going on and *you're* letting it happen!"

This time there was no pat to the shoulder, there was a sharp sting to Jase's left cheek he welcomed because Rustin was right. "If she's different, it's because she's the holy grail of trophies! This isn't high school, son! She isn't the virgin you were trying to deflower. Forget the Heisman! College is over! This is the damn NFL, she's an accountable adult responsible for her own actions, and you're a shoo-in for the playoffs! Quit hook-sliding like a pussy! Lower a shoulder and plow through the defense like a REAL quarterback! Headfirst, baby! Make 'em capitulate! Who wants to go to the Super Bowl? Woo!" Rustin clapped his hands in Jase's face.

"Anyone ever tell you what a dumbass you are?"

Jase laughed and shoved Rustin back onto the couch opposite him. "Now clean up your mess, Jarhead."

"Coronado cock-blocker." Rustin conceded back to his normal good nature. He grabbed the larger throw and set about folding. "Sure, the stakes are high, but can we at least enjoy the time on the clock before you take a knee, please? I miss this." Rustin was genuine. How long since they'd had an epic bender waking up with women they'd never remember the names of? What a dilemma. Kinsley wasn't one of *those* women. If he treated her anything close to them, he'd loathe himself for what that might do to her and their chances as a couple. Not to mention, the wrath of Tyndall would forever be upon him. On the flip side, now that he'd shown Kins how he felt, he couldn't risk slumming without hurting her. *What to do?* Rustin still needed some celebratory liberty after the move. Maybe Mel or Dan could be his wing man?

Rustin's throat cleared to bring Jase back to attention. "You already know … girls like that, they're the wildest when you unleash them. Daddy's girl. Buttoned up tight, all repressed and obedient. Slave to the rules. The pressure mounts, they explode."

"Rustin, what the hell is your point? She's a good girl. Not the slut you don't call back after smearing her Barbie world." Jase hated that Rustin was spot on.

Kinsley was a ticking bomb, and they knew because Daddy's girls were one of their specialties, not to mention how receptive she was of that smooth douche bag who was making everything in Jase's life his business, girl included.

New shame gnawed at his gut. "I can't. I shouldn't have gotten involved with her."

"Give me a break. If you don't, someone else will and is planning on doing so as you twiddle your thumbs. At least *you* care about her, but good girls go wild. No matter how put together or stubborn or book smart, Kinsley can't see the forest for all the surrounding trees. Home field advantage doesn't mean jack if you aren't willing to stake your claim and build your barriers to keep the insurgents out."

"Stop, okay. Just stop. I need to think about this."

"*Think* about this? Damn. You don't just care about this one. You *love* her."

"Whoa, whoa, whoa … hold it right there!" Jase held his hand up in warning. "Tread lightly with that word."

"Whatever, Jase. Level with me. Ask yourself if she's worth it. If she is, then go for her and quit thinking so much. Nowhere in there did I hear a denial on the shit I called. Is she worth it?"

Jase chewed his cheek. "This is all too heavy. I don't know."

"Yes, you do, and yes, she is." Rustin rolled his eyes and adjusted. "Stop making this so heavy and let's have fun. Let's give *her* some fun before *her* life gets too heavy, know what I mean? Maybe let me help you with the weight …." He rubbed his hands together.

The two stared off in a showdown, pushing the other's buttons until the corners of their mouths twitched. Wasn't as if they hadn't learned the value of teamwork and sharing over the course of their friendship.

Rustin read Jase's mind. "Remember summer break freshman year? As I recall she was a redhead, too. Our first. Foreshadowing destiny."

Jase snorted, but nodded with a slight smile pulling into a relaxed one. "That became a competition, though. We were so bad for so young. Crazy. Doesn't feel that long ago."

"Doesn't have to be that long ago. She didn't seem to mind how our throuple played out." Rustin shrugged. "Just sayin', our parents worked hard to teach us that sharing is caring, Jase. You don't have to bear that burden all on your own. It'd be like honoring Pop's memory." He laughed and bore the brunt of the pillow Jase nailed him with.

"Shame on you, man, pulling your dad and his high moral teaching into this. 'Just say' all you want. This is dangerous. The whole thing. How did I get myself into this mess? And where do I get off pulling her in with me?"

"Hey, things are a mess either way. Eye on the ball, man. Eye on the ball. Now, about last night …."

"Yeah, that bastard's playing dirty, and she still smells like him even covered in coffee," Jase agreed and lowered his voice. He sensed a spy and stood with a finger held up to silence Rustin, but his rebellious friend peered past his shoulder toward the hallway.

"You in love, Jase? Kins your girl?" Rustin stared at him alight with a purpose and ready to make fun work of playing in the mud.

Jase narrowed his eyes at his friend's sordid tactics and nodded. "All in and no going back. The only easy day was yesterday."

34

Ugh! I exercised every ounce of patience not to kick the door shut in disgust. Spying on them had cost me precious minutes. I wasn't pleased with the return on my investment. After all the football references, how did I reconcile that Jase hadn't denied he loved me with what sounded like *sharing* at some point? What the hell?

Adjusting the knob to the hot spray, I got in the shower and a memory that might be more than what I'd imagined came unbidden with possibility that this may have begun years ago. The sweet naïve freshman in me would never forget, but perhaps she should examine a bigger picture. *Can't see the forest for all the trees, eh?*

My eyes narrowed as I sudsed shampoo through wet tresses and recalled washing the bonfire scent from the hair I'd butchered back when I was fifteen. The night Jase may have tried to sleep with me.

Nine years ago, Tyndall Taylor and I sprawled on our tummies in a tent. I listened as she gushed over two of her brother's best friends, senior boys who paid little mind to freshmen like us. She sighed with dreamy hopelessness and recounted all five words Devon the Douche had said to her that night. I rolled my eyes as she rolled to her back.

"Maybe he'll talk to me on Monday in the halls. You're mighty quiet. You want to go inside?" she asked. "You uncomfortable?"

Her nose crinkled when she grabbed her ponytail to sniff her hair. Both of us reeked of invisible hours around a bonfire clustered with gossiping upperclassmen. The smell didn't bother me so much but putting my hair up once more would have been nice.

"What's there to be uncomfortable about?" I blew my breath toward the bangs that fluttered as I drove my frustration home.

"You're only uncomfortable because you haven't broken-in your new look yet." She ruffled my bob. I pushed her hand away and twisted a ribbon of red around my index finger.

"Guess I better get used to this. It's trashed for, what, like the next year, at least? Angela won. Now maybe my bully will move onto another innocent life and shatter theirs instead of stomping on the broken pieces of mine," I pouted. "If I'm ugly, she has to leave me alone, because there's nothing left for her to take." *Right? How fun would school be without Angela Ansley's daily concoctions for Kinsley misery?*

"Kins." Tyndall gazed up at me. "You're only kidding yourself if you think this makes you ugly. Now you have a pixie bob to match your fae body. Guys will call you cute. Girls will adore you. I do."

I scrunched my nose. "You're biased. Girls will be even more condescending, and guys will treat me like a lap dog. Fun times."

"You shouldn't worry about people at school when your mom's gonna kill you when you get home. You'll be dead by Monday. Problem solved."

Although I smiled, my throat swelled with emotion.

She was right. My mother would cry when she learned I'd lopped off eighteen inches for Locks of Love without her permission. At least one good thing would come of this if Angela didn't halt her ways.

"Aw, Kins, I was kidding. I'm sorry. Your hair grows fast and she can't stay upset forever." She shifted from sympathetic to angry. "Oh, this is all so screwed up. I think we should tell your mom the truth."

"No. This is bad enough without the extra lecture on not caving to those who threaten you. And if she goes up to the school, things will get worse."

"Kinsley, this bitch accosted you in the bathroom with a pair of scissors. She could've stabbed you rather than threaten to cut your hair in exchange for stopping rumors she started for no reason, based on lies. I wouldn't put it past her. She's psycho enough. Who does that?"

"Who gives in?" I countered with fresh shame. "I'm such a coward and that's the worst."

"Damned if you do, damned if you don't. At least you had it cut by a professional and donated to a good cause. You turned her evil into something good. If you hadn't done it, she'd spread new lies. Wish I'd been there. They'd have suspended me for breaking a mirror with her beauty queen bitch face. I can't believe she's here. She wasn't invited. She piggy-backed on someone else's invitation. Makes me want to lure her to my bathroom upstairs to finish her. Mother, may I? We can sneak into her tent and cut her hair while she's asleep."

"And have you arrested and charged with assault? Your dad sued by her cop father? Nope. Old business. Bad blood. Nothing to do with you. I'm tired."

"Whatever," she grumbled, but wrapped me in a hug. "It's late, you're exhausted. You'll feel all better in the morning when you wake up and see your hair is prettier than you give it credit for and her evil intention bites her in the ass."

Her fingers played through my hair and coaxed me to relax. Before long, small streams of tears ran down the sides of my cheeks and dripped on the nylon floor in the darkness.

What if this didn't work? Angela would make life worse and I'd be out of options. Why couldn't things be simple? Go to class. Learn. Get an education instead of worrying about bullying. Go home. Have fun. Repeat. My whole life felt like a constant struggle.

Could I ever just rest?

At least she hadn't noticed me thanks to the hat I'd worn to disguise myself. Wonder how pretty everyone would think she was if they had any idea what me and other minions endured when she trapped us. *Would Jase have allowed her here if he knew?*

Tyndall's hand rose to swipe at the tears she didn't give me a hard time for. "Shhh, sleep."

There was no point in arguing. I yawned and feigned sleep while she drifted off that easy with no looming problems or cares. Lucky. The biggest issue Tyndall faced came in the form of big brother beating down a dude for coming onto her in the hallway. She'd grown so tall and curvy over the summer. He was nervous about graduation. Who would look after his sister when he left for boot camp?

I should tell him how much she'd learned from all their childhood fights. He might take comfort knowing she wasn't afraid to smack a jerk. School would seem empty without him. Not that he paid me attention other than the passing comment or nod. He was so much quieter at home than at school, almost thoughtful. I didn't mind quiet. I was quiet, too, unless hanging with my close friends like Tyndall and Jack.

My longing sigh blended with Tyndall's soft snores. Jack Carter. He'd been quieter, too, and wasn't enjoying the transition into high school. We'd invited him to come hang out tonight, but he'd snubbed us. When Tyndall went to class, I'd asked why he refused.

He'd said, "Because. Let's be real, it's not a Homecoming party, it's an orgy for Jase Taylor. I'm tired of hearing about him like these girls just found God. It's sad and gross. I hope you don't turn out like them, Kins."

"No way. I need more than a pretty face. And I'm waiting for marriage. No orgies for me." I'd smiled, hoping to disarm him. To my happiness, Jack had smiled in relief then asked whether I'd be at the dance instead of Jase's house. "Well, no one has asked me."

"So." He'd shrugged while I hoped he'd take the bait. "No one asked me either, but I figure we only get four of them. You should come and we can be wallflowers together unless you'd like to dance together outside of a studio? Maybe invite Tyndall if she doesn't want to go to her brother's sex fest."

Yikes. I didn't want to be like everyone else to him, but I also wondered what to make of his mixed messages. I wanted Jack to see I had more substance than the gorgeous girls that guys like Jase always had under their arms. Maybe we had a mutual hope and an important thing in common.

Last night at the dance, he'd asked me to the floor a couple times, but seemed conflicted about something he didn't want to talk about. I didn't have the heart to tell him that Jase's party wasn't until tonight.

What if he found out? How would he react to my haircut? At least we slept beneath the same sky and this too would pass, although, he was right about sex. I could hear the faint sounds of coupling in various tents. This sucked.

Unable to shut my mind off, I unzipped the tent to sit beside the smoldering glow of dying embers in the fire pit. I held my hands up to the soothing heat, and my hair fell forward against my jaw. When I shoved the strands back behind my ear, my hair loosened once more, too short to stay put. I gulped against the lump of regret and pulled my legs to my chest, chin burrowed into my knees to stop the tremble.

"Hey, sweet Kins. Why are you awake?" Jase's muted voice quizzed from somewhere over my shoulder. I craned my neck, shocked he wasn't one of the mating rabbits.

"You cold?" he asked. Without an answer, he slid his Letterman jacket off and draped the skin-warm fabric over my shoulders. I guided my arms inside the leather sleeves. My heart hammered as his nails brushed my neck. When he sat down, his much longer leg leaned against my own as his knees mimicked mine, his elbows setting atop.

Holy crap! We were touching! And I was wearing— practically swimming in— Jase Taylor's letter jacket! With his body heat! The material smelled like him even over the fire! I hoped he couldn't see the butterflies he'd set free! From the corner of my eye, I sneaked a glance. Without his hat, his hair shadowed his eyes to his cheek bones, not much shorter than my own. The observation made my heart clench, and I tried placing a lock behind my ear again, failed again.

He hooked a finger beneath my chin. My breath sucked up as his free hand ran through my abbreviated wisps. His soft smile radiated warmth where mine warred with so many foreign sensations. No guy apart from my daddy had ever run his fingers through my hair or touched my face. More than anything else, my aching pain was on display, and the shallow king of high school hotness was taking this in like an art appraisal.

"Breathe, baby."

My held breath whooshed against his finger. He licked his lips and brushed a fraction of my cheek with his thumb. I tried to form an explanation for why I was out here, but I hurt for more reasons than before. Jack would be so disappointed in how weak I was as Jase's head tilted while his eyes examined my face.

"Your hair will grow back." He soothed. "I admire what you did. I can't name anyone else who would cut off even two inches of such beautiful hair so that some poor cancer patient might have such a neat color as yours. Courageous."

Tears burned and brimmed. He sighed over my pathetic bull. In Jase Taylor's world, the only crying I bet he ever dealt with was when he had to break-up with someone who'd picked out the dress and written her vows. Shame only stung worse as I imagined there weren't many emotional girls to take care of in the land of beautiful, mature, young women. They were all so developed, so outgoing, so confident with their perfect teeth and hair.

Captains of drill team, color guard, cheerleading … those girls weren't weak. They had everything going for them while I had little boobs, wore braces, and now bore this mess I'd made of my head. What a disaster.

"I see that face. Are you calling me a liar, sweet Kins?"

Jase dubbed me that way since day one. I didn't know another girl he'd nicknamed apart from Tyndall. I relished the endearment, even if I fell to the sister zone. Not like I had a chance at being more. But with how he looked at me now, how close he stayed, his skin in contact with mine, I could imagine the weight those other girls buckled under.

His honey eyes grew thick with warmth and sincerity. I managed a smile that didn't suck as bad as the last one.

"No, no, Jase. I would never … I'm sorry, it's just …."

"Your hair was a part of who you were. Now, without it, you feel confused and insignificant?"

"Yes," I whispered and cursed my braces lisp when his gaze lingered on my lips once more. *See, even he couldn't quit focusing on the stupid metal mouth!* "Everyone knew me as the ginger with the long pretty hair. Now ....." I trailed off lacking the guts to say there was nothing more to feel pretty about.

"Kinsley, that's where you're wrong. Baby, you don't need long hair to be beautiful." As my girly awe went haywire, he looked down, then cleared his throat and met my eyes again. "Only a true badass would've done what you did today. Besides, it's only hair. Like I said, it will grow back. Here." He rested his back on the leaves. "Lie down."

"Huh?"

"I want to show you something. Lie down."

"But your jacket—"

"Will be fine."

I silenced the warning bells my dad had told me about, because Jase didn't see me that way. I laid down.

"That was easy." When I lifted my finger, he chuckled and grabbed my hand. "Don't worry, nothing else to do with you is easy. Now check out the stars."

No problem there. Stargazing was my favorite thing to do at Tyndall's house, because they were so numerous and much brighter in the country. I'd long since memorized the locations of major constellations on previous sleepovers.

"You see that pink one?" He released my hand to make a box with his over my point-of-view.

I grinned and found the red planet before he helped.

"You mean Mars?"

"Sure." He smiled beside me as he whispered. How surreal to have this perspective of him. "They might've mentioned Mars in one of my Science classes but who cares about planets when I can blow things up with chemicals?"

"Shame." I fought a laugh. "So, we're looking at Mars, and?"

"Well, she's a red planet in the middle of the stars. Doesn't matter how pretty they are, she stands out. You're like Mars."

I gasped. My gaze swung from Mars to his face where I saw the dumbest grin I never knew could melt a heart in pain.

"Hey, don't give me that face. That's the 'aw, he's not a total dick' face, but you'd be wrong because only a total dick would tell you he could relate."

"Oh? How?" I leaned away for a better look at him, unable to hide my braces or ignore the tension in my cheeks from smiling. *Jase Taylor said I was beautiful and compared me to Mars! Whoop, whoop!*

"Yeah, I used to wear my hair to my shoulders before my dad forced me to cut it. I mean how the hell will I pull off a Kurt Cobain 90's grunge without that hair? The only other option is baby oil to make it look greasy, and I have limits." I giggled in the face of his corny play, and he sighed as he studied me. "See? My work here is done. You're laughing again, sweet Kins." Warmth like the fading embers filled my cheeks. What a caring and playful side to an otherwise predictable guy. Why keep this side to himself?

"Do you miss your hair, or did you figure out a new character?" I asked with renewed hope. His face brightened. He shook his head, the leaves crunched beneath him.

"Nah. Now, I have to pretend that if Kurt had lived, he'd have had hair like this. In the meantime, I'll take being able to pull off *Smells Like Teen Spirit* in the shower. Crazy to picture him conforming to preppy ways though. Sorry, Kurt, wherever you are …." He winced in mock defeat. "I've become a traitor and conformed to The Man. But have you seen the car The Man helped buy? Cutting my hair was well worth the prize."

"No joke," I said. "I'll shave my head if my dad wants to do the same when I'm old enough to drive."

We both laughed too loud. I covered my stainless steel-girded mouth with a playful cringe he mocked with eyes of fear, forcing me to laugh all over again.

"Kins, you have the best laugh," he told me. "You want to come hang in my tent, so we don't risk disturbing the others with your crazy loud ass because I am so damn good at cheering you up? I mean, I'd love to do this all night. You're such an easy audience, and my self-confidence is in the toilet. I wouldn't mind the pick-me-up. If I fall flat, we can always play thumb wars or something."

"Or I'll fall asleep on you." I joked but worried I'd wake in a sleepwalking state to find I was dreaming this.

"Ha." He lifted his arm and gestured with his chin. "Pillow's right here if you want to snuggle up, but I'll probably fall asleep because you're warm and content now."

Holy crap! Did he seriously offer to cuddle?

"Kins." Tyndall sounded nearby. "Guess I'm not the only one who can't sleep through all the gross body smacking. This sucks. Let's go back inside."

My heart plummeted to my toes as I jerked upright like a guilty fool. She hated when her friends crushed on her brother.

"Jase, you're usually banging in a tent with some slut. What the heck are you doing out here?" she demanded with suspicious disdain. "Kinsley's not *your* type."

My eyes apologized to both, even as I prayed the ache in my unrequited heart wasn't showing.

Jase ignored her tone and insults. "Nah, it's not like that. I heard movement and wanted to make sure no one was screwing with your tent. When I saw Kins, she looked sad. I thought I'd offer a shoulder to cheer her up," he told her. "It's always worked for you, Tyndall."

She softened and gave him a silent nod of gratitude while we both realized this wasn't what it looked like. I stood to brush the pine needles from my bottom and shrug off his Letterman, but he sat up and waved me off.

"Keep the jacket. I'll get it at church tomorrow."

My heart pounded with elation as I draped the jacket back around my shoulders. His gaze ran over where the hem hit my lower thigh. I was much shorter than him. Did I look stupid for wearing shorts when the temp had dropped to frosty? I felt like a fool.

His eyes traveled to my face. "Night, sweet Kins. You dream of me, I'll dream of you, and we can play thumb wars that way, okay?"

For a moment, I decided not to care how dorky I seemed. He'd lifted my spirits. I braved my brightest smile. "Well, in that case, sweet dreams, Jase."

"Impossible to be anything but sweet if you're there, baby." He winked and granted the lopsided grin reserved for melting hearts in the hallways.

"Nuh, uh, mister." I shook my head and waved a finger, knowing he was still cheering the charity case.

Tyndall and I turned away. The cream leather sleeve crinkled as I fanned my fingers over my shoulder while I sent a last grateful smile his way. Jase waved bye with a soft one in return. That thoughtful expression shadowed his face as he watched us go.

Holy crap! I would have loved to pick his brain all night! What things lurked inside someone who played at being shallow? My laughter must've been what awakened Tyndall, not the sex sounds. My heart ached at my stupidity.

"Are you flirting with my pathetic brother?" Tyndall elbowed my ribs as we held hands and tromped through the woods to the house. "Because he *was* flirting with you."

"Psh. No way. He was just cheering me up. Don't worry, I'm not one of those posers, Tyndall. I love you, girly. Your brother is part of the package." I leaned into her as her arm wrapped around my shoulders for a side hug.

"Well, for what it's worth, I know he meant what he said. I came to your rescue right in time, especially if he put you in his jacket. He doesn't share this with anyone. Not even me. You're the first and only chick to wear this, baby." She mocked her brother, then popped my bottom. "And church, too? Mom's gonna invite you over every weekend! You're a miracle worker."

Happy dance! Thank you, God, for this amazing night!

35

Once I finished dressing in the here and now, drying my hair, applying makeup, I found Bayleigh sitting beside the star of my memories in the living room. Her feet propped on my coffee table, she was comfy as she ribbed with Jase and Rustin. When she saw me, she gave a cat call and checked her invisible watch. "Damn, you look super-hot for our breakfast date, babes. I should have blown my hair out, too, so we'd match. I know I'll be the envy of many a lesbian today."

I chuckled while the guys did a double take, then shot accusatory glares my way. Bayleigh always knew how to disarm me in a snap. Her plan was all new to me but rolling with her was best since my phone displayed multiple unanswered texts I'd received from her during my marathon of primping-on-purpose. We were going out for coffee based on some card she found in the stack I'd given her yesterday.

"Hey, don't look at me like I changed the channel during your Super Bowl." I shouldn't have said that, should've resisted the dig, but couldn't. The guys shared a glance while Bayleigh stood to loop an arm into mine.

"Did they ask you out before I did?" Her eyes fixed on them. "Because we've had this planned for like a week, guys."

"Nope," I said.

"I was about to ask you to breakfast after you finished in the bathroom, baby." Jase's miffed gaze scanned my appearance. *Mmhmm ... I'm the quarterback of this game.*

"Better luck next time." Bayleigh shrugged and cheesed at me.

"You promised me a date last night," Jase pointed out. Some of his charm mixed with conflicted frustration. He was trying to stay cool about this unexpected turn of events, which pissed me off that he *had* to try. *Had he no shame?*

"You can have your date when you ask me sober, yeah?" I reasoned. "Be specific. I have a busy schedule." Bayleigh and I laser-beamed the calendar adorned with sloppy notes. The dry erase needed major updating with all the meets and invitationals I had on the docket, including tomorrow's.

Jase raised an eyebrow like I wasn't serious. With Bayleigh there, I remained resolute and nodded.

"Today?" He grasped at straws. "How long will you two be?"

"A while. I didn't make a timeline of events," Bayleigh said. "We're going out to Treasure Island."

"What the hell is way down there?" Jase demanded. Rustin's eyes flashed wide with warning. Jase changed his tune. "All right, fine. I want lunch. You have breakfast, do your girly thing, and when you're done, our turn. Fair?"

The guys shared a scowl, then Rustin grinned. "Need a marker?" he asked to the tune of a snarky smart-ass. *Nice.*

"*Our?* As in both of you?" I shot back like they'd piddled on the carpet. This game needed a new playbook.

When I got no response, Bayleigh tugged us toward the patio. "Sounds great, lovers. After I've gotten my fix, she's all yours. Now let's go, Kins." She snapped her fingers and headed straight to the door. We paused for the guys exit first. I locked the deadbolt, then she backed us out of the drive a few minutes later. "What the hell, girl?" She wasn't asking though. She was talking to the space filled with the same question I hadn't asked. "Oh, come on. They want to follow. How will we get this taken care of?"

Before I quizzed her, she held a finger up and insisted I wait until she lost them in traffic. "I need to concentrate. Jase is freaking stalker material." After flooring the accelerator on the I-4 West ramp, her coupe zoomed ahead, but Jase's loud-ass monster truck kept right up.

"He's onto you." I noted in the passenger side mirror. "Thank you for picking me up, Bayleigh. I need a break."

"What do you mean? Did Jase do something stupid last night?" A severe 'bitch will cut a fool' expression replaced her jovial norm. She wove in and out of traffic like a Formula One driver, hoping that the truck would never fit in gaps her Mini Cooper did. "He still has advantage. He's high up with the lift kit on that truck. Doesn't matter how far ahead I get or what highways we take. He has an overhead view, dammit!"

"No, nothing stupid I'm aware of, but A) they spied me doing a dance to some Mötley Crüe this morning. B) I may have dumped scalding-hot coffee all over my boobs, and C) I overheard them talking locker. You were right. Jase is into me, but they may have something competitive going, then even seemed to consider sharing instead. I'm pissed."

"Damn. A three-way? If it were anyone else, I'd say fine, but Kins that's a lot of drama you don't need. You're not that kinda girl …." she trailed, bothered. Wow. Not what I expected from her. "It's also weird they wanted to come out with us since Treasure Island is not right around the corner. You're welcome to hang with me all day. I promise somehow, someway, we *will* lose them on the beach." Her eyebrows waggled, naughty mischief alive in her aquamarine eyes.

"There's my adventurous girl." I couldn't handle Bayleigh going heavy on me when she was a source of easy-peasy I needed.

"I have an extra bikini in the trunk. Might have sand in your ass crack if you don't shake it out well." She filled the drive time by informing me on why there was nothing sexy about sex on the beach. "Kins, the movies are such a crock of BS! My hustle was ruined for a week and had nothing to do with how good this dude was, and everything to do with sanding my crack," she muttered.

I cupped a laugh that burst forth. *Only Bayleigh* ….

"Oh, you laugh." We wove through the last part of town before driving onto the causeway. "I had to swipe diaper rash medicine from my niece's diaper bag because my bum was raw. My sister had a fit when she couldn't find it." She snickered. "For the record, that junk burns, too. Those crooks manufacturing that stuff should be ashamed torturing poor infants with that fire ointment. Anyway, I'm fully recovered and ready to throw on a suit and hit the waves! Wha'd'ya say?"

"Yeesh." I cringed. "You know how I feel about bikinis. Thanks, but no thanks."

"Seriously? I confessed that my ass was chapped for a week, and had to butter my butt to carry trays at work, now you're sneering about bikinis? If I wore one-piece's I'd let you have that one instead, but my sister is living proof you flaunt it while you got it." She peeked at me while we inched along the always clogged bridge. There were faster ways to get to Treasure Island.

"K, well do you have a cover-up I can throw over the bikini? You know how I feel about this thing." I pointed to the spot beneath my left boob, then slapped my forehead and stared out at the water while shaking my head. Jase and Rustin saw me in my bra, which means they saw the ugly mark. Man, I couldn't win today.

"Oh, BFD on the birthmark front!" Bayleigh griped. "Your track uniform shows almost as much skin!"

"Almost being the operative word," I said with a smug grin that didn't reach my eyes.

"Quit effing texting and driving!" Her hand flew up when the car at our rear slammed on his brakes inches from her bumper as we stopped. Jase behind him honked in warning. Protective as always. "If we didn't have *stupid* tourists who couldn't operate roundabouts, this would be smooth!" She gestured to the river of brake lights ahead of us. "Don't Yankees have more of these things than we do in the south? They should know better," she muttered. "Bet that Brit handles this like a pro." She glared at the car in her rearview mirror.

"I didn't get his number. I didn't ask for it …."

"Why not?" I gasped in surprise.

"Well, for one, he's diggin' *you* hard. If Jase keeps going, I will have to take the shovel from the Brit's hands and hit him over the head with the spade to get you out of there! *Then*, I might have a chance. And … if we're both honest, I see the way you look at him. There's chemistry there. For *both* of you."

"Bayleigh—"

"Ease up, we don't have to talk about him. Just felt you should know I'd never go out with someone you even have a hint of attraction to. Plenty of other dudes out there."

"You're a good friend, Bayleigh Blue."

"You sound like my mom. She's the only other person who calls me that."

"Because of your eyes? That's why I do."

"No, because that's the color my balls would be if I had them."

She beamed and jostled my hand while we shared a laugh. I looked out over the glittering bay and the pedestrians making progress past us as we inched along. The boats in the marina by the aquarium bobbed with the freedom to speed away for hours, wind whipping hair, waves rolling out a carpet of adventure as the gulf spilled wide without an obstacle.

Then, there was the guy on the houseboat welcoming guests while his carnivorous barbeque pit billowed. My stomach growled when the aroma of cooking meat permeated the air. Anything appealed more than traffic slow enough I could crawl faster. Spring break was gonna be insane. Whether I was with Jase or Bayleigh, we would have to keep to our clocks to make extra time for getting off the island to drive to work later.

"Kins! Earth to Kins, I'll ask you one more time. Want to lose the spies and bikini phobia and go to the beach with me?" Her fingers snapped. "Jase can have his date another time while we get a tan and hand out cards to pull some of this crowd to the bar. Yes?"

"Yeesh, sorry girl. The water's glittery today. Attention Deficit— Ooh Shiny!" We giggled. "All right, but after coffee? I'm in desperate need of caffeine and some ointment of my own after spilling on myself." I drew my feather-light top away to examine my still-pink chest but busted a cackle when Bayleigh not only entered the roundabout but circled three unnecessary times in a row for fun before heading down the wrong street. "Way to lose our spies!" I beamed with total pride, craning my neck to peer out the back window. "You did it! But we should head that way, too."

"Mmhmm. He's ensnared in the Coronado hotel trap and are you sure you wouldn't rather have a Bloody Mary?" We stuck our tongues out at each other. "The ointment is somewhere on the floorboard if you're up to digging, but I'd go for something lighter. Don't wanna ruin your top. Love the open cut-outs in the back, but no bra? That's not like you. I know you wore those shorts and wedges to punish Jase. Did you see his face? He's hurting bad." She gave a villainous laugh.

"Yes, to punish him, but I admit I'm wearing pasties because I really did burn myself. I'm lucky it hasn't blistered, but my bra hurt too bad when I put it on. I look trashy, huh?" I chewed my cheek and regret my decision.

"No way. With this crowd, you're still overdressed. Rock them while they're still standing on their own, girl. And speaking of punishment ...." She tapped the Bluetooth as her phone rang. "Jase, we missed the turnoff. As soon as I find a place to turn around, we will be right behind you." She crinkled her nose with a silent laugh in my direction. When she hung up on a perturbed Jase, she said, "He'll be stuck there for at least thirty minutes before he realizes I lied. Besides, my friend told me to park in her condo spot while she's at work. They won't be able to find my car."

"Well done." I grinned, feeling lighter. "Since we aren't going to Treasure Island, where *are* we headed, and why did we drive here to drink coffee instead of the Cuban place we love?"

"You have to promise to stay chill. We aren't going to a coffee shop as much as a beach bar." My skepticism wore on my face as we shut our car doors. The condo building was across the street from a small shopping center with a popular bar that had an open roll-away door and colorful outdoor tables built into the facade. We jogged through the park, the stalled lines of traffic, and into the fragrance of cooking bacon. "I've been as uneasy with the secrecy as you. I sought answers. Tracking down the horse to hear the truth straight from her mouth wasn't easy, but ...." She trailed off as we entered.

Chairs printed with beach scenes and sunsets begged patrons to sit and have a drink or ten, no matter the time of day. Totem poles and tiki lamps surrounded the full bar that sported a couple lazy daisies watching classic Rolling Stones music videos as they slurped coffee and cut into omelets.

Bayleigh and I stood in wait of service. The bartender/waitress/hostess for the morning shift lazed through the door from the kitchen with a paper sack she extended to a man 'for his wife.'

When she turned, she faltered in surprise, then regrouped and resumed her greeting. "You found me." A now brunette Sara smiled and cast a watchful glance over our shoulders. "Is it just the two of you?"

"It is," Bayleigh told her. "Jase is on a wild goose chase."

"Good deal. Want to sit at the bar, or by the window?" She grabbed menus and napkin-wrapped cutlery. We opted for the window. I ordered coffee while Bayleigh ordered two sinful pastries no one planning on wearing a swimsuit in public ought to consider.

"Big appetite this morning?" Sara asked her.

"No, one's for Kins. Can't you hear her stomach roaring? I could barely hear the radio in the car."

"I can't eat that, Bayleigh. My coach would kill—"

"Live a little! Besides, I saw uneaten Pop-tarts on your counter." Bayleigh gave her attention back to Sara. "I'll have some orange juice and we'll both have a side of water."

"Sounds good. I have a break coming soon, Little Red," Sara told me. Marcus had rubbed off on her. "You need to be aware of a possible problem."

She left and returned minutes later with two plates of stuffed French toast. My stomach growled while I scowled at the consequences and weighed them against the beautiful temptation.

"Take a bite. You'll be a changed woman. Honestly, I don't know how you survive. If I wasn't having sex, I'd be eating everything in sight. You're not bulimic, are you?"

"What? No, Bayleigh," I said, offended.

"I'm sorry, but you're looking at that food like you're tempted to eat it and puke it up when you're done. If it's not that, what's your secret? How do you stay skinny?"

"My secret? It's called self-discipline," I told her and chewed my bottom lip. "And, twenty-plus hours of conditioning per week. Just because I don't eat junk doesn't mean I don't eat. I probably eat at least twice the calories you do every day. I have to be cautious what type I consume is all."

She stared at me like I'd told her a tragic story and reached out to squeeze one of my hands in empathy.

"You must be dying to graduate!"

I shook my head and stared at our surfboard table.

All the tables were surf boards.

"I see what you're doing. I'm not eating until you do." She set her fork down and crossed her arms over her chest. "Although I do like the boards for tables, too."

"Seriously? Fine, mom." I cut into the toast and sighed when sweet cream cheese oozed over strawberries. She cut hers the same, then counted from three. We forked bites into our mouths together. When I hummed and closed my eyes, she gave a playful growl and told me how sexy I was when I ate. Again, I didn't want disarming, dammit. I grinned at her and threw caution to the wind with another indulgent bite. Once Bayleigh and I were halfway through our plates, a manager relieved Sara when other customers had vamoosed, and the place was empty.

"Ya did good, kid. You ate half and that's all I can ask." Bayleigh winked and pat my hand, then sauntered outside for a cigarette. Since she didn't smoke, she knew the info Sara was about to divulge.

"She's worried about you," Sara told me as Bayleigh's blonde ponytail disappeared around the corner. "I never considered the risk until she said you both picked up on something."

"Yeah, she threw me into Marcus's office last night over some dude who's been coming in asking about you. What gives?"

She took another nervous survey, her eyes full of remorse. I was glad my Brit was looking out for me.

Who was looking out for her, or looking *for* her?

"The short version? My soon-to-be ex-husband fell into addiction. His personality shifted about a year ago. I learned the hard way he'd developed a cocaine problem which expanded to a meth problem, then he started dealing. I had no clue how bad off he was until he didn't have the money to pay our utilities and I smelled something weird when I came home after work one night. I mean, something was off, but I'm a good girl, Kins. I didn't grow up around drugs. I was ignorant."

Her eyes filled with tears she looked away to blink back. I was such a blind fool. *Why did I assume she had a great marriage?* I'd never met her husband. She had always insisted him coming into the bar was against their rules since she had to flirt to make generous tips but seemed happy.

Her expression hardened as she looked at me again. "Can't help who you love, Kins, but I tried to help him with the twelve-step program, rehab. Didn't matter. The addict must be willing and ready to change. You can't push a rope. Not long after, he worked me over for my tips. Let me tell ya, you never forget taking a punch for the first time, and going home every night afterward expecting a beating? That's hard. Especially when you're trying to hide the bruises. I kept our son with friends and family as often as possible. I stashed money in cushions and the toilet tank to keep food on the table. Had to get another job besides the bar. Filed for divorce, and he flipped out. High as always. Our son was home when his dad attacked me. Noah tried to stop him. Patrick broke Noah's nose, and I snapped."

She peeled cutlery away from a napkin to dab at her eyes. I gripped my fork too hard while visions of stabbing the bastard with the tines danced in my mind.

Her poor son!

"Somehow, I broke the Swarovski vase we got for our wedding over his head to knock him out. If I hadn't stashed that thing, no doubt he'd have sold the crystal for drug money. Lord works in mysterious ways. Right place, right time. Can you believe *he* pressed charges against *me* for domestic violence? That's what I get for never calling the cops all the other times. I had no way to prove I wasn't the abuser."

"Good grief, Sara. I never saw bruises. Never knew you were captive in your own life." I wanted to cry. "Are you facing jail time?"

She gave a bitter laugh. "The tricks I learned with makeup would blow your mind. And my court-appointed attorney helped me file a restraining order on him and to document every mishap, but he keeps attempting to get to me through other people."

"What about the cops? That violates the rules on the restraining order, right?"

"Oh, Kins ... to still be wide-eyed and trusting. The cops can't act unless I can prove intent, and even then, bureaucracy prevents them from moving on my word against his. Now, here's the part you need to look out for. This guy who harassed me at the bar wore an Inferno vest. I reported the incident, but if the cops are bribed, they won't touch certain groups. They'll turn a blind eye. If their silence is not bought, they're threatened or scared. When you look at the bigger picture— murder, rapes, drugs, burglaries—domestic incidents are low on the list of priorities and the most dangerous calls they get. Women end up beaten to a pulp before a uniform shows up. Can't win."

"Don't say that." I took a desperate breath. "Sara, why not tell someone we know? Get a witness. What about Jase? He swore an oath to defend this country against threats, both foreign and domestic. Sounds like domestic terrorism in my book."

I shoveled a huge bite into my mouth to shut myself up. My temper raged while I wrestled back a rant that would make things worse.

Jase couldn't have known about her abuse and not done anything ... *right?*

36

Sara interrupted my thoughts. "No. Jase is one man, tough, but this goes deeper. Patrick's a firefighter. Though most are good, there's a high chance he's a prospect—"

"For Inferno?" I interrupted.

"Yes." Sara nodded. "That is why I am not telling our local heroes like Jase. Their egos are too big. They go all country justice. When you're dealing with domestic violence, you stay silent not only because you're scared to speak, sometimes it's about protecting others from the psycho who comes after you. They punish those who help. I can't let that happen to my parents, to my friends."

Where the hell did that leave me, dammit? And Patrick? Please, God, tell me that 'Pat' wasn't his shorthand!

"The guy who came into the bar unnerved me because up to this point, I had received threats through letters and shouts from car windows. Since I moved, the harassment stopped. Noah and I are sharing a two bedroom with my girlfriends, but this is such an expensive area, Patrick would never think to search for me here."

"Did Bayleigh park in your spot?"

"My roomies' spot. I got rid of my car to throw Pat off my trail. I borrow their cars when I need to take Noah to school or pull shifts at the bar. My parents put Noah in a great private school. It's like signing out the crown jewels to pick your kid up early."

And there you had it: Pat. My stomach soured while she rattled on about a big threat like the danger no longer pertained to her since she'd moved. She bounced from worried to capricious, jaded to her circumstances, then fearful. Inconsistent.

"But I'm done and ready to fall off the map," she continued. "The bar is Patrick's last way to track me. I'm quitting. After your time with

Jase, come by my place to grab my uniforms. You can get ready there and I'll take you to work."

Um, riding with her to the place where her stalker ex was searching for her?

Our eyes diverted when we heard Bayleigh's flirtatious cackle. We couldn't see her, but we shook our heads since we didn't have to. The brunch crowd trickled in over the course of our conversation. Sara's manager eyed her in need of assistance.

"Want me to grab a tray?" I teased to lighten things.

"Right?" She smiled like what she had been talking about hadn't been terrible. "Okay, just a minute," she called over her shoulder when she got the signal. A large group of guys walked in, their sandy flip flops clapped against the floor, beach bodies shiny with tanning oil, hair sun-bleached and slick. We expected Bayleigh to saunter in with one of them, but she hadn't returned yet.

"Quick, Kins." Sara dropped decibel close to my ear while I chewed and stared at the doorway. "That night at the bar, I was taking out the trash. This guy offered to throw the bag into the dumpster for me, then said I had something *he*—as in the guy who put him up to this — wanted, and that if I was a smart girl, I'd forget about it. Which doesn't make sense, right? Because if I had something he wanted, wouldn't he demand it from me? Anyway, at first, I worried that Patrick stiffed a dealer for some take. Then, this prick asked what was so special about my ... uh ... well ...." She gestured below the belt. "Claimed he was in the market for a redhead and wanted to know if the carpet matched the drapes. It shocked me since—" She paused and told the group of guys to sit anywhere, that she'd get their drink orders in a moment. "— he'd been nice. But I told him to kiss my ass because he had the wrong girl. That's when it dawned on me. He was threatening me to take our son. Screw him and Pat. Made me more vigilant. After that, I ran to tell Marcus, but Kins, the guy grabbed me and shoved me up against a car in that blind spot by the dumpster. I was lucky the car alarm went off, because he backed off, but he warned I'd better be careful who I messed with, and that he'd be watching."

He was!

Didn't matter which one was Pat. They weren't only watching, they were hunting, and *I* was easy prey, afraid in ways I'd been angry at Marcus for questioning me about. Tonight, I'd have to own up and confess my trepidation.

"Kins, watch your ass. I'd feel awful if anything happened to you." She turned with her pen and pad in hand, but I reached out and snagged her arm.

"Hey. Is that why you left the card? Like a secret ploy to get me here to fill me in? Is that why you waited until now?" I didn't understand how she let this information wait this long.

She looked at me funny. "What card?" she asked but left before her tip dwindled.

Bayleigh walked back inside giggling away while I ground my teeth through another bite way too large for my mouth in renewed frustration, anxiety, hell, I'll take adjectives that depict stress for five thousand, Alex.

Why did Bayleigh mention a card if Sara hadn't left one? Was he watching us now?

Everything no longer seemed as carefree. I re-mulled the beach incident, wondering if someone was already stalking me aside from Looney Lucy.

On a watchful look around, my food lodged in my throat when I saw the sexy Brit talking to Bayleigh as he walked up to the bar. *Oh, come on!*

In seconds, my cough drew attention from the guys at Sara's table, which then led to Bayleigh and the Brit looking up from their banter. His pleasant surprise morphed to concern, money in his hand paused mid-way to the counter.

The manager tending bar left her post to help, but I shook my head and waved off her Heimlich, then hauled outside around the corner to gag up what I choked on. And … some of what had me hungover.

"Ewww!" Spring Break douche bags side-stepped as they sniggered and pointed. "Hashtag Spring Break Clearwater Beach!" one joked and snapped a picture on his phone. When I stood to shoot them the evil eye, I caught that the side of the building was full of open windows, too. I'd just put on a gross show for everyone inside.

"Why, God? Just why? This what I get for taking bites too big? Ugh! That's not even a proper sentence!" I spit one more time and forearmed my mouth like a bloodied MMA fighter charging inside for more.

"I was coming to check on you," Moonlight told me when I reached the threshold. "Here." He handed me a wet dishtowel courtesy of the bar and ushered me to the stool I'd been sitting on. Bayleigh appeared to be missing in action, big surprise. "The loo," he teased my thoughts. "You all right?"

"You following me?" I croaked as I dabbed my mouth and face so as not to ruin my makeup. The coffee cooled to a lukewarm but flushed the acid stinging my esophagus. I caved and chugged some water.

"Perhaps I should ask you the same, Kinsley, though I believe this is pure coincidence. If I'm making you uncomfortable, I can leave."

His sincerity shoved my guilt to the forefront for projecting my anger onto him. Considering his protective help at the bar, I wondered if I'd sent out the bat signal and drawn him to today's peril.

"No, please stay. I'm sorry, it's not my best day. Hungover." Lame excuse, but true enough. He nodded and gave me a pass. "Want to sit? Guess Bayleigh had a less than ladylike emergency?" I grinned, hoping he'd laugh. He did, and I swear the effect carried the same intensity as last night.

His skin was a smooth shade of pale that would bronze over the next few months but didn't need to for him to be beautiful. Drunk goggles had nothing to do with how handsome I'd thought him to be. *Praise the Lord I wasn't under the influence this time!*

Maybe this day wasn't total crap, because I'd thought of this man, the asshole pirate, for the past two years, and now here he sat! In the flesh. Right in front of me during daylight hours. No sunglasses! No costumes! No hat! I was almost dumbstruck.

"So." I cleared my grimy throat and celebratory thoughts. "At last we meet outside of the bar. And elevators. No obstacle courses." His lips quirked at my pun. "I'm sorry if I've ever served you before and didn't remember." I confessed. "You can't imagine the people who come and go, even those with accents, but I should've recognized you. I thought I recognized you at the beach but chatting during exercise is bad form. Your scent did the trick. Can't forget that. Please, shut me up." *How embarrassing!*

"Ferme la bouche."

Whoa! My lips clapped together in shock. His tone hadn't changed, but deploying French? *How did he know?*

"Whoa, easy there. Only jesting." He held his left hand up, his right wrapped around the cup of coffee Sara delivered. She spoke to him like he was a regular and asked about some charity tournament while I studied his hands for jewelry before he spied my inspection. All bare— a good sign. "Refill?" he asked. I refocused on his face and nodded. He seemed pleased.

When she walked away to grab the pot, he smirked. "You curse in French sometimes when you're working, and no worries on the recognition. I admit I didn't distinguish you without smeared mascara and leather pants there for a while."

My jaw dropped, but the smile came too bright.

"Asshole."

"In case I had any doubt, there she is." He laughed, an easy sound that settled me more comfortably on my stool, my arms folded onto the table.

Sara's eyes smiled in knowing as she refilled my mug. "Holler if you two need anything," she sang.

"Yeah, a search party for Bayleigh if she doesn't show in the next five."

"Right." Sara snickered over her shoulder. I rolled my eyes and doctored the coffee with the creamers on the table while wondering how she seemed chill.

"Kinsley, you look spry for being hungover. Fresh. We should all be as lucky. Your hair is beautiful, like shades of fire in the sun." My hair was down, blown out and curled at the ends in my earlier attempt to wait the guys out with no luck. Now, I blew on my coffee and tried not to blush at his kindness.

"Thank you." Considering his brand of humor, I shied receiving his compliments because they were almost hard to handle. Not to mention, he was too handsome and refined. I was almost twenty-five, yet still felt too childish for this male's attention.

I guess my face changed with my inadequacy because he spoke up with his head dipped to my view. "You seemed upset when I arrived. Is something bothering you? Anything you need an ear for?" the Brit asked, his free hand gestured to himself. When I glanced at his intense eyes, the sun showcased them like a spotlight, and the contrast of dark lashes with such a light, stormy gray was like sunshine on an impending thunderstorm … captivating. *I should be so lucky.*

Without answering, I shrugged.

"Very well, I won't pry." He looked out of our open window. "Beautiful day for the beach."

I snorted at the smart-ass change in subject, and he seemed happy this time.

"Well …." I trailed and peered at Sara to see she busied herself pouring booze before seating back-to-back tables. How to resist the ear he lent, especially after how he'd handled the biker last night? I found my longing to pick his brain for a solution festered stronger than the guilt I carried at betraying her confidence. Factor in she never planned to tell me at all? Yeah.

"There's this guy—"

"Blast!" Moonlight's fist tapped the table while he looked away like aw, shucks. "There's always a guy."

I cackled with how silly he was—playing the grief-stricken card well, full animation, chewing the same fist he'd used to hit the table with.

"Go on, I can handle this. It's that bloody Taylor guy, right? After all, he took you home last night."

"Hey, it wasn't like that." I waved a finger in playful warning. "For real, though, this isn't about him. I can't tell him this …."

"Ooh …." He rubbed his hands together, his eyes alight with adventure, making me smile like a fool.

"Pray tell, lay it on me. Means I have a hand up."

"Or you're in the dreaded friend zone." I gasped with a hand over my mouth and round eyes he mirrored before we both chuckled. "All right, you gonna focus, boy? You with me?"

"Rep," he teased like the dog I'd made him into.

This guy … who imagined he could be this light?

"Rokay, Raggy." I quit playing *Scooby Doo*, cleared my throat, and relayed Sara's situation. His humor took a hike and replaced with calm neutrality.

"What does this bloke look like?"

"My guess is that he's one-in-the-same as the biker you took off my shoulders last night." I gulped as I had to ask. "Where did you get that awful tip with the writing on it? You placed the money on the bar knowing I'd see."

He offered a nonchalant shrug, but there was a stoic ice cooling his gaze. "Found a twenty on the floor. Saw your name. Did the math." Relief swept my fear in the trash. "I wanted to show you that his actions weren't going unnoticed, that I'm paying attention."

"Oh, crap!" My relief dissolved. "You saw my name! He wrote my name! That means it's no mistake due to dim lighting. Patrick sought me out on purpose! Why?" I cupped my face as realization threatened to steal what little remained of my breakfast.

"Hey." He reached out and stole my hands, gripping them in a way that sedated the adrenaline rush. "If he's into redheads, 'tis possible he has a type and that's all. Let's not over think his motive until there's irrefutable evidence. He may have decided you remind him of the wife he loves and can't control, however, that doesn't mean he has a shot in hell at anything with you. We don't know for certain that he's the

Patrick she's talking about. Or perhaps he's a fanatic and this has nothing to do with her. I gather you're used to those?"

I nodded, holding to his eyes the way I had in the stairwell and Marcus's office. His authority soothed, which was great because I wasn't telling my father about this. Or Jase. Sara was right. If he knew I was in danger, he'd act, no doubt.

Moonlight cleared his throat, snapping me from my head. "Bartending has drawbacks, but where to draw the line? Does Marcus know about all this?"

"Marcus? Yeah. I'm the last to find out, as always. Oh, hold on." The phone beside me buzzed with several texts: each text one word. "Nice," I muttered.

"What?" he asked while I thumbed through. I lifted the device to show him.

"It's that bloody Taylor guy." I mocked his accent and watched him roll his eyes through a reluctant grin.

Kins

will

u

go

2

Putt

Putt

With

us

When

ur

Done

With

Bay?

"He's forcing me to pay attention by over-texting, because I agreed to a lunch date with him." I recounted my morning, then what Bayleigh had to do to get me here.

282

His laughter echoed over the crowd. Butterflies took flight from my belly like wisps I might have captured between us.

"What? You telling me you don't do your own karaoke to Mötley Crüe? Spoon mics in the privacy of your own home?"

Yes, I'd shared the whole story. His smile was radiant while he stared outside to compose himself.

"For the record," my voice snagged his eyes, "the worst of it was wasting a pumpkin spice K-Cup I'd gotten with some fantastic roses for Valentine's Day. To spill that coffee after saving it for just the right occasion?" I swear, he looked like the shy one for a wonderful moment as if he enjoyed my play but was uncertain with navigating the attention. *How was that possible when there were bikinis checking him out on the regular?* "Do you know how hard those are to find after autumn?" I jostled his resting elbow.

"I might have an idea …." He beamed at the table, then met my eyes. "Are you going to go?" I searched for any clue of how that made him feel. He threw a great poker face. Dang it.

"Since Bayleigh freaking bailed, I will have to." I looked around in frustration. *What if this guy was a creep?* Not smart. She needed a lecture.

I began texting Jase for the location. Moonlight placed his hand to my phone and pressed the device to the table before I hit send.

"Shall we think about this for a moment?"

"What do you mean?" I rested my chin in my hand, my elbow on the surfboard.

"Well, I understand your reservation, especially after their guy talk. Taylor appears to have had everything feminine come to him the easy way, while you seem the type to make a man work for your attention, unless *I* was the only one you wanted to punish?"

I cackled and clapped my hands, but his eyes appraised my reaction like he hoped his summation was correct. My body hummed with shock and longing to be myself for a new reason.

"While you *are* fun to punish, you're right. Plus, I have goals, and I'm so close to graduation, I can taste the victory from here, therefore,

I don't date." I glanced at the ceiling with an innocent grin. "Although, there was this one guy I met a couple of years ago … I was in a relationship, but he made me realize I wasn't ready to commit and somehow the sky wasn't falling by breaking up. Kind of an asshole, but he snapped me out of the clouds and back to my schooling. Now, here I am, shy of my masters instead of someone's happy housewife." I confessed since he'd revealed that he'd thought of me, why not return the favor?

"Wow." He exhaled a deep breath. "Goals are good … important." His finger traced the hibiscus flower on the surfboard. "To clarify, are you saying you dumped one man over another?"

"Bold question, sir." Our eyes met. He had his answer without my word.

"Sounds complicated." His eyes took on the glow of a man issued the ultimate challenge. *Kitty growl!*

"Simple is boring," I pressed to intensify that look of his.

"Seems Taylor would be a simple choice …."

A slow smile warmed my face. "Smooth. I suppose in some ways you'd be right. But he's plenty complicated in others. If I don't respond, he'll come find me." My tone taunted.

"I suppose you have only two choices."

"Oh?"

"I can either offer you a ride to wherever he is expecting you, or you can reschedule with him, making him work harder for the goal *he* can almost taste." He glanced down to emphasize Jase's goal was below my waistline. "Or we escape to anywhere you'd like, Kinsley. You've got this weight on your mind, and you're not confident about telling him. Difficult to plaster that facade for the moment?"

Wow. He'd knocked my rook off the board.

My phone buzzed with more texts, but everything inside paused at this man's courageous insight. Sara came to offer more coffee and our check. "You all right, Kins?"

I ripped my eyes from the Brit's depth, realizing he'd never looked away. He wasn't afraid of me, nor intimidated. He pushed me toward scary terrain I'd never navigated.

"Yeah. I'm okay. Did Bayleigh leave any messages?" I struggled.

"She did." Sara tapped the paper, a small handwritten note: *See you at work. Here's hoping you need diaper rash ointment* ☺.

I laughed.

"Ever the match maker, that girl." Sara smiled up at the two of us. I read her expressions with him. She seemed at ease in his company.

A finger up to him, I hopped off the stool and took the check to the bar. Sara followed.

"You know he paid your bill, right? Bayleigh wouldn't have left you doing dishes," she teased. I rolled my eyes and leaned closer. She knew what was coming. "He's safe, Kins. Not a creep. A good ally to have in your corner. If you confided in him, I'm glad. If you want to go spend a few hours in his company, go, do it. But give me your phone. The whole restaurant can hear the constant buzzing. Bayleigh said Jase is a little too strong today. He's out of his element with you, but I'm with that guy. Don't let him have anything easy. I say leaving with him," she gestured with her chin, "will make Jase prove himself— that, and I don't want Jase finding out. Too dangerous. Take a cool down."

She was right, the phone was going crazy. Jase— you're like Mars—Taylor might have already picked up on something being off and be experiencing alarm bells of his own. Rustin would read my mind and I'd be screwed. I had to get out of here before he tracked my dang phone.

"Kinsley. Remember, come to my place to get ready for work and I'll take you later. Now you have an insurance policy. Go have fun. You never let yourself do anything and maybe you'd do wonders with a different view?" I saw the dreams she didn't live out swimming in her eyes. I couldn't help but pray that she'd have another shot at love with someone who wasn't crappy.

Ugh! My phone was incessant. I didn't bother reading all the texts, just responded that something had come in the way and we'd have to reschedule.

Sara held her palm out, but I gripped her fingers instead of placing the phone into her hand.

"Sara …." My look was pleading. She turned her attention to Moonlight. He no longer sat at the table, but hovered beneath the open roll-away door, hands in the pockets of his cargo shorts. With a kind smile, he conceded and lifted his hand in a wave, then disappeared into the sun. My heart clenched. Sara's grip on my hand was like the swat to my bottom my team landed when they needed me in gear.

I lifted the phone. "Take a picture in case you have to show the cops who I was with. I'll see you later?" I gave up the device. She pocketed the buzzing phone and whispered the condo number in my ear.

"You'd better use that sprint before he's gone," she called. "Don't pull a hammy chasing after him."

What a loaded statement!

37

I sprinted outside, dashed through the heavy traffic, ignored blaring horns. "Hey! Wait!" I shouted. Moonlight turned in shock, prepared to lunge before a car to protect me.

"Are you *daft*?" He snatched my hands, pulled me near a white Tesla behind him. My palms tingled. "Kinsley, you might've injured one of your medal-winning legs, then where would you be? Goals and the lot. After you just recovered." His sincerity made me smile. A look like that one might tempt me to put myself in danger more often ….

"Not to worry. I'm not foolish enough to race something I can't beat," I said while I caught my breath.

"Bloody hell." He released my hands to rub one of his across the back of his neck and zoned on the pavement to calm his nerves.

"Oh, stalker, did I fail to mention I'm a trained professional?" I teased like a smart-ass, my head dipped into his line of sight. The hand at his neck rose with his head.

"Guilty," he cracked in kind. "I'm a fan as you're well aware." *Whoop whoop!*

"Yeah, I could've hurdled that car for ya, but I figured why show off? Humility is the best tack," I reasoned.

He ran his tongue against his cheek to fight a dumb grin.

"Where to? I have to be back at Sara's in about four hours to get ready for work, but that bloody Taylor guy can wait until he comes in the bar with a search party."

His whole face shifted into elation.

My cheeks almost cramped at the realization I'd caused his joy. *Me?* Lucky indeed.

"You're coming with me?" he asked.

I nodded. "We've already had coffee …." I gestured to the Tesla in question. He chuckled with a look over his shoulder and shook his head, his lips formed that sneaky smirk he kept sporting last night. A key dangled from his finger, but he nodded beyond that handsome car, and tossed me off my game.

"You up for it? Bringing a car into Clearwater during spring break would be madness and there's no way in hell I'd be caught dead in a Smart Car or a tiny Fiat to get into a parking spot."

I struggled for the right words. *Could I go there?* "I've never done this before. How can I get on that thing when I don't even know you?" All that awesome bravado gave way to a scared girl who'd left herself wide open to misinterpretation. *Ugh!*

He dragged his teeth over his lower lip. "Would you like to *know* me, then?"

Holy crap! Had he asked me that last night or something? Why did that seem familiar?

"I'd love to be your first."

Shades stole over his smiling eyes. I gulped, not only at his sex appeal or the scandalous innuendo. An expensive blue crotch rocket parked on the sidewalk sapped my courage. We'd be as close as possible with fabric between us. The forbidden chemistry we shared ready to flare once more. Maybe this time we wouldn't end up arguing?

Well, crap. Would I rather wrap my legs around a total stranger than the guy I'd known for a decade?

I looked back at the beach bar like my last chance at sanity. Somewhere in there, Sara was watching to see if I had the balls to take a chance on someone outside my realm of safety. When I turned back to him, he sat on the bike, his key inserted, one of his Topsiders sitting on a peg.

"What? No helmets?" My question drowned out as the motorcycle growled to life. A sound like that ate butterflies for breakfast! This was birds of prey screaming thrills and chills throughout my body that gravitated his way despite my hesitation. His hand gripped a handle. He revved the engine with a wicked quirk of his brows, a dimple creasing his cheek as his brilliant smile ignited. My father would kill me, but dammit, *I didn't want to be that little girl anymore!*

"Screw it." I ran to him when I caught sight of Jase's monster truck looming down the line of crawling traffic. If he was looking for me, I was ready for a game of hide-and-seek and we had seconds to get out of here!

Moonlight noticed the same thing and stood to give me enough space to pinch in as close as possible. Thank God for flexibility because stretching my leg hurt like mounting a horse without the stirrups a saddle offered. His bike was tall and intimidating, then again, he was too. I snugged up while trying to pretend everything wasn't lighting up at the foreign intimacy.

"What do I do with my bloody hands and feet, love?" I mocked his endearment near his ear with a huge smile. All my childish fear vanished for an exhilarating moment. We hadn't even moved, and I already had a rush akin to whipping ass on the track!

"Anything you want, my sweet!" *A new endearment!*

I tossed my head back on a full laugh and nailed his bicep. "I'm for real!"

"Well …." He looked at my feet and kicked out pegs behind his. "I'll let nature take your hands, but you'd better hold tight. And whichever direction I lean, you need to lean with me."

"Huh?" I looked down to plant my feet on the pegs, then squealed as the bike lunged forward and gained in momentum while I clawed to hold on. Angry pedestrians leapt out of his way. An evil sort of glee sounded from him as he steered us off the sidewalk through a narrow space between parked cars and took a split-second shot through the traffic heading in both directions. Didn't take me long to adhere every available fraction of myself to his body! I didn't even feel pain from my burns anymore.

"Holy hell!" I shouted at his ear. "You were talking smack about *me* back there? You're crazy!"

"Damn right!" he called, leaning the bike as he threaded in and out of creeping cars. My chin rested against his shoulder, fingers dug into his chest, thighs clenched against his lower back. Everything felt too alive and radiant with adrenaline. Bayleigh would hate me. I had her to thank for this euphoric lapse in judgment.

"He's gonna be so pissed!" He boasted as we flew past Jase. I bit my lip through my guilty smile. *Let's see how the quarterback fared after a tackle!*

"I'm not the only redhead in the world, sir!"

"Ha! Trust me, *you're* the only one that matters in his! And you didn't tie that insane mane back. It's waving like a battle flag. Better make this worth the grief!"

Jase wasn't my boyfriend. For the first time, I relished the flavor of being a free woman. Didn't matter how long this lasted, I wanted the thrill of a pursuit before a man placed a ring around my finger. Jase could use torment in the fan girl department. If he wasn't up for the chase, he wasn't the right guy. Not that the one wrapped in my grip was either, but I was twenty-four-years young! I longed to toss my head back and throw my arms out to celebrate this foreign intoxication.

When we neared the roundabout, he slowed and crawled through the unpredictable amateurs in line. I sat up to twist my hair into a bun and tied a knot as his feet inched us along the pavement.

"What do you think?" he asked.

"Exhilarating!" I gushed with unconcealed enthusiasm.

"Oh, Kinsley, we're still strangers. Wait till you really know me," he purred.

My head tossed on a cackle. "Don't you wish!" I told him and added the final changes to my bun. "There. Now I'm not as easy to spy."

"Impossible." He glanced back and shook his head. Good grief, his face was radiant, even with shades on! As I absorbed him, I refused to believe anyone else was having as great a time as me in this moment.

Wild fun swelled all around us. Music blared from each vehicle we passed, windows down, almost everybody clad in a swimsuit. Pedestrians of all ages, shapes, sizes, ethnicities, some with dogs on leashes, some cruising through on roller blades or skateboards roamed the crosswalks, crowded toward Pier 60, jaywalked between sitting cars that vied for a spot in the circling mass ahead. Horns honked and had nothing to do with angry drivers and everything to do with making connections for parties or volleyball games. The atmosphere was a perfect conglomeration of what I loved about living in Florida. Though reserved, I wasn't exempt from the lure of a crazy time. The risk was too great to let my guard down. There always lurked a predator ready to steal an opportunity or take a damning photo or video. Screw allowing anyone that type of power over me.

Somehow, I felt safe to relax for the first time in too long. Something about Moonlight told me he had enough intimidation to scare creeps and a strong enough grip on his body to keep his hands to himself until a woman gave the order. *What would that be like* ….

A loud whistle through someone's fingers diverted my dangerous thoughts.

"Let's go, Mi-cro!" The chant that matched my moniker at track meets sounded from a male in a nearby jacked truck. Another dude leaned across the driver to shout, "Woot! Woot! That girl loves to fly, and that Ducati's got wings! Sexy!" Their horn honked extra. Numerous horns joined to create a chaotic chorus. Though I wanted to face-palm, I couldn't help my huge smile as I tucked my cheek next to Moonlight's even though we weren't moving. Gotta love college guys.

"You're a real master of disguise, love."

"Damn right." I mocked, but how cool to have clout in front of him and prove that they hadn't a chance in hell next to this guy! He enjoyed the same thing because I could feel the vibration of his chuckle beneath my hand on his waist. I threw my index finger up in the number one like a cheerleader to pump their enthusiasm and shamelessly confirm *Micro Machine* was indeed the girl on the back of Moonlight's bike.

They reciprocated, but then a chick shouted from the backseat, "Who's the guy? Are you together?"

"Yikes."

"Yes, Ms. Hayes, inquiring minds want to know." He teased me over his shoulder as we approached the front of the line. I gulped as his face was intimately close to mine when he looked at me.

We waited our turn for the incessant humans to cross the street. "Time to lose the paparazzi," I half-joked. Who knew what the rumor mill would be by Monday?

"As you wish. Pull your hair back down, braid it, and tuck it between us." When I hesitated, he said, "You heard the bloke. I've got wings. We're about to take flight. Trust me." I cringed but obeyed in anticipation of the rush he promised. *How scary fun!*

No sooner had I finished, did he rev the bike and startle the crowd enough to create a narrow clearing.

He had the shot, he fired, and left my cheering fans and their prying questions in the dust.

"That was awesome!" I shouted and loved the rise in his face as he smiled against me and maneuvered like a lunatic through the moving vehicles in the circle. My fingers itched to run up his chest and tuck around his shoulders. I took a cue from Rustin's advice to Jase and quit thinking. I did what I wanted. Just like my pirate had done with the pedestrians. When his chest swelled, my eyes closed, and when he fired the bike ahead once more, I sensed a different urgency in how he meandered through the traffic. Every lean with him was more terrifying than any ride I'd ever horrified myself on at the theme parks! I struggled not to scream the way I did on roller coasters when that same dip tickled my belly.

As for our destination, I didn't ask where he was taking me. Would he take me somewhere typical or throw me for a loop? When I opened my eyes, I prayed he didn't throw us both off the bike while we wended through the cars on the causeway. Thank God the traffic wasn't too thick on the outbound side leaving the island.

Back on the mainland, the path through town went well. When he took the ramp onto the highway, I squeezed my eyes shut in new horror. To this adrenaline junkie, the speed limit was only a suggestion, and a whole other level of scary! The faster we went, the more he leaned down until I leveled over his back like I could sleep my way to wherever we headed, but no way was I relaxed!

38 | ♀

Once we left the greater Tampa area, he headed north where the outbound traffic thinned. I wasn't sure how he would get me back to Sara's in time even though we'd only made lift off thirty minutes ago. The southbound influx into downtown already bottlenecked at a standstill. He still drove like a bat out of hell, but I learned to trust his skill. He knew his bike the way Rustin knew his guitar. I settled against him and savored being a bird in the breeze scented of Complicated Moonlight in the sun.

When we took an exit for a road I seldom traveled, I perked up. Was he taking me to the Big Top flea market?

No. He slowed but kept driving until what little remained of small-town outskirts morphed into sporadic gas stations and backwoods bars.

Were we headed anywhere particular, or did he want to take a joyride with me on his pretty bike? Either way, I reveled in the mystery. At the same time, how did he feel familiar to my touch? As if I'd touched him before. How could that be? The journal entry from the day I'd met him haunted my mind, the chemistry I'd written about. I should have burnt that in a ritual as well, because as much as I loved this, he had to be a heartbreaker. Why else would he be single?

I hated that I anticipated the ending before anything began. My brain was always working, analyzing, weaving through outcomes the way this lonely road twisted through a forest of trees on either side until signs for the Hillsborough State Park came into view. *Hmm, would he take me to a park this far away when there were others much closer to where we'd started?*

The entry opened on the left, but he turned right onto a gravel drive I'd not noticed.

An iron bar used for a gate was open, but I saw no other cars. *Should I be nervous?* Now Bayleigh wasn't the only one who needed a lecture.

The bike crawled to an empty clearing and came to a stop. The engine killed altogether. Sounds of nature filled the deafening quiet where the wind and his motor had stolen my ability to hear. For moments neither of us moved.

Should I ask him what we were doing? Would my query pop this bubble blowing bigger with each silent second?

I dragged my stiff fingers from his shoulders down to his waist. His inhalation almost scared the birds. I exhaled against his neck where my face rested. He released his hold on the handles and dropped both hands to his side, which also happened to be on my thighs.

Danger! Danger! Sensation sizzled where his fingertips touched my skin. All at once I dashed from the motorcycle with the grace of a foal getting her legs for the first time. His laughter echoed off the twisted oaks and wild palms while he nudged a kickstand free.

"Your stems were in the way of my pockets, love. What were you thinking?"

I glared while scraping away grasshopper guts glued to my knee, re-situating the ribbons laced from my wedges up my shins and adjusting the way my shirt had bunched and twisted during the ride. Well, hell. No bra today. Pasties only. No wonder he was making moves. I hadn't even thought about the ways the back of my top had lifted beneath the force of the wind on the way here. He smiled like a man who'd known before extending the invitation. Moonlight dismounted and sauntered over without a care, ruffled the mushroom of loose and puffy hair on my head.

"You look ready for more karaoke." He grinned as I growled and unbraided this mess. He stole one of my hands to lead me toward a mowed trail between the foliage.

"Is this a good idea?" I blurted by mistake, swallowed in unease.

"You're going to stop trusting me now? After everything else? If I wanted to kill you, I could have tossed you from the bike to look like an accident. I'd have evidentiary scarring from your claws, though." He jostled my arm. My palm in his sweat like crazy.

"There are other crimes against women aside from murder, sir." My tone wasn't nice. He gazed down like he was proud. *What the hell?*

He tapped his temple and said, "Exactly."

I jerked my hand from his and halted. He shrugged his shoulders and put his hands in his pockets, kept walking with the gait of a visitor enjoying nature without a time cap. I crossed my arms over my chest and gnawed my lip as I watched him go. Not once did he turn back. When he rounded a corner hidden behind grass tall enough I'd disappear, my view of him vanished.

Shoes scuffled on the trail behind me. A man in period clothing from about one-hundred-and-fifty years ago bobbed toward me. "Are you lost, young lady?"

Was I dreaming?

I found my voice as confused alarm covered my reservation about the gray-eyed-man's intentions. "No, sir. I'm just catching up with my company." I directed my hustle to his last known whereabouts.

"Festival's not 'til tomorrow. You're not supposed to be here." He called after me. I pretended not to hear him and turned the corner in a near jog. Treacherous for a professional sprinter wearing wedges on unstable terrain. The Brit's almost black head of hair bobbed into my line of sight. I chastised myself for not asking his name. I couldn't shout for 'Moonlight' to wait so I didn't re-injure my ankle or get booted out. *Did he realize he was breaking the rules? And what kind of festival took place in the middle of dense woods?*

"Oh!" I dropped behind the tall grass and covered my head as the unmistakable sound of gunfire riddled the air. Bullets echoed through the trees. I froze, unable to detect their origin. My chest heaved as I sought to make sense of this. *Hunting season ended. What was happening?*

"Love." Moonlight's hand appeared before my ducked head. I gripped his fingers like a lifeline and surged to wrap grateful arms around his neck.

"You came back."

One of his hands wrapped around my back. Déjà vu slammed my senses: *darkness, cologne, warm lips, harm's way ... Henley.*

Had I conjured an alter ego to dream of in Moonlight's place?

"She okay?" The man in period garb trudged past.

"Yes, sir. The gunfire startled her." I felt his chuckle through my chest. The other man's joined the sound.

"Well, if you didn't tell her, I see why." *Oh, hell no!* I ripped myself from his arms again.

The man walking away laughed anew when Moonlight thanked him for ruining his game.

"Is that what you're doing?" I demanded.

"You threw your arms around me, not the other way around, woman. Maybe I should fear your motive to get in my pants."

"Well, what am I supposed to think?" I gestured to our seclusion. When more shots rang out, I leaped beside him in reflex. He created space between us. His finger came up much the way I'd treated him during our first encounter. The gray resolve in his eyes matched the steel in his expression. My breathing shallowed.

"There's a difference between flirtation and an angle. When I'm gunning for your knickers, Kinsley, you'll bloody well know beyond a doubt. That's a promise."

He presented his back and hiked down the trail once more. Heat spread through my face. I hated this sting. Something about his resistance bothered me like I'd made assumptions he wasn't comfortable with and lumped his attention with, well, boys. Analyzing everything might not be such a great idea.

"Wait!" I hated the gun shots. He didn't flinch, where I prepared to crawl on sticks and dirt that would ruin my legs for a week. Moonlight halted without turning, just stood while I scurried to his side. I rounded to assess his expression and placed my hands to his chest. "Please, I'm sorry. Remember what I told you about the guys? I'm on defense. I misjudged you."

"Did you?" he asked with a smoldering gleam in his eye. Shifting and unpredictable. I sighed and gripped his hand with an order he guide the damn way and quit playing head games. "You like them, admit it. The blokes around you are predictable prats."

"Okay, I don't even know what that word means, but—" I gasped when a town of fabric tents and camp sites dotted our dead end. A small village populated by men, women, and children in period costume roamed the area the way this land must have looked centuries ago.

How cool!

Our banter forgotten, I drew his face down to plant a grateful kiss to his cheek for being legit. He wasn't pulling me into a trap, he'd opted for time travel and grinned with gratitude at my affectionate response.

"The guns and their *blanks* are on the other side of the fort. See the wooden beams of the structure up ahead?" he asked.

I nodded while looking around in awe.

We walked through their world like modern day intruders invading their blast from the past. Fur trading, selling of homemade goods and commodities, handmade jewelry, even Seminole reenactors striking deals with the pale-faced militia. The fort wasn't like any fortification I'd ever been to. I'd expected a stone edifice to appear through the trees. "This looks like a bunch of green pencils sharpened and secured together with a deck and houses built into the corners," I observed aloud. He nodded in agreement, pleased that I liked what I saw.

"They're practicing and setting up for this weekend's Fort Foster Rendezvous & Reenactment. If you'd like to browse, I'm sure I can talk them into selling us a few items?"

"No." I shook my head. "I don't deserve that after my behavior, sir. And I didn't bring my wallet."

He ignored me and nodded at a woman in a tent who invited us to look around. His voice lowered. "Let me be a bloody man and buy you something because I deserve to pay for my devious behavior." *Huh?* "You're not an errant child. Don't apologize for being mean to me when you were nervous. If you hadn't been nervous, I would have been. I say you've permission to leave the feminist back on the beach where people know you and enjoy being an incognito female for a moment."

Was he serious? Was that all a test?

"I'm not a feminist," I muttered and moved to look at a row of vintage pocket watches.

"Aren't you? Can you say you aren't a slave to the trend to avoid scrutiny or judgment from your peers? College is the worst for peer pressure. Sad, considering you're surrounded by grown adults in this phase of life."

"Do I come off that weak?" I wasn't offended, though I diverted my attention from the watches to his face. "While you make an excellent point, I don't care what others think."

"Oh? You wanted your wallet so I wouldn't pay."

"I'm independent."

"Bollocks. I was hoping to score a free meal next time," he teased. I rolled my eyes with a reluctant smile.

"When was the last time you wore a dress?" he asked.

"I wore a dress to church just last Sunday, thank you very much."

"And was that because it was expected of you, or because you wanted to?" *Dammit.* "Admit it. I'm right," he said in that arrogant way.

"You're not. If by feminist you mean the freedom of a woman to choose her own life with equal salary and liberties as men, yes. But if you mean penis-envying manhater, no way." I squealed and leaped away when he tickled my ribs, but I bellowed through my words when I couldn't escape. "I wear dresses!"

"But no heels."

"Yes, heels, you lunatic! Please!" If he didn't stop soon, I would snort in public!

"I don't believe you, Kinsley. Say the words. I'm right," he sang with a beautiful smile.

"I'm right!" My cackle pierced the quiet space. I grasped his arm to still his naughty hand, but his choice to grant mercy was his alone.

"You have to stop! I said it!" The tickle torture halted. I bent to hold my knees and catch my breath.

"Can't win," he muttered to an amused woman and passed from one tent to another. I shimmied after him while he smirked over his shoulder. "I'm only playing with you, love. Makes no matter whether you envy my penis or hate me. I'm your ride, and an undaunted one at that. Although, I am biased when I say you should wear more dresses and I'd love to see you in heels. Your legs are far too beautiful to hide."

"Sir." I waved my finger at his flirtation and focused on a new set of tables. "Oh, wow. Garrett would go nuts for the stuff in this place!"

"The bartender?" he asked.

"Yes. I love that I don't see any garden variety tourist trinkets here." These items were handmade and historical artifacts. Old locks and skeleton keys, brooches, Wild West Sheriff's stars, Pony Express badges, whore house coins from Tombstone.

"Three cents?" He winced. "Steep for a whole night." He snickered as he rolled a coin in his fingers. "Cheers to inflation, eh?"

"Shut up, you dork."

He cringed and showed me a lewd coin. "Perhaps feminism began a long time ago." We both cracked sneaky laughs at his dry humor. Heads of the coin: *Good for All Night*. Tails: *A prize for the biggest cock*, the cock being a rooster, of course.

"Screw wet t-shirt contests," I joked and elbowed his ribs. He chuckled and rubbed the spot I'd tickled. My belly fluttered at the ability. "Can you imagine? How do you think—yeah, let's keep that thought train at the station."

"We'll buy this one for you in case the opportunity should present itself. You need to have something to give to the winner."

My turn to run my tongue over my teeth. When he wasn't trying to piss me off, he was fun to talk to. He didn't give the typical first date interview. In fact, the only questions he asked pertained to my opinion on pieces he'd pick up and examine. He didn't hover but explored the same tent at his own pace and allowed me mine. How contrary to the feminism bull he'd given me. This was unlike any first date I'd ever been on.

Was this a date?

A man walked past and told him they were about to practice another skirmish. Moonlight, who refused to tell me his name until he 'knew' me better, paid for various trinkets he tucked into his pockets, then led the way through the square of Fort Foster. We ducked through a doorway near an old cannon to come out on the other side. A wooden bridge over the Hillsborough River was flanked by opposing forces. The Seminole Indians opened fire on the troops reenacting the 1836 defense of the supply point during the Second Seminole War.

As we watched the cannon and gunfire, some men dropping and others advancing, I wrapped my fingers around his as I thought about him coming to my aid last night. All jokes aside, the things Sara told me, combined with my inebriation and capricious attitude toward Marcus, ate my guts over the sheer foolishness of having my guard down too many times. Rustin Keane wasn't the stupid one, I was.

Though my mind wandered, our attention as the only modern-day viewers never wavered. How surreal. Moonlight secured a backstage performance for a date he hadn't planned, with a girl in need of an escape in more ways than one. A bittersweet gift. I felt honored and undeserving at once even if he enjoyed giving me a hard time.

The actors finished. Women ran to the field to tend to the wounded and cry over the deceased. The period-dressed children from both sides rushed toward the banks to fish together from the river. Such a contrast between the battle and their joy. Sometimes childish glee was an enviable alternative to the realities adults created.

Moonlight drew my attention to the small Indian village on the opposite side of the bridge where we jaunted across to explore. This was entertaining and informative. The quiet distinction after the fighting created a tranquil refuge. Not a single phone charging station or vehicle in sight. No devices or modern amenities. People engaged in face-to-face conversation working the land and their posts with only their hands. I longed for a simpler time and hated putting the village behind me as we traveled closer to modern problems with each passing minute back across the bridge.

"This is so peaceful," I told him. We stopped halfway over the bridge to lean against the railing overlooking the river. The kids extended poles right at the water's edge, undaunted by the possibility of alligators and snakes. I searched the water, as I did everywhere except the beach, for eyes breaching the surface. The water appeared safe for the moment.

"Very peaceful," he said, "but do you understand why I brought you here?"

My hand gestured at the entire place. No explanation necessary. He shook his head.

"Kinsley, sometimes people find themselves in wars they didn't ask for, but to do nothing means a guaranteed loss. People have a basic human right to defend their lives when threatened. If you fight back, there's always a chance you'll win." My head turned to study his face. "If you're threatened, don't cave. You didn't ask for Inferno sexual harassment. Their misbehavior came to you. If inappropriate advances come to you again, be an unapologetic bitch. Why do you think I teased that side out of you once more?"

He asked the rhetorical question like a stern commander to troops facing a giant. The thought sent my mind to all the what-ifs. Being a bitch to him on our first encounter was easy because for all his intensity I had a gut feeling he wouldn't hurt me. Inferno liked provocation with their women. A good fight like foreplay. No matter what, I was screwed.

"Tell that head to hush so you might listen better, Kinsley." He softened some.

"Are you sure you don't want to tell me your name?" I whined and tried to change the subject. I didn't want to taint this realm with the real world.

"And spoil the mystery? No way. You'll learn when the time is right." No innuendo or teasing. "Just know it's not Henley." He winked, and the flirt was back.

"You ready, love?"

I said no but tilted his wrist to check his designer watch. Only an hour left. "You're gonna drive like a demon again, aren't you?"

A chuckle filled the space, then his face cleared. "Is there any other way?"

Though he played at scaring me, he had done a great job monitoring our time, and admitted to always having his watch set for one hour ahead of the actual time so he was never late for a meeting. This meant the ride back lacked urgency. He only cheated in traffic a few times, taking shoulders to cut in line, the idiot you cursed and hoped you didn't accidentally kill as you obeyed the law. Instead of giving him a hard time, my lips rested at the back of his neck. His hair tickled my nose, but I breathed him in for as long as I could to memorize his cologne, the feel of his skin and body beneath my hands, to prolong this high. My arms around him held more like a hug than from necessity the closer to the causeway we traveled. To make me laugh once more, he lit the bike up through the roundabout. I cheered with no question of his competence on the steel horse.

Back on the island, the sun hung low to the west. The ocean peeked between structures. Silhouettes of bodies shadowed along the water. I envied their ability to go all night in whatever direction the breeze took them. I'd miss this breeze in ways unmatched. I was now a huge fan of a motorcycle and this mystery man.

He jumped the curb to park onto the same sidewalk we'd started at. The engine cut. We sat still for even longer than we had at the fort. A lump formed in my throat as I released my grip. We got off the bike easier than the first time.

While walking together across the park toward the condos, he scanned our surroundings on automatic patrol. I tensed. This entire facade of safety seemed more like a dream, along with our time together. Every step closer to Sara's was one step further away from his protection. *How could I be a bitch when the fallout might be disastrous?* I couldn't help worrying.

The hallway was hollow and devoid of anyone else when we got to Sara's door. I prayed she wouldn't answer before I knocked. When I leaned against the wall, he placed a hand upon the brick beside my face and studied me with the deepest expression he'd had all day, dark, tired, longing.

"Thank you for today," I offered.

"Thank you for taking a chance on a stranger," he quipped to stoke that mystery and snap me from my sorrow.

"You're a cold man, sir."

"You're a hot woman, love."

"Things could become warm between the two of us, yeah?" I gave a soft smile at my cheesy joke, then froze when he bent his face to mine. My eyes fluttered shut as the heat of his breath steamed the windows of my mind. The feather-light graze of his lips was the epitome of self-discipline. He was in control, period. *Ooh lala!*

"I'd love to do this again sometime, Kinsley." His lips brushed mine through his speech.

"The date or the kiss?" My voice trembled.

"Both." He ran his nose along the length of mine as though he sensed I might combust from stimulation.

"I'd like that," was all I choked. His mouth captured my response then spread into a small grin.

"You'll be the death of me, woman." He leaned back to study my face in a fuzzy memory game I wanted to play again soon. *Was I solid pink?* Not from embarrassment, but pure desire? "Make him pine. It's all about the grand gestures, be them what they may. Have a good night at work. Be a harsh, penis-envying, man-hating bitch."

Fear snatched my laugh and everything wonderful today had been. I wasn't sure why unease compounded by the minute. *Intuition?* "Even to Inferno?" I whispered. "I'm scared. I've never been an outright bitch to anyone who might harm me."

He stood to his full height, shoulders pulling back, chin lifting, eyes stormy. I longed to ask him to come into the bar just in case, but how realistic was that? I had to man-up.

"Especially to Inferno, Kinsley. Never become a willing victim. That's an order." One finger rose and his other hand rummaged a cargo pocket. "Should you get into a situation you're afraid you can't get out of, use this." He tucked something into my hand. "I will say no more on the matter, so don't ask. Use the card *only* in a real emergency, understand?" His everything was autocratic. I nodded. Without thinking, I wrapped my arms around his waist, my cheek pressed to his chest. His arms hung in surprise for a beat before he exhaled and reciprocated, even ran his nails over the cut-outs on my bare skin to soothe. I released a slow breath as the sensation worked against me.

"Just to be clear, this isn't coddling. I'm thanking you, sir."

His chuckle reverberated against my ear. I loved the sound. "That's great, because I'd rather you be ready to throttle a bloody miscreant, than have you going soft."

I *was* soft over how hard he urged me to be. I'd met no one like him. "Ditto." I forced a brave front and grinned up at him as I stepped away and tucked the card with my hands into my back pockets.

"Touché, my sweet."

Oh, the knowing irony in that endearment. I summoned every glimmer of restraint to keep from grabbing his face to force him to kiss me like there wouldn't be another chance.

"I mean what I say and say what I mean, Kinsley," he directed. "Emergencies only."

I sighed with an obedient nod. He knocked on the door, then lifted my hand to his lips for a deeper kiss than the one we'd shared. When he turned my hand to kiss my palm, my eyes closed against the electricity and a stray moan escaped my lips. He hummed. "That's what I like to hear."

"Hey!" Sara gushed, interrupting any retort I may have thrown to dispel my obvious weakness. "We need to hurry girl. You're gonna be late. Did y'all have fun?"

"We did," we said in unison. I blushed, he laughed, and we parted. But he looked back with a brilliant smile and fanned his fingers over his shoulder to mock me.

When Sara shut the door, my knees buckled as I melted against the wood. "Oh, Sara!" I sighed like the biggest sap. "What's his name?"

She gaped at my pathetic softness. "You mean, you went out with him and didn't even know his name?" When I nodded, she beamed.

"I asked, but now he's made it a game of mystery."

"Then I'm not ruining the surprise. Now let's get ready and get out of here."

39 | ♀

When Sara dropped me at the curb, I felt odd going inside the bar by the front door while in uniform. "Looks like a gold strike," she joked and kissed my cheek with a wish for a fantastic, but safe, night. "Gonna miss these shifts. If things ease up, I'll be back."

"I'd love that." Because the peace would have been restored in Oz again. "You sure this isn't too much?" I asked her with one last check of my makeup in the passenger side vanity mirror. "Looks like I'm being dropped off by my pimp."

She giggled as I smoothed a finger over the silver glitter glazed across my blackened eyelids.

"You'd make me rich. Ignore the assholes and keep an eye out for the ones I warned you about earlier. Gotta go," she called through the window as I shut the door behind me. "Quit tugging on that top. Stand up straight, shoulders back, ass out. Pretend you're me if that makes your character easier."

Yeesh, that was the last thing I wanted to do. This whole appearance package took a huge step in the wrong direction. I realized way too late that I looked more like her than myself. Add to that, I needed to make a name tag as soon as possible to cover the embroidery of her name over my breast, and I'd become the volunteer bait.

Before I could ask for a picture of Patrick, she waved and drove away with a single beep. Her taillights melted into the mix of traffic. I looked down at the bows beneath my knees where my wedges laced. She'd applied concealer to a couple places I'd had to pick bug guts from my legs after the motorcycle. We'd both marveled how I'd felt no pain due to Moonlight's Novocain presence.

The wedges were usually tame, but in this combo, they were less beachy cute and more ho-bag fabulous. The Spanx, otherwise known as the booty shorts I wore, climbed the crack of my butt, but I did what she told me as best I could instead of digging them out. At Gus's signature whistle, I turned and let him hustle me past the line that folded around the side of the building.

Reminding myself that those who worked on the beach had worse chaos than I did, I owned my slutty appearance and tried to ignore the insecurity and built-in conviction as I passed throngs to get to the bar. My daddy wouldn't only kill me if he saw me like this, he'd cry. Hopefully, he and my mom would be well asleep by the time I got home.

Bayleigh was an even darker character than my own, her top cropped to little more than a glorified sports bra with her height, skin and strips of fabric, eye makeup so heavy her lids hung low and sexy.

Chad's head bobbed on-stage under the black lights as he mixed popular tracks for Spring Break's hedonistic horde. He preferred downtown's hype or the larger beach clubs and bars, but our unique crowd got his name out to those who didn't yet frequent his hot spots. The other deejay who did our gig was the same way, but Chad was *my* favorite, and he always knew how to get me into my job. For now, the mood was light and fun, not slutty and dirty. A welcome relief, and I aimed for the bar while dancing to Alexandra Stan's *Lemonade*.

"Damn! I thought Sara changed her mind about coming in," Marcus remarked when I clocked-in.

"Well, don't be excited I'm here playing by your awful rules." I grinned while I set about my personal preparations before I could get to work. Even if he teased, I was relieved in his presence. "I need to make a name tag. Is the labeler in your office?" I asked and pedaled through counting bills.

"Why do you need a name tag when I had your name stitched into the shirts? That was the point." He tilted his head then narrowed his eyes in confusion as he read the cursive. "She's quitting without even calling and using you to get word to me? She is nervous," he muttered. Alarm skittered up my spine. He saw the fear on my face.

"She told me what happened. I'm sorry I didn't take you seriously."

He waved me off. "Relax, Little Red. I've got eyes on the situation. I'm excited to see you've taken a walk on the wild side. I'll have to dig out the labeler if we even still have it. Maybe throw your hair over her name for now?"

"Good idea." I did as he said. He gestured to my appearance and clapped his hands together, pretending to thank the heavens while I laughed and waved a finger. "The Lord knows better, mister."

He crossed himself like a Catholic and took his perch to supervise from the hallway. He looked mighty happy tonight. Some of my trepidation dissolved, though I still needed to speak to him in depth about Sara's conversation.

My time with Sara hadn't been all heavy.

After the date with Moonlight, we'd had a more fun girl talk. She picked my brain about where he took me and whether he'd made a move. Even when she mentioned Jase, somehow his name didn't weigh like a burden. I found that as I wended through rounds and tables, I searched for him, nervous the quarterback might toss the ball to the ground and walk off the field altogether. While I wasn't sure what I wanted from either of these men, I did know I'd never want Jase walking out of my life. I'd told her as such but feared his reaction.

"If you pissed him off, big deal," Sara had told me. "You had a fun time today. You don't have a boyfriend and Jase didn't ask you out before Bayleigh showed up. He intruded on your plans. *You* get to be pissed at *him* as well. Presumptive of him to expect you to be at his disposal like one of his booty call groupies."

I'd chewed my lip. "You're right, but I still hate upsetting him."

"Please tell me you won't allow your guilt to cause you to give into him." She'd stopped and waited. Ugh! How little faith my girlfriends seemed to have in my ability to keep my goals intact, spiritual included! Felt like everyone eagerly awaited any opportunity to point fingers and shout, 'See! I told you! It was always a crock!'

"My ice cream ain't free, Sara. I will not start a giveaway because some singer I've crushed on since ninth grade decides I might be his current craving."

"Well, how much are you gonna charge him for a sample?" We'd both smiled as I'd followed her into the bedroom where she kept the uniforms. I couldn't tell where her roommates' things ended, and Sara's began. The place blended with exotic colors and scarves hanging over lamps, incense burners with ash in trays. The bathroom overflowed with makeup littering the long counter. She'd placed the regular uniforms on the only spare area—on top of the toilet. "Here's the one you wear tonight. The others are here. Change, then we'll do your face and hair." She'd held a plastic bag. "Pass your clothes and I'll put them in here."

"I think you're crazy for even taking me to work."

What if something happened to us because I was stupid enough to wrap us in a targeted package? I should have asked Moonlight to drive me home on his bike. Why hadn't he said anything about that or offered after his bossy protective speech?

"I thought you wanted to avoid the bar." I'd held up shorts small enough for a kid. "Mine are bigger than this."

"I know. Tonight, wearing them will help keep Marcus off my case by you dressing how he wants us to without extra hassle. I know you swapped your extra small sets for shorts you bought at a department store. Who do you think kept Marcus off *your* back about them? Please? Besides, you'll force Jase to prove himself after how I'll fix you up."

"What if he doesn't show?"

"He'll show. If he's half the man I know him to be, he'll come out of hiding and throw down the price you demand. Your trick is to keep the currency steep under his influence, you hear me?" She'd looked more maternal than I'd ever seen her before. Sara's cost for my ice cream was extortionate. Her method of advertisement was to place the product in everyone's faces so they would line up for a taste. No way was this my style—this was dirty.

At the end of the night, I preferred being the girl that stuck out as the one that wasn't willing to leave with someone. Lower key, pretty in my skin, and if a man didn't notice me, he wasn't the type I wanted to notice, simple as that. If I lingered in the mind, I won in the grand scheme. I loved winning. Let the men have their fun with their snacks, eventually appetizers wouldn't fill them.

Sara trashed all my rules by making me look like I should be doing tricks on a pole. Somehow the dichotomy was the elixir she prescribed the moment Jase walked into the bar. He and Rustin searched for me as they gave handshakes and guy hugs. Heads turned to gesture toward my whereabouts while I pretended to be too busy to notice. *Were they mad?* They didn't seem too upset. Then again, I had no way of knowing from a distance. *How the hell did I play this? At least I had bodyguards just in case.*

Bayleigh and I danced in tandem routines while she relayed information as she studied the guys for me to disguise my interest. "Two sluts. One wearing a bikini top with a leather skirt and red lipstick. Came to play. Wants Jase, but will settle for Rustin or Dan. I say you go over there and give her and the prostitute she hired the sweetie treatment. Flaunt your assets."

"Bayleigh, there's no way I can flaunt them anymore than I am!"

I awarded the gentleman across from me with a gorgeous grin on purpose and tucked his shy response and tip into my apron.

"Yeah right. You're still free-balling. She can't compete with that."

"Bayleigh, she is free-balling too if she's wearing a bikini top, hello. Sara is a double D. It was either I free-ball or stuff two cups worth of toilet paper into one of her bras. May as well go *au naturel*."

She tossed her head on a laugh, and said, "Anyway, that's not what I meant." She worked her body to the beat and blew an air kiss at Chad when he started her favorite Cuban song in a remix of something else I'd never heard. I passed him a sweet smile. He rolled his fedora down his arm like a showoff. He used the hat to fan his face while mouthing a 'damn girl' at my appearance. When I giggled, he cast a pointed glance in Jase's direction. I shook my head in disapproval at his wicked intent.

"Kins, I'm talking about that passive-aggressive angel-in-disguise thing you have. Drives guys mad but pisses off hookers even more."

"Bayleigh, what would I do without you to teach me how to be a jerk?"

"Ha! The natural talent is all yours. I'm here to teach you how to use the gift to your advantage." She booty bumped my hip and forced me out to their table with a tray packing four tables worth of drinks. Time to rip the bandage.

"Plenty of breasts and thighs on tonight's dinner buffet, eh, gentlemen?" I weaseled in between the group of men crowding Jase's table after delivering the others. Rustin grinned in genuine surprise. His arm wrapped around my shoulders as if we were together. At the faked smile on the girls' faces, I obeyed Bayleigh's advice and looked them in the eye the same way I did the guys, referred to each male by name to sharpen the clear edge their blunt jealousy hated. "Rustin?" I asked when I arrived at his turn.

"Yeah, I'm hungry. Looks like spicy is on the menu. But I'm in the mood for legs tonight," Rustin told me. "Yours are f—"

My empty hand shot to cover his mouth. "Nuh, uh, uh. Easy on that language, sir." I grinned in that charming way that Bayleigh said made a man putty in my unknowing hands. Genuine, girl next door, 'have no idea what you mean by that, mister' kinda smile. "Have to be sensitive around virgin ears." Ugh. I loathed when girls said this crap.

Jase's eyes snapped at the word like I'd cracked a whip. From across the table, he seemed uncertain that I wasn't a virgin. *Cheers to Bayleigh.*

His tongue glossed his lips while he lifted a girl's hand from over his and took aim. "It would be an honor to help you out with that, baby." His friends hooted and exchanged fist bumps. His air breezed light enough to prove he was also playing mind games. He didn't seem mad, but *was* he beneath there?

"Right …." I turned with a fan of fingers over my shoulder and an innocent smile to disarm him. "Be back with that order!"

"Better be …." Rustin abruptly snatched my wrist and captured my waist to stabilize me in my wedges. We pressed too close, his hand not releasing mine. "Nix the Bud. Make it a Slow Screw," he drawled. My mouth dried. I swallowed. *What did he say about moving in on turf earlier?*

"I've never made that before." I didn't fake my innocent ignorance.

"If you want, I'll teach you," Rustin slathered.

"No thanks, I'll ask Bayleigh," I breathed and tried to pull away.

"Even better."

When I pressed against his chest, he released me and enjoyed the guys applauding his audacity. *Holy crap!*

"Bayleigh, I don't think your ploy is my friend," I told her as I crossed behind the bar and asked how to make a slow screw.

She cracked up. "Sloe as in Sloe Gin, vodka, and orange juice." I watched her instruct her trainer. Sigh. "There." She beamed. "As for his crap, hit him where it hurts." She leaned into my ear and told me how to exact vengeance with another type of naughty mixed drink, but did I want to play these stupid boy-girl love games?

While I distracted myself with other patrons, wormed through gaps crowds left between cliques, I lost myself in the music Chad played as if knowing I needed the fun. He had a good view from there. Could he see my struggle when the throngs were this rambunctious?

Guys turned with their drinks to dance in ways that begged me to join. I smiled and kept at my routine while longing to salsa with the Latin locals working their partners in an impromptu competition. Men outnumbered women as the floor swelled, tables cramped, and the doors allowed the mean, lean, and spiffy clean to join the mayhem. Some had that starched Mafia vibe going. Gold teeth and gold chains here and there. Smooth in how they surveyed their surroundings. Interesting. Reminded me of how Moonlight looked around when he walked me to Sara's. He had the same mean confidence.

I glanced at Marcus. No conversations with a disguised Moonlight, but I wondered if the bouncers had a motive for the crowd they pulled the rope for. *How long had junk in the bar been under my nose while I enjoyed my blind world? Maybe I watched too much crime TV?*

Just before I reached Jase's table with drinks, Looney Lucy caught and spun me in a huge hug. I applied dance skill to keep the tray balanced! She introduced her less than pleased friends while I tried to brush her off without being an annoyed jerk.

"Y'all belly up to the bar and order a round on me, okay?" I told them over the music.

"Belly up to the bar? Who says that?" I overheard one of her hipster friends ask another. They exchanged amused disdain before staring at my uniform the same. Sad. Poor girls didn't even realize how out of place they appeared. And Lucy never registered there was anyone else in the world who didn't feel about me the way she did.

"Hey, baby! Sorry to interrupt." Jase placed a hand to my waist and extended his other to Lucy. "Hi, I'm Jase." She and her group choked on awed laughter and greetings. Lucy grabbed his hand with way too much excitement.

"Hi! I'm Lucy. I'm Kinsley's exclusive track manager and basically like her personal assistant between heats," she gushed while I fought a gape at the title she'd created for herself. *How many other introductions had she made with that description?*

"Glad to meet you." He gave a tight but kind smile and waited for Lucy's group to disperse into the rest of the crowd, then cast a very warm grin down at me. "Was about to go in after you. Didn't want anyone to step on you."

Then quit trying to walk all over me!

"I bet it's the other way around in this, though." *Damn straight.* Jase's eyes hooded with lust.

"You look … uh …." Without finishing, he cleared his throat and took drinks from the tray, passed them out to a cluster that doubled with groupies. Obvious to see the bouncers let the women in by their lack of clothing. I'd bet Lucy and her snobby friends had used my name to get in. My jaw clenched with ire at the drinks they enjoyed without knowing me.

"Yoohoo …." Jase snapped twice, clearing my thoughts.

"My, my, Kinsley. Who says you need practice to be perfect when you nailed it your first time?" Rustin interrupted and took my wrist to kiss the soft flesh.

I tried to smack his cheek. Jase captured my hand mid-motion and said, "all right. Gauntlet thrown, asshole!" He was laughing one instant, then grabbing my hips to pull me against the metal button on his jeans that felt full. When he nuzzled his nose against mine, I tilted my chin to study his eyes for hints of jealousy. "Show them, baby. Show them they have no chance." His vodka breath burned too hot and close to my lips, the way Moonlight's had only hours ago.

Could I show them? Was that even fair? The jury in my courtroom said no, but Jase stole the judge's gavel and overrode the verdict like he was ready to throw me into a cell. His mouth swept fervid and dewy for the briefest of seconds, then parted on my inner war, sentencing me to the prison of my criminal thoughts. As my eyes shut, visions played of these people vanishing. His arm swinging out to knock away the bottles and fruity cocktails, my back meeting with the lacquered surface of the table. Rustin looking on with jealousy. Moonlight pulling up just long enough to emit a triumphant laugh and declare victory to both of their faces.

Record skip!

I ripped away. My fumbled, "Not while I'm on the clock," almost came out wrong.

When I scurried around the bar, Marcus grunted and told the bitch server to take my tables for a while. Heat licked up my cheeks. He didn't seem happy with me.

That made two of us.

40

Marcus raised his eyebrows. "Don't look at me that way, Kinsley."

"Marcus, can we drop it?" I begged. "What did you expect with the role you want us to play in these trashy uniforms? If you don't want him all over me, where's your guy? Otherwise, the only problem is my own." I fired off like the bitch Moonlight demanded. Misplaced target, but I wasn't up to taking heat for a situation I hadn't yet navigated.

"Fine," he grumbled, "but you're off his table for the rest of your shift." There was no use arguing. My body needed a time-out. I accepted that this might be God's way of granting that. "Don't be mad, Little Red. I'm watching out for you. I'm not playing favorites. Taylor's cool, but I want to be sure you aren't compromising yourself."

Bayleigh cast a side glance with thin lips and shoved a loaded tray with instructions on table numbers. She wasn't certain whether to tell Marcus to bite a butt cheek, or to agree. Neither was I.

After scrutinizing Marcus's sincerity, I found him legit and granted a soft smile. "Thank you. I understand. Mind if I catch you on my break?" I asked.

"Sounds good, baby girl. You're doing great. Keep going."

"Yes, sir." We shared a smile. He stepped aside as I hoisted the tray and hit the back section.

Over the next two hours, Jase's attention rarely wavered even as he goofed with his friends and danced with a few women like he sensed I might be put off by his hot pursuit. Jealousy and relief created an odd mixture. When two men in Inferno vests took stools at a vacated table in my vicinity, those emotions took a hike as fear took root. I didn't think I'd have to say a word to Marcus, but I found him too busy helping Bayleigh and Garrett fill orders and trays as fast as myself and three other servers could deliver them.

I crept into Marcus's hallway alcove to search for bouncers. Jarrell held the side door as the other two hauled brawlers outside. Gus was out front. Well, hell. That meant I had no choice but to go in.

The things Sara said haunted me. My limbs weighted with dread as I struggled to be the woman Moonlight commanded. One certainty after this long on the job, the smell of fear reeked akin to chum in shark infested waters. I played at chill and set down two cocktail napkins while I held my empty tray at my side. Up close, I recognized the one who had made my skin crawl last night.

Oh, Moonlight, where are you?

41

Kinsley set a tempest of complication into motion. Her fear compelled me to immediate action. I'd given Marcus my word. She'd told me face-to-face that she was afraid. Time to follow through.

Sara Scott's abusive husband was a recent prospect for the Infernos which made her situation impossible to find safety unless she became one of the gang's ol' ladies. She couldn't hide forever. Such was the nature of the business. Patrick Scott's abundant resources stacked against her lack of such. Between honorable public servants and the dishonorable, they shared a commonality: firefighters took care of their own. Though they rivaled with the police, they kept their ears to the ground for anything damning.

My source, a firefighter on the right side of the law, shared that this went far deeper than a custody issue.

Patrick Scott needed to pay bills. He had dangerous debts with ruthless collectors.

If his debt belonged to Nightshade, he'd have died weeks ago, which meant he was being hunted. If I didn't get rid of him before this *hunter,* Sara wouldn't live much longer. Neither would her son. The whole family would suffer for the sins of the father.

My suspicions of Kinsley's role in Patrick's game were confirmed, the sheet of proof crushed in my fist the way I'd love to crush his skull. No way I would sit on my hands and let him exchange Kinsley Hayes for a debt he wasn't willing to put his battered wife up for.

While Kinsley and I had played at Fort Foster, a few miles south, my lieutenant, Eric, used a drone to get the lay of Patrick's preferred Inferno biker bar. The building sat as empty now as when we'd driven past earlier. If she'd noticed Eric following us at any point, Kinsley hadn't given a hint. He'd turned off while we'd cruised further up the road.

We now sat in Eric's Jeep studying the footage on his tablet, preparing to fire the first shots in a war that shouldn't be. My men protected their servers. Since their leader displayed an obvious softness for one last night, they seethed rabid with desire to defend what I honored. Time to remind the underground who controlled them. Nightshade wanted the order.

Eric held a stylus and the tablet between us. "From what I can tell, Patrick is the bitch in charge of babysitting their playground while he earns their trust. The Infernos have a scheduled ride up to Daytona for trades of the human trafficking variety with some truckers along the I-4 corridor. Word is, they're making a detour. Patrick informed them that his 'payment' would be delivered to Tallahassee tomorrow, specifically to the athletic department at Florida State University."

He grabbed the paper I'd crumpled and unfolded the schedule. With a pen, he circled a time code, then used his stylus to open a window on his tablet and circled the scheduled time for relay races.

My hand scrubbed my mouth. "I'm gonna kill him, Eric. Really, really kill him. Bad. *Really* bad."

"I know."

"Do you? *Really?*" I demanded, balled my fists. "Because right now I don't have a weapon or Patrick Scott's neck between my hands. My palms are restless with the need to rid Kinsley of this problem."

"Do your breathing exercises to conserve your energy. You taught me it does no good to lose your head, because that's when mistakes are made. I'm willing to bet you don't want anything less than perfection on this one."

"I know. I know. You're right, Eric. Let's see what you've got."
I ran my sweating palms against my shorts, then bounced my knee.

He noticed and arched an eyebrow at my body language.

"Eric, come on. Ignore my shit."

He nodded. "Sorry, boss. I've never seen you fidget." His gaze diverted back to the tablet. "Inferno finished a business meeting yesterday. The bar should be empty while they're on the lam. There's a swamp area over here." He drew on the tablet. "Shouldn't be hard to draw the alligators into a feeding frenzy." He spread his fingers over the screen to zoom in. I thought of Kinsley searching the water for gators like a protective mum over those kids. "See these two trees? A rope will suspend right over the water. We can cut the hemp once the deed is done and burn the remnants. I've opted for natural fiber in case any are left behind they'll be native to the environment, not to mention, it's weaker than synthetic. Easier breakaway for gator prey."

"Perfect. Did you rhyme on purpose?"

"Aye said the fly. Thought you'd like that."

I rolled my eyes at this idiot.

"Relax, Klive. We've got this. The punishment will fit the crime and the message will send clear to all the right entities. Now, if we park out here, we can hike in through—"

My phone rang. I lifted the display. "It's Marcus."

We shared a knowing look and buckled up. "Go time." As he backed us out of the area, I pulled my phone to my ear. Marcus spit curses about how to intervene with Inferno without repercussions.

"Don't intervene. I'm on my way."

"*Don't* intervene?!" he asked. "For how long? How far away are you? Did you put anyone else on her? What the hell?!"

"I have Joey on her. I'm ordering him to stand down. I need you to do the same. *No one intervenes*, do you understand me?"

Marcus sputtered fractions of words as he couldn't make sense of my order. Eric looked to me like I'd lost my mind.

Where Kinsley Hayes was concerned, perhaps I had.

I ended the call with Marcus to call Joey with the order. The call lasted less than five seconds.

"Klive …." Eric's voice was nervous. "There are other ways to be a hero."

"Eric, do you know what Joey said when I told him to stand down?" I asked, my chin lifted. He remained silent. "He didn't question my reasoning or demand an explanation, he simply said *yes, sir*. As he should. Tread with caution, Eric. I'm no hero. This is a chance for someone else to prove how villainous he might be. Trust me. I have everything under control. Drive faster."

"Yes, sir." He floored the accelerator.

Inferno stared while I feigned pleasantry. "Good evening, gentlemen. What'll it be?" I asked. "Just a minute." I held a finger up to a table that wasn't signaling. I refocused like I was busy as hell because I was.

"You guys have pub grub on the menu tonight?" One Inferno with a voice box full of gravel asked while the other's eyes roamed without the rebuke of scary eyes to keep him in check. My body wound tight as I wondered if this might be Patrick in the flesh. Without a doubt, I'd seen both of them before.

"Pub grub is Sundays only. I'm sorry."

"That's a shame, eh, Patrick?" The guy with the voice confirmed my nauseous suspicion. No way the fear wasn't eating into my calm. "I was in the mood for some legs and thighs myself."

Effin Marcus better be seeing the negative fruit of these uniforms right now!

After placing his eyes on a fast, Patrick smiled with a kindness that didn't seem forced just like the times he had flirted with me before I knew his name.

"Yeah, this place has the best legs in town." He glanced at my overexposed thighs for a beat as if his innuendo needed spelling out. The sinister intention running beneath that friendly exterior impossible to miss. When he ordered a beer for each of them, also a Rusty Nail for his friend, I turned too eager to get out of there. Not like I wasn't quick on my toes throughout my shifts, but I'd poured blood in the water.

When I beelined for the bar instead of going to the table beyond them, I'd given myself away and was screwed. Marcus sounded ready to kick an ass as he spat curses into his phone from the hallway.

Should I keep walking and haul to my car to get out of here?

"Hey, you okay? You want me to take their drinks?" Bayleigh growled ready to run damage control the way tall girls were free to do. She threatened jerks on the regular. They acquiesced or surrendered, while I got looks like I was an adorable bitch.

How did Moonlight think this would work out?

"No, it will only make things worse. I've chummed the water, though. Make me a Rusty Nail, please?" I reached into the ice for their brews. Then I remembered the card. I'd only peeked once, then hidden the square away. Matte black with nothing more than a cloud of smoke. No lettering. Blank. Soft touch. How that secured my safety or how he would know when the offering transferred hands was anyone's guess, but knowing I had his mystery threat in case of emergency, I shook off my fear and squared my shoulders, their bottles in one hand, Rusty Nail in the other. No tray.

Think feminist bitch, Kins.

I set the drinks on the table and switched for my bottle key. *Holy shit! The card wasn't in my back pocket. No! Where did it go?*

"How come you never called me?" Rusty Nail asked with an intense focus on my face. "You know, the twenty with the writing?" The key in my fingers shook as I held only to the bottle and no secret weapon. *What? That didn't make sense if the other guy was 'Pat'….*

"Had bills to pay," I told him.

"I can relate. Gotta do what you gotta do to keep the collectors away. Here," Patrick said. His fingerless riding gloves grabbed my hands to do the motion for me. I wasn't sure how to be mean when I was paralyzed. "Bet your tips are great tonight. Sexy uniform."

Oh, God, please!

With the way I leaned over the table and how he held my hands, my hair might have fallen forward and exposed Sara's name!

"You seen Sara?" he asked like he heard my thoughts. "She's supposed to be on duty. You look like her with your makeup done like that. Never seen you do yours that way before."

"I've never seen you on a Spring Break weekend before, either." I swallowed. "I haven't seen her," I managed. "She called in sick."

"Your hands are sweaty." He lifted my hands from his beer and moved them over to the other guy's. His thumb ran hard against my palm before fitting my key over the cap.

"Your hair looks almost wind-blown," Rusty Nail said. "Like you've been on a motorcycle after all."

"You might be coming down with something, too, yeah, Kinsley?" Patrick asked. "A little sweaty and green around the gills."

I hated that he knew my name!

"Need help, baby?" Jase's baritone sounded at my back. I ripped my hands from Patrick's. Jase jerked the beer from Patrick and popped the cap with his thumb, slammed glass against wood in a clear threat.

Just like that, I'd made the mess I'd feared the most.

"She's doing her job just the way I like." Rusty Nail sneered like Jase was stupid for interrupting. I risked a glance at him and startled when Rustin walked to the other side of their table. He leaned in between the men like all was fine.

"She's done doing her job for you," Jase told them and took my hand, guiding me behind his back. My worried eyes traveled up to the stage and met Chad's stare. He wasn't concentrating on music anymore. Several starched men on the dance floor held their partners, but watched the scene, paying little attention to my role.

"Young lady, please come with me."

The Nightshade member who'd bragged about his ring placed his hand to my back as he moved me away from the table. *What the hell?* I looked at Jase, but Jase wasn't looking at me. He was ready to do damage. *Pas bien! Not good!* These bikers differed from a drunk with naughty hands!

"Is everything all right?" I cried when we walked past Marcus and down into the hallway toward the back door. Marcus didn't remove me from this man's company. Bayleigh stood rooted behind the bar biting her lip. Garrett looked on and served drinks. I freaked.

"Oh, shit!"

"Relax for me. I will not hurt you, and I will make sure they don't either. Think of me as a guardian angel of sorts." He smiled at me in deceptive cordiality, like a stockbroker or banker here to chill but acting as a good Samaritan.

I yelped and lurched back against him when the rear employee door ripped open just before we reached the handle. The gray-eyed man stormed inside, nearly plowing over us, his aura much darker and somehow scarier than Jase's.

"Kinsley, you all right, love?" he demanded. His anger breathed like something I might've touched in the air around us as he grabbed my shoulders to steady me. I nodded and chewed my lip to hell. His eyes softened. The guardian backed away. Moonlight took my hand and walked me to the mouth of the hallway once more. I leaned into his body's support like he would make this all disappear if I hid there. Damn, I wished he had a coat to tuck me in at this moment.

"Kinsley, show me who was fucking with you." But I didn't need to. He stared straight at them. When the bikers saw him, the threats fell from their faces. Their pallor paled and shifted to panic.

"Them," I squeaked. He looked down at me and his expression softened.

"Do not fear me. I'm not angry at you. I'm sorry if I scared you back there. Did you use the card?"

"No." I couldn't tell him I didn't know where I'd put his gift. "I'm sorry." My voice broke, but I pressed on. "It's Patrick. He was asking me about Sara. The guy who orders Rusty Nails asked why I didn't call him and said I looked like I'd been on a motorcycle today! Patrick told me I looked like Sara tonight and that I might be coming down with the same illness she was! I'm sorry! I tried to follow your instructions but froze! I started shaking! I couldn't open his beer. He used my hands to force me to pull the caps from their bottles!"

Moonlight nodded while I fought against tremors.

"Shhh, everything is okay." He tucked me close, my face hidden for a moment. I felt him moving like making silent orders with his hand. "Look at me, love."

I forced my face from the cologne and shirt I wanted to ball up in to cry this out. His eyes were serious, the same firm they'd been when we'd been in the elevator.

"Yes?" I whispered, guilty for things that made no sense.

"I want you to do me a favor. Can you do that?" he asked as if I were a child. I felt as doe-eyed and fearful while I peered into his reassuring, but scary, face. I nodded. He put a hand to my cheek like he needed me to focus hard. The warmth of his palm helped, the metal of a ring cool by comparison. "Do you trust me?"

"Yes," I breathed, my chest heaved. I trusted him.

"You came back."

"I did. I'm here." His stormy eyes traveled between my teary irises. I silently begged him to make this go away the way my daddy always had with monsters under my bed. He told his friend, "Get her out of here."

"Yes, boss."

"Kinsley?" Moonlight sought my focus, funny since I couldn't recall the last time I'd focused on anyone's eyes the way I was on his now.

"Mmhmm?" I asked in a hum with the shiver of a camper caught in a snowstorm desperate for warmth.

"I want you to let your boyfriend take you to his house," he whispered. "Marcus will clock you out. Eric will escort you outside."

"Mmhmm." I couldn't speak.

"Good girl." He whistled through his fingers, and Jase and Rustin rose. The one I'd been walking with came and took me again.

Dear God, what had Sara mixed me up in?

43 | ♀

My feet shuffled with the man's strides, the rest of me was along for the ride. "Eric?" I asked.

"Yes, Kinsley. That's me. Pleased to officially meet you, sorry for the circumstances." We walked out into a night strikingly calm when compared to the craziness inside. I continued trembling despite the humidity and heat.

"I'm sorry. I seem to be overreacting, but I can't stop shaking. This probably looks pathetic," I said.

"You have nothing to apologize for. Trust your gut," Eric said. That almost made the trembling worse.

Jase's truck parked to the right, my car further down, but Eric steered us left with his fingers at my wrist to count my pulse.

"But—"

"It's mine, Kinsley. Let's go," Rustin ordered. He jogged ahead to pull the door open on a red Dodge truck with KC lights and mud tires. Eric lifted me under my arms like I was a child instead of allowing me the option of getting into the truck on my own.

"Right here," he instructed me to look at his phone's flashlight. He gave a grunt of approval and shut the door at once. I caught a mask of anger as soon as he turned away to give Rustin muffled instructions. He had that same shift I'd seen in Moonlight.

Rustin's tires spit gravel as he wasted no time backing the truck out. We fishtailed onto pavement seconds later, then gained speed through an area riddled with idiot tourists.

"What about—"

"Quiet. Don't speak right now."

I nodded. The tears at last spilled over. Didn't matter if I'd been trying to keep my composure or whether he seemed mad at me. He checked the rearview mirror several times as we flew through local areas at a rate that broke the law.

"Screw it," he said. A camouflaged light strip strobed to life, a siren sounding. Cars cleared and pulled over, creating space for us through intersections. When he reached the interstate, he turned the strip and siren off and put the pedal down. "Yes, I'm a cop. Yes, what happened back there is bad. Yes, Jase is staying since those douche bags know his vehicle. He doesn't want a tail. No, I do not care to comment on Inferno, Nightshade, or anything else. Let me focus."

"Yes, sir," I whispered. Opting to stare at my hands worrying on top of my clenched thighs, tears rained down my cheeks and made dark splats on my fists.

Rustin sighed as he changed lanes. His hand reached for one of mine. I gripped his fingers. "Kins, I'm not mad at you. I'm in action mode, that's all. We all were. I'm sorry men can be pricks."

"Not your fault," I mumbled.

"I'm not talking about the guys who crossed the lines. With them, that's expected. I was apologizing about those of us who came to your defense. You have a lot of people looking out for you." He sighed in reluctance. "You're something special, Kinsley." He squeezed my hand, and this might be the only time I'd let him touch my thighs without feeling like he wanted to keep crawling in between them.

He drove two exits past the one for the house I remembered Tyndall and Jase growing up in out in the country. The highway became dark and deserted. He exited but turned the headlights out as he did. After the U-turn beneath the overpass, he didn't wait long before he had the lights on once more to navigate the maze in the middle of the woods. Only someone who lived out here knew all the unmarked bends and curves, the different turns onto adjoining farm roads. Rustin admitted to taking several attempts to learn the route without Jase.

When we veered onto the hidden driveway that slithered like a snake through the dense forest of old oaks and wild palms, he turned the KC lights on to spot trouble.

"I'd be shocked if anyone found this place or was screwing around, but you can never be too careful," he said.

Drapes of moss hanging from trees cast dancing shadows that played tricks while we passed. When Jase's two-story family house came into view, the strain in my shoulders relaxed a fraction. How unbelievable that I should revisit under such tense circumstances for the first time in years. I wished Tyndall waited inside with a stack of movies and a bucket of nail polish like she did when my dad used to drop me off for sleepovers. Mike, their dad, always came out to visit with mine. Sometimes they'd drink a couple cold ones, then Daddy would kiss my forehead and tell me to have fun until we'd meet back up at church on Sunday morning.

Mike didn't come out. Tyndall wasn't here. My daddy would be ready to commit murder and make me quit my job. I wanted him bad but wanted to keep my mouth shut more.

Rustin opened the truck door and gave me a hand to help me hop out.

"Thank you."

"Of course," he offered.

Rustin's truck chirped as he armed the alarm and locked the doors. Cicadas filled the silence. Lightning bugs flashed in the trees beyond the clearing around the house. My heart clenched with an odd homesickness as we walked toward the familiar front door. Rustin reached down for my hand again. I let him. If he hit on me after all this, he was an even bigger jerk than I'd estimated. I hoped he would use this opportunity to redeem himself.

The keys thumbed through his free hand. He glanced up with an apology but stopped everything to wrap his arm around me, guiding my face against his shoulder.

"Dammit, Kinsley. I'm sorry I was insensitive." His tone softened, his leather jacket and cologne vaguely familiar. "Know what's hard?"

"Please tell me this isn't some awful innuendo," I whined.

A relieved laugh shoved out of his mouth. He took one of my hands, separated my index finger, told me to lick the tip. I gave him a deadpan glare. He pressed my fingertip to my tongue then brought my painted nail up between us to draw a line in the air. "One for you, Mizz Hayes." The humor drained as his face sobered to an authority I now associated as his cop look. That's the face of the guy who asks if you know why he pulled you over.

"What's hard, Kinsley, is holding back when someone naïve is scared. Assholes get off on the fear, but for those of us in charge of protecting and serving, our animal instinct is to do away with the threat as fast as possible rather than allowing due process to run a drawn-out course. The law gets frustrating when it's in the way of your instincts."

Naïve? I guess I was ... how pathetic and foolish.

He inserted the house key, pressed the door open a moment later. I scrubbed beneath my eyes to find my thumbs smudged black. Sometimes I hated makeup.

"I'm sorry if I got mascara on your jacket."

Both thumbs rose in display. He chuckled and gestured I go inside ahead of him.

"You're not the first woman to cry on this shoulder. You gonna be okay?" He closed the door behind us. His keys dropped into a dish on a console table in the foyer. I caught sight of my reflection in the mirror above the table and cringed.

"I think I want to shower and rest. Morning clarity will help discern how much of what happened grew from my panic and how much I need to flip out about. What a long day."

We went into the living area like I'd never left, only the space was cleaner than I remembered.

"His parents don't live here anymore. They live in the suburbs closer to town."

I nodded. He must have read my curiosity. I wanted Jase's mom, Bianca, to come out, dishtowel in hand, to give me a hug. The kitchen gleamed dim and spotless, one of her old dishtowels dangled off the stove handle.

"Too bad, might have been nice for his mom to whip up some hot chocolate like old times." I smiled over at him. He looked relieved to see normalcy in my person.

"I can make you some if you like. I'm sure we have some," he offered and strolled into the kitchen. The lights turned on. I told him I was teasing. "Okay, but if you change your mind, tell me. In the meantime, let's get you settled in for the night."

"I'll take Tyndall's old room, if that's okay?"

"No. Jase would want you to have his room." He came around the island to take my hand again. We walked down the hallway to the left of the foyer, toward Jase's parents' old room. I swallowed against the anxious intimacy of entering Jase's domain when the space was now his master bedroom.

Much different from the teenaged boy with posters of nude girls on bikes and bikinis with nip-slips on hoods of hot-rods. No body odor or dirty boxers lying on the floor. No Playboys or Penthouses cluttering the nightstands. No plaid sheet thumb-tacked over the window.

"Wow."

Clean, grown up, simple. Not a shred of bachelor pad geared for seduction in evidence.

"Yeah, he keeps a tight ship here at his house. Anyway, take his bed. The shower should have whatever you need since he's such a prima donna. You can find something in his dresser to sleep in. Make yourself at home and don't hesitate if you need anything."

When I looked up at him to ask if he was sure about this, he smiled and nodded. What a relief to see him relaxing into his country chill again!

"What about Jase? Is he coming home? Where's he going to sleep?" I bit my lip like a kid in trouble to stop all the questions he'd warned me not to ask. "I'm sorry."

His hand came to my chin to make me look up at him. "Hey, don't apologize. You're not in trouble. I meant what I said. I was in go-mode. We're safe here. *You're* safe here, okay?" I nodded and took a deep breath to force my body to believe his words. He continued. "Jase will be home in a few hours, and where do you think he's gonna sleep?" When I gasped in alarm, Rustin chuckled and drew an invisible tally. "Gotcha. That's two points I've got to your one, now, Mizz Hayes. Jase will take his old room. I'm in Tyndall's."

"Huh? How come you took hers instead of his?"

"Smells better."

I smiled at the floor. He ran his hands over my biceps trying to jostle the tension in my frame.

"Relax. Shower. Sleep. Everything will be all right in the morning. If you need something, I'm taking the couch until Jase comes home."

Rustin didn't give me the chance to respond or argue. As he left the room, I saw him reach back and lift his shirt to remove a gun from a holster on his belt. The door clicked behind him. I was alone with my thoughts and Jase's things.

44

I didn't feel like I had permission to touch anything. Everything Constance had surmised about Jase having Obsessive Compulsive Disorder matched with how the pillowcases and sheets of the bed were crisp and tucked with perfect corners. I checked off another box as I walked into his parents' en suite bathroom. *His* bathroom. The white quartz countertop gleamed empty like a hotel vanity, the mirror so clear, the only blemish came from one you brought on your face. I opened a drawer beneath the sink. Custom wood dividers separated his hygienic items.

Bianca's beauty products used to litter the vanity to the point of hogging Mike's sink, too. The only products I saw out in the open were the ones lining the shelf in the shower, and in there, was an organizer. A place for everything. Best of all, not a single feminine item in existence.

I recalled my folded uniform on the foot of my bed, *was that really this morning?* and knew Jase was responsible. His obsessive example became my format as I peeled this trashy uniform from my body, afraid to even shed them to the floor since they looked out of place like black sin against the pristine white tile. Instead, I disrobed and stacked the uniform on the floor beside the nightstand. My accessories and phone placed on top like they'd shatter if I didn't put them down with precision. I was stiff as hell and ready to shrink back into my skin, my clothes, my routine.

The shower pelted the negative emotions like the pressure could beat my nerves into a submissive relaxed state. Rather than wincing under the spray hitting my tender chest, I absorbed the pain left by the hot coffee mishap to distract my worried mind. Track would be the only thing to help me cope. Tomorrow's invitational, despite four driving hours upstate, gave me a thrill if only for the escape. Had I known this morning that my world would implode, I'd have planned to compensate and packed extra panties. How in the hell was I going to get out of here that early? The buses on campus would pull out of the lot. Coach would flip his crap if I wasn't on-board.

Jase's shower only had guy scented product, thank God. At least he had conditioner to match his shampoo.

My hair was a bloody mess after all that time on Moonlight's bike. Not to mention, Sara hosing me down in hairspray earlier. *How had the Rusty Nail guy known about the bike? Or maybe he didn't and was trying to get the same rise out of me he'd caused the last time? Why did he ask me about calling him when Pat was the name on the bill? Ugh! Stop thinking!*

I tilted my head back to rinse and tried to not to think of how scary intense Moonlight looked when asking who had been messing with me. There was a lot of protective anger there, almost possessive. He had a very commanding presence. I loved most that he'd been the same from the day we'd warred in the elevator, but *why would Inferno fear him? Why were members of Nightshade friends with him? Hadn't Eric called him boss? Then again, Jase calls a lot of men boss like I call them sir. And all the guys had been scary commanding, not just Moonlight, and they weren't Nightshade.*

I deserved none of their provision. *Why go to this much trouble? What happened after Eric and Rustin had whisked me off to safety? What was Moonlight going to do? How was Jase compliant to any of his orders when he copped an attitude with Marcus over stupid stuff sometimes?*

"Ugh!" My growl echoed off the large white tiles in the shower that matched the flooring and counter. *I didn't want to think anymore! Too much information stimulation!* I couldn't stand the idea of any of them being bad.

I scrubbed my face three times, got out, wrapped a thick towel around my body, another around my hair, and eyed the squeegee hanging on the shower door. If I didn't remove the water droplets from the crystal-clear glass shower frame, I'd be a disrespectful guest. This sucked but gave me something else to concentrate on. While I set about the chore, I made sure that even the soap didn't have residue beneath the bar, though soggy, wet and used. If my parents saw all this effort, they'd keel over in shock.

After I finished playing housekeeper—and fretting over how to jump these damp towels onto hooks that hung too high for a hobbit to reach—I did what Rustin told me to: I rifled through Jase's dresser in search of something to sleep in. Heat warmed my cheeks as I sifted through boxer briefs in his undie drawer, pushed aside unopened boxes of condoms, something rubbery, body oil. *Crap.* This was too intimate and embarrassing! *Had he used that oil on someone? The condoms? What was that thing? How did he make plans for sex, or did he never plan and fly by the zipper on his pants?*

I hurried through and settled for microfiber boxer briefs, then peeked into another drawer like every one of them would tell a secret I didn't want to know. An undeniable ache took root in my heart. Jase liked cheap fixes. I wasn't sure how to not feel cheap if he wanted me. What an awful thought.

To my relief, this drawer contained about a hundred impeccably folded shirts from places all over the Middle East, Asia, South America, emblazoned with tour titles, missions, insignia. Choosing something that seemed a special part that no one touched inside him felt wrong. Jase never wore these, or those hats with the flags and emblems, ribbons and such that hung on hooks over his bathroom door. Seemed the war was a private part of his life. The condoms were almost easier to handle.

I settled for an over-sized jersey in another drawer. Bleh. My father and my team would shun me if they caught me dead in Florida State gear, especially since that was the exact place we were heading in mere hours. If I didn't dominate, superstitious curses would adhere to this jersey forever. If I did, maybe I'd wear this with bragging rights. I snickered to myself.

This was better than searching through more drawers and stumbling upon more foreign objects, or even dirty movies or magazines. No way that pervert from high school didn't keep similar stimulation just because he didn't display his desires on his walls and night stands anymore.

I brushed my hair, eyed the bed and tried not to think of the women who may have slept in these sheets or on top of him. *Hadn't Constance said something about Jase not liking anyone at his house?* I prayed that when I peeled the heavy quilt back, I might be one of few who snuggled into his mattress and smelled the cologne on his pillows.

How crazy, I thought, and stared at the 'companion' pillow on Jase's bed. Technically, I'm on the companion pillow. Weird.

I turned out the lamp and rolled to my back. A long growl emitted from my stomach. Acid followed. Dammit. I wanted to tip toe out to the kitchen and grab a snack, but Rustin was sleeping on the couch, that gun at his side. No way in hell would I cause a disturbance that might make him reach for the trigger in a sleepy stupor. I wasn't familiar enough to know what type of sleeper he was. Too dangerous.

For distraction, I dipped down to snatch my phone and turn the display on for the first time since this morning. About a zillion texts buzzed like a restaurant pager. The device almost vibrated out of my hands with Bayleigh asking me many questions throughout the day, how things were going, whether I'd gone out with Jase or blown him off for Complicated Moonlight, if I was coming in to work still, if I was all right after what happened with those guys. Her last one read: *Moonlight is FLOORED! Scary! Bouncers grabbed them and followed him out the back. Jase went with. Where are you?*

She'd still be awake and working. I texted her where I was and begged her to pick me up at the butt crack of dawn.

My father had texted to ask if I was ready for my meet tomorrow, pumping me up with his cheerful support. *Oh, Daddy ….*

Coach sent two mass texts to the team about tomorrow's invitational and bus times.

Eliza texted to warn that Lucy and her little group were planning a trip to see me at work. Well, that would've been nice to see earlier.

Crap! Bayleigh texted: *I'd love to pick you up, but I'm babysitting my sister's kids overnight as soon as I'm done working.*

That meant I would have no choice but to ask my daddy to pick me up. Whatever. I manned up and texted him, admitting I was out at Jase's but hanging with several old friends, sleeping in Tyndall's old room, and needed a ride in the morn.

Daddy: *Why don't you have your car?*

Me: *Why are you still awake? Rode with friends in case of drinking.*

Daddy: *On a night before a meet? Okay, honey. I'll see you in the morning. Be a good girl!*

Sweet relief he didn't press on the lecture he'd deliver soon.

Me: *I promise, daddy. Love you.*

Jase's texts were next and a crap ton of annoying during that whole thing he'd done this morning. One-word-at-a-time offers to go workout on the beach after putt putt and lunch to get me in gear for my meet. *Aw! He'd paid attention to the sloppy calendar.* His texts ended with an angry emoji and a: *screw it, Kins, you wanna play that way? Forget our date!*

An apology came after. Nothing after that.

Anxiety and sadness stole my appetite. I programmed my alarm and set my phone on the nightstand. I fell asleep easier now that I wasn't thinking of myself as an eventual notch on this bed post.

45

I wasn't sure of the time when I roused from sleep, but the alarm hadn't sounded.

Something else had.

Rustling.

Someone in the room!

I gasped.

"It's okay, baby," Jase whispered. "It's me, shhh, shhh, shhh." He caressed my cheek. His silhouette took form as my eyes adjusted to the darkness.

"Jase?" *Where was I?* "What are you doing here?"

"It's me, yes. I'm sorry I spooked you, but I live here." *Live here?* His lips brushed my forehead. I smelled body wash. "I didn't mean to wake you. I needed a shower. Go back to sleep."

"No. Please, don't leave yet." I reached for the lamp and blinded myself into cognition. We sat blinking back spots for a moment. "Sorry," I stammered.

"No worries, Kins." He knelt by the bedside, a towel around his waist. Wet hair licked at his cheekbones. Stray water droplets glistened over his fresh skin. "You okay after everything?" His brown eyes held such genuine concern.

I nodded.

"You're really late."

"Yeah." He offered nothing more. I wanted to press but lacked the right. He wasn't my boyfriend. I wasn't his girlfriend. I would not make demands of the free bird, even if I slept in his bed.

"Are you still mad at me?" The patterns in the quilt became my focus instead of his face. "I'm sorry I upset you."

He sighed; the gentle concern fizzled into frustration. "You stood me up, *sweet* Kinsley Hayes." He stood up to drive the words home and walked from my side of the bed around to his dresser. I gasped when he dropped the towel. His naked bottom, pale next to the deep tan over the rest of his body, stood out and stared at me in chiseled glory. His skin appeared untainted elsewhere, but small scars marred a good part of his butt and upper thighs. To see anyone in this capacity was overwhelming but seeing a side of *Jase* I didn't know in such an intimate way ….

My cheeks burned in scandalized surprise and sadness at him turning this side on me, at whatever caused those marks.

He opened his underwear drawer and snorted with bitterness. Once he found a pair, he jerked them up his legs. I turned where I sat to face the wall, placing my feet on the floor. I couldn't look at him. *This was too intimate! He was being an asshole!*

"Oh, you're gonna turn away from me as if you're the virgin sweetheart you make me believe? No, not you. For your information, I almost killed someone because of you today, well, yesterday." My head snapped in his direction. I ripped my eyes from how Jase Taylor looked in a pair of skintight boxer briefs. With his wet hair and attitude problem, he could earn a fortune on a runway. His left hand held to his hip, but he wasn't doing the turn and model walking out of the room in a cloud of arrogance. He waited for an explanation, but I asked first.

"What do you mean you almost killed someone?"

He scoffed as though I sat blind to the obvious. "After douche bag flew by with the finest redhead this side of Orlando wrapped around his waist, I did a double take because Rustin called you out. Unbelievable. I even tried defending you, but after jerking the steering wheel with my head into oncoming traffic, I almost creamed a little Beetle because he was right. Do you know how embarrassed I was to have that happen in front of my best friend?"

"Like being put on the spot to say yes to a date in front of one of mine?" I shot back.

He swallowed, blinked hard, and we appeared frustrated for the same reasons, different causes.

"I'm sorry I hurt your ego."

"My *ego*? What about my *feelings, Kinsley?"*

"What does that even mean, *Jase?* Why am I finding out about your supposed feelings when someone else shows an interest?"

"Don't do that, dammit." He strode to his side of the bed and leaned on the quilt with his fists. Everything came alive in conflict as the sinews of Jase's arms protruded with the pressure he put on the mattress. I stood and backed away from temptation. His eyes had the briefest touch of a smile, but he cleared his delight. "What's wrong, Kins? Scared of me? My scars? What I stand for? What I do to your body? What you'd *like* me to do to your body?"

I swallowed. I hated that he was right about most all those questions. When I nodded, he stood and rounded to where I backed against the wall, I pressed into the texture and his fresh skin pressed close to mine.

"We can't." I turned my head to stare at the bedroom door instead of his intensity.

"Can't what? Be attracted to each other? Want to share our lives before marriage? Tell me, Kinsley, how long down the timeline you have created for your life is your wedding date? You got it all planned like Tyndall? Have one of those stupid scrapbooks for all your wedding plans but no boyfriend?" He taunted in a way reminiscent of what I had dealt with in high school and hurt me the same. "Did you know in the Old Testament, all a man had to do to call a woman his wife was to claim her? He wasn't a sinner for banging her because they didn't have some expensive ceremony."

"Oh, can I fact check that real quick?"

"Still you play while I wonder what it's gonna take for someone to stake a claim on you? Sure, go fact check, but riddle me this: you think God will hate you for the feelings he gave you? Huh? Tell me."

"Stop it!" I stomped my foot, humiliation consuming me under his words, but he captured my chin.

"No, *you* stop it. Stop pretending you don't feel shit for me. Stop treating me like all I am is sex you should avoid at all costs. I am a human and it's simple. Sex is my body joined to yours. Claiming yours."

"I'm *not* sleeping with you." My defiance was a stern set in my jaw and the refusal to look anywhere but his eyes as I held to my most pressing goal for the second. Didn't matter how hot my cheeks were, or how fierce he was. Moonlight's pep talks on feminist bitchiness surged forward. Hours too late, but here she was.

"Good, because *I'm* not sleeping with you, but we will get one thing straight right now."

"What's that?" Air was scarce, at least the type that didn't smell of Jase's soap. Fresh tears stung my eyes, but I refused my body the pathetic pleasure of releasing them over this jerk drawing them out with his resentment of my faith.

"How mad I am about you, sweet Kins …." The tone morphed into a tender whisper as he surrendered his weapons of words.

The frustration in his expression weakened. His nose and lips drew close, brushed my skin with the same reverence as he did the mic on a blues session. "I'm so mad about you, baby. You're the *only* girl I'm mad about." His hands came to either side of my face, cupping my cheeks, then he saved me from deciding by opening his mouth on mine. At first, I only opened my mouth to gasp, but he seized control, and I followed his lead.

"Jase." I mumbled, willing him to be wrong, fighting the pulsing sting ripping through every sexual place on my body, desperate to ignore the way his muscular chest seared against breasts too sensitive under a jersey with his last name printed on the back like the claim he described.

Feminism be damned, this couldn't be! I wasn't ready for this!

Grand gestures. Make him pine. Make him work.

He was working on me well. He didn't even have to touch the areas my body wanted him to!

God, please! How can something that feels good be wrong?

The more he ran his tongue against mine, the more mine complied, and the more compliant my body became when leaning against his. All at once, he wrapped his arms around me like a barbarian plucking up the female he wanted.

When I hit the bed, he came down on top of me. This marked the beginning of the end. I wouldn't be able to argue against my body's wishes. The more urgent he became in his kissing, the more I wanted him and fisted his hair, pressed him in tighter.

His hands roamed down my stomach, his fingers bunched the jersey. As he dragged the material up, cool air kissed my sensitive skin and I fought to cope with the sensations I denied myself. He felt like a flashlight pinched between us, and while him pressing into my belly hurt, I found I didn't care.

"I want you, Kinsley. *I* want *you*."

I wanted him, too!

His fingers gripped the waistband on the boxer briefs I wore. I begged God's forgiveness. *This was inevitable!* Shame and desire warred inside, but I couldn't tell which would lose. Jase's skin was a hot brand on mine, his tattoo beneath my nails too vivid to be a dream. He wanted me. *Me!*

I'm sorry, Lord. Please!

The phone vibrated and chimed right as Jase tried to tug the undies down. He jerked up and assessed the noise as a would-be intruder he needed to kill.

Exhaustion, relief, disappointment, and bewilderment punched me like a bitch doling an excruciating blessing.

"What is that for?" he demanded, his lips swollen, eyes heavy, hands not ready to release me.

My breathing huffed like the finish from my fastest sprint. "It's my alarm. I'm going upstate. The bus leaves in two hours. My dad is coming to get me."

He let a slew of curses fly, then, "It's unhealthy to run on low sleep that way."

I scoffed at the absurdity. Even *I* knew boot camp put the best through drills on fumes. This was nothing. "Jase, I'm *not* missing a meet. Do you know who'll be there watching?"

He grumbled something I didn't make out, then sighed in defeat. "What are you planning on wearing out of here? This thing is blasphemy, right?" Neither of us smiled at his joke about the jersey. The smog of lust and irritation hung too heavy.

"I changed at Sara's. I have my clothes."

"No, you don't. Remember, they're at the bar if you brought them. You sure weren't carrying them when Klive came through the door and forced you to leave like I couldn't handle that shit."

"Who?" *Was that Moonlight's name?*

He rolled his eyes and pushed up. I tore my gaze from his body, from the adjustments he made and the size of that flashlight. The underwear left nothing to the imagination. I needed to get the hell out of the beast's lair if I planned to make the meet with my integrity intact.

"Text your dad." Jase sighed. "I'll take you home, so you don't have to do the walk of shame."

Sure, he was disappointed about not having gone as far as he'd have liked. I doubted he *only* cared about that, but I didn't know what I didn't know. I didn't want to ask. Instead, I did what he asked, because whether I came home sporting Jase's traitorous jersey and my work shorts or wearing last night's uniform, I would be in trouble. Re-dressed in Sara's uniform, I waited outside in the dewy fog without fear of my father hauling me home like the whore leaving a house call I looked like.

Outside, siphoning the fresh air, I said silent morning prayers. *Thank you! Thank you! Thank you, God! Can you even hear me after that episode? Guess so since you came just in the nick of time. Thank you. I'm sorry. Please forgive me ...?*

Could the country be more beautiful?

Low fog crept off the distant pond, through the barren cypress trees, over the grass in the pasture beyond the house. Birds of all feather chimed in the most beautiful chorus from the surrounding forest. The sun glowed hot pink and orange behind a set of spindly oak trees. Yellow finches fluttered in the birdbath when Jase exited the house. He locked the door then coughed too loud and sent the flock scurrying.

"Did you do that on purpose?" I asked. He cheesed at the deadbolt and tugged his key while I shook my head. "I'm sorry, Jase. Maybe Rustin can take me if you're too tired?"

"Stop. Don't be sorry, sweet Kins. Might be different if I'd fallen asleep, but after that, I'll be an insomniac for hours. Rustin sleeps like a bear, in case you didn't see the floorboards peeling from his snoring."

I managed a laugh on the way to his truck and watched the birds fly back into their bath. Speaking of baths, his truck needed one. The tires caked with mud though the ground was dry. We hadn't had rain in a week. What the heck?

"Don't mind my attitude," he told me. "*I'm* sorry I'm a dick when I'm overtired. I've never been stood up. It was a humiliating experience," he admitted.

While I'd had valid reasons for what I'd done to him yesterday, I hated realizing I'd made him feel the way Nate had made me feel when he stood me up at Gasparilla.

The locks clicked. He opened my door, then helped me into the passenger seat since I didn't bring a ladder.

This truck was crazy.

"As far as that date, I may have lost my temper in text, but I *will* be rescheduling. Count on it." When we were out of his driveway, he reached for my hand. His smile warmed my sadness. "You are a really great kisser. Anyone been teaching you?"

Anyone meaning this guy, Clive?

"No, Jase. Just because *I'm* not making out with someone at the bar every time *you* look up doesn't mean I must suck or be elementary. There is such a thing as paying attention to cues and following a leader. Deeper connections. It's not all about marriage …." I trailed off and looked out the window. Dew droplets blew away from the glass as we entered the highway and picked up speed.

"Fair enough. This meet, does your father always go to them? Is that who you were talking about being there watching?"

"Yes, him and local papers. Sometimes sports casters, but they usually wait until the tail of the season to see if I'll follow through to the end. Two years ago, an Olympic scout sought me out and filled my head with big dreams of being the next Allyson Felix."

"Damn, that's amazeballs, baby."

I giggled at his stupid word after he was serious.

Back and forth this man swung as a pendulum. "Why didn't you take the opportunity?"

"Meh. Ever have a gut feeling that something awesome might not be as awesome as you imagine? Nothing wrong, per se, just not right for you?"

"Yeah. Probably like a shoot-to-kill mission on an HVT, but you don't have all the intel. Hard to refuse, but wise in the long run." He winked. I stifled questions I wanted to ask about those shirts. "HVT meaning High Value Target, that is. Can I come to one sometime?"

"To a meet?" I asked with a smile. "You don't have to ask. They're public events, but that would be great. I prefer that start to the one we almost had. No offense, but we've not spent enough time in this new capacity. You may not even like me outside of the bar."

He snorted and shook his head but gave into a smile. "If memory serves me, I knew you before the bar was back in business and long before you were legal to sell liquor, little lady."

"Fair enough, sir. Still, life changes people. Sorry, this is kinda heavy before coffee. Mind if we just chill and let things work themselves out as we go? I'm chronic in the analysis department, then that leads to assumption rather than fact. And you know what they say about assumptions."

He glanced over with that lift of the corner of his mouth. "Can't punish you for your honesty. Want some music?" When I nodded, he turned on the radio and the morning talk came over the air.

"Authorities say the deceased may have been the target of gang violence—" He changed the station.

"Firefighters confirmed the victim as thirty-seven-year-old volunteer firefighter, Patrick Scott, survived by his wife and son. Their names have not been released. Police are trying to determine the motive, but say gang violence may have—"

He hit another station and found a song.

"Patrick Scott?" I couldn't breathe!

"That's Sara's husband, right? Ironic. Maybe there is a God."

Jase stayed out all night.

Jase had been one of the last people seen with Patrick. So had Moonlight.

"Jase, it's nearly seven. Where were you all night?"

"With you."

My eyes bugged as I stared out the window and contemplated rolling the glass down to avoid puking in the truck. Goosebumps broke out over my skin. *Would he go that far, then use me as his alibi?*

He watched the road as he sang along with the radio, then did a double take at my expression. "Calm down, baby. A guy like him makes easy enemies with many people. You heard the radio. Gang violence." He seemed … *indifferent.* "Kins, this is good news. You're safe now." He caressed my hand with his thumb, then fell in with the chorus. "*Don't Close Your Eyes.*" He drummed on the steering wheel. Bum. Bum. Bum.

He grinned. I gulped.

The same words my father warned me with.

Was this a cosmic warning bell, or the ultimate grand gesture?

46

When we parked in the circle drive, Jase got out of his truck to divert my father's attention.

Daddy worked on swapping a rusted link in the chain that held our porch swing. I understood his passive message, we needed porch time. Jase blocked Daddy's view of me while I hauled ass upstairs. I slammed the door to my apartment, focusing too much energy into packing my uniform into the track duffel, grabbing protein bars like I'd have an appetite ever again.

Patrick was dead! Did Sara know yet? She'd have to, right? To give permission for them to release his identity? Again, maybe I watched too much crime TV.

Most women were eager to toss their bra and let the girls go free, but I snaked into a bra and secured the clasp like a painful hug from a friend. I'd just struggled into a tee with my university's logo when the knock I expected from my father drummed. Didn't matter what I pulled from my shorts drawer, I shimmied some on, ran for the door and tugged my hair from beneath the shirt.

Jase grinned when I opened. "Came to kiss you good morning, baby." He leaned over the threshold and took my chin. I couldn't pull away before his lips parted on mine. *Oh gosh! Was my daddy watching?* Under normal circumstances I may have had butterflies, tingles, something awesome. These weren't normal circumstances. *Did the man kissing me kill someone last night?*

When he stood back, his eyes were dark. One of his fingers traced my cheek down to my jaw. "So mad about you, Kinsley."

"Goodnight, Jase. Thank you for the ride home and whatever else …." My gaze found my bare feet and inspected the boots he wore. Bits of mud caked to the bottom, dried with tiny clumps of moss. Like his truck.

He'd not only *driven* somewhere muddy.

"You're welcome. Kick ass on your races, baby." His thumb tipped my chin. "Don't worry about Patrick. If someone took him out, he deserved what he earned. I only hope he got a taste of being pounded to a pulp before the deed was done."

He knew?

He had a point. With Patrick's death, I wasn't the only one secure in the aftermath. Sara and Noah were. They were more important. Hope sprang through my eyes while I searched his.

"You're right," I agreed. "She's safe now. This is a blessing in disguise. Thank you. Want me to give Tyndall a message for you?"

His whole face lit. I loved how he loved her. "You're headed to Tallahassee? Well it's a fantastic thing we got you out of that jersey, then."

I snorted without forcing the sentiment. *Yay!* "I am, and yes, a superb thing."

"How about you tell Tyndall about Patrick, then tell her to avoid douche bags who act like good guys."

"Uh, is she dating someone new?" I asked, curious if he knew about Tyndall's deadbeat boyfriend. Better for her if I played dumb.

My hands wrapped my hair into a ponytail to hide my nervousness. He tapped my lips while I secured the elastic.

"See you when you get back, baby. Be safe." He jogged down my stairs and left me confused, then polluted the quiet neighborhood in a cloud of audacious noise too early on a Saturday. My dad stood beside his BMW with his hands in his pockets.

"Gimme a ride to the buses?" I begged.

"That's what I'm here for, Kinsley Fallon." Short tone. He waved me on. I hustled to grab my duffel, snatched my effects and slung the bag over my shoulder before running downstairs and hopping inside his car. He chose not to look me over until we were on the highway. I was bent putting my socks and shoes on. He cleared his throat. "You seem energetic for staying out with friends."

Yup. Like Jase, I felt I'd be an insomniac for days to come. *Who needed coffee when your boyfriend, ish, may have done something bad?*

"I'm psyched about running today, Daddy. Aren't you? We don't have much longer to enjoy this. Instead of pouting the way I did last week, I'm absorbing the experience." I smiled to disarm him as he assessed my honesty.

"None of this has anything to do with you staying the night at Jase's house and him kissing you before he left?"

"Daddy, if you'd gotten to hang out with mom at her house, even with her friends, then she kissed you goodbye, would you taint the experience with the speculation of others, or would you relish the moment as long as you could?" I asked. "Didn't you want this?"

"Kinsley, I want you to find love, sure, but I don't want to fill your head with an idea your heart doesn't agree with. Just be …." He trailed off. I didn't give him the chance to find the right words because we stopped in the lot where the buses waited. No mistaking I was the last to arrive. I kissed my father's cheek and asked for prayers.

"Love you!" I waved over my shoulder. Coach tapped his watch from the bottom step. I saw relief in his eyes as I bounded on-board.

Before I plugged my earbuds to ignore Lucy, she plopped beside me in a cloud of peppy that grated on my frazzled nerves.

"Have you had a chance to see the news?" she asked. "Crazy stuff about that guy dying after threatening you, huh? I bet you're relieved! I was worried when you were leaving last night." There was an honest conviction in her face, but somehow, she didn't put together how awful her statement sounded. *Could she be that dumb?* "Your job is dangerous," she continued. "Good thing you're graduating soon. Though I'll miss you. Any word on the new internship?"

Yes, she was that dumb. She droned on rather than wanting an answer. Coach gave me a silent reprimand that said she may annoy us but had a valid point about my being a bartender.

"Ugh! Lucy!" I kicked the seat back in front of me. "I was up late last night. Let me get some bloody sleep, please!"

Coach's assistant leaned up and plucked earbuds from his ears, his cap pulled low like he'd been asleep.

"I'm sorry," I rushed. "I shouldn't have done that."

Lucy bit her lip through a smile instead of letting my attitude affect her. "You sound like that British guy. He works in the same building I do. I gave him your name when he wanted to send you roses. His name is Clive. When I misspelled it on his cup, he corrected me. He uses a K for Klive instead of the traditional C. Isn't that unique? You're both K's. But that guy who sings? He's hot too. Cool to meet him last night. I think he has a crush on you."

"Lucy," I snapped. "Don't you think if *Klive with a K* was trying to do something sweet, you might have just ruined it? Or if he'd been a creep, you compromised me?" I felt awful that I had no patience, but things were too crazy. I needed rest! I did appreciate the information confirmation: *Klive*.

The guy in front of me shook his head, then burrowed back down in his seat the way I wanted to.

"Lucy, if I lose because you wouldn't let me sleep, your ass is grass."

The girls who'd been a symphony of siren gossip silenced in shock since I reserved my mean state for the track. *Why couldn't my bitch have come out on Patrick last night? Would my attitude have made a difference or made this worse?*

"All right, Luce. Go on." Coach gestured with his head, and she moved. He took the spot beside me. I leaned against the window. "Need an ear?" he asked.

"Nope. Frankly, I could use at least one guy who isn't complicating shit up. Just be yourself." I stared, hoping my tired eyes said the rest. I expected him to rub salt in my wound with a self-righteous lecture. However, for once, he said, "All right, kid. Rest up." After that, I napped like the dead.

The meet went okay. My spirits picked up with the ability to run away from my inner turmoil, but my body weighed down with too little training, the stuffed French toast mistake from Bayleigh, stress, dehydration.

When I came off my final race, sweaty and nasty, but somehow victorious and holding the stitch in my side, Tyndall threw her arms around me. She was an open traitor to her alma mater. We snickered at the mean mugs she received from those in her school colors.

"Soooo proud of you, Micro Machine!" She grinned and jostled my ponytail. I traded the baton for a water bottle Coach ordered me to drink.

"Glad you claim me in public." I elbowed her ribs while I caught my breath and choked on water I couldn't down fast enough. I didn't feel too good.

"If I didn't claim you, I'd lose out on all the free shots at the after party," Tyndall teased. "You're staying in town afterward, right?"

"I dunno, Tyndall. I have a ton to tell you," I confessed. "Too much. And I'm not myself."

"I know that tone!" She scooted close like I wasn't turning green. "There's a guy!"

"There's a guy." I confirmed but stared somewhat bewildered by the hope clouding her eyes to the obvious. *Maybe if I puked on her feet, she'd leave the boy-crazy bimbo back at the dorm?*

Before I elaborated the way she begged me to, Coach ordered Lucy to get a towel with ice. She complied. Where Tyndall seemed blind, Lucy passed the ice to me with worry. Coach Walton ordered me to hold the towel against the inside of my elbow to stave off the nausea.

Closer to my ear, he whispered that he knew I was favoring my injured ankle. Dammit.

"Act natural, kid. We'll treat the issue when we get back to Tampa. Don't let them see." I held his eyes with a nod.

"Yes, sir." Act natural I did as the normal fans came to congratulate me while I packed my duffel and changed from spikes to tennis shoes. New fans mixed in while Tyndall and I tried to sneak conversation.

Over the next fifteen minutes I shook hands, took pictures, signed hats and newspapers. I also avoided the glares of others who had sore loser streaks like mine. Another chick famous for her sprint signed tees and took pics as well. She was the one to watch this season. I would not hand over my record in the final stretch. That didn't keep us from having to take a picture together as if she were my successor for the wrong school. Fun times.

Tyndall stayed in my company, confessing from the dry side of a shower curtain about how her loser lover had come through twice in a row since Valentine's, then we made plans for when she was coming to town for her spring break.

"All right, Kins, enough small talk. I can't take it anymore. Your turn! Tie your hair up and come out with it already!" She doled the order as I finished drying and dressing speedy moments later.

"All righty. Look at this, Tyndall. I haven't even seen this pic yet." I bent to the duffel for my phone, shoving the nasty uniform into a plastic bag inside. Tyndall stole the device, thumbed through to find the photo I asked Sara to snap yesterday. We walked back toward the track still filled with stragglers.

"She snapped quite a few," she mumbled, zoomed in. "A motorcycle, Kins? Oh, he's—"

"Excellent job, love," said the British accent I'd know anywhere! "Looks to be a promising season."

Tyndall and I jolted. She ripped the phone behind her back. Our expressions were of similar panic. He grinned to prove we were caught in his suave web. Sunglasses covered his eyes, his hair sculpted like a prima donna who'd broken all the casual rules. *Would she recognize him?*

Moonlight handed me a single rose the way others lifted their hand to say hello, casual and friendly.

"Tha— thank you." I stammered, though my smile grew bright even as the memory of last night hovered too close. "What are you doing here?"

"I'm a fan, remember?" He pointed to his shirt bearing my university's mascot, none of that scary guy anywhere. "You thought I was blowing smoke yesterday?"

"Yesterday, huh?" Tyndall shoved her hand like an axe between us, her tone something I couldn't peg. "Hi, I'm Tyndall Taylor, Kinsley's best friend in the whole universe." He received her palm in his with incredulous surprise.

"Tyndall Taylor?"

"I'm sorry, do you two know one another?" I asked as I examined her mirrored appraisal.

"No, Kinsley, but if a guy this hot is into my bestie and travels four hours to bring her a rose, I'd say I better know of his *existence* …."

Yikes! Did she have no shame in calling things how she saw them? As if he needed his ego pumped. Her gorgeous smile came off more a growl in my direction. *C'mon, I'd been trying and how could I tell her he was who he was with him standing right here?*

"How did you two meet?" Her eyes traveled between us. Someone had better ante up.

He chuckled and released her hand on a shrug. I rolled my eyes and waited to hear his response.

"I'm pleased to make your acquaintance, Tyndall. From my understanding, meeting a girl's best friend can be more important than her parents. This is an unexpected and pleasant surprise. To answer your question, she took her anger out on me instead of the other guy. Just another casualty of that temper. The rest is history."

"You're a glutton for punishment, Mister …?"

He tapped his lips and shook his head, a flirtatious smirk at me. "I'm afraid Kinsley and I have a game going. Until it's done, my name has to remain a mystery."

Her mouth dropped open with an enormous smile. One check of my face said she was putting the pieces of the Valentine's puzzle together on her own.

I wanted to ask if his name was Klive, but he was too much fun in his play for me to ruin that side. *What a relief to have him back to his friendly persona!*

"Hey, Micro Machine, you coming to celebrate tonight?" Eliza asked as she walked past, fresh and clean now, too. "Hey, Tyndall! Ooh, pretty rose, Kins!" Tyndall waved at Eliza and suppressed her smile at how Eliza formed a claw behind his back.

"Yeah, I think I might join you guys later," I called. I struggled to keep a straight face myself as I refocused on him.

"Oh, I'm gonna go run interference," Tyndall said.

Dammit. My father lingered instead of taking my mom out like normal afterward. Tyndall jogged away to throw her arms around my daddy. Funny how both Taylors had created diversions for me in the same day. I glanced away from them and up to Moonlight. The rose rested against my lips. I sniffed the bloom while I waited.

His face cleared of humor but remained kind. "I came to check on you after last night. I'm sorry you saw me that way. You all right?"

"I am. Thank you," I admitted. "I'm not sure what your place was in all that trash, but I'm grateful." The memory of how both bikers paled at the sight of him made me wonder how afraid *I* should have been of him. I wasn't. He didn't scare me. I was glad to see him now, and I'd been glad to see him last night. "*You're* all right?" I asked.

His laugh floated like bubbles blown off a wand. "After seeing you have done so well today, yes, I'm quite pleased you didn't allow last night to steal from your talent."

"Thank you. Did you *do* something?" I dared. As I searched his face, mine shifted to a determination to flesh the truth. *What would I do if he had?*

"Let's say I have a powerful influence and leave it at that." *Really?* "Did *you* do something?" he countered. I knew what he meant. He wondered whether I'd given up the goods to the boyfriend whose house I'd spent the night in. The same boyfriend's house he'd ordered me to go stay at. In that moment, I considered how frustrated he must've been to send me into the lion's den to protect me. I thrilled at how he didn't mask his hope. Also, with how he chose not to question me about the missing card ….

He licked his lips and looked to the ground. I did, too, but took that time to inspect his shoes, too clean. *If he was asking about Jase like he thought I'd spent the whole night with him, did that mean they hadn't done anything bad together?*

"Hey Mr. King." Lucy interrupted our awkward moment as she trudged by. She sold him out on purpose, that bitch. My attitude came out in an instant, and she kept stepping. His eyes closed for a long beat.

"Well, love, I guess some mysteries spoil too soon." The bitterness in his tone surprised me. His jaw muscle flinched as we stared at one another.

"Never fear, your majesty." I adopted his accent to needle his silly to the surface. I let the rose fall upside down. The petals tapped against my body, below the belt. "Not *all* mysteries were spoiled."

Relief filled his eyes as he understood that I hadn't slept with Jase. My cheeks heated in remembrance of how close I'd come, though.

The rose lifted to my lips. I didn't ask him his first name. Some things were worth waiting for. If I wanted the luxury of not giving everything up to someone, extending that courtesy to someone else was mutual respect, even if Jase and Lucy had given everything away.

"So, Mr. King, I'll see ya around? After all, you might be worth getting to know better."

I hoisted the duffel onto my shoulder, searching him for signs of playful relief.

He unleashed an elated smile. "Bet on it, Ms. Hayes."

Oh, sweet heaven! I reciprocated with a mega-watt smile of my own. When I turned to jog where my best friend and father waited, I waved over my shoulder.

Klive King kissed two of his fingers and delivered butterflies like a promise.

There was much to tell Tyndall.

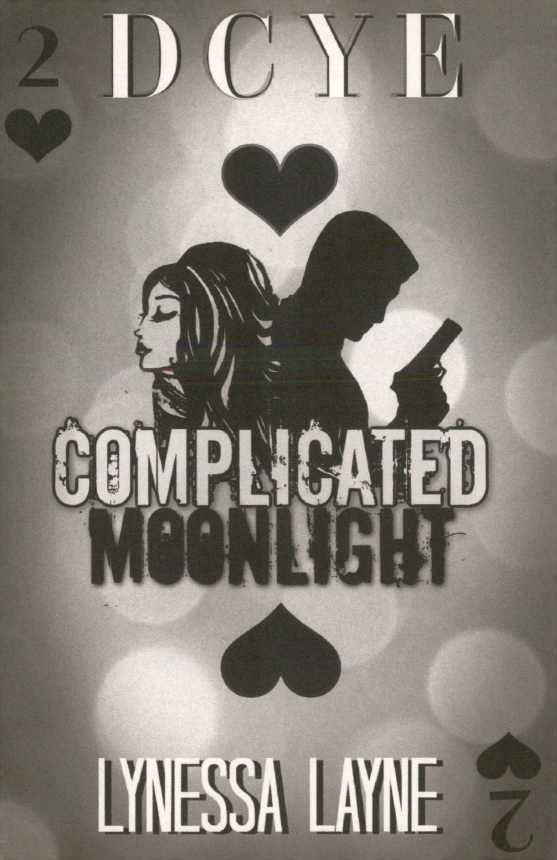

1 | ♂

Kinsley smiled over her shoulder as she skipped away with the exuberance of a giddy five-year-old. She held the rose like a girl ready to pluck the petals and ask whether *he loves me, he loves me not.* I kissed two of my fingers and waved, unable to help relishing her joy. *I caused that? What a feeling!*

When I turned from Kinsley, the man who'd stolen my freedom pilfered the fleeting happiness from my soul as he sauntered down the stands. A smirk of knowing lit his wholesome veneer as he stopped before me.

"Cheatham, how are you?" I asked but couldn't give a damn.

"Not as well as you appear to be, Klive, especially after last night." He peered beyond my shoulder. "She's talented. Quite attractive. A little young, don't you think?"

"Hobbies always are." I smirked in kind.

"Rumor has it this is more than a hobby. You're breaking protocol." He shook his head as though we discussed some travesty, concerned empathy replacing the smirk. "Klive, I'd hate for the collateral damage to be on such a scale, but she'd make a great martyr. Track fans would gather on their social platforms to mourn their small-time icon while pledging war against whomever we pin the blame. She might draw more attention to her sport dead than she has alive. A great legacy."

My eyebrow lifted as I half-smiled. "You want to go there over a rumor? I don't think you want my trouble on your doorstep, Cheatham. There's mutiny in the ranks. I am not inclined to allow disrespect a foothold. Perhaps you're the cause of it?"

He chuckled and relaxed his demeanor, shook his head, but I could tell his eyes were on her once more. "I see why you showed up. She has very pretty legs for being short, doesn't she?"

1

Testing my temper. *Always testing!* I continued undeterred. "She's a server at a Nightshade bar. The second server within three weeks taking shit from Inferno. Either I draw the line that I won't put up with boundary-testing by those beneath us, or we risk looking weak and allowing a biker gang to overthrow Nightshade. Up to you. What should it be? Unless that's your plan?"

"And what of your plan? I still own you for two more months. I'd hate to increase that sentence because you chose disobedience in the final stretch."

"Enough. If I want to get laid while defending my territory, 'tis nothing different from anyone else. Your threat implies a motive for causing the divide. In which case I have a right to defend myself and anyone else in the face of *your* mutiny."

"That a challenge, Klive? Remember who created you. Do you think you're the only *golden boy* at my disposal?" He tilted his head to see her better. "If you screw anything more than this girl, I'm removing the distraction. And if I'm not mistaken, her little friend looks awfully familiar … haven't I met her before?"

My jaw clenched, but I thought of Jase Taylor, the damage he would do if he had any idea that his sister, Tyndall Taylor, was threatened. Cheatham didn't know I had *golden boys,* as he called hitmen, of my own.

He eyed my face and said, "Gotcha. Heed my warning. Best to stay away from the girl. I don't want a war within the underground. Let Inferno have their whores to pay their debts. That's an order. You violate, you know the penalty."

"No. She's not a whore. Their debts are their own."

"Oh, Klive, haven't you learned? Most women are whores for the right price. Inferno's debts will become yours if you say no to me ever again."

He bypassed me and jogged right up to Kinsley. I didn't have to hear to know he asked for a photo after having the gall to shake her father's hand like a friendly admirer of her gifted sprint. His phone rose before he pulled her close for a selfie just like several others had before him.

Now Cheatham had her face as his way of marking her for any *golden boys* assigned to remove her.

Would they be foolish enough to do so if they knew they'd have to go through me *to get to her?*

I jogged down the stands and mixed into the crowd departing the venue. My personal security detail, Joey, kept eyes on Kinsley. Eric, my Nightshade lieutenant, played a convenient body double as he wore what I was. He walked toward my vehicle without looking over his shoulder to give me time to study Cheatham's actions from the shadows.

Beneath the stands, I unzipped the backpack Eric left for me, changed my shirt, pulled on a shaggy brunette wig, added a ball cap and a pair of sunglasses. I licked the back of a temporary tattoo and placed the symbol to the inside of my left wrist.

In truth, I wasn't as worried about Cheatham's threat as much as what he was setting into motion on my end. *What was his goal? Forcing me into more time?* Something more was afoot.

I fished for a set of keys in the bottom of the bag, then zipped the tines closed and pulled the strap over my shoulder.

From beneath the stands, I couldn't help spying Kinsley between the beams of metal. I crouched and crept closer until I was close enough to hear her conversation with her father.

"—will Jase think?"

"Daddy, Jase isn't my boyfriend. The guy was just another fan. What's the big deal?"

"The big deal is your career vanishing because of a crush on an older man."

"My career *vanishing*?" She waved the rose I'd gifted her like a sword between them. "I just won every heat. What have I lost? You act like he's forty or something."

"What if he is? What then?"

"Daddy, what if he's just a fan and you're overreacting? Seriously. Just, next time maybe don't come. I'm out of here."

"What about Tyndall? I thought you were staying with her."

"She has her boyfriend now. Like most of my friends. Some are even— gasp—married with kids! And their lives aren't ruined because they gave up extracurricular activities for real life!"

I gave a silent whistle and turned my head. A redhead sat nearby cupping her mouth. *Kinsley's sister?*

Kinsley waved her father away and turned toward the locker rooms once more. Her father called out, "Don't you need a ride home? You never said where you were going!"

"I'm riding the bus with all the normal girls! And you're right, I didn't say."

"Kinsley Fallon!"

"Hayden Andrew Hayes," the redhead cursed his full name. *Damn! A tone like hers had to be from a wife.*

"Oh, Clairice." Andrew Hayes wilted by her side as she wrapped arms around his broad shoulders. "My baby. Where's my baby girl?"

"Andy. Can you imagine what a fool you've made of yourself if she's telling the truth about the guy with the rose? It's not the first time someone's given her flowers after a win. Why this one? When will you realize she's not a baby anymore? She's an *adult*. Your baby girl, yes, but a grown woman. You said you'd give her space, but maybe that's easier said than done?"

He placed a hand over one of hers on his shoulder. "No, I know this guy, Claire. Ben invited him to lunch with us a few times to get his advice on difficult client relations. He knows his stuff, has a silver-tongued charisma when he isn't busy snubbing those beneath him. He's far too young to be so successful. The British accent makes it worse."

"You accuse Kinsley of crushing on an older man, now you say he's too young. Which is it?" she asked. "Did this man not work for this success? Was it just handed to him because of some social standing?"

He sighed. "From what I've gleaned, he's worked for every title and penny he's earned."

Well, thank you very much, Mr. Hayes. What the hell is bad about that?

4

"In conclusion, he's a successful, driven, powerful snob and you're afraid he's going to work at earning our daughter's attention by driving hours upstate to give her roses after showing her support at her track meet? And, by the way, he seems to have a knack for dealing with difficult people which we both know you've trained your little girl to be." She hummed while her husband frowned. "I think he deserves the benefit of the doubt. Kinsley hates snobs. Do you really think your partner at work would befriend a snob?"

Andrew Hayes gave a bitter laugh. "Ben *is* a snob."

His wife slapped his hand. "I don't know what's gotten into you, but Ben is perfectly kind. I'm sure whoever this man is may have something more than charisma and an accent going for him."

"Hell, Claire, he does. Remember my birth—"

"Andy? Claire?" Kinsley's friend, Tyndall, jogged back in from the parking lot and held her side. Kinsley's parents looked at her. "I screwed up. I already sent Kinsley packing on the bus because I have a date later, but since you're in town, you mind grabbing a bite with me to catch up?"

"Please, Tyndall, if you wouldn't mind, we'd really enjoy your company," Claire told her.

"Yeah, not to be rude, but I could tell papa's kinda freaking out. Maybe I can allay your fears?" Tyndall offered.

Wow. I'd heard enough.

I walked out from under the beams beneath the stands and straightened the wig. The hair fell somewhat over one eye.

Eric's black 911 Porsche was front and center in the lot. Rather than heading for his car, I found the barista who worked at the coffee shop in my building. The ultimate test. I cleared my accent and lowered my voice.

"Hey, it's Lucy, right?" I asked when she exited the locker room. The group of girls on her heels gaped, one elbowed Lucy's ribs. I rolled my eyes behind the reflective glasses.

"Yes?" Lucy asked, excitement lighting her face at a male's attention singling her out among the throng.

"Is Micro Machine inside? I was hoping to get a picture with her before—"

"I'm not taking any more pictures today," Kinsley said as she emerged. The group of girls gasped, some blushed. Kinsley stared them down as she ignored me and passed them. "Sorry. Not feeling well." She paused and faced me. "Lucy's not my handler. You'd do better to ask my coach if you're ever looking for me. Some people just claim to know me when they're just piggy-backing the ass of the racehorse."

Damn!

She was *very* angry. In ways I'd not even experienced on the lift when we'd first met!

What the hell caused such a dramatic shift from the bubbly girl I'd left on the track? Surely, not just the bit with her father?

"My mistake. I'm sorry. Yes, next time," I told her and waved, prepared to be on my way.

"Wait. Please, forgive me. Get your picture." Kinsley's bag fell off her shoulder to the ground. She walked up while I hurried to raise my phone and put my arm around her. When she leaned close and smiled, she inhaled. Her face inspected mine. After a couple snaps on my phone, she rushed to pick up her bag.

For the second time, I'd made the mistake of wearing the cologne she responded to like a drug.

"What kind of cologne do you wear?" Kinsley asked with no hint of flirtation or interest. "Smells nice. Would love to get some for my father."

Lucy hadn't recognized me, but did Kinsley?

Was this her passive anger turning on me with the daddy card, or was this the way she treated guys she wasn't interested in?

Did her kindness toward me mean she was interested the way her father feared?

"Sir?" she interrupted my internal questions. I realized she'd been crying. Her nose was pink, and she sniffled a couple of times.

"I can't recall," I told her.

"That sucks." She waved with cautious indifference.

6

"Hey, are you okay?"

"Yep. Seasonal allergies."

I nodded and allowed the distance to grow between us, but Cheatham could kiss my ass if he thought I'd stay away for long.

About the Author

Lynessa Layne is a native Texan who grew up in the small town of Plantersville, home of The Texas Renaissance Festival. She's a fan of cosplay, exploration, loves the beach and is always game for devouring a great book. A military wife, she's bounced around the US, including the settings in DCYE, currently landing in the heart of sweet home Alabama where she and her husband are raising their blended family.

Lynessa is a certified copy editor, a member of TWIG, WFWA, FWA & AWC with work featured by *MysteryandSuspense.com* and *Writer's Digest*.

For more information on upcoming releases, swag, events, visit lynessalayne.com

Facebook: facebook.com/authorlynessalayne
Twitter @LynessaLayne

Read her blog entitled The Dark Side of Light (DSoL) on Wordpress.com

Reviews & ratings on Goodreads.com

CPSIA information can be obtained
at www.ICGtesting.com
Printed in the USA
LVHW040353230321
682153LV00001B/1